About the A

Kayla Perrin has been writing since the age of thirteen. She is a *USA Today* and Essence bestselling author of dozens of mainstream and romance novels and has been recognised for her talent, including twice winning Romance Writers of America's Top Ten Favorite Books of the Year Award. She has also won the Career Achievement Award for multicultural romance from RT Book Reviews. Kayla lives with her daughter in Ontario, Canada. Visit her at KaylaPerrin.com

Rebecca Winters lives in Salt Lake City, Utah. With canyons and high alpine meadows full of wildflowers, she never runs out of places to explore. They, plus her favourite holiday spots in Europe, often end up as backgrounds for her romance novels because writing is her passion, along with her family and church. Rebecca loves to hear from readers. If you wish to email her, please visit her website at: cleanromances.net

Kate Hardy has been a bookworm since she was a toddler. When she isn't writing Kate enjoys reading, theatre, live music, ballet and the gym. She lives with her husband, student children and their spaniel in Norwich, England. You can contact her via her website: katehardy.com

Sports Romance

Sports Romance:

On The Pitch

KAYLA PERRIN

REBECCA WINTERS

KATE HARDY

MILLS & BOON

First Published in Great Britain 2025
by Mills & Boon, an imprint of HarperCollins*Publishers* Ltd
1 London Bridge Street, London, SE1 9GF

www.harpercollins.co.uk

HarperCollins*Publishers*
Macken House, 39/40 Mayor Street Upper,
Dublin 1, D01 C9W8, Ireland

MIX
Paper | Supporting
responsible forestry
FSC™ C007454

This book contains FSC™ certified paper and other controlled sources to ensure responsible forest management.

For more information visit: www.harpercollins.co.uk/green

Printed and Bound in the UK using 100% Renewable Electricity
at CPI Group (UK) Ltd, Croydon, CR0 4YY

UNDENIABLE ATTRACTION

KAYLA PERRIN

For May-Marie Duwa-Sowi, founder of Illuminessence magazine.

Your vision is extraordinary and awe inspiring. I know your big dreams are about to come true. I'm proud to call you a friend and say, 'I knew you when.' Keep illuminating!

Chapter 1

Melissa Conwell's hands tightened on the steering wheel as she passed the familiar sign along Interstate 90 west. Sheridan Falls. She was almost home.

Home home. Not Newark, New Jersey, where she lived now, but the small town in upstate New York where she'd been born and raised. Normally, seeing that sign caused her heart to fill with happiness, knowing that she would soon be seeing her parents, sister and young niece. But today, the fact that she was almost home had her throat tightening.

It was an illogical reaction, especially since she was returning to Sheridan Falls for a joyous occasion. It was sure to be *the* event of the summer, a big wedding that was bringing family members together from across the country. And yet joy was the last thing she was feeling.

She was anxious. Terrified, even.

Because this time she was going to have to see Aaron Burke. Small-town boy turned international soccer star.

International heartbreaker, more like.

She hadn't needed to read the tabloids to learn that Aaron had had his share of women and had broken his share of hearts. She knew that from firsthand experience. Eleven years, nine months and ten or so days ago, Aaron had crushed her teenage heart and left her reeling.

Not that she was counting or anything.

Melissa's fingers began to hurt, and she loosened her grip on the steering wheel. Why she was getting all tense at the thought of seeing Aaron was beyond her. She hadn't spoken to him in nearly twelve years. He wasn't part of her life, by any stretch of the imagination. So why was she acting as if seeing him was going to disrupt her world?

Because she didn't *want* to see him. Ever. Not after how things had ended between them. She might be over him, but they weren't friends, and spending time with him was going to be awkward at the very least.

But that's exactly what she was going to have to do. Over the next few days, she was going to be seeing a lot of Aaron—at the welcome dinner, at the rehearsal, at the wedding. And worse than simply seeing him, she was going to have to interact and play nice, because not only was Melissa in the wedding party, Aaron was, too. And for some unfathomable reason, Tasha had paired Aaron with her.

"What's the big deal?" Tasha had asked when Melissa expressed mortification over the wedding arrangements. "The other pairings made more sense this way. Besides, you and Aaron used to be close."

"Exactly—*used* to be," Melissa had said. "We haven't spoken in years. Are you forgetting what he did to me?"

"But weren't you the one who decided not to follow him to Notre Dame?" Tasha asked, sounding confused. "You said he'd be too busy with his soccer scholarship and you didn't want to get in his way? Then things fell apart after that."

Melissa had been glad that she and her cousin were speaking on the phone, three thousand miles between them. Because she didn't want Tasha to see her face.

The story that Melissa was the one who'd decided not to go to Notre Dame had not been entirely truthful, but it had been much better than admitting that Aaron had rejected her. She'd been trying to save face when she'd told her close friends and family that she was the one who'd chosen not to follow Aaron to college. The truth was, Aaron had been the one to ask her why she would travel across the country for school when there were better social work programs closer to home. Melissa had been stunned. Didn't he *want* her around? Didn't he love her?

Melissa's heart had been beating out of control as Tasha

had gone on to talk about how Melissa being paired with Aaron would be fine, that years had passed and she was sure there would be no tension between them. Melissa hoped her cousin was right, but she wouldn't bet money on it. How did you play nice with someone you'd tried to eradicate from your memory?

Melissa gazed out at the familiar landscape. The trees along the interstate were a vibrant green and in full bloom. The sky was cloudless and a gorgeous cerulean blue this early-summer day. The weather for the weekend was supposed to be perfect.

If only she could feel good about it.

Her mind ventured back to the one thing she couldn't escape—the fact that she would have to see Aaron. Did she hate him? No, hate was too strong an emotion, but she certainly didn't like him. Once she'd learned that Aaron had done the unthinkable—he'd married Ella Donovan, the one girl in high school she couldn't stand—any remaining respect she might have had for him instantly died. He'd given Melissa the song and dance about how they were young, it was time for them to concentrate on their careers, that the distance between them would eventually become a factor.

Yet somehow he'd ended up making a relationship work with Ella? Ella had stayed in Sheridan Falls and worked for her father, who'd been the longtime mayor of the town. When had Aaron had time to forge a relationship with her?

Unless they'd been involved while he and Melissa had been. Every unthinkable scenario had crossed Melissa's mind, and she'd ultimately been livid with herself for falling for a Burke brother. Hadn't she known better? During high school, she'd heard all the rumors about the four Burke boys, how they dated whomever they wanted, were too popular to be faithful and women were supposed to take what they could get—*if* they were lucky enough to catch the eye of one of the Burkes. Which was exactly why Melissa had always vowed to never be like the other women in town, who seemed to lose their minds whenever in the presence of Aaron, Keith, Carlton or Jonas. Yes, the Burkes were hot, but it was pathetic how googly-eyed women became around them.

And then Melissa spent a summer with Aaron. They were both hired by a local camp at the end of their senior high school year as counselors charged with entertaining kids twelve and under. Melissa and Aaron had spent a lot of time together, time in which she'd gotten to know him. And he'd seemed so different from everything she'd heard. Caring. Funny. Engaging. Truly interested in the kids. Relatable. A good listener. He didn't seem conceited at all. And somehow, Melissa had fallen for him.

Her first love. Her first heartbreak.

Dreams shattered. Her innocence lost.

The best summer of her life had turned into her biggest regret.

Though Melissa had tried to the best of her ability to avoid following Aaron's career and his life over the years, she hadn't been able to avoid everything. She had seen the photos of him in various highlights on the news about his soccer achievements, and of course about his happy marriage to the mayor's daughter.

It was rare that she didn't find a story about Aaron whenever she looked up news in the online version of the *Sheridan Falls Tribune*. In their town of seven thousand people, Aaron Burke was a local hero. Even him buying a new car made the paper.

Melissa had fallen for him before he'd ever become successful, though he had always been legendary. He was the son of Cyrus Burke, a local celebrity who'd had a long and celebrated career in the NFL. Not that Melissa knew anything about Cyrus's personal life, but every time she'd seen him in town with his wife, Cynthia, he seemed like a man in love. Always holding her hand. Opening doors for her. Gazing at her fondly, as though there was no woman more beautiful in the world.

There'd never been a hint of scandal about Cyrus's fidelity, something Melissa had reflected on after she and Aaron had become an item. She'd figured like father, like son, and had assumed that if Aaron became successful as a soccer player, he would be like his father. Instead, he'd proceeded to behave exactly like the majority of highly paid professional athletes out there—parties, women, a string of broken hearts.

Melissa had read all about it in the tabloids. Seen pictures of him on yachts in the Mediterranean with other soccer players and a horde of bikini-clad women. She'd seen how female sports reporters would look up at him with the same googly eyes she'd witnessed on the women from Sheridan Falls. It had been hard for Melissa to stomach.

And then Aaron had married Ella in some big event in Sheridan Falls, and Melissa had stopped paying attention to what Aaron did with his life. She'd spent too much time over the years thinking about him as it was, and if he could marry the one person who'd made her life hell in high school, he didn't deserve a second thought.

"Enough of this nonsense," she said to herself. Vowing to forget about Aaron, she turned up the music on the radio and bopped her head to an upbeat tune. Her eyes ventured to the lake as she crossed the city limits into Sheridan Falls. That was the lake on which she'd spent her last summer of high school as a counselor.

The summer she had fallen in love with Aaron Burke.

"Oh, for goodness' sake," she all but yelled. "Stop thinking about Aaron! He's ancient history."

Suddenly, it hit her what the real issue was. She didn't want to see him with Ella, who she knew would rub in the fact that she had snagged a Burke brother. Having to stomach Ella gloating over her coveted prize would be more than Melissa could bear. In high school, Ella had lived to steal other women's men, as though it were a competitive sport. If only Aaron had ended up with anyone but her. Ella, who'd never suffered from self-esteem issues to begin with, must have an ego as large as the state of Texas now.

Dealing with Ella's gloating would be bearable *if* Melissa were heading home with a hot man on her arm. But sadly, she was single. Her relationships over the years had all died before any real promise of a happily-ever-after. Her most recent relationship had started off with hope, in part because of the fact that Christopher worked in the social work field, as did she. But hope had faded as quickly as the initial spark, and the relationship had ended without so much as a fizzle.

"You don't need to return home with a man," Melissa said. "All you have to do is ignore Aaron. Pretend like he doesn't exist."

Because he didn't. He hadn't existed in her life for over a decade, and that wasn't about to change just because of the wedding.

Chapter 2

A slow smile spread on Melissa's lips as she pulled into the driveway of her parents' home, the house in which she had been born and raised. Gone were all thoughts of Aaron as she saw her mother sitting on the porch swing. As Melissa exited her navy Chevrolet Malibu, her mother got to her feet, her eyes lighting up with excitement.

"Melissa!" her mother exclaimed. "Ooh, come here, child."

Melissa quickly closed the car door and rushed up the porch steps. Her mother's arms were already spread wide, and Melissa threw herself into her embrace. Her mom hugged her long and hard against her large bosom. Instantly, Melissa felt a sense of comfort, the same way she always had as a little girl when her mother had wrapped her in her arms.

The weekend was going to be okay. Why had she been worrying herself silly?

"My baby." Her mother broke the hug, leaned backward to check her out and took both of Melissa's hands in hers. "Looks like you could use some good home cooking. You're getting a little thin."

Her mother had grown up in the South, and practically everything she made had a stick of butter or lard in it. It was a diet Melissa tried to steer clear of, for the most part. "I've been working out."

"I'll get some meat back on your bones," her mother promised. Then she said, "It has been way too long since you've been home. It's like you've forgotten your father and me now that you're living in the big city."

"You know I could never forget about you and Dad," Melissa said. She squeezed her mother's hands affectionately, then released them. "I meant to come back after Christmas, but I've been so busy with work."

"Some days I wonder about that job of yours."

"I love it," Melissa said quickly, walking into the house. "Even the crazy hours and the emergencies." Being the program coordinator at a group home in Newark was deeply rewarding. Melissa made an impact in the lives of troubled youth, helping the kids get back on track.

"I know your job is important. But I don't like that you have to devote so much time to it. All work and no play, you'll never find a nice man."

Melissa offered her mother a small smile, though what she wanted to do was roll her eyes. Her mother would never be fully happy until Melissa had been married off.

Though her mom should know by now that marriage didn't mean happiness. Her sister, Arlene, had just endured a nasty divorce. Her parents had viewed Craig as the son they'd never had, only to be devastated when he'd turned his back on not only Arlene, but also on them. He'd cheated with his secretary, then had the nerve to be unapologetic about his actions. The ensuing scandal had caused much embarrassment for Arlene and the family.

"Where's Dad?"

"He's lying down," her mother said, and now she was the one to roll her eyes. "The crazy fool tired himself out retiling the basement bathroom. I told him to hire someone, but *no*, he swore he could do it himself. I think he threw his back out, but he'll never admit it."

Oh, yes. Melissa was home, all right. Her parents always bickered, sometimes from sunup until sundown, but despite their small disagreements, their deep love was never in doubt.

"I'm about ready to tell him that if he doesn't call in a professional, I'm leaving him. This time I mean it."

Melissa chortled. "Mom, you know you're not going

anywhere. You always threaten to leave, but you never will. And you know why? Because you and Dad would be lost without each other."

Melissa crossed through the living room en route to her parents' bedroom. She found her father lying in bed, his eyes closed, but when he heard her, he opened them and immediately smiled.

"Melissa," he said warmly, starting to sit up.

Melissa hurried over to him. "No, Dad. Don't get up. Mom said you threw your back out."

Her father made a face and waved a dismissive hand. "I'm fine. Ripping out tile is hard work. I just needed a little nap, is all."

"You didn't pull your back out?"

"Of course not," he scoffed, his tone saying the idea was ridiculous. But he winced after speaking the words.

Melissa leaned down and hugged her father, then sat on the edge of the bed. "It's good to see you, Dad."

"It's always good to see my favorite daughter."

"And what do you say to Arlene?" Melissa asked, raising an eyebrow in a feigned gesture of seriousness.

"That she's my favorite, too. A father is allowed to have two favorites."

"Only two?" Melissa asked.

"Two favorite children. And numerous favorite grandchildren."

"Hmm, that's convenient," Melissa said. Then she grinned down at her dad. "I love you." She got up off the bed. "You need anything?"

"I'd tell you to get me a beer, but your mother is watching me like a hawk. She thinks if I cut down on beer, my belly will disappear."

"How about water?" Melissa suggested.

"How about a new wife?" her father shot back.

"Sure. Should I go into town and pick one up for you?

Bringing her home could be tough, though. It could get ugly with Mom."

"I'll have some water," her father said grudgingly.

Melissa smirked, then exited the bedroom. She heard her cell phone ringing and quickly ran to the front of the house, where she'd dropped her purse. Seconds later, she had her phone in her hand and saw her sister's smiling face flashing on the screen.

"Hey, sis," Melissa greeted her.

"You here?" Arlene asked without preamble. "In Sheridan Falls?"

"Yep. Just got to Mom and Dad's."

"Great. We need you here ASAP."

A loud wail sounded in the background. "Where are you?" Melissa asked. "And what is going on?"

"We're at the bridal shop," Arlene told her. "Tasha is having a meltdown. She's worried your dress won't fit, and there's only a short time left for alterations. Tasha's maid of honor put on ten pounds and her dress has to be altered."

"I'm sure my dress will be fine," Melissa said. "I sent in my exact measurements for every part of my body, and my weight hasn't changed. I might have lost a couple of pounds, actually."

"Yeah, well, nothing's going to appease Tasha unless she sees it with her own eyes. How quickly can you get here?"

"I'm on my way."

Melissa arrived at the upscale bridal shop twelve minutes later and found the bridal party in the back. Tasha was slumped in a velour armchair, two of her bridesmaids on either side of her. Maxine, Tasha's older sister, stood to her right and held Tasha's hand. The friend who must be Tasha's maid of honor was on her knees beside the chaise. She was also holding Tasha's hand and worrying her bottom lip.

"How can you tell me everything will be all right, Maxine?" Tasha demanded. "Bonnie's dress doesn't fit. And she's my maid of honor. She has to look amazing."

Tasha shot a glance at the woman on her knees. Yes, she was definitely Bonnie. "It's only the zipper," Bonnie said. Her plump face lit up with a reassuring smile. "Enid already said that can be fixed. Plus, I'll eat only salad for the next two days."

"But what about Melissa?" Tasha countered. "What if her dress doesn't fi—"

Tasha's words died on her lips as her eyes ventured beyond the women trying to console her and landed on Melissa. Tasha immediately eased up in the chair. "Melissa?"

"Hey, you." Melissa beamed as she moved toward her cousin. The moment Tasha got to her feet, Melissa took her in her arms.

"You're here," Tasha said, then burst into tears.

"Hey," Melissa said softly, easing back and taking Tasha's hands in hers. "What's this all about?"

"I just want everything to be perfect, and if your dress doesn't fit…maybe they won't get all the alterations done in time."

"It'll fit," Melissa assured her.

The attendant, a red-haired woman with a worried expression on her face, whom Melissa had briefly noticed as she entered she shop, tentatively approached the group. "I'm Enid." She looked Melissa directly in the eye. "I take it you're Melissa."

"Yes."

"Oh, thank God." The woman's shoulders slumped with relief.

Melissa fully turned to face the woman, asking, "Where's my dress?"

"It's hanging in dressing room number four." Enid pointed toward the door. "You can try it on any time you're ready." Then she leaned close to Melissa and whispered, "But sooner would be better."

"Got it," Melissa said, facing her cousin and giving her a bright smile. "Everything's going to be okay. Don't you worry."

Tasha nodded, but her glum expression said she didn't believe Melissa's mollifying words.

Melissa greeted the other women with smiles and hellos, then briefly hugged her sister before heading into the dressing room. The bridesmaid dress was hanging on the back of the door. Melissa's eyes widened as she checked it out. It looked even more beautiful in person than it had in photos. The lavender dress was a floor-length, one-shoulder stunner. The charmeuse fabric was soft and shimmery. The bodice of the dress was covered with a layer of lace, and a ribbon of satin surrounded the dress's waist.

A lump of emotion suddenly formed in Melissa's throat. She'd always thought that by thirty, she would either be married or on her way to being married. Yet here she was, single with no prospects, while her twenty-seven-year-old cousin had found the love of her life.

Melissa disrobed and put the dress on. It was meant to be fitted from the waist up and flowed elegantly from the waist down. There was a slit in the dress that came to midthigh.

"Do you need any help?" the attendant asked.

Melissa opened the door. "If you could zip me up…"

The attendant eased forward and zipped the dress at the back, then Melissa fully exited the dressing room and moved to stand in front of the floor-to-ceiling mirror. The rest of the bridesmaids gathered around her. Through the mirror, Melissa could see their eyes lighting up. That was when she fully took note of her outfit, giving it a slow gaze from the top of the one shoulder, along the lace-covered bodice that somehow managed to make her breasts look more shapely, and down to the length of the flowing skirt. A smile spread on her face. It fit her perfectly. And she looked beautiful.

Tasha came up behind her, and her eyes filled with fresh tears. She had already cried a lot, given how puffy and red her eyes were. But at least these tears were happy ones.

A bubble of laughter escaped Tasha's throat. "It's perfect. You look gorgeous. Just stunning."

"I told you not to worry," Melissa said.

"You look so beautiful."

Melissa turned and faced her cousin, the gown swooshing around her bare feet. "But not nearly as beautiful as you'll be. The picture you sent me of you in your dress… you're going to knock Ryan off his feet."

"You think so?" Tasha asked, a hitch in her voice.

"I know so." Melissa reached out and tucked a strand of her cousin's curly hair behind her ear. "How could you not?"

Tasha beamed. "Everything's going to be fine, isn't it?"

"Of course it is," Melissa said. "Why wouldn't it be? You're marrying the love of your life, and he absolutely adores you. Everything is going to be perfect."

Tasha wiped at her eyes. "You're right." Then she glanced at the rest of the bridal party. "I'm sorry I've been such an emotional mess."

Maxine looped an arm through her sister's. "You've just got the prewedding jitters. It's perfectly normal."

"But Bonnie's dress—" Tasha said.

"Will be fine," Enid said, stepping forward. "There's enough room to let the dress out at the sides so that it zips up. I'll be working as long as necessary to make sure that everything is just right."

Tasha inhaled and exhaled deeply. "You've been so good to me, Enid. Working overtime to make sure that all is perfect."

"I'm happy that you gave our boutique the opportunity,"

Enid said, smiling. "A big wedding like yours... I thought for sure you'd find a boutique in Buffalo or New York City."

"Never," Tasha said. "You and I go way back. Fourth grade. Of course I'd give you the business." She squeezed Enid's hands, then glanced at her wristwatch. "Ooh, we only have a couple of hours before the welcome dinner. We should really get out of here so we can get ready."

Melissa glanced at Enid, seeing relief wash over her face. "The alterations will be started immediately," she said in an effort to allay any possible concerns that Tasha might have.

Melissa waved a dismissive hand. "No worries. We'll be back tomorrow for the dresses."

Tasha wandered back over to the armchair where she'd been sitting, lifted the champagne glass from the table beside it and finished off the contents. "Okay, ladies. My meltdown is over. Let's get ready for tonight's dinner."

Chapter 3

Tasha was marrying Ryan Burke, part of the Burke family dynasty in Sheridan Falls. He was Aaron's first cousin, which explained why Aaron—and his brothers—were in the wedding party.

Melissa slowed her car as she approached the sprawling house where the welcome dinner was to be held. The Burke estate.

She had never been there before, but she'd driven past it when she was a teenager. She and her friends had marveled at the mansion where the town's most famous family lived.

The Burke home was in an exclusive neighborhood in the city's west end. There were only three homes on this court, and the Burkes' house, in the center of the court, was the largest. It was arguably the largest house in town.

Though Ryan was Cynthia and Cyrus Burke's nephew, the welcome dinner was being held at their home because of its large size, plus its location on the lake, which made it an ideal spot.

Melissa pulled up behind a silver Lexus SUV. Her pulse was racing as she exited her car and made her way to the massive cobblestone driveway leading to the house. It was a Georgian colonial-style home with a gray stone and white wood exterior. There were two stately pillars standing on each side of the red front door, which provided a pop of color in the center of the house. The four pillars held up a rectangular balcony on the second floor.

There was a circular fountain in the center of the driveway, around which was a bed of colorful flowers. A myriad of luxury cars filled the space. Mercedes sedans and SUVs. BMWs. A classic Corvette was parked at the front of the house, before the main door. Canary yellow. That was Cyrus's vehicle. Melissa remembered him driving around in that sports car when she was young. The paint was shiny and polished, and there wasn't a blemish on it. If she hadn't known it was an older car, she would've thought it was brand-new.

Melissa counted approximately thirteen cars in the driveway, not including the ones parked on the street. The place was clearly packed. There were more people here than she'd expected for a welcome dinner, but she'd heard that the extended Burke family was vast.

Melissa took her time heading up to the house, acutely aware of the fact that she would be seeing Aaron any minute now. She wished more than anything that she had a man on her arm. It was silly, she knew. But she wished she could look outrageously happy with a gorgeous and affectionate man when she saw Aaron for the first time in years.

"You have nothing to prove to him," she told herself as she made her way along the stone path that led to the front door.

She could hear music coming from the back of the house and hoped that someone would be able to hear the door. She rang the doorbell and waited.

Less than a minute later, a man dressed in a black suit, white shirt and black bow tie answered the door. "Good afternoon," he said, greeting her with a warm smile.

"Hello," Melissa responded. "I'm here for the party."

"Of course. Take this hallway on the right, then take a left when you reach the kitchen. When you walk through the kitchen, you'll see the patio doors that lead to the backyard."

"Thank you." Melissa made her way to the right, following the instructions. She looked around in awe at the vivid paintings of landscapes on the walls, along with some African-inspired art, and wondered what it was like to live this kind of life. Everything about the house was grandiose. From the double staircase in the home's entryway to the wainscoting on the walls and the absolutely massive kitchen filled with gray-and-black marble, this place was absolutely gorgeous, and immaculately decorated.

To their credit, Cynthia and Cyrus Burke did not seem pretentious, even though they were clearly living the dream.

Melissa passed staff in the kitchen preparing trays of hors d'oeuvres. The waiter pouring champagne into flutes caught her eye, and she offered him a smile before continuing on to the patio doors, where she paused and looked outside. She exhaled softly.

Wow.

She stood with her hand on the doorknob, taking it all in. Just outside the doors was a massive deck. Palm trees— yes, palm trees—stood in all corners of the deck, providing a contrast to the white wood. The tree trunks were decked out in strings of tiny white lights. Happy people congregated on the deck, drinks and plates of appetizers in hand.

Melissa opened the door and stepped outside. She made her way to the back of the deck, where a staircase led to the lawn below. The yard was massive. There was no other word to describe it. The lawn extended for at least a couple hundred yards, where it ended at the lake. There was a dock there, with a pleasure boat moored to it. Melissa remembered that years ago when they'd watched his parents cruising on the lake one summer day, Aaron had said the boat was a Boston Whaler.

A huge white tent was set up in the middle of the backyard, and inside it Melissa could see tables and chairs. Just within the entrance to the tent was a table with a giant silver punch bowl, from which punch was flowing as if it were a fountain. Well-dressed people were mingling outside the tent, some inside. Classical music played through the speakers, creating a lovely ambience.

Melissa started down the steps. Most of the people here she either didn't know or hadn't seen in years. Where were the members of the bridal party?

And then she spotted Carlton Burke, Aaron's older brother. He was walking across the lawn on the far right side of the tent with a couple of other people. Melissa swallowed.

"Hello, there."

At the sound of the warm female voice behind her, Melissa turned. She saw Cynthia Burke, wearing a simple white dress with flowing sleeves, moving toward her with the grace of an angel.

"Is that you, Melissa?" Cynthia continued, her eyes lighting up. "All grown up?"

Melissa smiled at the friendly face she hadn't seen in years. "Yes, Mrs. Burke. It's me. How are you?"

Cynthia pulled her into an impromptu hug. "It's so good to see you again." Releasing her, she took Melissa's hand in both of hers. "My, you've grown up so much since your days working with Aaron as a camp counselor."

"Yes, ma'am," Melissa said.

"I'm so glad you're here." Cynthia beamed as she released her hand. Then she looked up at the sky. "And I'm very happy that the weather cooperated for this dinner."

"Yes, it's a beautiful day," Melissa agreed, glancing around. She felt an odd sensation and knew that it was the fear of seeing Aaron. He could appear at any moment, and she wasn't prepared for that.

"Help yourself to some punch," Cynthia said, pointing toward the tent. "Or if you'd like something from the bar, you can get a drink right there." She gestured behind her to the left. There was a patio area along the entire back of the house, complete with a number of white wrought iron tables and chairs. A full-service bar was set up. Two bartenders, a man and a woman, were busy making drinks.

The walk-out lower level of the house boasted floor-to-ceiling windows, and Melissa could only imagine how lovely it was to wake up each morning and start your day with a cup of tea or coffee while enjoying the view here.

"Thank you," she said to Cynthia. "I think I will get a drink."

Just as she spoke the words, the waiter she'd seen in the kitchen filling champagne flutes appeared. He extended the tray, and Melissa took a glass.

Slowly, Melissa walked in the direction of the lake, continuing to survey the massive property. Every tree on the property also had angel lights wrapped around the trunk. There was the fragrant scent of roses in the air, coming from several strategically placed pots filled with lavender-colored roses, which matched the color scheme for the wedding.

In the distance, the lake shimmered beneath the sun's rays. The beauty of this place was breathtaking. It would be a perfect spot for the wedding, if Tasha and Ryan had wanted to have it here.

Melissa took a sip of her champagne and gazed out at the lake again. In the distance, there were other homes that backed onto it. The lake bent and veered to the right a few hundred feet in the distance, and it was around that bend that the campground was.

The camp where Melissa and Aaron had worked as counselors the summer they'd fallen in love.

Well, *she* had fallen in love with him. She doubted that Aaron had ever been in love with her.

She sipped more champagne, needing something to help take the edge off her nerves. No matter how pleasant the view and the music, Melissa hated that she had to be here at the Burke residence right now. She wished she could skip this welcome dinner, but that wasn't an option.

"This is certainly going to be one interesting weekend," she muttered.

"It sure is."

A jolt hit Melissa's body with the force of a soccer ball slamming into her chest. That voice… A tingling sensation spread across her shoulder blades. It was a voice she hadn't heard in a long time. Deeper than she remembered, but it most definitely belonged to *him*.

Holding her breath, she turned. And there he was. Aaron Burke. Looking down at her with a smile on his face and a teasing glint in his eyes.

"I thought that was you," he said, his smile deepening.

Melissa stood there looking up at him from wide eyes, unsure what to say. Why was he grinning at her as though he was happy to see her?

"It's good to see you, Melissa."

Aaron spread his arms wide, an invitation. But Melissa stood still, as if paralyzed. With a little chuckle, Aaron stepped forward and wrapped his arms around her.

Melissa's heart pounded wildly. Why was he doing this? Hugging her as if they were old friends? As if he hadn't taken her virginity and then broken her heart.

"So we're paired off for the wedding," Aaron said as he broke the hug.

"So we are," Melissa said tersely. She was surprised that she'd found her voice. Her entire body was taut, her head light. She was mad at herself for having any reaction to this man.

"You're right, it's going to be a very interesting weekend indeed," Aaron said, echoing her earlier comment.

He looked good. More than good. He looked…delectable. Six feet two inches of pure Adonis, his body honed to perfection. Wide shoulders, a muscular chest and brawny arms fully visible in his short-sleeved dress shirt. His strong upper body tapered to a narrow waist. A wave of heat flowed through Melissa's veins, and she swallowed at the uncomfortable sensation. She quickly averted her eyes from his body and took a sip of champagne, trying to ignore the heat pulsing inside.

Good grief, what was wrong with her? She should be immune to Aaron's good looks. And yet she couldn't deny the visceral response that had shot through her body at seeing him again.

It was simply the reaction of a woman toward a man who was amazingly gorgeous. She wasn't dead, after all. She could find him physically attractive even if she despised him.

Although *despised* was too strong a word. He didn't matter to her enough for her to despise him.

Still, she couldn't help giving him another surreptitious once-over. He had filled out—everywhere. His arms were bigger, his shoulders wider, his legs more muscular. His lips were full and surrounded by a thin goatee—and good Lord, did they ever look kissable...

"I can't believe it's been ten years," Aaron said.

He didn't even remember. Why was she surprised? And worse, why was she irked?

"Closer to twelve," Melissa corrected him. "Eleven years, nine months. Something like that." She shrugged, hoping he didn't think that she had kept track of the exact date that they'd stopped talking.

"You're right," Aaron said, nodding. "It is almost twelve years. Wow, time flies."

"It sure does."

Melissa could hardly stand this. She glanced away, and relief flooded her when she saw her sister and Tasha. They were chatting with a group of guests about thirty feet away.

"You look good," Aaron said. "Amazing, actually."

His eyes roamed over her face, then her dress, and heat erupted inside her. Oh, how Melissa wished she could pretend the heat was simply anger, but it was more than that. She could see in Aaron's eyes that he thought she was beautiful, and her body was reacting to that reality.

Betraying her was more like it.

"It really is good to see you again."

Somehow, Melissa stopped herself from snorting. Was

it really nice, she wondered. If he was so happy to see her now, why had he cut off all communication with her years ago?

Melissa looked in Arlene's direction, and finally her sister saw her. Arlene's eyes lit up, and she waved.

Melissa waved back. Arlene was a lifeline at this moment, and Melissa took it. "Ah, there's my sister. I have to talk to her about something."

"Oh—"

"Later, Aaron," Melissa interjected, then strode off without giving him a chance to say another word.

She didn't dare look over her shoulder. Her heart was still pounding, a ridiculous reaction. So what if she'd seen Aaron Burke again? He didn't have the power to hurt her anymore. Her feelings for him had died years ago.

Was he watching her walk away?

Why did she care?

She *didn't*. But if any part of Aaron felt a measure of regret at cutting her out of his life, then good. She relished that thought.

He was happy to see her…as if! Why would he even say that? Was he trying to make nice after all these years, pretend that he'd never hurt her?

Well, if he thought there was a chance the two of them could ever be friends, he had another think coming.

Melissa inhaled deeply as she neared her sister. She was finally regaining her composure and her dignity. So what if Aaron was sexy? One of the sexiest men she'd ever laid eyes on, granted, but what did it matter when his character left so much to be desired?

She hoped he was happy with Ella, but she wasn't about to ask him about his wife. Nor was she about to spend any more time with him than was necessary. She didn't want him asking her about her life, and she didn't want to ask him about his. She would be paired with him for the wedding, deal with him as minimally as possible, and then go home to Jersey and forget all about him.

She had done it once. She would do it again.

Chapter 4

Ryan Burke clinked a fork against his champagne glass, effectively getting everyone's attention. Tasha stood beside him, a permanent smile on her beautiful face.

"Excuse me, everybody," Ryan said, looking around at the crowd of people. "Will you all please head into the tent and take your seats? Dinner is ready, so I hope you haven't indulged too heavily in the amazing hors d'oeuvres."

Ryan patted his stomach, as if to say he was guilty of exactly that. There were chuckles among the crowd.

"As you make your way into the tent," Ryan continued, "be aware there are names on the tables indicating where you're to be seated. We figured this way there'd be less confusion and less scrambling. It's buffet style, so please wait for your table to be called before heading into the line." He gestured toward the tent, indicating that everyone could proceed.

Melissa and Arlene wound their way into the tent with the rest of the guests. Melissa was already getting a bad feeling about the seating arrangements, and she crossed her arms over her torso as she glanced down at the first table to find her name.

"Oh, here we are," Arlene announced.

Melissa hurried to her sister's side. As she looked down at the names on the table, her stomach sank, her fear confirmed. Aaron Burke was seated to her left.

Oh, good God…

Not that she should be surprised, since they were paired off for the wedding. But still, this was too much for her to deal with.

When most of the guests were seated, Ryan and Tasha stood at the front of the tent. "We'll commence with the buffet line in a minute," Ryan said into a wireless microphone. "But Tasha and I would like to say a few words first. As you know, this is a welcome dinner for all of you who have come from far and near to be here with us for our special day."

Melissa glanced over her shoulder, saw Aaron entering the tent and quickly took her seat. As she did, she continued to survey the crowd. Where was Ella? As Aaron's wife, shouldn't she be here? Melissa would expect the woman to attend if for no other reason than to gloat. To show off to all those who had returned to town just how special she was because she had snagged a Burke brother.

Aaron and his father, Cyrus, were standing near the entrance of the tent chatting. An old classmate, Douglas Hanover, walked past them, heading in Melissa's direction. Before she knew what she was doing, Melissa was jumping to her feet and practically throwing herself into Douglas's path.

"Douglas?" she all but squealed. "Douglas Hanover!"

"Melissa?" His eyebrows raised as a question flashed in his eyes.

"Yes, it's me." She beamed at him. "Oh my goodness, it's been so long." She hugged him and noticed that he was stiff for a moment before hugging her back. "I see you on television all the time," she said as they pulled apart. "I always trust your forecasts."

"You watch me on the morning news?"

Douglas was employed by a network in New York City, and Melissa watched him every morning as she got ready for work. "Every day," she said. "I'm in Newark."

"Ah, okay."

She glanced beyond Douglas's shoulder at Aaron, trying to not make it obvious that she was looking at him. He was staring at her, watching her with curiosity. Even when she'd left him and joined her sister and Tasha, she'd noticed Aaron looking at her here and there.

"You always said you wanted to be a weatherman," Melissa said and grinned widely. Did she look idiotic? Or like a woman flirting with a potential new guy?

Aaron and his father were walking toward the front of the tent now—and heading right in her direction. "We should get together for coffee sometime," Melissa said to Douglas, speaking loudly enough for her voice to carry. "I get into the city quite a bit."

"That would be awesome," Douglas said. "Here, meet my wife." Douglas extended an arm, and a gorgeous woman Melissa had noticed heading in their direction sidled up next to him. "This is Diana. She's one of the producers of the morning show."

"Oh…" Melissa wanted to slink into her chair. Not because she cared that Douglas had a wife. She was happy for him. But because she had hoped to find someone— anyone—with whom she could flirt. There was something about the intense gaze Aaron had been leveling on her that had her distinctly uncomfortable. If she had someone else with whom she could spend some time, maybe he would throw his wandering eyes in someone else's direction.

"Very nice to meet you," Melissa said, shaking the woman's hand.

Diana's smile seemed forced, and Melissa couldn't blame her. To her, Melissa must have seemed like a threat. A woman determined to pounce on her husband.

"Lovely to meet you as well," Diana said, her voice professional and poised but lacking sincerity. "Sweetheart, we should go get our seats."

"Of course," Douglas said. "Melissa, we'll talk later."

No, they wouldn't. Melissa had already made a fool of herself. She felt bad for her pathetic display of flirtation, but seeing Aaron had gotten to her.

She glanced at her old flame again, saw that he was indeed looking at her even as he spoke to another guest. She quickly sat back down.

"What was that about?" Arlene asked, her gaze following Douglas.

"I just… I guess I reacted as a fan," Melissa lied. "I watch him on television every morning."

Arlene didn't look entirely convinced, but Melissa was saved from having to answer any more questions when Ryan began to speak again.

"Thank you, everyone, for taking your seats," Ryan said as the last of the stragglers found their tables. "And thank you all for being here. Isn't it a great day?"

People clapped, and some cheered.

"Tasha and I are glad that the sun is shining and that the forecast for the weekend is clear skies all around. I put in a special request to Douglas, and he delivered!"

There were chuckles among the crowd, and Douglas waved a hand.

"But more importantly," Ryan went on, "Tasha and I are happy that each and every one of you is able to join us for our special occasion. This wedding wouldn't be the same without you here. So we thank you so much for taking time out of your schedules to be a part of this."

"There's nowhere else we'd rather be," someone said, raising a wineglass.

There was a round of *hear hear*s, and people raised their glasses in turn.

Ryan smiled. "Many of you here are in the wedding party, and some of you are dear family and friends. All of you are important in our lives in some way. So this welcome dinner is as much about thanking you all for being here with us as it is a cause for celebration."

Aaron slipped into the seat beside Melissa. She twirled the stem of her wineglass, pretending she hadn't noticed.

"Some of you asked why we're not having the wedding

here," Ryan continued. "And this is certainly a stunning location. But aside from the fact that this house might not hold all the guests my wife-to-be wanted to invite…" Ryan glanced down at Tasha, who was now seated, and she gave him a sheepish smile. "It's also very important to Tasha and to me that we have our wedding in a church. We want God's blessing on our union, and we feel that's the right way to do it."

"Amen," Cynthia Burke said. Beside her, Cyrus patted her hand.

The one thing that Melissa had always liked about Cyrus and Cynthia was their absolute devotion to each other. Even as a child, she had seen how much they loved each other. How odd that their sons had become such players, despite the example of their loving and doting father.

Why was she even thinking about this?

But she knew why. She could feel the heat emanating from Aaron's body beside her, and it was stressing her out.

Tasha got to her feet and took the microphone from Ryan's hand. "But despite the number of people attending the wedding, it will still have an intimate feel. Because we love each and every one of you so much. Blood or not, you're all family."

Melissa lifted the bottle of Riesling that was on the table and poured some into her glass. A whiff of Aaron's cologne, musky and masculine, wafted into her nostrils. The heat from his body continued to radiate toward her, and she had to swallow.

He was entirely too much man. The problem was, he knew it.

She should be counting her lucky stars that their relationship had fallen apart. God forbid, what if they'd gotten married? He would've broken her heart the way he had Ella's.

Ella had fought so hard to snag a Burke brother, no doubt

for the bragging rights, but she'd had to endure Aaron's infidelity. Successful soccer player, wanted by many women around the world—it was no wonder that he had such an inflated sense of ego and had not been able to remain faithful.

At least Melissa had avoided that very life, a life she would not have been able to deal with. She didn't care how successful a man was; she demanded fidelity. She would not stand by her man as he cheated on her, just to keep the facade of a happy home and to maintain whatever luxuries she had become accustomed to. Material things didn't matter when your heart was breaking over and over again.

"Melissa, will you pass the wine?" Aaron asked.

A simple request, yet Melissa wanted to pretend she hadn't heard him. But a nanosecond later, she knew the evening would be that much harder if she played this game.

So she raised the bottle and poured him a glass.

Carlton appeared at the table then and took a seat on her right. She had already learned that he would be paired with her sister for the wedding.

"Melissa Conwell," Carlton said, smiling warmly at her. "It's good to see you again."

"It's good to see you as well," Melissa said, and she was glad that she had Carlton to chat with. It saved her from having to spend more time talking to Aaron.

"I can see that the staff is itching to take over," Ryan said, glancing at a man standing off to the side who was dressed like a butler. "But despite the table numbers, I'd like to ask that the table with my parents, grandparents and our gracious hosts for this evening, my uncle Cyrus and aunt Cynthia, make their way to food line first. Please, everyone, give them a round of applause."

People clapped as two generations of Burkes stood. They acknowledged the guests with warm smiles before making their way over to the food.

A hum of chatter filled the tent. Wilma, Tasha's aunt,

was seated with them because she was in the wedding party, and Melissa was glad that she was. Wilma was a talker, the type who liked to be the center of attention. She regaled the table with a story about how she'd been out with one of her sons in Buffalo and people thought they were dating. Wilma was in her fifties, but looked no older than her late thirties. She loved that no one was able to guess her age.

"So, Melissa," Aaron said.

She started to turn toward him, but the butler called their table then, announcing that they could proceed to get their food.

Melissa was the first one to jump up.

Anything to escape Aaron.

Chapter 5

She was ignoring him.

Aaron had made that determination shortly into dinner, when Melissa turned her attention to those on her right and kept it there throughout the night. She threw her head back and laughed many times, as though the conversation on that side of the table was utterly fascinating. She barely threw him a second glance as she proceeded to have the time of her life engaging with everyone at the table but him.

Which meant only one thing. She was angry with him. Maybe she even hated him.

Almost twelve years had passed since he'd last seen her, and apparently those years had not been long enough to bury any animosity between them. He had hoped that now, years later, with both of them more mature, they could re-kindle their friendship. Even though things had fallen apart between them, he'd missed her friendship.

She had been a godsend in his life that summer when they'd dated, especially when he had been able to open up about the tragedy that had shaped his life. His little sister, Chantelle, had drowned. On his watch. He'd never been able to forgive himself.

Every great milestone he'd achieved had been marred by guilt. Good things were happening for him, yet Chantelle was dead. Did he actually deserve happiness when it was his fault that his sister had drowned?

That dark cloud had hung over him his whole life, even now, no matter how hard he'd tried to shake it.

That night he'd opened up to Melissa, she'd assured him that he did deserve love, happiness and success. And he had so wanted to believe her. Their relationship had seemed perfect, but perfect never lasted, did it? He'd learned that with Chantelle, so before it was too late, he'd ended the relationship with Melissa.

"Did you try the cheesecake?" Arlene asked, extending the plate of bite-size desserts past Carlton and toward Melissa. "This is to die for."

"No, let me try one."

Melissa took the plate of desserts, plucked a cherry cheesecake, then placed it beside the fruit on the small plate she already had. She didn't bother to extend the dessert plate to Aaron; she just put it down.

Aaron smirked slightly. Yeah, she was upset with him.

At the front of the tent, Ryan stood and spoke into the microphone. "Just so you all know, the party's not over. Please join us for some dancing. DJ, hit it!"

The next instant, a funky old school tune exploded from the speakers. People were standing, sitting or chatting, and some now made their way out of the tent, jiggling their bodies as they did.

"Please, enjoy the bar, the dance floor, the music," Ryan went on. "The dinner is over, but the night is young. And the wedding is in two days, so you can sleep in tomorrow."

Melissa quickly got up from the table and walked over to Arlene. They shared some conversation that Aaron couldn't hear. His eyes were on her, watching her every move.

She was mesmerizing. She was as enthralling as she had been when he'd known her years ago. If she had come here hoping to avoid him, she should have picked anything other than the sexy red dress she was wearing. Because she had his attention. And he couldn't keep his eyes off her. She was the most gorgeous woman here.

The dress was stunning. The formfitting, stretchy fabric highlighted her hourglass figure. She was the epitome of a sexy vixen, with those large breasts, narrow waist and voluminous hips. The black pumps she was wearing had a streak of red on the underside, and Aaron found himself thinking about sex.

With her.

As soon as he could get her naked.

Her hair was pulled up into a chignon and he wished more than anything that he could hold her in his arms, release the hairpins and let those raven strands down. He was tired of her frosty reaction to him, and he wanted to help her warm up to him and unleash her inner vixen.

The first song faded into another upbeat tune. "Ooh, that's my song!" Bonnie exclaimed. She took both Melissa and Arlene by the hand and pulled them out from the tent. The three women made their way to the dance floor that had been set up while everyone ate dinner. Aaron watched them go, his eyes fixed on the shapely figure in the red dress.

Out of nowhere, his brother Keith, younger by a year, appeared and plopped himself down on the chair that Melissa had vacated.

"Have you finalized the plans for the bachelor party?" Keith asked.

Aaron nodded. "The limo's arriving at eleven."

"And he knows nothing about it?"

"Ryan is clueless."

Keith smiled. "Good."

Melissa had had enough, and she kicked off her heels. She wiggled her bare toes, hoping to bring circulation back into them. The shoes were beautiful, one of her rare splurges, but she could only wear them for so long. She had passed the threshold of comfort quite some time ago. There was no way she could continue on the dance floor in these.

"Whoever invented high heels wanted to torture women," Melissa said above the music. She was dancing with Arlene now, as Bonnie had bopped off somewhere else.

"That's why I wear flats as much as I can," Arlene said, then raised a foot to show her sensible flat sandals.

Melissa typically did sensible, but today, she'd wanted to do something different. Wanted to come back to Sheridan Falls and make a certain someone realize what he'd missed out on. The beauty of it was, Aaron could only look but not touch, because he was married.

Speaking of married, where was his wife? She hadn't been here all evening.

Arlene leaned close and asked, "Are you going to the bachelorette party?"

"I'm here, so I guess I'm going to join everyone as we make the rounds."

"I'm not sure I'll be able to make it." Arlene frowned. "Craig says he's busy tonight, and he's giving me a hard time about being a neglectful mom. I might have to pick up Raven from the babysitter's."

"Neglectful mom? What the heck is he talking about? You're an awesome mother."

"He's just…he's finding any excuse to pick a fight with me. I don't know if I have it in me tonight to argue with him."

"How's he even going to know if you go out?" Melissa asked.

Arlene's lips twisted as she looked at her. "This is a small town, remember?"

Her sister was right. The smallest of news spread like wildfire in this town.

"He's been on my case about having the babysitter watch her too much. I don't know how he expects me to hold down a job…"

"Why don't you ask Mom and Dad to watch her?" Melissa suggested. "He can't complain about doting grandparents."

"They're always coming through for me. Sometimes

I feel guilty for leaning on them too much. I don't know. Tonight I might just stay home."

Melissa's eyebrows shot up as she looked into Arlene's eyes, trying to gauge her sister's mood. "Everything okay? Is there more going on than you're telling me?"

Arlene shrugged. "I'm just a little bit stressed. Working, being a single mom…it's not easy."

"All the more reason for you to come out with us tonight and enjoy yourself."

Melissa knew that the plan was to head to Buffalo and make the rounds at several bars. Tasha was ready for her big night, complete with an outfit that would let everyone know she was a single woman about to be married. The bridesmaids were going to treat her to her last big hurrah, so to speak. Perhaps there would be some flirting, but nothing outrageous. They weren't going to have strippers or anything like that. Just enjoy a great time bonding before Tasha's big day.

"I'll see," Arlene said with a shrug.

The music had changed from a hip-hop beat to something slow, and Melissa watched as Ryan pulled Tasha into his arms in the middle of the dance floor. A smile tugged at Melissa's lips. It was nice seeing her cousin so happy.

"Mind if I steal you?"

Melissa's spine stiffened. Certainly Aaron was *not* speaking to her.

Swallowing, Melissa glanced up and over her shoulder and saw that her ears had not been playing tricks on her. "Steal me for what?" she asked.

"To dance with you."

Was he out of his mind? "Arlene and I are discussing something."

"No, you go on," Arlene said. "Dance. I'll talk to you in a little bit."

"But…" Melissa's protest died in her throat when Arlene smiled at Aaron, then headed off the dance floor.

Melissa wanted to scream at her sister. Why would she encourage Aaron dancing with her? She knew how much he had hurt her years ago. Besides, he was a married man, so dancing to a slow tune with him was inappropriate.

Aaron stepped forward and slipped his arms around her waist. Melissa stood as still as a rock.

"I won't bite," Aaron said, trying to urge her body to sway to the music. Then he leveled a charming smile at her.

Melissa could almost imagine his unspoken words. *Unless you want me to…*

Oh, he thought he was smooth!

Because she knew it would look ridiculous to stand ramrod straight while Aaron tried to lead her in a dance, Melissa moved with him. But she eased her body backward as far as possible so that people watching them wouldn't get any crazy ideas. The last thing she needed was to come back to town and be embroiled in any sort of scandal.

"So," Aaron began, "we finally have a moment to talk."

Melissa said nothing.

"Are you still going to give me the silent treatment?"

Melissa made a face as she looked at him. "What are you talking about? We've talked all evening."

He raised his eyebrows and pursed his lips. "You've barely said anything to me."

"I don't know what you expect me to say. I haven't seen you in years."

"True." Aaron was silent for a moment as he turned with her, edging her ever closer against his body as he did. He leaned in and said softly, "It really is good to see you again. You look amazing."

Melissa glanced up at him. She felt a tingle of warmth as she saw the expression in his eyes, something that looked a lot like attraction.

He held her gaze for a long moment, and God help her, the warmth turned to a searing heat. Why was he looking at her as though he wanted to...

To kiss her?

No, she must be imagining things. Maybe he was just fascinated that he was seeing her again. Maybe there was even some level of regret on his part, knowing that he'd let a good woman go. She could only imagine what his life was like with Ella. Despite that Aaron was rumored to be a playboy, she couldn't imagine that Ella made his life easy.

But that had been his choice, hadn't it?

The reality that he'd rejected her hit her anew, killing any bit of physical attraction she was feeling.

When was this song going to end? She couldn't handle this anymore.

"It certainly looks as though life is treating you well," Aaron said.

"It is," Melissa said, exaggerating the excitement in her tone. "My life is amazing. I have no complaints."

"That's good to hear. I always wanted good things for you."

Melissa wanted to roll her eyes and tell him not to be patronizing. What, did he think she'd lived a boring and unhappy life because he hadn't been with her?

"You're single?"

"That doesn't mean I'm not happy."

Aaron looked at her askance. "I didn't say that."

No, he hadn't. Melissa was being far too sensitive. She inhaled deeply and told herself to calm down.

"I'm glad you're happy, that life is going well for you."

"Thank you." Though Melissa didn't want to be conversing with Aaron, she figured she ought to offer something to the conversation. "And you've been very successful. Soccer worked out well for you."

"It did, yes."

"Well, that's what you always wanted. Congratulations."

"Thanks." Aaron released her to take her by one hand and twirl her around. Then he pulled her close again. "You know, when I found out you were going to be in the wedding party, I asked Ryan to make sure we were paired up."

Melissa couldn't help gaping at him. "You did?"

"I figured it'd be fun."

Was he out of his mind? *Fun?* Was that what this was to Aaron? A game?

She didn't know what was going through his mind. Maybe he was flirting with her because he was one of those guys who wanted to feel that no woman could resist him.

The very fact that he was dancing with her like this was disrespectful to Ella.

Again, Melissa wondered where she was. How had the Ella she'd known in high school given up this opportunity to gloat on the arm of her husband?

Aaron splayed his fingers across her back, making her skin tingle. He pulled her close as the slow song came to an end, and for one insane moment, Melissa reveled in the feeling of her body pressed against his. She luxuriated in the heat that consumed her.

But only for a moment.

Because the next instant, she pushed herself backward, though he refused to release her.

"I think that's enough," she said, looking up into his eyes. Why did he keep looking at her with that smoky gaze, as though he wanted nothing more than to get naked with her?

"It's not nearly enough," Aaron replied.

Melissa glanced around uncomfortably, certain that she would see disapproving gazes everywhere. Instead, she saw Tasha looking at her with happy curiosity.

"Maybe this is just your...*way*," Melissa said distastefully, "but I'm not going to become a point of gossip for this town."

"We're dancing," Aaron said, and when Melissa tried to extricate herself from his grasp, he used the opportunity to twirl her around again.

Oh, he was infuriating!

Even though the tempo of the new song was upbeat and didn't lend itself to slow dancing, Aaron snaked a hand around her waist and pulled her against his body. Despite her irritation with him, a fresh wave of heat washed over Melissa. She looked up at him, aghast, and saw that the edges of his lips were curled in a grin. He thought this was funny!

"Aaron, that's enough," Melissa said, her voice firm. She knew what would happen tomorrow. Phones all across town would be ringing, people gleefully sharing the news that Melissa Conwell had been getting all cozy with Aaron Burke at the welcome dinner for the wedding.

Finally, Melissa wiggled her way out of Aaron's arms and glanced around, trying once again to ascertain just how much of a spectacle she'd become.

"What's the matter?" Aaron asked.

Melissa guffawed. "You're not serious."

"I'm dead serious. I was hoping you'd be happy to see me."

Melissa wanted to give him a piece of her mind, but instead she forced a neutral look onto her face. Leaning forward, she said in a low voice, "I know that you're used to women fawning all over you, but this isn't Europe, where no one cares. This is Sheridan Falls. Everyone here knows you're married."

Instead of looking even a little embarrassed for his unflattering behavior, Aaron chuckled.

"I can't believe you think this is funny. Consider your wife. And what people will say. By tomorrow, all seven thousand residents in this town will be talking about us and our disrespectful behavior on the dance floor."

"If you'll stop for a minute, I have something to tell you," Aaron said.

Melissa frowned. "Tell me what?"

"Ella and I are divorced."

Chapter 6

"What?" Melissa exclaimed, and she was glad that another upbeat tune had started to play, drowning out her voice to those within immediate earshot.

"We divorced a year and a half ago," Aaron explained.

Melissa knew she must look stupefied. "You and Ella are no longer married?"

"Actually, that's not true," Aaron said, and Melissa's heart pounded furiously. "We split a little over a year and a half ago," he went on, "but our divorce was finalized six weeks ago."

She stared at him, blinking but saying nothing. He was lying. He had to be. Melissa would have heard.

But why would he lie about that? In this town of seven thousand people, there was no way he could get away with saying something so untrue.

"I heard you guys were having problems, sure. But I also heard that you retired and returned to Sheridan Falls to work on your marriage."

"There was no saving our marriage when I retired last year," Aaron said, "but that was the spin on the story."

Melissa frowned. "If you got divorced, then why haven't I heard? It's not like anyone can keep a secret in this town."

"Ella and I kept this one," Aaron said. "I was tired of everything I did becoming fodder for the rumor mill, so I made a deliberate attempt to keep the news of the actual divorce very quiet. I didn't want the headache of the press salivating over every perceived sordid detail. For Ella's part, I don't think she was too keen on spreading the news either, especially after she got a lot of negative feedback for some of what she said about me to the press previously. So she agreed to keep things quiet. We went to another city, got it done. Only our families knew, and they were sworn to secrecy. This is my first official event as a divorced man, and as such, I've finally been letting people know."

"Wow," Melissa said, stunned. "I'm completely shocked. I'm sorry, by the way."

Aaron waved a dismissive hand. "Don't be sorry. It was a long time coming."

Aaron and Ella had split. Melissa's head was spinning. What exactly had happened? Who had ended things?

Maybe it had been Ella who'd ended the relationship, finally tired of Aaron's womanizing. Or had he grown bored of her?

She didn't care, so why was she even thinking about this?

"I'm sorry nonetheless," Melissa said. "I'm sure it wasn't easy."

"Thank you," Aaron said. "These things happen." He shrugged casually, as if it was no big deal.

And maybe for him it wasn't. The little she'd read about him in the tabloids indicated that fidelity was something he wasn't interested in. Maybe Ella had finally gotten smart and put her foot down.

Aaron narrowed his eyes as he regarded her. "Do you really think I'd be dancing with you like this if I were married?"

Melissa hesitated. She wanted to say no, but how could she? Celebrities were a different breed, and their behavior often left a lot to be desired.

"Don't celebrities live by their own code?" she countered.

"So that's a yes? Even with my parents here?"

"You're a grown man. They certainly can't stop you from doing what you like."

Aaron narrowed his eyes as he regarded her. She wasn't sure what he was thinking, but she could see his disappointment.

"I wouldn't bring dishonor to my parents, Melissa. I thought you would know that."

I know nothing about you was what she wanted to say. But when she saw Arlene whizzing toward her behind Aaron, her body sagged with relief. Thank God. She needed an excuse to escape Aaron and this uncomfortable conversation.

But as her sister neared her, Melissa's relief turned to concern. "Arlene, what's wrong?" she asked, seeing the stress on her sister's face.

"I need a ride."

"What is it?" Melissa asked.

"Aaron, I'm really sorry to interrupt you guys," Arlene said.

"No problem," Aaron told her.

Arlene took Melissa by the hand and led her away, throwing an apologetic glance over her shoulder at Aaron. "I'm sorry, Mel."

Melissa waved at her concern. "No, don't be sorry." In fact, she could thank her sister. Her interruption was perfect timing. "What's wrong?"

"I came here with Maxine, and I don't want to disturb her. She's having fun." She blew out a harried breath. "I need to leave."

"Why?"

"Raven is pitching a fit and I've got to go deal with her. The babysitter says she won't settle until she sees me. Who knew four-year-olds could wield such power?"

Melissa's worry abated. She'd feared something worse was going on. "She'll probably calm down in a little bit."

"She's been acting out since Craig and I split," Arlene explained. "She's having quite the tantrum, apparently. I'd really better go now. If we're going out later and I can get her down, I can have the babysitter stay with her for the night. I know this is inconvenient, but do you mind giving me a ride?"

Melissa threw a glance over her shoulder at Aaron, saw

that he was still looking at her. He probably wanted to pick up the conversation where they'd left off.

No, thank you.

Melissa faced her sister and gave her a reassuring smile. "No problem at all. Let's go."

"Thanks, sis. You can always come back."

"Naw, I'm good. Plus, I'll see the girls later tonight."

"Let me say goodbye to Tasha and Ryan and Cyrus and Cynthia," Arlene said.

Together they found Tasha and Ryan, then the Burkes and said their goodbyes.

"It was so lovely to see you again," Cynthia said, holding both of Melissa's hands. "It's nice to have you back in town."

"It's good to be back," Melissa said. She couldn't help wondering if there was something to Cynthia's smile and warmth. Had she jumped to conclusions seeing her and Aaron together?

"Okay, let's get out of here," Arlene said.

Melissa fell into step beside Arlene. Only once they were on the deck and away from the guests did Melissa ask, "Did you hear that Aaron and Ella divorced?"

Arlene's eyes grew wide. "They did?"

Melissa had asked the question in part to gauge her sister's response. Though she doubted Arlene would know and say nothing. Arlene genuinely hadn't heard. Aaron *had* managed to pull off the impossible—keep a secret in this town.

"He told me when we were dancing," Melissa explained.

"Oh my goodness! I knew they were separated, but Ella always told anyone who would listen that they were working on their marriage. Obviously, none of my friends heard or *someone* would have told me." Arlene paused. "Can I share the news?"

Melissa shot her sister a sideways glance. "You just can't wait to start making calls, can you?"

Arlene couldn't help smiling. "Well, this *is* big news."

"Aaron said they've finally started letting people know, just now, so it's not a secret."

"It's not surprising," Arlene said. "The stories of his cheating were rampant. I guess despite what Ella said, she finally had enough."

"I guess so."

Melissa led the way across the driveway and out to the street where her car was parked. Aaron clearly had a way with women. Not only was he gorgeous, he was charming. And successful. With his level of success came a certain amount of confidence. Of arrogance. Of expectation.

It was why he'd so easily put his arms around her and pulled her close on the dance floor, as if he expected that his mere presence would drive her crazy. She didn't want to know how many women he'd seduced with that easy smile and just the right touch.

Still, her body couldn't quite shake the hint of excitement his touch elicited.

Good grief, she was pathetic.

She pulled her keys from her purse and unlocked the door, then tried to shake off the memory of Aaron's arms around her waist. A memory that brought her back to twelve years ago. Twelve years ago on the lake, under a moonlit sky, tenderly kissing the young man she'd thought she would love forever.

Losing her virginity to him.

That was ancient history, a very long time ago.

Melissa would do well to remember that.

Chapter 7

"I'm getting married!" Tasha exclaimed to everyone on the street as the bridal party exited their third bar.

There was some hooting and cheering from passersby, and Tasha threw up her hands and gyrated her body. She'd had at least three or four shots and was clearly feeling no pain.

It was just after midnight, and the bridal party was making the rounds in Buffalo's downtown core. Arlene had begged off, deciding to stay home with her daughter, who had been fussing a little too much and wouldn't settle. Melissa had also tried to politely decline the evening's festivities, claiming that her long drive from New Jersey had left her tired, but Bonnie had insisted that Melissa attend.

"Tasha wants you there. She *needs* you," the maid of honor had stressed. "This night is about all of us bonding as much as it is about Tasha's last big night as a single woman. If everyone starts bailing, how's she supposed to feel?"

Melissa had gotten the point and agreed to go out. She didn't have a child to use as an excuse, after all, and figured that at least tonight she could truly unwind and relax.

Unlike during the welcome party, where she hadn't been able to fully enjoy herself with Aaron around.

The five of them walked into bar number four, Tasha leading the way. Heads turned, just as they had when they'd strutted into the first few bars and when they'd walked down the street. All it took was a glance to realize that their group was out for a bachelorette party. Tasha was decked out in a plastic crown and veil, the word *bride* written in sparkling silver glitter on the crown. Strings of cheap plastic beads, Mardi Gras style, hung around her neck.

Wilma, Tasha's aunt, walked right up to the bar and found a space between two people sitting on bar stools. No one could accuse her of being shy or lacking self-confidence. Despite being in her early fifties, she had as much energy and spunk as the thirtysomethings. She'd already had to fight off male admirers—which really seemed to please her.

Melissa and the rest of the bridal party gathered close behind Wilma. "Ah, a bachelorette party," the attractive bartender said, his eyes volleying from Wilma to the rest of them.

"Yes," Wilma said. "My niece is getting married."

"Niece?" The man's jaw nearly hit the bar. "You mean she's not your sister?"

Wilma blushed. Melissa got the feeling that if she weren't happily married, she would leave a string of broken hearts in her wake. She probably had in her youth.

"You're too kind," Wilma said. The man sitting on the bar stool to Wilma's left got up and walked away, and Wilma quickly took his seat. "We'd love a round of shooters. Flaming sambuca."

Melissa opened her mouth to protest, but then stopped when the rest of the bridal party began to hoot and holler in agreement. They were having fun, and she wasn't about to be the party pooper. Especially since they'd taken a limo to Buffalo for their night on the town, meaning they could all drink and not worry about driving. Wilma's idea.

Besides, she was enjoying the camaraderie that she never got much of these days. As the program director at the Turning Tides group home in Newark, her days and nights were often filled with emergencies, bad behavior, court dates and dealing with one crisis after another. But it had been a long time since she'd gone out, let her hair down and had some fun.

"Five flaming sambuca shots coming right up," the bartender said. "By the way, I like your shirts."

Tasha beamed. "Thank you." She had wanted everyone to wear T-shirts that announced their role in the wedding.

They were lavender, one of the wedding colors, and *bride*, *maid of honor* and *bridesmaid* were printed in a white cursive font on the corresponding shirts. There was no mistaking that they were celebrating an upcoming wedding. They all had feather boas slung around their necks, adding to the look.

Bonnie leaned in close to Wilma and said, "We can't spend too much time in here."

Wilma glanced at her watch. "We've got a bit of time."

"What's going on?" Melissa asked, picking up on the air of secrecy. Bonnie and Wilma had been sharing quiet conversation for the last half hour or so.

Wilma raised her eyebrows and smirked as she looked at Melissa. "Just a little surprise for Tasha."

Melissa regarded her with suspicion. "What kind of surprise?"

Wilma raised a finger to her lips and indicated for Melissa to be quiet.

Oh, goodness. Were male strippers a part of tonight's plans? Melissa had *not* signed up for that! The last thing she needed was someone snapping a photo of her in some sort of compromising position and putting it on social media. Sure, no one would likely know who she was, since all of her social media accounts were set to private, but still. She'd never liked the idea of half-naked men dancing in front of her. What was the point?

Tasha sidled up next to her. "Shocking news about Aaron. I can't believe he got divorced and no one knew."

Aaron's divorce had been the topic of conversation during their drive to Buffalo. The news had spread like wildfire.

"You think you two will hook up?" Tasha asked.

Melissa's eyes bulged. *"What?"*

Two more people vacated seats at the bar, and Tasha hoisted herself up onto the stool beside Wilma's. "I saw you and Aaron earlier. You both looked pretty cozy, like you were having a good time. At the time I wondered what he was thinking, but now that I know he's a free man…"

Melissa's face flamed. Then she chuckled uncomfortably. "Um, I have no clue what you're talking about."

"The two of you on the dance floor, getting up close and personal." Tasha wiggled her eyebrows.

"What are you talking about? We were certainly *not* getting up close and personal."

"You looked real comfortable to me," Tasha insisted.

"Comfortable is the last thing I was feeling," Melissa stressed.

"You could have fooled me," Wilma chimed in.

Melissa's head jerked toward her. "What?"

"See," Tasha said, "I wasn't the only one who noticed." Wilma reached beyond Melissa to high-five Tasha.

"You two are killing me," Melissa said. "A woman can't talk to a guy in our small town without it being scandalous?"

No one responded to her, because at that moment the bartender placed five shooter glasses on the bar in front of them and said, "Five flaming sambucas for the most attractive bridal party I've seen in ages."

His eyes held Wilma's for a long while before passing over the rest of them. Oh, he was a charmer.

And his charm was working. Wilma took a number of bills from her wallet—far more than were necessary. She was going to leave him a big tip.

"What's your name, sweetheart?" Wilma asked.

"Peter," he answered, then skillfully filled the glasses, which were set directly beside each other so that their rims were touching, with one long pour. Tasha watched wide-eyed, as though this was the most fascinating thing she'd ever seen. And when Peter then used a lighter to set each drink aflame, Tasha cheered and clapped, followed by the rest of the bridal party.

Except for Melissa. Though she was having fun, Tasha's

comment had her feeling a little…flustered. She hadn't looked cozy with Aaron, had she? How could she? She'd been the complete opposite of cozy.

"Come on," Bonnie said, pushing a drink in the direction of each woman. "Drink up, ladies."

This night was taking Melissa back to her college days, though she'd never been a wild partier even then.

Tasha lifted her drink and held it high. "To Melissa getting reacquainted with Aaron," she said in a singsong voice. "Who, I must say, is sexier than he's ever been."

The women all lifted their drinks and downed them, but Melissa didn't. She stared at each of the women in turn, her stomach filling with dread. "What are you guys talking about?"

"We all noticed it," Wilma said. "You and Aaron getting close…the way he was looking at you."

"How was he looking at me?" Melissa regretted asking the question the moment the words left her lips.

"Um, as though he'd like to get naked with you!" Bonnie answered and started chuckling. "I've never even met the man before today and I could see the lust in his eyes."

Melissa wished her sister were here to defend her. She would tell them all that they'd been imagining things.

"Quick, drink your shooter," Maxine told her.

Melissa threw her head back and drank. Warmth immediately spread across her face. But whether the heat was from the alcohol or her embarrassment, she couldn't be sure.

God, leave it to people in small towns to jump to conclusions. This was ridiculous.

"I haven't seen Aaron in nearly twelve years," Melissa said. "We danced. We talked. Is that what it takes to get people excited in Sheridan Falls?"

"Are you seeing anyone?" Bonnie asked. "Tasha tells me that you and Aaron dated the summer before college."

Melissa tried to suppress her frown. She didn't even know Bonnie, Tasha's best friend who lived in California with her. How had Tasha managed to fill her in on *her* life?

"I always thought they'd make it work," Tasha said, and her expression became wistful.

Melissa wondered when this evening had become about her. Wasn't it supposed to be about Tasha?

"You aren't seeing anyone, right?" Tasha asked, her eyes lighting up with hope.

"Not right now I'm not," she answered. "But what does that matt—"

"That's a start," Bonnie said. "You're single, and now so is Aaron. So there's nothing to stop you from reconnecting."

Why any of this was of interest to Bonnie, Melissa didn't know.

"I just want her to find love," Tasha said, and Melissa suspected it was the alcohol talking. "I want everyone to find love."

"Who's talking about love?" Wilma asked. "If I were fifteen years younger and single, I know what I'd be doing. Heck, if I were just single…it's a good thing I'm happy with George."

"Now that's what I'm talking about," Tasha said. She high-fived Wilma, then Bonnie.

Melissa frowned. What was this? Some sort of conspiracy?

"You all are crazy. Actually, you all are drunk," Melissa corrected herself. "I see a guy again after twelve years and you think that I'm going to what—get married?"

"Get naked," Wilma clarified, and chuckled.

Melissa felt hot again, and was desperate to change the subject. She turned to Maxine, Tasha's older sister, and the one who didn't seem quite as boisterous about her and Aaron.

"What about you, Maxine? Have you been dating since your divorce?"

"I kinda chased Carlton for a while," she said, speaking of Aaron's older brother, the oldest of the four Burke boys. "But I just made a fool of myself. I don't know about that guy—he seems to have eyes for no woman."

"You don't think he's gay?" Bonnie asked.

Melissa doubted it. News like that would have definitely gone through Sheridan Falls like wildfire.

"No," Maxine said. "I just think he's…moody. He seems to focus all his attention on running the inn. Plus, since his wife left and went back down to Arkansas, he's kinda been a recluse."

Melissa couldn't help thinking that this felt a lot like old times. Girls talking about the Burke brothers. Which one they liked. Which one they hoped to be fortunate enough to date.

It was pathetic.

She had been one of those pathetic girls, but her interest in Aaron had never been about landing a Burke brother. Yes, the Burkes had been the most talked-about bachelors in town back in the day, and apparently they still were. They came from a great family, were successful in their own right, and their sexy looks only added to their appeal.

Melissa's connection with Aaron had been forged from a mutual bond of friendship that grew over that summer twelve years ago when they'd worked together. In fact, at the start of the summer she had vowed to never date Aaron, or any other Burke brother, for that matter. But something about him had gotten to her, and he had touched her heart. His compassion for the kids they were counseling, his easy humor. And like a typical girl, she'd fallen. Hard.

Dammit, why couldn't she stop thinking about Aaron? This was stupid.

"Another round of shooters?" Maxine asked.

"Actually," Bonnie said, sneaking a glance at Wilma, "we should be going."

"Already?" Tasha asked. "I like this bar." She glanced around at the decor, which ran toward Mexican paintings and artifacts. "I feel like I'm in Cancún."

"It's nice, but we've got to get going," Bonnie said, and helped her down from the stool. "We've got a tight schedule to keep."

"Thank you, Peter," Wilma said, her voice low and flirtatious.

"You ladies don't do any serious damage now," he cautioned playfully.

"What fun would that be?" Wilma asked.

"I wonder what the guys are up to right now," Tasha said as Bonnie led her to the bar's exit.

"Don't you worry about the guys," Bonnie said. "Ryan's celebrating his last night of freedom, and so are you."

Melissa could only imagine what the guys were up to. Probably something raunchy. Naked women dancing all over them. Aaron was undoubtedly reveling in the experience.

It was ludicrous that anyone was even talking about there being any spark of attraction for her on his part. They'd dated—and he'd dumped her.

All Melissa knew was that she was older, wiser and not about to be flattered by a guy looking at her, even if his smoky eyes were the sexiest she'd ever seen.

And now that she knew that the bridal party was practically taking bets on when she would bed Aaron, she was all the more determined to give him the cold shoulder over the next couple of days. Let someone else become victim to his charms. Melissa was past that.

Chapter 8

"Why are we stopping?" Ryan asked.

Beside him, Aaron clamped a hand on his shoulder. "You'll see, cuz."

Ryan shot him a suspicious glance. "I thought we were heading to a bar in another part of town. Isn't that what you said when we got back on this bus?"

"Actually," Aaron began, "some guests will be joining the party."

Music was blaring in the party bus and the drinks were flowing. The party was in full swing.

"Hey…" Ryan frowned. "I specifically told you guys no strippers."

"Just sit back and relax," Jeremy, Ryan's older brother, said.

"Jeremy, I promised your wife we wouldn't do anything scandalous. Not to mention I promised Tasha."

Dave, Ryan's friend and best man, made his way to the front of the bus. The song playing on the speakers changed to an old favorite, and the seductive words "Do you mind if I stroke you up" blared through the limo.

"You all ready?" Dave asked.

The doors opened. A twirling feather boa was the first thing that appeared. Aaron looked at Ryan, who was shaking his head. "Come on, guys. You know this isn't what I wanted for tonight. I just wanted to hang with the guys."

"Ryan," Aaron said, "stop talking."

"Wait, what?" Ryan asked when the woman fully appeared. She strutted farther into the vehicle, heading toward Jeremy. "What is this?" Ryan asked.

"Your surprise," Aaron answered.

Then he heard, "This isn't our bus," and his breath stopped. That was Melissa's voice.

"Sure it is," Bonnie said.

"Are there strippers on this bus?" was the next question. "Because I didn't agree to—"

Bonnie yanked on a hand, pulling the protesting woman up the steps.

Melissa.

Aaron swallowed. Though he'd seen her earlier, as his gaze settled on her now, he felt a fresh stirring inside his body.

Her hair was down, hanging just past her shoulders. She'd curled it, and it looked amazing, with soft tendrils floating around the front of her face. Her eyes were narrowed, her confusion evident as she checked out the occupants of the party bus. Aaron's eyes went lower. Her purple shirt clung to her breasts, and the white jeans she was wearing were like a second skin.

Wow, those curves.

His breath caught in his chest. She was beautiful.

Wilma shimmied her way over to Jeremy, while Tasha appeared next. Her eyes lit up, and then she began to giggle. "Ryan?"

Maxine entered the bus last, and she too started to laugh. Then, as was the plan, all the women in the bridal party headed toward their respective partners and began to dance in front of them.

Everyone except Melissa.

Aaron made eye contact with her and raised his eyebrows, hoping she would catch his drift that she was to play along.

Ryan, looking awestruck, hurried to Tasha. He pulled her against him and started to dance. Then he faced his groomsmen. "You guys got me. I thought you had strippers entering the bus. I was about to kill you all."

Tasha looped her feather boa around Ryan's neck. "You're not disappointed, are you?"

"Absolutely not," Ryan told her. "I couldn't be happier."

As the two started to kiss, the other men started to dance in front of their respective partners. Melissa stood, staring awkwardly around.

Wow, so she wouldn't even be a sport and dance with him?

Aaron slow danced his way over to her. He saw the flash of panic in her eyes. Was she really that unhappy to be around him?

Or was she feeling something else?

She crossed her arms, her lips pulling into a tight line. She seemed completely unhappy.

Aaron knew that things hadn't ended in the best way between them, but they'd both been much younger at the time. He'd hoped that this wedding would give them a chance to reconnect.

He stopped in front of her, but kept his body moving to the beat of the music. "Come on, Melissa. Smile."

"I… I thought I was being lured onto a bus with male strippers."

"Are you disappointed?" Aaron asked.

"No. Of course not. Just…taken aback. I need a moment."

Aaron glanced around at everyone else on the bus. They were either dancing or pouring drinks. Having a good time.

"We decided to have a little fun with the bride and groom," Aaron explained. "Make them both think we'd ignored their wishes and had raunchy things and debauchery waiting for them."

"Cute," Melissa said, but the tone of her voice told him that she thought the stunt was anything but cute.

Wow, she was a tough cookie. Despite the happy partiers around them, she stood still, as if determined to be miserable.

That wouldn't do.

Aaron slipped an arm around her waist and pulled her close. "Come on, don't be a poor sport."

She glanced around, and seeing everyone else having a

good time, she began to sway to the music with all the enthusiasm of someone with a gun held to her head.

"There you go," Aaron said, smiling. "It's not killing you to dance with me, is it?"

She said nothing, but at least she didn't pull away from him. He tightened his grip on her, his breath catching as her soft breasts pressed against his chest. Man, she felt good, smelled good. And even with annoyance in her eyes, she looked irresistible.

"You don't have to hold me so tightly," Melissa said, squirming a little.

Oh, she was feisty. Aaron wondered how that attitude played out in the bedroom.

"You're not interested in getting to know me again?"

Instead of answering, she cut her eyes at him. She was trying hard, but Aaron felt something simmering beneath her outrage.

Passion.

She was fighting the obvious attraction between them.

Aaron urged her closer. "You feel good."

"Aaron, please."

"Please what? Whatever you want, I'll do."

Her eyes widened in horror, but he caught the flash of a spark. There was heat in her horrified gaze.

Good. He needed to know that he wasn't the only one feeling the pull of attraction.

"I'm not asking you to…you know that's not…" She could hardly get her words out.

He swayed with her slowly, looking down into her eyes. She glanced back at him awkwardly, then around at the others. It was clear she didn't want to look into his eyes.

Was she afraid that her frosty exterior would melt?

"Hey," Aaron said softly.

She slowly lifted her gaze, a question in her eyes. Her

chest rose and fell with a heavy breath, and her lips parted slightly.

Heat zapped his groin. Damn, he wanted to kiss her.

Aaron didn't know what he'd expected when he'd seen her again, but he hadn't really been prepared for this reaction to her. He had hoped to reconnect and renew their friendship. But this visceral pull? This was more than he'd anticipated.

All he could think about was getting her naked.

"I'm not the same guy you knew before," Aaron told her, his voice low.

"I know," she said. "I've read the papers. Seen the news stories. You've led quite the life as a star."

Aaron frowned. "You can't believe everything you read in the paper."

She rolled her eyes. "I'm sure."

"What have you heard?" Aaron asked. Though he pretty much knew. Everything he'd done had been reported—and exaggerated—in the media. If he had coffee at a café in Rome with a female friend, the paparazzi wondered who the new "flame" in his life was. Heck, some of the stories had been downright lies.

The piercing sound of a whistle sounded on the bus. All eyes went to Bonnie, who stood at the front. "Sorry, y'all, but it's time to go. We have to get back to our respective partying."

"Nooo," Tasha protested, but Bonnie was already locking arms with her.

"What have you heard about me?" Aaron asked Melissa, hoping she would answer.

Instead, she pulled herself away from him. "We've got to go."

And not a moment too soon for her, Aaron surmised. She was no doubt happy for the chance to escape.

"We'll continue this conversation later," he said.

"No. We won't."

She angled her jaw, trying to look defiant. But Aaron could see that she was flustered.

He knew the feeling.

Seeing her again had shifted his world off its axis. Gone was the shy, somewhat awkward teenage girl he'd gotten to know that long-ago summer. She had blossomed into a radiant beauty. A sexy, mature woman.

One he wanted very much to get to know.

Chapter 9

"**I**'ve never forgotten you. Never forgotten our time together."

Aaron's voice was husky, and his fingers were warm as they traced her face. Melissa's lips parted on a sigh. She could look into his eyes all day, every day and not get bored. How was one man so darn sexy?

"You don't have to say that," Melissa whispered.

"I'm not saying anything I don't mean." Aaron angled her face upward, lowered those full sexy lips and softly captured hers. The kiss sent a jolt of electricity racing through her body, and delicious heat tingled through her veins.

"Baby…"

Melissa reached for his face. But all she felt was air.

Her eyes flew open, a sense of disorientation and panic instantly hitting her. For a moment, she was confused. One minute she had been with Aaron, his lips on hers. His hands gently touching her face. Now…

She was in her old bed in her parents' house.

She'd been dreaming.

About Aaron.

For a long moment, she lay there, her chest rising and falling with harried breaths. Hadn't it been bad enough that she'd had to see Aaron? Now she was dreaming about him?

She needed her head examined.

Melissa turned onto her side, and that's when she felt the first stab of pain in her temple. Good Lord, her head hurt.

Then she remembered. The night before. Making the rounds at different bars in Buffalo. Having one too many shots.

Suddenly, there was a noise, some sort of blaring. It took

a full couple of seconds for Melissa to realize that it was the alarm clock on her cell phone going off.

She rolled over in bed and fumbled for the phone on the night table. Another few seconds passed before she was successfully able to swipe the screen and stop the annoying noise.

Then she dropped backward on the pillow.

For the first time in years, she was hungover.

Worse, she was aroused.

"I'm never drinking again," she muttered, then got out of bed.

Melissa took a long, cool shower, but it still felt as though her brain were in a fog. The throbbing headache would not subside. No surprise there. She hadn't had that many drinks in a long time. At her age, she could no longer drink like a college student.

She wanted to regret the previous night, but the truth was, it had been fun. And just what Tasha needed. Her cousin had had an amazing time, and she was no longer worried about the wedding and things going wrong. The night on the town had been worth it just to see her cousin happy—even if at the end of the night Tasha had ended up weeping, talking about how much she missed Ryan and that she couldn't wait to see him and never leave him again.

Melissa couldn't help chuckling at the memory as she got into her car. It was nice to know that her cousin had found that special kind of love. From everything she knew about Ryan, he was a stand-up guy. Unlike his cousins, there had never been a hint of scandal about him. She felt confident that Tasha was going to marry a man who truly did love her and would always honor and respect her.

The bridal party was to meet at three in the afternoon for coffee and pastries. Melissa would need the largest coffee she could get, with at least a couple of espresso shots.

Hopefully the espresso would help fully sober her up—and keep thoughts of Aaron from invading her brain.

All the women appeared to be in the same boat when they arrived at the coffee shop—hungover and badly in need of caffeine. Wilma wore dark shades that she didn't take off. Unlike the night before, she was quiet. She downed two cups of coffee in no time, but Melissa got the feeling that she would have preferred to have it injected into her arm.

Melissa would have preferred that, too.

But despite everyone's clear fatigue and recovery mode from last night, there were some smiles and a definite sense of satisfaction throughout the group.

"Does anyone know whatever happened to all the beads I had?" Tasha asked.

"You started giving them away to random guys," Melissa said. "They gave you a kiss on the cheek, you gave them a bead. It was all very...cute."

"Why do I have no memory of that?" Tasha asked.

"Because you had way too much to drink, my dear," Maxine said and patted her hand.

Only Arlene was completely fine today. "Sounds like I missed quite the night. I could have used it."

"You can still let loose at the wedding. There are plenty of good times left to be had," Maxine told her.

"I, for one, am not drinking again," Melissa said. "I'm too old for this."

"Hush," Wilma said. "We've got a day to recover."

After enough coffee to keep them going and pastries to fill their stomachs, the bridal party headed to the nail salon. The salon owner had put out a big sign offering congratulations to Tasha in the back of the shop, and every seat that was reserved for them had a string of flowers adorning the sides and top. It was a nice touch, and the tears that welled in Tasha's eyes had them all collectively saying "aw."

Melissa gave Tasha a spontaneous hug. She was finally getting caught up in the excitement of the wedding. One more day, and her cousin would be married off.

Melissa wasn't excited about the rehearsal, however, which was to take place at seven o'clock at the church.

After last night on the bus with Aaron, Melissa felt even more awkward. Seeing him tonight and tomorrow at the wedding was going to be hard to endure.

Already, he was starting to invade her thoughts, and not in a good way. Why on earth had she dreamed of him? Imagining his lips on hers, his fingers softly skimming her skin… It was too much to handle.

She didn't know what it was about being back in this town and seeing Aaron again that had her so…flustered. It wasn't like her to even feel hot and bothered. She certainly hadn't spent restless nights dreaming of her last boyfriend.

As she watched the rest of the ladies settle into the chairs for their pedicures, it hit her just what was going on. Being away from work, her brain was unoccupied with the various crises she was used to and the day-to-day business of running the group home. Which meant she had all the time in the world to think about the here and now. And surely the alcohol didn't help—she was not used to drinking so much. Coupled with the fact that Aaron really was the sexiest man she'd ever laid eyes on, her subconscious brain could not stop her from thinking about sex.

Whoa…*sex*?

Though the women around her couldn't read her thoughts, Melissa shot nervous glances at them. She hoped that her eyes and facial expression didn't indicate what was going through her mind. She sat in the pedicure chair and tried to relax.

"I'm thinking of having one of my nails painted blue," Tasha said. "You know, for something blue."

Melissa tuned them out, her thoughts wandering back to Aaron. Was she really thinking about sex with him?

The zap of heat that hit her told her what she didn't want to accept.

Illogical, yes, given that she didn't even like him anymore. But she knew it was true.

Here she was, thirty years old and smart, and somehow Aaron's charm and good looks had gotten to her. The way he'd held her, moved his body against her when they were dancing, the scorching looks he'd leveled on her...

Melissa's brain and her libido were not in sync. Her brain knew that Aaron was bad news, but her libido...well, her libido had been turned on.

It's okay, she told herself. *Thinking about sex is fine. It just proves that you're still alive.*

And honestly, when it came to sex, she hadn't felt alive in years. Not even with her last boyfriend, Christopher. Her libido had come roaring back to life yesterday, and that was a good thing, wasn't it? She'd allowed an important part of her to essentially die.

Maybe when she got back to New Jersey, she would do what her best friend, Teresa—who was also the receptionist at the group home—constantly suggested: fill out an online dating profile and finally put herself out there. She did need some excitement in her life.

Two hours later, their nails and toes were done in lavender shellac, guaranteed to look perfect for the next day and beyond. From there, the women headed directly to the church.

"I'm sorry I didn't go out with you guys last night," Arlene said to Melissa when she got into the passenger seat beside her. Melissa had decided to leave her car in the salon's parking lot, and Arlene was driving them both to the church.

"You missed a fun time," Melissa told her.

"I could use some carefree fun. Craig has been driving me crazy. The thing is, I'm kind of worried that he's going to try to use anything I do against me. Like if I party too much, he'll say I'm an unfit mother."

Melissa's eyes narrowed as she looked at her sister. "Are you guys still fighting over custody? I thought you already won."

"He's not happy I was awarded primary custody. He does get Raven on the weekends, and I make lots of time for him to spend with her outside of that. But he still seems hell-bent on making my life miserable."

"Don't give him the power. You're doing everything you should be and more. You're a great mother. Don't let him drag you down."

"I'm still so hurt that he cheated. And he wasn't even original. He had an ongoing affair with his secretary." Arlene snorted. "She got pregnant—which is probably the only reason he told me about the affair. Then she lost her baby. I think he expected me to stay with him after that, and he's lashing out because I didn't. I mean, as if."

Melissa reached across the seat and patted her sister's shoulder. "I know it's tough, but just try to ignore Craig's rants and put-downs, whatever he's saying to you. It can only affect you if you let it."

"Honestly?" Arlene shot Melissa a quick gaze before returning her attention to the road. "My self-confidence has taken a beating."

"Come on, sis. Don't let him do that to you. That's exactly what he wants, by the way. Thank your lucky stars that you're free of him. There's someone out there who will appreciate you."

"I don't know. Maybe I should have just tried to make the best of things."

Melissa reeled backward. "You can't mean that. You know you did the right thing."

"Did I?" Arlene asked.

"Yes." Melissa squeezed her hand. "Never doubt that."

"But there are times when Raven asks me where her daddy is, and nothing I say seems to mollify her."

"But when she gets older and understands exactly what happened, she will know how strong you were. Your example that you shouldn't put up with anything just to stay in a relationship will be so important to her in the long run."

"But she's been acting out. There are times I worry that she's so unhappy, she'll be scarred for life."

"She's going through a period of adjustment. That's normal. But trust me when I tell you kids are resilient. Just show her constant love and she'll be fine. If the kids at my group home had constant love from their parents, they'd do so much better." Melissa paused. "Stop worrying. Everything will be fine."

Arlene sighed softly. "I hope so."

"I know so."

Arlene pulled into the church parking lot, and Melissa's pulse started to race. At least for a little while, she'd been able to put Aaron out of her mind.

But they were at the church now, and soon Melissa would be seeing Aaron again.

She wasn't looking forward to this.

Chapter 10

When the bridal party entered the church, the men were already there. Tasha speed walked down the aisle and straight into Ryan's arms. She hugged him tightly, as though it had been ten weeks since she had last seen him, rather than only half a day. Ryan dipped his head and kissed her softly on the lips.

"I missed you, baby," Tasha mewled.

Bonnie playfully rolled her eyes. "Girl, you've got the rest of your life to spend with him."

"Young love...so sickening," Wilma commented, then chuckled.

Maxine threw her a sidelong glance. "As if you're one to talk! You and George always out on date nights, holding hands and sneaking in kisses everywhere. You think word doesn't travel?"

"Of course I know it does," Wilma said. "I like to keep the gossips happy."

Maxine shook her head, but she was grinning.

"Hey, don't hate just because I keep the fire going," Wilma added, then snapped her fingers.

There were more chuckles, and Melissa quickly scanned the groomsmen. Aaron wasn't there.

Where was he?

And then she knew. The night had been young when the women had left the guys in their party bus, and who knew if they hadn't actually met up with strippers after that. And if not strippers, Aaron had likely met someone when they were out. A woman who was only too willing and eager to spend the night with him. He was gorgeous, and women no doubt threw themselves at him even if they didn't know of his celebrity status. Aaron was probably still exhausted and recovering from a night of pure carnal excitement.

No sooner had the thought entered her mind than the church doors at the back opened. Aaron breezed in, looking as though he had just stepped off the cover of a magazine. Dressed in a pale blue dress shirt that was open at the collar, Ray-Ban sunglasses and black pants, he looked drop-dead gorgeous.

He slid off the sunglasses and his grin illuminated the room. "Hey, sorry I'm late. Everyone been here long?"

"We just got here," Wilma told him, and Melissa noticed how the other woman's eyes lit up. Yeah, there was something about the Burke brothers that had women losing her minds. Even happily married women couldn't keep their eyes off them.

"Good, then I'm just in time," Aaron said.

He made his way down the aisle to the front of the church, and Melissa couldn't help noticing that even his walk exuded a sensual confidence. He looked good, and he knew it.

"How's your neighbor?" Ryan asked.

"She's better now," Aaron replied. "The doctors said that she has a mild concussion, but she's lucky she didn't fracture a hip."

"What happened?" Tasha asked.

"Aaron's neighbor, Mrs. Langley. You remember her. She taught fifth grade."

"Yes, of course," Tasha said.

"She fell this afternoon," Ryan explained. "And it's a good thing Aaron was there to help."

"Oh, no," Wilma said, her eyes narrowing with worry.

"Her house is across the street from mine, and I was walking to my car when I saw her heading down her front steps," Aaron said. "She went straight down, hitting her head on the concrete. I raced straight over to her, and she was nonresponsive. But she came around after about a minute or so. I didn't bother waiting on the ambulance. With the help of a couple of other neighbors, I got her into my car and took her to the hospital right away. That's where I'm coming from now."

"You're a hero," Bonnie said, smiling, and the rest of the wedding party shared their chorus of agreements. Some even slapped Aaron on the back, congratulating his efforts. Melissa stood rooted to the spot, a foul taste filling her mouth. It was the taste of shame. She had judged Aaron wrongly. She'd jumped to the conclusion that he had barely been able to tear himself away from some sexy vixen, while the truth was that he'd actually been helping out an elderly neighbor.

And Mrs. Langley, to boot. One of her favorite teachers in grade school.

"That is so sweet," Maxine said, laying a hand over her heart.

Aaron moved forward, heading straight toward Melissa. She realized then that she was the only one in the room who hadn't really acknowledged him. "Hi," she said, hating how breathless she sounded.

"Hi."

There seemed to be a glint in his eyes as he regarded her—or was she imagining things? "So, Mrs. Langley will be okay?"

"Yeah, thankfully. She'll have to take it easy for a while, but she's expected to fully recover."

"It's a good thing you were there, then," Melissa said.

"Sure was."

The rehearsal got underway. Even though they were just practicing for the big day, Tasha's eyes filled with tears nonetheless. It was obvious to anyone looking at her and Ryan that they had a real and special love.

Melissa's own eyes got misty as she watched Tasha walk down the aisle to join Ryan. She'd always hoped that by this age, she would have found her own special man. A man who would love her forever.

She glanced at Aaron. Saw him looking at her. He winked.

She quickly averted her gaze, but the heat that zapped her body lingered, leaving her feeling flushed.

Sex with Aaron when he was a young man had been amazing. What would it be like now that he was a full-fledged adult?

Saturday morning dawned bright and beautiful. So that all the ladies could be together and get up early to get ready for the big day, Tasha had the bridal party staying at the town's historic inn. The men were banned from going anywhere near its premises. Tasha didn't want to run the risk of Ryan seeing her in her wedding dress before she walked down the aisle.

"Something's wrong," Tasha uttered, looking around the hotel suite with a panicked expression. She was dressed in her off-the-shoulder mermaid-style gown, which was simply stunning. The bodice was decorated with shimmery beads and pearls. So were portions of the bottom of the gown that flared just above her ankles. Her makeup was flawless, her hair elegantly put up in a chignon with soft tendrils framing the sides of her face.

"You've got everything," Melissa told her. "Something old, something new, something borrowed, something blue. And you look…*wow*. I don't think there's ever been a more beautiful bride. And I'm not just saying that."

Tasha worried her bottom lip. "No, something's not right. I don't know what it is. I just… I feel it."

Bonnie went over to a drawer, opened it, withdrew a gift box, then approached Tasha. "It's probably this," she said.

She extended the small white box, delicately wrapped with a lavender bow, to Tasha. The box was attached to a small envelope.

A look of surprise on her face, Tasha accepted it. "What is this?"

"A gift from Ryan. I told him I would give it to you when the time was right, and assured him I would know when that time was." Bonnie offered her a reassuring smile. "That time is now."

Opening her eyes wide, Tasha began to fan her face. "You give this to me now, after my makeup's done?"

"I'm still here to do any last-minute touches," Lizzie, the makeup artist, chimed in.

"Open it," Melissa urged, smiling. She'd been surprised earlier when a gift from Ryan *hadn't* arrived. Not that one was necessary, but she had figured that Ryan was the type who would send one.

Tasha took a seat on the sofa, and the women gathered around. She pulled the envelope off the small box, then opened it and withdrew a white card accented in gold.

"'For the love of my life,'" Tasha read, and her eyes filled with tears. "'My grandfather gave this to my grandmother on their wedding day, and now I'm giving it to you. All my love, Ryan.'"

Tasha set aside the card and quickly opened the box. And when she did, she gasped. "Oh my God."

"Let me see," Maxine said and angled her body behind Tasha's to get a better look.

In the box was a pair of teardrop earrings—one large diamond surrounded by tiny coral-colored diamonds.

"Oh my God," Bonnie said. "Those are gorgeous!"

Tasha was crying now. "I love Ryan so much. And now my makeup is ruined."

"Don't worry," Lizzie said. "I've got you."

"Help me get these earrings off. I have to wear Ryan's grandmother's."

Bonnie quickly got to work, removing the earrings

Tasha was currently wearing and replacing them with the ones from Ryan.

Tasha got up and walked to the mirror. When she saw her reflection, she beamed. "There. Now everything is just right." She glanced around at her bridal party before looking into the mirror once more. "This day is going to be perfect."

And it was. From the heartfelt personal vows Ryan and Tasha had written for each other, to the fact that there was hardly a dry eye in the church, the ceremony was deeply moving. Melissa had to hold back tears on several occasions.

More times than not, when Melissa looked in Aaron's direction, he was looking back at her. And even when he wasn't, she found herself checking him out. That long, lean body with its perfectly honed muscles. That chiseled jaw, those full lips. His smoky eyes that so easily lit her skin on fire.

He looked *good*. More than good. He was as hot as they came. Especially in that suit that fit his lean, athletic frame so well. Had any man looked sexier?

All the men were dressed in gray suits with lavender vests, ties and a flower to match the bridesmaids' dresses. The color combination was sharp and unique.

Ryan's suit also had tails, distinguishing him as the groom. He definitely looked handsome—but he had nothing on his taller, more athletic cousin.

Unlike the last two nights, Melissa wasn't freaking out every time her eyes connected with Aaron's today. The undeniable sizzle between them didn't send her into panic mode. She was past denying that she was attracted to him. The way her skin flushed when he locked his gaze with hers made their attraction incontestable.

In fact, somewhere along the line, she'd started liking the attention from him. Every time Aaron leveled his heated gaze on her, she felt a little thrill. She felt alive in a way she hadn't in ages.

Aaron was making her feel like a sexy, desirable woman. It was a nice feeling, and for now she was going with it.

"Are you still trying to pretend that you and Aaron aren't attracted to each other?" Wilma asked her when the bridal party followed the photographer onto the bridge overlooking a brook.

Melissa cast a sidelong glance at Wilma. Then she said in a hushed voice, "I never said I wasn't attracted to him."

Wilma's eyes grew wide. "Ooh! Okay, then."

Melissa chuckled. And wondered why she had just been so vocal about her attraction. Especially after spending the past two days denying it.

Maybe because she'd learned that Aaron was no longer married. Not that that changed how she felt about him in a romantic way, but something about his heated gazes and his seriously attractive physique was making her think about sex.

A *lot*.

Even at the garden when they were taking pictures, just a gentle touch from him on her arm or on the small of her back had her almost losing her mind. Her body was so ripe to be touched.

By Aaron.

Not until this weekend had she realized just how starved for affection her body was.

"Girl, he's single, you're single," Wilma said. "The two of you keep staring at each other like there's no one else in the world. I say go for it. I know I would."

Melissa glanced in Aaron's direction. As if sensing her gaze, he turned and looked at her. Then he smiled.

Such a simple smile, but it was breathtaking. The edges of his lips curled only slightly, but that was enough to light up his face. Lord, he was sexy.

And in that suit…he truly looked like he could be a model for a top Italian designer.

"Ladies on this side, men on this side," the photographer announced, helping arrange them alongside the bride and groom.

"This has to be the last picture," Betsy said. She was the wedding planner, and for the last half an hour she had been losing her mind. "We're already running twenty minutes behind, and we have to head to the reception hall. People are waiting. Let's get the show on the road."

The photographer ignored her and snapped off a few shots. "Groomsmen, stand behind your partners." When Betsy made a sound of derision, the photographer shot her an apologetic glance. "This is the last one, I swear."

The men and women rearranged themselves. Even before Aaron gently pressed his body behind hers, Melissa felt the heat. And when he placed his hands on her waist, her eyelids fluttered.

She swallowed, trying to center herself.

Every innocuous touch turned the heat up another notch—and they still had the reception to get through. How was Melissa going to handle another four or five hours being this close to Aaron?

The two of you keep staring at each other like there's no one else in the world. I say go for it. I know I would.

Chapter 11

Aaron wasn't sure when it happened, but at some point during the evening, he knew he would be spending the night with Melissa. She'd been giving him a certain look, playful and flirtatious, quite unlike the way she'd looked at him before today. Even her body language was signaling to him that she was interested. The way she would throw a glance over her shoulder, brush her finger against her lips. All subtle things that others wouldn't notice, but for him, the cues were loud and clear.

She wanted him as much as he wanted her.

That knowledge made it incredibly hard for him to get through the evening when all he wanted to do was sweep Melissa into his arms and out of the reception hall. But, of course, he would have to wait.

Somehow he'd made it through the hours of toasts and the dinner and the obligatory dances, his sole thought on when he and Melissa could ultimately get naked.

And finally, Aaron was seeing some light at the end of the tunnel. Tasha was about to throw her bouquet, then Ryan would throw the garter, and then he and Melissa could hightail it out of here.

"All single ladies to the dance floor," the DJ announced. "It's that time of the night!"

The single women obliged, most going willingly onto the dance floor, though some were dragged by friends.

"That's it, ladies! Who is the next one who will get married? It's time to find out!"

Aaron watched as Arlene had to pull Melissa onto the back edge of the dance floor.

The DJ began to play Beyoncé's "Single Ladies," and Tasha teased and tempted, raising the bouquet high, then lowering it a few times, causing the women to gently push each other, vying for position to catch the flowers.

Except for Melissa. She stood near the back, looking bored.

Finally, Tasha threw the bouquet. It went flying over the heads and hands of eager women and straight to Melissa. Aaron watched as her eyes widened in surprise. Then she did the only thing she could—she reflexively put her hands out and caught the bouquet, looking completely stunned that she now possessed the coveted floral arrangement.

People clapped and cheered, then Melissa forced a smile onto her face and took a bow.

"Okay, guys. You know what that means. It's your turn. Once Ryan accomplishes the task of removing the garter!"

Someone brought a chair onto the dance floor, and the DJ played a sexy tune. Tasha made her way onto the chair. Ryan stood several feet in front of her, grinning. As the music played, he did a sexy strut toward her, gyrating his hips. And when he bent onto his haunches and slipped his hands beneath Tasha's gown, some of the guys hooted and hollered.

"Get it, cuz!" Aaron's brother Keith yelled.

Ryan made the removal of the garter a seductive art, smoothing his palms up Tasha's legs and ultimately using his teeth to drag the garter down. The applause and cheers were raucous.

"Okay, where are the single guys?" the DJ asked. "Head onto the dance floor."

Aaron made his way onto the floor with his brothers and the other unattached men in attendance.

Ryan did the same thing Tasha had, teasing the eager guys by feigning that he was about to throw the garter a few times. And when he finally tossed the blue garter into the air, almost all of the guys leaped and tried to get it.

It was just about to land into the hands of another guy,

but Aaron jumped and stretched his body, much the way he would on the soccer field, and felt his fingers ensnare the silky fabric.

He emerged victorious, holding the garter high. He did a victory walk around the dance floor, the other grooms-men patting him on the back in congratulations.

"All right!" The DJ sounded excited. "Now, someone bring the chair back. Where's the lady who caught the bouquet?" The DJ found Melissa in the crowd and pointed. "Yes, you. Come take a seat on the chair."

Melissa's eyes widened in alarm. Bonnie and Wilma both gave her a gentle shove in the direction of the dance floor.

"And you." The DJ pointed at him. "You know what you're going to do, don't you?"

The DJ began to chuckle. And Aaron was getting a pretty good idea.

"That's right," the DJ went on. "You're going to put the garter *onto* her leg!"

Aaron shot a glance at Melissa, who looked like a deer caught in headlights. She had not been expecting this. Neither had he—but he couldn't deny the rush of excitement that shot through him at the prospect of smoothing his hands over Melissa's shapely legs.

Melissa looked mortified, while Wilma and Bonnie were already cheering. And when the DJ began to play R. Kelly's "Sex Me," the cheering became a frenzy.

The crowd wanted a show, and Aaron was going to give them one.

He moved his body to the beat, slowly approaching Melissa. God, the way her eyes widened as he neared her...he couldn't wait to be alone with her.

Aaron swiveled his hips slowly, in a motion meant to turn her on. Right now, he was her private dancer, the crowd be damned.

Melissa blushed, then covered her mouth. Aaron held her gaze and twirled the garter around on his finger. Then he gyrated his hips until he was lowered onto his haunches before her. He slipped his hands beneath her dress and lifted one leg. The crowd went wild.

And damn, his pulse went into overdrive. Her skin was bare and smooth, and just touching her like this was getting him aroused. He looked at her toes, painted lavender to match her dress, and he felt a zap of heat in his groin. He wanted her in nothing but these silver shoes later at his place.

Aaron met her eyes, and there was that look again. Beneath the hint of embarrassment that they were doing this in front of everyone, he saw an undeniable flash of longing.

He slipped the garter over her shoe and pulled it up to her ankle. Then he extended his hands, making them visible to everyone watching, and used his teeth to pull the garter up to her knee.

The groomsmen hooted. Someone whistled. Melissa's eyes grew as wide as saucers.

Easing his head back, Aaron offered her a smile. Then he used his hands to pull the garter just above her knee, keeping it rated PG. He winked at her. She continued to meet his gaze, and he didn't miss the way her sexy chest rose and fell with a heavy breath.

Aaron stood tall, raised his hands in triumph, then bowed as people applauded. Glancing in Melissa's direction, he saw that she was still seated on the chair. He knew she was frazzled, but he was betting that it was in a good way.

He walked back over to her and offered her his hand. She accepted it, and he helped her to her feet. But he didn't release her when once she was standing. Instead, he pulled her body against his and leaned his head to her ear.

"You're driving me crazy. What do you say we get out of here?"

* * *

Heat rushed through Melissa's body with Aaron's words. Her body was practically an inferno. After that erotic garter escapade, she was barely breathing.

Aaron touching her leg, using his teeth to pull the garter up it…that was more foreplay than Melissa had had in nearly two years.

She was driving *him* crazy? He was making her crazy with need.

Her attraction to him was fierce. Something she could no longer deny. She'd been fighting a losing battle since she'd arrived in town.

The battle to resist him.

"You're good at this, aren't you?" she asked.

"Good at what?"

"Good at being so darn irresistible," she admitted.

There. She'd said it. She couldn't deny it any longer, and she didn't want to. The truth was, she wanted Aaron. She wanted a taste of him again. Maybe then she could fully get him out of her system.

"You find me irresistible?" His eyes lighting up, he drew his bottom lip between his teeth, indicating to her that he knew just how enticing he was.

"You're good at making a woman weak with need," Melissa said softly. "Good at making her want you."

"Baby, you ain't seen nothing yet."

The words were a promise. A promise that Melissa wanted him to fulfill.

One night with Aaron…it wasn't something she'd ever imagined before she'd arrived in Sheridan Falls, but right now she wanted nothing more.

She would satisfy an itch that needed to be scratched, then go her merry way.

"I can only imagine," Melissa said softly.

Aaron splayed his hands over her back and urged her

against him. Then he looked into her eyes for a long moment, and it felt as though they were the only two people in the room. "You don't have to imagine," he said.

Melissa glanced around, wondering if prying eyes were checking out their interaction. "You really want me to leave with you?"

"Am I in some way being unclear?"

He whispered the words in her ear, and Melissa's body shuddered. No, he wasn't being unclear. Not at all.

But she was hesitating. Was she really contemplating spending the night with Aaron?

Heck yes, she was. One night of carnal bliss...she needed it.

"What do you say?" Aaron whispered, and Melissa's eyelids fluttered shut.

She gripped his shoulders, needing to hold on to him before she swayed on her feet. He was having that much of an effect on her. Looking into his eyes, she said, "I don't want the night to end."

Aaron's lips curled in a slow, satisfied grin. "Good. Because I don't want it to end, either. I'm just trying to figure out the right moment to get out of here."

He pulled her closer and edged his face lower. But he seemed to catch himself and remember that the roomful of wedding guests surrounded them. So instead of kissing her, he whispered into her ear, "I haven't been able to get you out of my mind since I first saw you again. You've been occupying my thoughts at night, during the day. Hell, even when you left the room, I couldn't stop thinking about you."

Melissa's face flamed. It was silly, but his words stoked her inner fire. The idea that he desired her to that degree was a huge turn-on.

So what would it hurt? One night with Aaron, and she could get whatever this was out of her system and head back to New Jersey and her life.

"Why don't you get your stuff and head out of the hall as if you're heading to the restroom? I actually brought my car here earlier, so it's out back. I'll meet you outside in about five minutes?"

A few minutes later, Melissa put the plan into action. She didn't bother to say goodbye to anyone, not wanting anyone to be the wiser. Eventually they would wonder where she and Aaron were, but she was certain that no one would be concerned.

Melissa waited at the side of the building, and when Aaron rounded the corner toward the parking lot, she smiled. God help her, he was gorgeous. Every time she laid eyes on him, he took her breath away.

He returned her smile. "You wait here. I'll go get my car."

"Did anyone seem suspicious?"

"I left them going crazy on the dance floor. I don't think anyone noticed me slip out."

Maybe not yet. But they would notice soon enough. Though, honestly, she didn't care. Even if there were witnesses from the local paper who would make their tryst front-page news tomorrow, she was going to spend the night with Aaron.

She watched Aaron walk toward the back of the parking lot, his strong and confident gait turning her on even more. She could only imagine how skilled a lover he was now.

Well, she wouldn't have to imagine much longer, would she?

She was about to get it on with Aaron.

And she wasn't going to regret it.

Chapter 12

A little more than ten minutes later, Aaron was pulling his Mercedes sedan into a long, semicircular driveway. Sprawling trees blocked much of the view of the front of the house, and in the darkness you couldn't see much of it anyway. Melissa could see that the house was a dark color, likely red brick, with a large wraparound porch. It was big, with a spacious front yard, the kind of house that Melissa could imagine being filled with kids.

Aaron stopped the car and put it into Park, and Melissa inhaled a deep breath. She wanted to do this, was excited about doing it, yet her stomach flitted from nerves. It hit her full force that she was actually about to spend the night with Aaron.

There was no turning back now.

And she didn't want to turn back. Honestly, she hadn't wanted anything as much as she wanted this in a long time.

Aaron exited the car and hurried around to the passenger-side door. He opened it for Melissa, then offered her his hand.

She exited the car, then hugged her torso as she glanced around at the property.

Aaron placed his hands on her shoulders, then rubbed them down her arms. "Are you cold?"

"No. Just taking it all in." She turned to face him. "I like your place. It's serene. Not at all what I expected."

"What did you expect?" Aaron asked.

"Honestly? I guess I figured you'd have a place bigger than your parents', somewhere everyone can see it."

"I'm much more into my privacy, especially these days."

Melissa took a step toward the house, then abruptly stopped. "Wait," she asked, turning to face him. "Did you live here with Ella?"

"No. The big house you mentioned—Ella has it. I moved

here after we split." He put a hand on the small of her back. "But I definitely do not want to talk about Ella."

Melissa glanced over her shoulder at Aaron. "Neither do I."

Keeping his hand on her back, Aaron guided her toward the house. It was dark, but strategically placed lights on the porch provided soft illumination.

Aaron removed his hand from her body only to unlock and open the door. Then he took her by the hand and led her into his home. He flicked on the light switch, and the foyer came into view. A mahogany-and-oak table holding a statue of a horse was to the left beside the wall. An abstract painting hung on the wall above it. The staircase was to the immediate right and curved as it went up to the second level. At the top of the staircase was a lookout to the lower level. A massive chandelier with hundreds of coin-size crystals hung from the high ceiling and looked dazzling as the light played off it.

"Your place is beautiful," Melissa said.

Aaron drew her into his arms. "Thanks. Now can we stop talking and do what we've both wanted to do all day?"

He pulled her into his arms, and within a nanosecond, his lips were coming down on hers. Melissa expected fast and furious, especially with the buildup of the sexual tension between them. But instead, the kiss was soft and slow.

Heat unfurled inside her just as slowly.

Aaron's mouth worked over hers gently as his thumb stroked her jawline. His other hand moved to the back of her neck, his fingers tenderly touching her skin. Then they went higher, into the tendrils at the nape of her neck. It didn't take long for Melissa to realize that he was searching for the pins that held her hair up. Deepening the kiss, he maneuvered her hair free. Melissa could hear the soft pinging sounds of the hairpins falling onto the floor.

Her chignon successfully loosened, Aaron groaned and

slipped both hands into her hair. He swept his tongue into her mouth and tangled it with hers. A rush of excitement shot through Melissa's body. She crept her hands up his strong biceps and then wrapped them around his neck and held on as her head grew light from the most incredible sensations.

"This is what I've been thinking about all day," Aaron murmured. "And not just all day. I've been thinking about this since I first saw you again."

"You have?" Melissa asked.

"Yeah." Staring into her eyes, he pulled his bottom lip between his teeth and covered one of her breasts with his palm. "I've been going crazy thinking about you."

Melissa exhaled a shuddery breath. His attraction to her was like an aphrodisiac.

He kissed her again, his mouth moving hungrily over hers. And then he scooped her into his arms.

Melissa let out a little squeal, then giggled as Aaron rushed up the staircase with her. He headed straight down the dimly lit hallway and through an open door. The fact that he couldn't wait to get her to bed was turning her on even more.

Melissa expected Aaron to quickly put her on the mattress, but instead he stood at the bed's edge with her. He brought his mouth down on hers once more. Suckling softly, nibbling gently, he lowered her until she was standing. And then he continued to kiss her senseless. The sensations tingling through her body were heady and exciting.

He broke the kiss and whispered, "As much as I want to rip this dress off you, I know I shouldn't. Tell me how to get it off so I don't ruin it."

"There's a zipper at the back," Melissa told him, surprised at the sound of her ragged breathing. Her body was on fire. And Aaron hadn't even touched her in the places she craved the most.

He turned her in his arms so that her back was facing him, and he found the zipper and dragged it down. Slowly. As if his entire goal was to draw out the teasing to make her even weaker with need.

Once the zipper was down, Aaron pushed the fabric over the one shoulder and down her arm. His fingers skimming her skin were like tendrils of electrical wire touching her, zapping her with jolts of lust. She was loving every second of this.

Melissa shimmied her body, helping him to remove the dress. He guided it over her hips, and the silky fabric fell to the ground around her feet.

Melissa stepped out of the dress, then turned to face him. As he regarded her, his eyes slowly widened and filled with heat. She was standing there in her strapless bra and thong, and she'd never felt sexier.

Aaron's exhalation of breath was audible. "Damn."

He reached for her hand, then pulled her forward. She landed against his hard body with a little *oomph*.

His clothes rubbed against her bare skin. She wanted him out of them.

"Come here," he rasped. And then his mouth was on hers again. As his tongue flicked hungrily over hers, Melissa slipped her hands beneath his jacket and began to push the fabric off his shoulders. He helped her, shrugging out of it, his lips still locked with hers. He let the jacket fall onto the ground. Melissa then felt for the buttons on the vest and began to undo them one by one. He continued to kiss her, holding her face in his hands as he did, and oh, God, the feelings that were raging through her. They were intense and delicious.

Though her fingers and body were getting weak from the assault of his lips on hers, Melissa found the buttons of his shirt and fumbled to undo them. Finally reaching the last one, she pulled the dress shirt out of his pants. Aaron broke the kiss and hastily got out of the shirt and vest, as though those items of clothing were on fire. He tossed them onto the hardwood floor.

As Aaron undid the belt on his dress pants, Melissa reached behind her back to undo her bra. "No," Aaron quickly said. "Let me. I need to take off your clothes."

Need... Had more seductive words ever been uttered?

She licked her bottom lip as she watched Aaron finish undoing his dress pants then kick them off. Standing before her in only black boxer briefs, he stepped toward her. He slipped his arms around her body, found the clasp of the bra and released it. He slipped it off her, then tossed it onto the floor. Melissa's breasts spilled free.

Taking a step backward, Aaron looked at her. His eyes did a slow once-over, taking in every inch of her. "Wow."

"You look pretty incredibly yourself," she said, practically breathless from the raging desire flowing through her.

Aaron moved forward and pulled her against him with force. He captured her mouth in a ferocious kiss. He put his whole body into it, his arms wrapping tightly around her, his groin pressing against her belly. Melissa gripped his shoulders and hung on as her legs turned to jelly. Good God, how could she be so completely attracted to this man?

Making a carnal sound, he lifted her, and she threw her legs around his hips and secured them at the ankles. He moved with speed to the bed, and leaning forward, he lowered her onto it. Melissa's back hit the soft mattress. Aaron's body was still on top of hers as she clung to him, and she reveled in the feel of his smooth skin and hard muscles.

He slowed down the tempo of the kiss and softly suckled her bottom lip. Melissa sighed against his lips. Her body was alive with sensation, and it was amazing.

Aaron slipped a hand between them, covered her breast, then tweaked her nipple. They both groaned in satisfaction at the same time. Then Aaron broke the kiss and brought his head to her breast, flicking his tongue over her nipple. Melissa cried out as it hardened.

"Yes, baby," Aaron said softly.

Then he covered her nipple with his mouth and suckled softly. Melissa's center throbbed. "Aaron…"

He tweaked her other nipple to a hardened peak while continuing to suck the other one softly. He gently grazed it with his teeth, and Melissa thought she would lose her mind. She arched her back as a moan escaped her lips.

Aaron smoothed a hand down her belly and into her panties. He was gentle as his fingers explored, found her nub. He stroked her in a slow, circular motion, and Melissa thought her body would explode. That's how good this felt.

"I need to taste you," Aaron whispered.

And then he was moving down her body, positioning himself above her hips. He pulled her thong down. Melissa bent one leg at the knee to aid him in getting the underwear off. He slipped it over one of her heels, then the other, then discarded it behind him.

"Oh, yeah," Aaron said, his lips curling in a smile. "Do you know how sexy you are? Naked on my bed, except for those hot shoes?"

As Melissa held his heated gaze, she felt like the most desirable woman in the world.

Aaron slipped a hand between her thighs and stroked her, and she exhaled a slow, lust-filled moan. Then he lowered his head, his tongue gently flicking over her most private spot. Melissa gripped the bedsheet in her fists and arched her back. The feel of his tongue on her most sensitive spot was thrilling her beyond anything she had ever known.

He added his fingers, driving her even wilder with pleasure. Her breathing became faster, sharper. The pressure inside her was building. Taking her to the edge…

A soft flick of his tongue, then a little suckle, and Melissa was letting go. Falling into the sweet abyss of delirious sensations. Aaron linked his fingers with hers as she rode the delicious wave.

Then he got up, kicked off his boxers and went to his bedside table. Melissa's body was so spent from her earth-shattering release, she barely registered that he was getting a condom.

Aaron rejoined her on the bed, easing her legs apart and settling between her thighs. Then he guided his shaft inside her, slowly. Inch by delicious inch, he filled her. Melissa cried out unabashedly. "Oh, Aaron…"

"Yes, baby." He kissed her softly, then brushed his lips across her cheek. He kept going until he reached her ear. He drew her earlobe into his mouth and sucked on it tenderly. And oh, the sensation! That, coupled with the feeling of his shaft deep inside her, was raising her pleasure level to a fever pitch.

Aaron picked up the pace. His thrusts were harder, faster. Melissa moved her hips against him, matching his rhythm. She ran her fingers up and down his back, and he thrust harder.

Her release caught her by surprise. It came swiftly, starting in her center and tingling through her entire body. She dug her nails into his back, and Aaron's strokes became bionic. He was breathing heavily, his thrusts a steady, fast pace. Within moments, he was exhaling a primal cry. His body tensed as he succumbed to his own release.

"Yes," Melissa murmured, stroking his back tenderly now. She nuzzled her nose against his jaw as he enjoyed the full pleasure of his orgasm.

Several moments later, the weight of Aaron's body came down on hers. His heavy breathing mingled with hers, the only sounds in the room. Melissa curled a leg around his slick body, wishing she could stay there with him like that forever.

Aaron had just given her a sexual experience she would not soon forget.

Chapter 13

Melissa's eyes popped open. Sun was spilling into the room—a room she didn't recognize—through sheer curtains. She tried to move and realized there was an arm draped over her waist. It didn't take more than a nanosecond for her to remember.

She was in Aaron's bed. She'd spent the night with him. And he had rocked her world.

A slow smile spread on her face. They'd made love three times, each subsequent session lasting longer. Melissa had barely gotten any sleep, but she wasn't complaining.

She felt amazing. One thing was clear. She'd needed that. She'd needed hot sex, more than she had realized.

The last couple of years without any action had left her desperate for a man's touch.

She stretched her body to see the time on the bedside clock. Aaron groaned and held onto her tighter.

Melissa swallowed. He wasn't even fully awake, yet he didn't want to let her go. It felt nice.

More than nice. Aaron had been completely into her, and in his arms, Melissa had truly felt like she was the only woman in the world. The only woman he wanted.

But now it was morning, and the fantasy of last night had come to an end. She'd gotten what she wanted. One night with Aaron. One night that could keep her warm until her next sexual encounter.

She strained her body against Aaron's arm, and saw that the clock read 8:34 a.m. "Eight thirty!" she exclaimed.

Her outburst startled Aaron, and releasing her, he rolled onto his back. She glanced at him, saw his sleepy eyes and confused expression.

"I'm sorry," she said. "I didn't mean to wake you."

Aaron rubbed his eyes. "It's okay."

"I have to go," Melissa went on. "I didn't plan to stay here that long."

"Why do you have to leave?" Aaron asked. His voice was groggy.

"I have to get back to my parents'." She frowned. "I should have returned before they woke up."

"What are they going to do, ground you for staying out all night?" Aaron asked, smiling at her.

"No. I just…well, I don't really want them asking me any questions about where I was."

"Just say you stayed at Arlene's."

"Good idea," Melissa said, that thought not having occurred to her. She was entirely too paranoid about anyone knowing where she'd spent the night and exactly what she'd been doing.

"Or you can tell them that you had your wicked way with me," Aaron said, then laughed.

Exactly what she *didn't* want. "Um, sure. That'll go over well."

Aaron eased his body forward and snaked a hand around her waist. "Since you can use your sister in order to not get grounded, why don't you stay in bed with me?" He held her gaze, then bit down on his bottom lip. "I'm not through with you yet."

Melissa's woman parts tightened. Giving him a coy smile, she stretched her body out beside his. "Now that's an offer I can't refuse."

The sounds of someone moving around in his room caused Aaron to come fully awake. He opened his eyes and saw that Melissa was standing near the foot of the bed, slipping into her dress.

"Where are you going?" he asked.

"I really do have to leave," she told him.

"I was hoping we could maybe go out for breakfast."

When she threw him a glance over her bare shoulder, he realized that she would never be able to go out for something to eat in that dress. "Or eat here. My fridge is stocked. And I'm a pretty good cook."

Melissa tried to zip up the back of her dress. "Sorry, I can't. I have some things to do."

"All right. Can I see you later, then?"

"I have a dinner with the bridesmaids."

"Oh, that's right. The thank-you dinners." Aaron had forgotten about the dinner he was supposed to attend with the groomsmen. Ryan and Tasha wanted to spend a bit of time with their wedding party before they headed off on their honeymoon. Aaron wished they'd opted for one dinner with the men and women, but Ryan and Tasha were having separate dinners.

"I'm game to see you after that..." Aaron suggested.

Melissa's lips curled in a smile. "I'll check my schedule. See if I'm available."

Aaron chuckled softly. "When will you let me know if your schedule is clear?"

She headed toward the bed. "Will you zip me up?"

"Sure." Aaron maneuvered himself to a sitting position, then zipped up the dress. "There you go."

"Thanks."

"Seriously, I'd like to see you again," he said. "Maybe we can go for a drink after dinner?"

"We'll just have to see, won't we?"

Oh, so she was going to be like that. Make him work for it.

"Let me get up. I'll take you to your parents'."

"There's no need. I already called a taxi. It's on the way."

Aaron frowned. "Oh. So no time for coffee?"

"No time." Melissa sat on the bed beside him, her eyes lighting up playfully. "Thank you for the night, sir."

"I hope we'll have another one."

"If I'm in town, sure," she said flippantly.

"What do you mean by that?"

"I may be heading back to New Jersey before you get the chance to see me again."

Aaron cast her a sidelong glance. She was playing with him. Making him work for it, as he suspected. "I definitely plan to see you before you leave. I'm going to need to." She gave him a little smile, then got up and collected her shoes.

"Give me your number. It'll make getting in touch with you much easier."

"You know where to find me...if you want to."

"You're really not going to give me your number?"

"This is a small town. I won't be hard to find."

Then Melissa took a few steps toward the bedroom door. Was she really going to leave like this?

She seemed to think better of it and turned around. She made her way back to the bed and gave him a soft kiss on the lips. "Really, I had a great time," she said huskily. "Thank you for last night."

"You're welcome."

Aaron wanted to wrap an arm around her and hold on tight so she couldn't leave.

But he would see her again. There was no doubt about that.

Aaron decided not to rush the chase. He'd give Melissa enough time to miss him. Though as the next morning rolled around, he wished that he could have seen her last night after the dinner with the groomsmen. His thoughts had been on her the entire time.

Aaron hoped that as Melissa had been enjoying drinks and dinner with the bridesmaids, she was also remembering her night with him. Because that's what he had been doing. Remembering every fantastic moment of their night together. The way she'd felt in his arms. The way she'd kissed him so eagerly. The first moment he'd gotten to see her amazing body without clothes on.

Even Ryan had commented that Aaron didn't seem "fully there" last night, which was true. He had been with the guys physically, but mentally, he'd been in his bedroom with Melissa, making her sigh and moan.

He was eager for round two.

She had to want the same thing, given the electricity between them in the bedroom.

Aaron rolled over in his bed and sat up. Time to stop thinking about Melissa and find her. They'd both had a night to miss each other, and that had been enough for him.

He got up, showered and dressed, then headed to one of the local cafés for coffee and a bagel. Afterward, he went next door to the flower shop, where he picked up a small bouquet. Nothing over-the-top, but enough to let Melissa know that he liked her. He hoped that she would agree to spend the day with him. Maybe they could head into Buffalo for lunch, follow up with a movie. Then they could head back to his place.

Aaron pulled up to the Conwell residence and parked on the street. He was well acquainted with the Conwells, not only from having grown up in this small community, but because of the summer when he dated Melissa. He'd dropped by often then to pick her up for work or to bring her home.

He exited his car, grabbed the bouquet, then made his way to the front door. He rang the doorbell.

Less than a minute later, Melissa's mother, Valerie Conwell, answered the door.

"Why, hello, Aaron." Valerie's lips spread into a bright smile. "It's so nice to see you."

"Very nice to see you as well, Mrs. Conwell," Aaron said.

"And you brought flowers." Her eyes twinkled. "They're

lovely. Would you like to come in for a moment? I've got some tea and freshly baked biscuits."

"That sounds lovely," Aaron said, just as the smell of the biscuits wafted into the room. "But I've already eaten. I was just wondering if Melissa is here."

"Oh." Valerie's face twisted in confusion. She glanced at the flowers, seeming to fully understand now. "Aaron, she left. She headed back to New Jersey this morning."

Aaron stared blankly at Valerie, unsure he understood what she'd just said. In fact, he was pretty sure he had misheard her.

"She didn't tell you?" Valerie went on.

Melissa was gone. She'd left town. Without even a good-bye.

Aaron cleared his throat, trying to mask his shock. "I knew she'd be leaving at some point, but... I hoped I would catch her."

"You two looked like you were getting very cozy at the reception," Valerie said. "I can't imagine why she didn't tell you exactly when she was leaving."

"Me neither," Aaron muttered.

"Why don't you give her a call?"

Aaron nodded, and tried to keep his expression light. "Yeah. I'll do that." Then he extended the flowers. "Here. These are for you."

"Why, thank you, Aaron."

"You have a good day."

"Let me grab you a biscuit," Valerie offered. "You came all this way, and they're nice and fresh."

Aaron was about to protest, but smiled instead. "Sure. They smell delicious."

Valerie hurried off into the house and returned a short while later with a paper bag. As Aaron accepted it, he could tell that she'd put at least two biscuits inside. Maybe three. "Thank you so much, Mrs. Conwell."

Then he turned and started down the steps.

"Call Melissa, dear," Valerie said to him.

Aaron raised a hand as he headed down the walkway. "I will."

He got behind the wheel of his Mercedes, where he exhaled sharply. *Call Melissa...* The words were like a slap in the face.

Of course, Mrs. Conwell had no clue that he didn't have a way to reach her daughter. She'd given him that whole coy act about not giving him her number, making him believe that she wanted him to track her down the old-fashioned way.

Do a bit of chasing to prove to her that he was truly interested.

What a joke.

Was this her plan all along? To ditch him?

Aaron started his car.

Well, he wasn't about to be deterred so easily. Maybe this *was* a game. She expected him to pursue her, even if she wasn't making it easy.

All right. Game on.

Aaron eased his car into traffic. He was heading to Arlene's house.

Chapter 14

The thing with small towns was that pretty much everyone knew where everyone lived. And if you didn't know where a particular person resided, it wasn't hard to find out.

Aaron was well aware of Arlene's address. She lived right next to the town's original antique shop, where she happened to work. If he didn't find her at home, he would surely find her at the shop.

Ten minutes after leaving the Conwell residence, Aaron pulled up in front of the small turn-of-the century house that Arlene owned on the west side of Sheridan Falls. It was a two-story wood structure. An array of colorful flowers added to the curb appeal, and a fresh coat of white paint had the house looking new. As Aaron pulled his car to stop, he saw that Arlene was sitting on the porch, her young daughter blowing bubbles on the grass.

Aaron exited the car to find that Arlene had gotten to her feet. She was looking at him with curiosity. Her daughter, Raven, whom he'd met a handful of times in town with Arlene, ran over to him, clearly happy to have a visitor. "Do you want to try blowing some bubbles?"

Aaron humored her. "Sure." He took the little stick from her and the container, dipped it in, and blew out a stream of bubbles. Raven giggled happily as she chased and tried to catch them.

Arlene sauntered down the steps toward them. "Aaron," she said, looking at him oddly. "What brings you by?"

"You're not working today?" he asked.

"I needed a day off." Her lips curled in a faint smile, and Aaron sensed some weariness. "Is there something I can help you with?"

"I was hoping to find Melissa."

"Here? No, she's not here. In fact, I'm pretty sure she already left. But if not, you can find her at my parents' place."

"I've already been there."

Raven held up the stick for her mother. "Mommy, you try."

"You continue blowing bubbles, sweetie," Arlene said softly to her daughter. "Give me a moment to speak to Mr. Burke. I'll be over in a little while."

Raven blew some bubbles, then happily went off chasing them. Arlene faced Aaron again. "So she did leave."

"Apparently." The reality stung. Aaron hadn't thought she would leave town without seeing him again, or at least speaking to him. "I'm trying to track her down."

"Why don't you just call her?" Arlene asked.

The million-dollar question, which only drove home the point that he had been way off base with his thoughts about Melissa. He thought she'd *enjoyed* their time together. Hell, he knew she had. He'd assumed that enjoyment would lead her to want to see *more* of him. That wasn't an illogical thought, was it?

Never before had Aaron had such an incredible night with a woman, only for her to disappear from his life. Indeed, he had been the one to have to gently—and sometimes not so gently—push women away. He would start a relationship and quickly realize it wasn't what he wanted. The woman in question, while beautiful and seemingly sweet, would start dropping hints about some lavish item she wanted, or some would suggest they have sex without a condom. Aaron wasn't stupid. From personal experience, he knew that there were women who would try to ensnare a man with a pregnancy, whether he had a lot of money or not. He had been devastated by some of the truths he'd learned about Ella, and the lengths she'd gone to in order to manipulate him into getting what she wanted. It still hurt for him to think about what she'd done. Because of that painful experience, he knew that he had to be careful to pursue a woman interested in him, not in his wallet.

That hadn't been his concern with Melissa, given their history. But he had not for one moment entertained the thought that she would not only *not* chase him, but actually run from him.

They'd had an incredible night, and now she was gone? It didn't make sense.

"Well," Aaron began cautiously, "she forgot to give me her number."

"Really?" Was Aaron mistaken, or did Arlene look amused? "With all the time you spent together, you never exchanged the most basic information?"

"We were...busy. I thought she'd be around today."

"Well, it looks like you're out of luck, then."

Why did Arlene seem so happy about that fact? "I was hoping you could give me her number. I'd like to reach her."

"If my sister wanted you to be able to reach her, she would have given you her number."

Aaron looked at her askance. He offered her his most charming of smiles. "Come on. I only want a number. Not her address."

"If my sister didn't give you her number, there was a reason for that. Sorry. I have to respect her wishes."

To drive home the point that she wasn't kidding, Arlene turned and wandered over to her daughter. He heard her ask Raven about trying to blow some bubbles now.

"Arlene..."

She looked at him over her shoulder. "I guess a charming smile doesn't always get you what you want, does it? Even the Burke brothers have to deal with rejection."

"What's that supposed to mean?"

"Honestly, I was a bit surprised at how well you and Melissa connected at the reception," Arlene said. "I thought you burned the bridge on any sort of relationship with her years ago."

Aaron narrowed his eyes. "Is that what Melissa told you?"

"Okay, I'm going to try to blow the biggest bubble ever!" Arlene exclaimed, clearly ignoring him.

And with that, Aaron knew the conversation was over. He reached into his wallet and withdrew a business card. "Here, please give my number to Melissa. Tell her I'd like her to call me. Or email me. You give her my information, and she can make the choice to contact me or not."

Arlene took the card from him and gave it a brief glance. "Okay. But no promises she'll get in touch with you. Like I said, I think she would have left you her phone number if she wanted to stay in contact with you."

Aaron gave her a gracious smile, but he was irritated. First the comment about the Burke brothers. For some reason, people in this town thought he and his brothers believed they walked on water. It wasn't true. They'd earned that reputation when they were younger, and some of it was valid. But most of it was unfair judgment, simply because of who they were—Cyrus Burke's sons.

People in this town had put them on a pedestal, and Aaron hadn't asked to be there. Escaping to Europe to play professional soccer had been a relief. Living in a city where no one had known him as the son of a football superstar, he had been judged on his own merit. But ultimately, the pitfalls of fame had infected his life. A failed marriage, paparazzi lurking in the bushes when he was at restaurants, hoping to find something scandalous to write about him. Stories about him had filled the tabloids, whether or not there was a grain of truth to them.

Arlene's comment made him believe that she thought he loved the so-called perks of fame, but she had no clue. For every perk, there was a downside. Aaron truly enjoyed a quiet life and peace. When he'd retired from soccer last year and returned to Sheridan Falls, that had been his goal. He wanted to do something with meaning, which was why he'd started a charity to give back to children in need. He'd also hoped to have children of his own. But his marriage to Ella had quickly fallen apart once he was no longer whisking her on exotic vacations.

"Please, just give her my information," Aaron reiterated, hoping that Arlene would. "'Bye, Raven."

"'Bye!" She waved at him enthusiastically.

Aaron headed back to his vehicle. He wondered if some of Arlene's attitude was because she was bitter, having divorced Raven's father in what could only be described as a huge public scandal. In fact, it had been the biggest scandal in this town in a few years. Craig had not only cheated; he'd gotten another woman pregnant. The custody battle for Raven had only recently ended.

He hoped that Arlene wasn't so jaded that she would discourage her sister from pursuing a relationship with him.

A relationship? As Aaron started his car, he frowned at the direction of his thoughts. Was that what he wanted with Melissa?

He liked her. That's all he knew for sure. That spark he'd felt for her years ago was still there, and he wanted to get to know her all over again. See where things might lead. And if they led to more of what they'd enjoyed on Saturday night, then he was all for it.

Chapter 15

Three days later, Aaron was beyond frustrated. He hadn't heard from Melissa.

Now, sitting on his sofa with his laptop, he stared at the Twitter page for Turning Tides group home, where he'd learned that Melissa was the program director. That was one of the few things he'd been able to find out about her. When it came to social media, she was practically a ghost.

Aaron had found no Facebook profile, no personal Twitter. There was a LinkedIn profile, where he learned that she'd worked at Turning Tides for the past seven years. But any sort of personal information had been completely lacking.

She was leaving him no choice. He'd messaged her on LinkedIn days ago, and he'd gotten no response. He wouldn't be surprised to learn that she didn't check the app.

Now Aaron would have to contact the group home. Instead of calling—which was what he wanted to do—he would send a message through the website. A simple message asking that Melissa get back to him at her earliest convenience.

Hopefully this would finally get Melissa's attention.

"This looks amazing," Melissa said to Teresa, one of the counselors at the group home and her best friend. Her stomach grumbled as she eyed the macaroni topped with melted cheddar and bread crumbs, and the salad on the side. "The boys made this all on their own?"

"Well, I helped," Teresa said. "But this was entirely their idea, and they wanted to do a baked mac and cheese because you told them that's the only *real* mac and cheese."

Melissa smiled. "They remembered. Sometimes I wonder what gets through and what they instantly forget. Please tell them thank you. I don't have time right now to step away from my desk, not with my meeting in an hour."

"Will do," Teresa said. "Though I think you should take a break from your desk, even for fifteen minutes."

"I wish I could," Melissa said. "I've got too much work to do. I'm going over my notes for the plan of care meeting for Tyler. I'm still trying to reach his father, but he's out of town and hasn't gotten back to me." She sighed, then lifted the fork and spiked a cucumber in the salad. "No rest for the wicked."

And then she tried to suppress a smile as she thought about just how wicked she'd been—in Aaron's bed. The thought still made her smile almost a week later. So did the knowledge that Aaron had been trying to reach her. But Melissa held all the cards now. She hadn't gotten back to him.

Finally, he was getting a taste of his own medicine.

Melissa stuffed the cucumber into her mouth and turned her attention back to the computer when Teresa turned to leave the office.

"Oh, I almost forgot," Teresa said, and Melissa looked at her. "There's a message on the Twitter account for you. Did you see it?"

"What?"

"Someone named Aaron. Aaron Bradshaw. No, Aaron Burke. Said he's trying to reach you."

Though Melissa had just swallowed the cucumber, it felt as though it was suddenly lodged in her throat.

"I know you typically don't check the Twitter account, so I thought I'd ask. I'll screenshot the info and email it to you."

"Did he…say anything…specific?" Melissa asked, her heart thumping hard in her chest. She hoped Teresa couldn't sense her panic. But if Aaron had said anything that alluded to their night together…

Of course he hadn't, Melissa realized. If he had, Teresa would be grilling her for details.

"No," Teresa answered. "Do you know an Aaron? The message was so brief, I figured you must know him."

There was no point lying. "He's someone from Sheridan Falls. I saw him again at the wedding after several years. I guess he just wants to say hi."

Teresa nodded. "Oh, of course. I'll send you the information now."

Melissa forced a smile. "Great."

It didn't take more than a couple minutes for the email to come through. Melissa was barely breathing as she opened it.

Hello. This message is for Melissa Conwell. Please have her contact Aaron Burke at 716-555-8034. Or she can send an email to therealaaronburke@europeansportsonline.com.

Melissa blew out a slow breath. At least there'd been nothing suspicious in the message. Nothing for Teresa to give her the third degree about.

But still…

Melissa emitted a groan. She wanted to ignore the message. But given that he'd gone so far as to contact the group home looking for her, she was fairly certain that if she didn't respond to him, he would continue trying to reach her. Perhaps he'd even call the group home next.

She was glad that he'd provided his email address, because she didn't want to talk to him over the phone. Though she needed to continue getting ready for her upcoming meeting, Melissa quickly drafted an email to him.

Aaron, it's Melissa. Sorry I didn't get back to you sooner. I'm not really sure why you want to contact me. We had fun, and I appreciate that night more than you know. However, I'm not looking for anything to come from it. When I'm back in Sheridan Falls, I'll be sure to say hello.

Melissa reread the email, wondering if she should change it at all. It was direct and didn't sugarcoat anything. Perhaps it was a little...tactless?

No, it was clear and to the point. She didn't want a relationship with him, so why give him the sweet version of rejection that would have him still pursuing her? Better for him to think she was a jerk and be done with her.

Besides, she had to get back to her preparation for the plan of care meeting.

She quickly hit Send, then got back to work.

Aaron reread the email from Melissa, his stomach sinking more with each passing second. He could hardly believe his eyes.

Had she really just given him a none-too-subtle brush-off?

Brush-off? Heck, she'd sent him a very clear "get lost" message.

It didn't make sense.

Frowning, Aaron eased back on the sofa and ran a hand over his head. He was baffled at the message. She'd spent the night in his bed, begging for him to touch her here and there, crying out his name, and *this* was what she sent him?

Aaron closed his laptop. He couldn't accept this message from her. *Wouldn't* accept it.

Had her sister gotten in her ear? Helped sour her opinion of him? No, Aaron couldn't see that. Why would Arlene do that? And Melissa was certainly her own person. She wouldn't be swayed by someone else's biased opinion. Because there wasn't anything negative Arlene could tell Melissa about him that would be based in fact.

So something else was going on. But what?

Suddenly, a thought occurred to him. Something that

had his jaw tightening. It would definitely explain this bizarre reaction after they'd had such a great night together.

Had Melissa lied to him from the outset? The more Aaron thought about it, the more he realized it was the only thing that made sense.

Anger flared, hot and intense.

During his online search for anything about her, he'd found a photo of her and some guy named Christopher Fieldcote. They'd been out at some event in New York City, and while the photo's caption didn't say they were a couple, Melissa and this guy had looked pretty cozy.

Was he the reason for Melissa's email? Had she been involved romantically with someone else and yet gone to bed with him?

Aaron's pulse was pounding. He stood and walked to the window in his living room. He looked out at the peaceful view of the trees in his front yard. But inside, he was feeling the farthest thing from peace.

If Melissa had cheated on someone else with him, that was unacceptable.

He needed to get to the bottom of this.

As soon as possible.

Chapter 16

Melissa rubbed her pounding temple. "I don't think you're understanding me, Mr. Stone. Your son was not the victim in this situation. He was the instigator. He threw the first punch."

"He's there for you all to straighten him out. Why don't you do your job?"

Melissa inhaled a deep breath and counted to three. "I fully believe in your son, but he's acting out. I think if you were able to participate in the counseling sessions with him—"

"That's not possible," the man said curtly. "My business requires me to be in Europe for the next four weeks. Talk to his mother."

"I have spoken to his mother," Melissa said. "She's involved. But I think it would be especially meaningful if you could be here, too. Perhaps we can arrange to have you on Skype? I think it would mean a lot to—"

Melissa heard the man speaking, but his words were muffled. It took her a moment to realize that he wasn't speaking to her.

"I have a meeting I'm late for," Mr. Stone said. "We'll have to have this conversation another time."

"When would be a good time?" Melissa asked. But when she got no response, she realized that Mr. Stone had already hung up.

Melissa held the receiver in her hand and stared at it. She wanted to scream. How could Mr. Stone be so blind? Didn't he realize that his son needed him? Sure, Tyler had made some bad mistakes, but at his core he was a good kid. A kid who needed the presence of his dad in his life.

In Melissa's opinion, it was critical for Tyler's success that his father be involved in this process. In fact, she wouldn't be surprised to learn that Tyler's involvement with a gang and the robbery that got him arrested had been a cry for attention from a father who didn't make time for him.

Instead of being disappointed in his son for his mistakes, Mr. Stone needed to see his son's actions as a bid for attention and respond accordingly. Especially with his court case coming up in mere weeks. Tyler needed to be calm and not act out at the group home if he hoped to have a successful day in court.

She placed the receiver back on the cradle and rubbed her right temple. A migraine was starting. She opened her top desk drawer, withdrew the bottle of pain medication and took out two tablets. She washed them down with lukewarm coffee.

The knock on the door had her exhaling harshly. She just wanted a break. For a few glorious minutes, she wanted no distractions on this Friday afternoon.

But she sat up straight, tried to regain her composure, and said, "Come in."

The door opened, and Teresa peeked her head into the office. "I'm sorry," she began without preamble. "I know you said no unnecessary interruptions, but you have a visitor."

"The math tutor is here already?"

"No," Teresa responded simply, a look of intrigue in her eyes.

"Is it an emergency?"

"Sort of. He says he won't leave until you come out and speak to him."

"What's his name?"

"He refused to give me one. I tried to get him to make an appointment, but he wouldn't. Honestly, I'd be more alarmed if he weren't so darned attractive."

Melissa frowned. "He's cute?"

"*Very.*"

Melissa's pulse quickened. It couldn't be...no, the thought was crazy. It wouldn't be Aaron.

"But he does seem a little upset," Teresa said. "Well, maybe upset is the wrong word. He seems...focused. I think you need to come out and talk to him. I'll keep my phone on hand in case I need to call the police."

Unsure what to make of Teresa's announcement, Melissa pushed her chair back and stood. Could it be Christopher? He'd called her a few times recently, asking if they could talk. No, Teresa should know what Christopher looked like. Even though she'd never met him in person, she'd seen a couple of photos of him.

Following Teresa out of the office, Melissa made her way down the hall that led to the front of the house. She heard the frantic pounding of footsteps racing up the staircase, then Omar yelled, "Hey, everyone—come downstairs!"

What was going on?

A couple seconds later, when she stepped out from behind the staircase and saw who was standing in the foyer, her heart leaped into her throat. Her eyes bulged, and she stopped midstep.

No...it couldn't be...

Her eyes flitted from Aaron, who somehow was here in her place of work, to Omar, who had just bounded down the stairs. Her stunned gaze went to Aaron again. His taut shoulders relaxed, and he smiled at her.

"What haven't you told me?" Teresa whispered. "Because you know him, don't you? Are you seeing this guy?"

"Aaron," Melissa said, her voice barely more than a whisper. Tyler, Mohammad and Ben raced down the stairs, huge smiles on their faces. "What are you doing here?"

"I knew it!" Omar exclaimed. "You're Aaron Burke!"

Aaron grinned at the boys. "Yes. Yes, I am."

There was a chorus of excitement, with exclamations

like "Whoa!" and "For real!" and "Oh my God!" The boys immediately began to high-five and hug him.

"You're seeing him, aren't you?" Teresa demanded in a hushed voice as the boys swarmed Aaron.

"No, I'm not," Melissa responded, giving Teresa a pointed look. This was *not* something she wanted to discuss right now.

Aaron held up a hand, saying, "I take it you guys like soccer?"

"I'm a huge fan," Omar exclaimed. He was grinning from ear to ear.

Melissa stepped closer to Aaron and his throng of admirers, anger making her face flush. This was not appropriate. Aaron should not have shown up here like this and caused a disruption to the day. There were routines here, work that needed to be done. Sure, it was a lunch break now, but the boys were supposed to be in the backyard getting exercise, not crowding the lobby.

What had Aaron been thinking?

"Boys, you know this is time for physical activity," Melissa pointed out.

"But this is Aaron Burke!"

"I know exactly who he is," Melissa said.

She faced Aaron now, her eyes letting him know that she wasn't pleased with this intrusion.

"Wait—you know him?" Tyler asked.

"Duh, obviously she knows him. That's why he's here," Ben said.

Before Melissa could speak, Aaron did. "Ms. Conwell and I go way back."

"Cool!"

"Awesome!"

"Are you her boyfriend?"

Melissa's heart began to race. How would Aaron answer that last question?

She couldn't let him, so she spoke quickly. "Mr. Burke and I knew each other when we were kids," she said. "He's…he's in town and decided to visit me," she added by way of explanation. "But no, he's not my boyfriend."

"Aw."

The chorus of disappointment surprised her. As did the look of discontent on Teresa's face.

Melissa glanced at Aaron, saw him give her a questioning look. Was he actually disputing the fact that they weren't an item?

Melissa hoped that neither the boys nor Teresa had picked up on that subtle look. Yes, she'd slept with him. But just because she had didn't mean they were an item. After all, they'd slept together twelve years ago, and that had meant nothing to Aaron.

Their wedding fling was just that—a fling, the kind of thing Melissa was certain happened all the time. She had scratched an itch. Satisfied her curiosity. She'd had a great night, but that's all it was. One night.

"Chase is gonna be *so* upset when he learns you were here," Omar said. "He's out with Counselor Mike right now. How long are you staying?"

"Not long," Melissa quickly interjected. "Mr. Burke, will you follow me?" She was trying her best to maintain a professional tone with him. Desperate to not have anyone think there might be anything suspicious going on between them.

"I'd love to," Aaron said.

Melissa led the way down the hallway and around the corner to her office at the back of the house. She opened the door and headed inside, and Aaron followed her. She closed the door behind him and faced him.

"What are you doing here?" she asked. Gone was the professional and dispassionate tone. Her heart was beating fast. She didn't understand what Aaron was doing here, especially after the message she'd sent him yesterday.

"You're a hard woman to reach," he said.

"Why did you come all the way to New Jersey?"

"After the email you sent me, I figured you owe me an explanation."

Melissa raised an eyebrow. "You couldn't ask it via email? Or call me?"

"You have a way of not responding that makes it challenging for guy to get in touch with you," he said, giving her a pointed look.

Melissa couldn't say anything to that, because it was true. She'd been avoiding him. If only she'd known that he would show up here, she would have answered his calls. And she definitely wouldn't have sent that email.

And now that he'd shown up here, she knew she wouldn't live this one down. Teresa would have questions, and of course the boys would be speculating as well.

"Besides," Aaron went on, "this is something I wanted to ask you in person."

"What could you possibly want to ask me that would have you coming here? To my place of work?"

"Why did you send me that email?"

Melissa crossed her arms over her chest. "Are you so unaccustomed to rejection that you flew out here to demand an explanation?"

"Rejection doesn't typically start with a woman clinging to me so tightly in my bed that she practically leaves scars on my back."

Melissa's face flamed. She quickly turned, unable to face him.

"Oh, no, no, no. You're not going to avoid this one." Aaron scooted in front of her. "I need to see your eyes when you answer me."

"We had a great night," Melissa said in a lowered voice,

hoping to God that no one was lurking outside her door in the hallway. "But it was one night. Surely you've had a one-night stand before."

"You don't strike me as the type to engage in a one-night stand."

"As if you know anything about me," Melissa quipped.

Aaron blew out a frazzled breath. "What are you doing tonight?"

Melissa narrowed her eyes as she looked at him. *That* was his follow-up question? "What?"

"Tell me," he said.

"I am so confused right now."

"So am I," Aaron said. "Now answer my question."

She could tell by the sternness in his voice that he wasn't going to drop the issue. But if he had some bizarre notion that she was going to spend the night with him, he had another think coming.

"I have plans," Melissa said. Though the only plan she actually had was to head home and take a hot bath, drink a glass of wine and perhaps watch a movie before going to bed.

"With Christopher?" Aaron took a step toward her, his eyes boring into hers. "Is he the reason why you've given me the brush-off?"

Chapter 17

Melissa stared into Aaron's hard gaze, momentarily caught off guard. Christopher...?

And then it hit her, and her eyes bulged. Somehow, Aaron knew that she had been dating a man named Christopher. But how?

"I need to know," Aaron said. "Is Christopher the reason you've been avoiding me? Is he your boyfriend?"

"How do you even know about Christopher?" Had he hired someone to look into her life?

"So you *are* seeing him," Aaron surmised. Then he swore under his breath.

He looked upset, something Melissa didn't expect. Did he actually care, or was this about his ego being hurt?

She could let him believe that she was involved with Christopher, though their brief relationship had ended eight months earlier. Maybe it would be easier this way. If Aaron thought she was involved with another man, he would leave her alone once and for all...

And yet she found herself saying, "No. Christopher and I are no longer involved."

Aaron stared at her long and hard, as if trying to decide whether or not he believed her. After several moments, his features relaxed.

This *had* been bothering him. Melissa was confused.

"So he's not the reason you sent me that email?" Aaron asked.

"No."

"And what about another guy? Are you dating someone?"

"You said you didn't think I was the type to engage in a one-night stand. Now you think I'm the type to sleep with you while I have a boyfriend?"

"Wine, music, a lapse in judgment. People do it all the time."

"I don't," Melissa said, unable to hide her irritation.

"Good." Aaron paused. "Because I need you to be my date tonight."

Melissa's eyes widened, even as her heart skipped a beat. "That's quite presumptuous of you."

"It's an event I hope you'll be willing to attend with me. It's for a good cause."

More like an excuse to get me naked again, she thought. Though she had herself to blame for Aaron believing that he could wiggle a finger and seduce her again. She'd been a far too eager participant last Saturday night.

"What is this good cause?" she asked, trying her best to keep her doubt from creeping into her voice.

"I'm in town for a charity fund-raiser tonight," Aaron explained. "Have you heard about a little girl named Rosella Nunez?"

The name sounded familiar. And in an instant it came to her. "Yes, that little girl who needs a liver. She's only two years old, and she's going to die if she doesn't have a transplant soon."

"Yes, that's her. Well, her father is a huge soccer fan. I know some of the guys who play for the New York Red Bulls. The team's actually based out of Jersey, right nearby in Harrison."

"Yes, that's a suburb of Newark," Melissa said.

"Anyway, some of the players heard about Rosella's plight and suggested holding a fund-raiser for the family. It's a tough situation. The parents have had to quit their jobs in order to provide round-the-clock care for Rosella, and they've exhausted almost every penny they have for medical care. Obviously this is a trying time for the family, and the fund-raiser tonight is to help lessen their financial burden. I was hoping you would accompany me as my date."

Darn it. Melissa had been prepared to shut down whatever Aaron might have asked her. But now, how could she?

She'd heard about this young girl. It was a heartbreaking story, and certainly the most worthy of causes. As much as Melissa wanted to refuse to be Aaron's date, his story about the fund-raiser changed everything.

"And this is actually tonight?" she asked.

"Yes."

"Jeez, you don't give a girl much notice."

Aaron raised an eyebrow. "I would have—if you'd responded to me."

Melissa said nothing. What could she say?

Aaron wandered toward the window and looked out at the backyard. His face lit up in a smile, and he waved.

The kids must have been looking up at the window, fascinated that Aaron Burke, real-life soccer star, was here.

"You really are a big star," Melissa commented.

"Did you follow my career?" Aaron asked, facing her. "Or did you forget about me?"

"I…" She swallowed. "It was all but impossible to hear nothing of your success," Melissa said. "Everything you do is big news in Sheridan Falls."

"I see."

What did he see? Was he offended that she hadn't become his biggest fan?

"I love that you ended up working with kids," Aaron said, once again glancing outside. "Just like we used to back in the day."

Melissa's jaw stiffened. She didn't want to hear him talk about that—the very thing that had helped them forge a bond twelve years ago.

"Why would you *love* that I ended up working with kids? Why does anything we used to do *back in the day* matter to you?"

"Okay, so there it is," Aaron said. "You're upset with me because of how things ended."

"One day everything was great, the next thing you were pushing me away."

"I was young. I didn't want to hold you back."

"How would you hold me back?" Melissa asked. She hadn't planned on having this conversation with Aaron, but the breakup had weighed heavily on her heart. She wanted answers. "I wanted to be with you. Why wasn't I good enough?"

"Is that what you think?"

"What am I supposed to think? And then you married *Ella*. Of all people."

"It's not you who wasn't good enough," Aaron said, and pain flashed in his eyes.

Melissa waited for him to go on, but he didn't. Instead, he turned away from her.

Something hit her then as she heard his heavy breath. Was he still carrying guilt over his young sister's death? The night they'd made love, Aaron had confided in her that he'd been torn up with guilt for years because Chantelle had drowned when he had been watching her.

"Chantelle," Melissa said softly. "You still feel guilt over her death."

"It was my fault."

Was this why he'd broken up with her? Melissa knew from working with troubled youth that sometimes when people experienced a tragedy, they were emotionally stuck—unable to move forward and be happy because guilt held them back.

Melissa was gentle when she asked, "Did you push me away because of Chantelle?"

Aaron turned to face her. "I don't want to talk about Chantelle."

"But if you're still holding yourself responsible—"

"What I said twelve years ago doesn't matter," Aaron said, and the firm tone of his voice made it clear he didn't want to discuss the issue further. "Will you go out with me tonight?"

So he was going to avoid the subject. He was sounding like the Aaron he'd been just before they'd broken up, when she sensed something was wrong and he'd refused to talk to her about what was bothering him.

That was the man who'd hurt her. If he still wasn't willing to open up to her, clearly he would hurt her again.

If she let him. The more time she spent with him, the worse it was going to be for her. She needed to end this, whatever it was, before it went any further.

"You know what?" she began. "I'm not sure I can make it tonight. I do appreciate that it's a great cause and that you came here to invite me. But it's such last-minute notice. I'll happily give a donation, however."

"I want you there with me."

The commanding tone to Aaron's voice caused Melissa's heart to flutter. Gone was the vulnerable man from just a few minutes earlier. Despite herself, she liked his determination. It had always been one of his most attractive qualities. Still, she didn't want to spend any more time with him. She drew in a breath, then said, "I don't have a single decent thing to wear."

"You don't need to worry about that," Aaron told her.

"Look at me." She spread her arms wide so that he could get a good look at her simple blouse, jeans and flats. "This is my typical wardrobe. Not nearly appropriate for a fancy shindig with lots of well-to-do high-society people. Maybe you can ask someone else."

"You're the only one I want to ask."

Melissa bit her bottom lip as he held her gaze. God, that look. It would be her undoing. She could see the heat in his eyes, as well as his determination. He wanted her in his bed again.

She'd already allowed herself one night with Aaron, one night that was to be her last. So going out with him tonight was a very bad idea.

"It's practically in your backyard," Aaron said. "And you don't have a boyfriend. Nothing to stop you from going with me."

"What if I just don't want to spend more time with you?" she found herself saying.

Aaron closed the distance between them in a flash. "You don't?" The question was a challenge. "Is that what you're telling me?"

Melissa gulped.

"Because I find it hard to believe you faked your attraction for me last weekend. And suddenly you're done with me?"

Heat zapped Melissa's body. She hadn't faked her attraction. Not at all. But she needed to protect her sanity. Spending more time with Aaron was a bad idea.

So she said, "Aaron, I would go, but honestly I don't want to go in any old thing. You have to trust me when I say I don't have the right kind of dress."

"I already told you, you don't have to worry about that."

"I don't understand how you can say that."

"Before I came here, I made a stop. The wife of one of the guys who plays for the Red Bulls owns a boutique. I stopped by and took a look at what she had. There's an outfit that I think would look incredible on you."

Melissa shot him a skeptical look. "Why would you go to a store to look for an outfit for me if you thought I had a boyfriend?"

"Because my gut told me you didn't." He held her gaze. "Not after the night we shared."

Melissa's face flamed.

"It's red," Aaron said, his voice husky.

Red…like the outfit she'd worn the night of the welcome dinner.

"Red looks incredible on you," he told her, stroking her face.

"Aaron, you can't—" Melissa took a step backward. "Someone could come in here right now."

"I need you with me tonight," he said, and Melissa could hear the yearning in his voice.

Her womb tightened. God help her, she was all but putty in Aaron's hands when she was around him. Why couldn't her brain take over and prevent her body from betraying her?

"You seriously picked out a dress for me?" she asked.

"I seriously did. And accessories. Everything you need to go along with the dress will be available for you at the shop. Though I'd really love for you to wear those shoes you wore with your red dress last week," he added in a low voice.

A shiver of delight danced down Melissa's spine.

"You're going to be the most beautiful woman in the room. Even if you go just as you are right now."

Melissa's resolve softened. "Aaron…"

"I took the liberty of making an appointment for you," he said. "Five o'clock. You'll get dressed at the store, and I can meet you there to pick you up. Then we can make it into New York for the event, which starts at seven-thirty. I'm looking forward to this night being one that the Nunez family will never forget."

Despite herself, a wave of excitement shot through Melissa. Aaron had actually gone to a boutique to pick out a dress for her? It was the kind of thing that she would never expect a man to do. Aaron was exhibiting a take-charge attitude, the kind that Melissa always thought she wouldn't like. But the truth was, it was kind of thrilling…

Aaron had come here with a plan. A plan to take her out and not take no for an answer. She felt a stirring of desire. What would it hurt to spend another night with him?

"All right," she said.

"I can pick you up and take you to the boutique, if you like."

"There's no need. I can get there on my own, and you can meet me there once I'm dressed. Let's say five thirtyish?"

Aaron's face lit up with a smile. "That'll work."

For a nanosecond, Melissa couldn't help thinking that she was giving Aaron exactly what he wanted. He'd come here with one goal in mind: to take her out, and she was certain that he didn't expect to take no for an answer. He'd succeeded in his goal with barely any resistance from her.

Because she wanted the same thing. Just seeing Aaron again had her body remembering their chemistry. The hot sex.

And now he was offering her another night out together, another evening where they would get dressed up to the nines, have a glass of wine. Maybe two.

Would they end the night making love again?

Did a zebra have stripes?

Melissa glanced at the clock. "It's one o'clock. I can probably get out of here around three thirty, head home and shower, get ready. Then I can head to the boutique."

"But you'll have to leave your car there." Aaron pursed his lips. "Why don't I have a car pick you up at your place and drop you off at the store? The driver can then get me, then swing back to the store for you."

Melissa nodded. "I guess that makes the most sense."

"All right," Aaron said. "I'll need your contact information, then."

"Okay."

"Start with your phone number," he told her, giving her a knowing smile.

Chapter 18

Melissa was hoping that Aaron could escape the group home unnoticed, but he'd barely made it out of her office before the boys were there, swarming him. Soon, someone was suggesting that he play a game of soccer with them in the backyard.

"I think Aaron has to go," Melissa said.

"Aw," Omar, the oldest of the boys, protested. Then he looked at Aaron and said, "Please, can't you stay a little while longer?"

"I've got a bit of time," Aaron said. There were cheers of excitement, and two of the boys took Aaron by the arm and led him toward the back patio door. He wore dress pants and shoes, not the proper attire to kick a ball around, but he followed the boys outside nonetheless.

Melissa watched them go, then headed to the back door and looked outside. The excited expressions on the boys' faces made her smile. It was nice to see them so happy.

Someone tossed Aaron the soccer ball, and he immediately started to do some fancy footwork with it, bouncing the ball first off his foot, then his knee. The ball went high, and he dipped his head to hit it, knocking it forward.

He made what he'd just done look easy, but Melissa knew it took skill. Omar tried to follow Aaron's example and failed. But Aaron passed the ball back, and with a huge smile, Omar tried again.

"So," Teresa said, and Melissa realized that her friend was directly beside her. Melissa glanced at her, saw that Teresa was looking out the window at the star of the hour. "Who is he and why have I not heard about him before?"

Melissa released a shuddery breath. "That's Aaron Burke."

"The guy who emailed you yesterday. Why is he here? Why did he come to see you?"

Melissa gazed out the window in time to see Aaron kicking the ball to Tyler and the boys racing through the backyard. He was making some sort of hand gestures, and the boys seemed to separate into two makeshift teams.

Even just observing him for these few minutes, it was easy to tell that Aaron was really good with kids. She wondered why he and Ella had never had any.

Just the thought of Ella caused a bitter taste to fill her mouth. She met Teresa's curious gaze and tried her best to manage a neutral expression. "I grew up with Aaron Burke. And…years ago we used to date."

"What!" Teresa's eyes grew wide. "You used to date that *fine* brother?"

"It was a summer fling," Melissa said, trying to minimize their affair. But the truth was, she had never felt as though it was simply a summer affair. It had meant a whole lot more to her.

"Wait," Teresa said, and her eyes lit up, as though something had just occurred to her. "He was at the wedding last weekend. And you two hooked up, didn't you?"

Melissa said nothing.

"Don't bother denying it," Teresa said. "I told you you looked different when you got back from Sheridan Falls. Didn't I say that? I told you that you looked…*relaxed*." Teresa chuckled. "Now I get it."

"It's not a big deal," Melissa said. She knew there was no point in lying. Teresa wouldn't believe her. "I hooked up with an old flame." She shrugged. "It happens all the time at weddings."

Teresa's eyes grew as wide as saucers. "No big deal? When was the last time you had sex?"

Melissa crossed her arms over her chest. "It's not like I'm in the running for woman who's gone the longest without sex. And can you keep your voice down? I don't want anyone hearing this."

"All the boys are outside with Aaron, and Dana and Courtney are meeting with that probation officer. No one's going to hear."

Teresa was right. Melissa was being paranoid, but she didn't want to talk about last weekend.

"So why did he come here? Obviously the sex last weekend had to be amazing!"

"He's in town for a charity event," Melissa said. Then she explained the details. "He wants me to be his date."

Teresa's eyes were practically dancing with glee. "So this is already getting serious!"

"The event happens to be in New York, and I happen to be right here in Newark. It's convenient."

"I'm sure he could have asked anyone else to go with him. And he could certainly have flown the date of his choice here if he wanted to."

You're the only one I want to ask...

"It's a charity event. Not a romantic date."

Teresa smirked. "Whatever. Talk to me tomorrow. Just don't leave out any of the juicy details."

Melissa's first wow moment of the evening came when the Maybach arrived to pick her up. She'd thought Aaron would send a regular limo, or perhaps a regular sedan. But a Maybach? The most expensive of the Mercedes line?

He wasn't in the car, and she wondered where he was getting ready.

It really hit her that she was about to have her own *Pretty Woman* type of moment in a boutique when the driver stopped in front of *Dazzle*. Just looking at the storefront, she could tell it was very high-end. The kind of store Melissa wouldn't normally step in, because a dress could easily cost her a year's salary.

But here she was. This was really happening.

The driver exited the vehicle, made his way to the back

door and opened it for her. There was a smiling woman standing just inside the boutique, behind a Closed sign, and as Melissa approached, she opened the door for her.

"You must be Melissa," she said, extending a hand.

Melissa shook it. "Yes."

"I'm Crystal."

"Very nice to meet you," Melissa said. "Thanks so much for having me. I didn't realize I'm coming after hours."

"Actually, I closed the shop for you. Aaron insisted. He wanted you to have my undivided attention as you got ready. And he's made it worth my while, trust me."

Given the smile on Crystal's face, Melissa could only imagine. And it made her feel warm and fuzzy inside. Aaron was certainly pulling out all the stops for her.

Crystal began to walk, and Melissa fell into step beside her. "I think you're going to love the dress Aaron picked for you. It's right there."

They rounded the corner into the dressing room area, and when Melissa saw the dress hanging on the dressing room door, she stopped dead in her tracks.

"Oh my God," she uttered. "That's the dress?"

Crystal grinned from ear to ear. "Yep."

It was an off-the-shoulder trumpet gown made of red satin. The neckline was adorned with black lace and black jewels. The same lace and jewels were also embedded around the dress's waist. It looked formfitting and flared outward at the knee.

It was gorgeous.

Melissa had wondered if her pumps would work with this dress, but the combination of black and red on the dress would match her shoes perfectly.

"Try it on," Crystal urged.

With an excited giggle, Melissa headed into the changing room. The look on Crystal's face said it all once Melissa had the dress on. Her mouth formed a perfect O and her eyes lit up.

"You look stunning."

Melissa made her way to the large wall of floor-to-ceiling mirrors, and when she saw her reflection, her heart fluttered. She *did* look stunning. How had Aaron picked out the perfect dress for her?

Red looks incredible on you...

"I already picked out some accessories that I think would look fabulous with this gown," Crystal said. "A necklace made with onyx jewels, and a matching bracelet. Would you like to try them on?"

"Yes, please."

Once Melissa had the entire outfit on, including her shoes, she was mesmerized by how incredible she looked. She'd curled her hair and pinned it up, and Crystal helped her finesse the look.

Melissa noted that neither of the items she'd tried on had a price tag, but she knew this must cost a small fortune.

"Am I supposed to keep all of this?" Melissa asked, gently stroking the teardrop onyx stone.

"It's all for you," Crystal said. "A gift from Aaron." Pausing for a moment, Crystal smiled. "He's a great guy. My husband has known him since college, and he has nothing but high praise for him. And from what I can see, he likes you. A lot."

Melissa expelled a shuddery breath. She couldn't wait to see the look on Aaron's face when he saw her in this dress.

Aaron arrived at the shop and exited the limo, anxious to see Melissa. He already knew she would look amazing, but the text from Crystal had him extra excited.

Wait until you see her!

Aaron didn't have to wait long. Within a few seconds, he saw Crystal heading toward the door. She opened it wide, and then Melissa came into view.

A slow breath oozed out of Aaron. "Wow."

Melissa's face lit up in a smile. God, she was a vision of loveliness. The red dress hugged her curvaceous hips and her bountiful bosom. She was gorgeous, classy and sexy all at the same time.

Aaron wanted more than anything to take her in his arms and kiss her until she begged him to skip the event. He wanted to smooth his hands over those curvy hips.

He wanted her.

"Hi," she said, her voice wavering.

Aaron finally stepped toward her. "You look incredible."

"Thank you," she said, and twirled so that he could see the entire dress.

"And you're wearing the shoes?" he asked softly.

She lifted the hem of the dress so that he could see. "Yes."

"Oh, your bag," Crystal said, then disappeared into the store.

"Honestly, you're the most beautiful woman in the world," Aaron said. He leaned down and gave Melissa a soft kiss on the lips.

He saw the way her chest rose with the deep inhalation of breath. Was she as happy to see him as he was to see her?

"You don't have to say that," Melissa whispered.

"Did you look in a mirror?" Aaron countered. "I'm going to be the envy of the ball," he added with a playful smile.

Crystal returned with a tote bag. She passed it to Melissa. "Your belongings."

"Thanks," Melissa said.

Aaron took the bag from Melissa. "Crystal, thanks so much for everything," he said.

"Any time. You two have fun."

Then he offered Melissa his elbow, and she took it. He walked with her the short distance to the Maybach and opened the door, and she got in. He put her bag in the trunk, then got into the back seat beside her and took her hand.

She glanced at him and gave him a little smile.

Damn, she looked incredible. Aaron was seriously tempted to tell the driver to head straight back to his hotel.

But he would wait. And the waiting would make it all the more exciting.

Chapter 19

The ballroom at the Waldorf Astoria was the most spectacular room Melissa had ever seen. The walls were illuminated in pale pink, and trees with tiny crystal lights were strategically placed around the room. The tablecloths were accented in gold, and gold candles sat in glass containers. Melissa felt as though she had walked onto the set of a fairy tale.

The various items listed for the silent auction were placed on tables around the perimeter of the room. Jewelry sets. Paintings. Sports paraphernalia. Unique art sculptures. Weekend getaways. There was an amazing lineup of items to bid on.

And the people she'd met so far were absolutely lovely. Melissa had assumed that the crowd of high-profile citizens would be stuffy and conceited, but to her surprise, they were kind and friendly.

"Hey, gorgeous," Aaron said, slipping a hand around her waist. "See anything you like?"

"So much of it is amazing," Melissa said. "And I saw that you donated your original soccer jersey."

"It was the least I could do. I hope it fetches a pretty penny."

"Let's hope." Melissa turned toward the item she was standing in front of. "I'm really drawn to this painting by Felix Virgo." She angled her head as she looked at the painting of a swan peacefully swimming on a lake among lily pads. "It's so serene. I'd love to have this hanging on my office wall. Just looking at it would give me a sense of calm."

"It's beautiful," Aaron agreed. He looked into Melissa's eyes. "And so are you."

His unexpected compliment caused her stomach to flutter. "Thank you."

"Seriously, you're the most beautiful woman here." He slipped his arm around her waist.

Melissa cleared her throat. "Um...should we be doing this here?"

"I don't see why not," Aaron told her.

Heat coursed through Melissa's veins. Being this close to Aaron, she thought she might lose her mind. "I can hardly concentrate on the auction items with you near me," she whispered.

Aaron beamed, seemingly amused by her answer. "I'll leave you to mingle in peace."

With that, Aaron turned and made his way into the crowd, and Melissa saw him almost immediately hug another athlete—no doubt another soccer player.

"Hello."

Melissa turned to look at the woman who'd sidled up beside her. She was beautiful, with an olive complexion, her dark hair styled in an elegant chignon. She had bright eyes and a big smile.

"Hello," Melissa returned.

"I'm Olivia Rivera," she said, and extended a hand.

"Melissa Conwell." She shook the woman's hand.

"You're here with Aaron Burke."

Obviously, the woman was stating a fact, not asking a question. But Melissa responded anyway. "Yes."

"It's nice to see Aaron dating again."

"Oh, we're not dating. We're friends. We go way back."

"Hmm." Olivia's eyes narrowed slightly, as though she was confused by Melissa's answer. "Well, it's nice to see Aaron out regardless. After things fell apart with Ella, we didn't see him for a while."

"I guess you're one of the soccer wives," Melissa surmised.

"Yes. I'm married to Antonio Rivera. He and Aaron

played for the LA Galaxy for a couple of years before Aaron went off to Europe. We were all very happy for Aaron's success."

Melissa nodded. "This is a great event."

"Yes. Lovely venue, and I'm sure a lot of money will be raised for the Nunez family."

Once again, Melissa couldn't help thinking that her judgment had been way off regarding the people who would be here tonight. When she'd first walked into this ballroom on Aaron's arm, she'd assumed that everyone would be stuck-up and accustomed to adoration. Instead, Melissa had found down-to-earth people who cared about the cause.

Seeing the slideshow of the young girl at the start of the night and hearing about the family's terrible struggles had really touched Melissa. She checked out many of the other items up for bids but found herself wandering back to the painting by Felix Virgo. She didn't know why, but looking at this picture made her feel good.

She lifted the pen and scrawled her bid onto the paper. It was a hefty amount, but it was for a good cause.

She hoped her bid would be enough to secure the painting.

Aaron watched Melissa from across the room. Two men were talking to her, and they looked enthralled.

Aaron couldn't blame them. Melissa was utterly ravishing.

And he couldn't wait a minute longer. He needed to get her out of this room. Now.

Aaron had a suite booked upstairs. And that's where he wanted to be with Melissa. Holding her, kissing her, making sweet love to her.

He crossed the room toward her. As if sensing him, she turned, and a smile lit up her face.

God, she was radiant. And in the outfit she was wearing, she was easily the most beautiful woman in the room.

"Aaron," she said. The two men standing with her parted, allowing Aaron to close the distance between him and Melissa. He bit down on his bottom lip as he looked at her. What he really wanted to be doing was biting down on her lips. He wanted to take her in his arms in front of this crowd and kiss her senseless. Kiss her until she begged him to make love to her.

He slipped an arm around her waist, pulled her close and whispered in her ear, "Let's get out of here."

"We're not going to wait until they announce the winners of the auction?"

"They'll let us know if we won anything." He tightened his grip on her. "I need to take you upstairs. Now."

Melissa's eyelids fluttered. She looked up at him with those beautiful doe eyes. Beneath that wide-eyed gaze, he could see her passion. And he could also sense her hesitation. The same hesitation that he'd gotten from her when he'd shown up at her place of work.

Their connection was fiery, and Aaron wasn't afraid of it. He didn't want Melissa to be afraid of it, either.

He wanted to brand her, make her his. He wanted to give her all of him.

"You're sure?" Melissa asked.

"Do you know how absolutely irresistible you are?" he asked.

"People are probably staring," Melissa whispered.

"All the more reason to get out of here now."

He took her by the hand and looked into her eyes, where he saw no more hesitation.

"Okay," she said softly.

Aaron whisked her out of the ballroom.

Melissa felt a rush of excitement as Aaron led her to the elevator. They were a respectable couple as they waited for the elevator to arrive, but once they were inside, and alone, Aaron swept her into his arms and planted his lips on hers.

His lips moved over hers hungrily, and his hands roamed over her back. His tongue tangling with hers, their heavy breaths filled the enclosed space until the ping of the elevator sounded. They came apart quickly, and Melissa was relieved to see that they were on Aaron's floor.

Still, that didn't mean that no one was about to enter the elevator.

But when the doors opened, no one was there. Aaron quickly took Melissa's hand and led her down the hallway. She giggled as she had to jog to keep up with Aaron's fast pace.

The electricity between them sizzled. She loved the way she felt when he looked into her eyes—the thrill of excitement that came from knowing just how much he wanted her.

Aaron opened the door, and Melissa entered the suite first. He quickly followed her inside, flicking the light switch on.

He pulled her into his arms, his lips coming down on hers before he'd even closed the door. Melissa sighed as his tongue delved into her mouth.

A lingering groan rumbled in Aaron's chest, and a sexual charge shot through Melissa. Knowing that he was turned on so much that he couldn't even wait until the end of the event to get her upstairs excited her even more. She looped her arms around his neck and held on, her legs growing weak as she succumbed to his sensual assault on her lips.

"Baby," Aaron whispered, and he brought a hand to her face. Softly, he stroked her skin, then cupped her cheek. All the while he was moving with her, walking her backward into the living room of the suite. Several seconds later, her legs ran into the sofa, and she stumbled. Aaron held her and gently guided her down onto the chaise lounge, then went down on top of her, holding his strong frame above her so that he didn't hurt her. Melissa straightened her body out on the sofa, and Aaron stretched his strong, masculine body over hers.

He kissed her jawline, then dipped his mouth beneath her jaw, to her neck. He skimmed her flesh with those beautiful, full lips of his, causing a ripple of delicious sensations to swirl through her.

Then his head went lower, and he planted soft kisses on her collarbone before trailing his lips to the area above her breasts. Melissa caressed his head as he softly suckled the flesh of her cleavage. Her internal body temperature was rising rapidly.

Aaron lifted his head and looked into her eyes. "Every time I touch you, I go crazy."

His words made her shudder. The way he was stroking her skin, the way he was gazing at her... Melissa felt like the only woman in the world. "Every time you touch me, you make me crazy," she told him, her voice but a whisper.

"Tell me you were thinking about this the moment you saw me today. Tell me you wanted to make love to me as badly as I wanted to make love to you..."

His voice held a pleading tone, as if it would crush him to hear anything other than that Melissa desired and wanted him as much as he did her.

"Yes," she rasped, meaning it. "I couldn't help thinking about you kissing me again. Making love to me again..."

"Oh, baby..." Aaron moaned. He kissed her deeply, his tongue tangling with hers. Melissa snaked her foot around the back of Aaron's thigh as much as her skirt would allow.

"As beautiful as this dress is, I need to get you out of it."

He got to his feet and pulled her to a standing position. Melissa immediately reached for the zipper beneath her right arm and pulled it down. She shimmied out of the dress and stood before Aaron in only her strapless bra and lacy underwear.

"Take it all off for me, baby," he rasped. "Except for the shoes. I love those shoes."

Turned on by his words, Melissa quickly undid her bra and tossed it onto the floor. Then she pushed her underwear over her hips and down her thighs and kicked them aside.

Fully undressed, she met Aaron's gaze. His eyes were darkened with lust.

His gaze was like a caress, sweeping over her from head to toe. He expelled an audible breath. "Oh, baby."

Melissa swallowed. She was a little self-conscious standing in front of Aaron like this, fully exposed, totally vulnerable. But as he stepped toward her, the obvious desire in his eyes melted away her insecurity. She was no longer thinking about her body's flaws.

"You're perfect," Aaron told her.

He spoke as though he was seeing her naked for the first time. As though they hadn't been naked and getting it on just last week. Those lips had already explored every inch of her body.

He pulled her into his arms and brought his lips down on hers. This time, the kiss was slow and hot, causing every inch of her body to tingle. Her hands encircling his neck, she sighed against his lips.

"I don't ever want you to stop talking to me again," Aaron whispered.

Why would he say that at a moment like this?

"You were avoiding me," he went on, answering her unspoken question. "But I can't live without touching you." He smoothed his palms down her bare back. "Without kissing you."

"Aaron…"

"I don't want you to fight this anymore, that's what I'm saying. Why fight something we both want?"

Melissa pressed her body closer to his. "I'm not fighting…"

With a primal sound rumbling in his chest, he kissed her

again, ravaging her mouth with his. He slid his hands down and over her behind and pulled her against him forcefully. Melissa could feel the rock-hard evidence of his desire for her pressing against her pelvis.

She dug her fingernails into his shoulders and raised one leg high around his thigh. Aaron secured his hands on her behind and lifted her, and Melissa wrapped both legs around his waist.

"Yes, baby…"

Aaron's mouth widened, and he deepened the kiss, their tongues mating at fever pitch now. He moved with her swiftly down the hallway, and Melissa slipped a hand between their bodies. She tried unsuccessfully to undo the buttons of Aaron's shirt. Her concentration wasn't what it should be, not with his tongue assaulting her senses and making her body weak.

Aaron took over, and with one strong pull ripped his shirt apart. It was a shocking action, and one that stoked Melissa's inner fire even more.

Aaron lowered her onto the bed, his tongue still twisting hungrily with hers. Melissa pulled and pushed the fabric of Aaron's shirt off his shoulders, reveling in the feel of his smooth skin underneath her fingertips, and of his muscular chest pressed against her breasts. As the weight of his body settled on hers, he moved his lips from her mouth to her earlobe, suckling the flesh, and Melissa gripped his upper arms as the sweetest sensations flooded her.

Her earlobes were an erogenous zone, something she hadn't known before her night with Aaron after the wedding.

Aaron covered both of her breasts with his hands. He took her nipples between his thumb and forefinger at the same time, tugging on them both. They hardened instantly at his touch.

"My God, Melissa. Everything about you is driving me wild."

Aaron moved his mouth from her earlobe and brought it down on her breast. His whole mouth covered her nipple, and his tongue twirled around and around the tip. Melissa gripped his shoulders as her body was lost in a sea of intense feelings. Then he began to suckle softly, making her even crazier with need. She felt the heat and wetness pool between her thighs. She was ready for him. Ready for him to take her to that magical place once again.

He moved his mouth to her other breast and twirled the tip of his tongue over the nipple before taking it deep into his mouth and sucking hard.

"Oh, Aaron…" Melissa tightened her legs around his hips, urging him to be even closer to her. She needed his clothes gone and him deep inside her.

He eased himself downward and spread her legs apart. "I need to taste your sweetness."

Melissa's breath caught when Aaron dipped his tongue into her navel. Then his lips moved lightly over her belly as his fingers caressed her inner thighs. His touch was exquisite.

Aaron's lips followed the path his fingers had taken, kissing her inner thigh, close to her knee. Far from where Melissa wanted his mouth to be.

Slowly, his lips moved over her thigh, going lower. Melissa held her breath, and when his tongue gently flicked over her sensitive flesh, she expelled that breath in a rush.

"Baby!" she rasped.

Aaron's tongue worked magic until Melissa was panting and gripping the bedsheets. "Aaron…oh, baby. I need you inside me!"

Aaron eased backward and quickly pulled at his belt, then the hurriedly got out of his pants and shirt. Her body weak, her breathing heavy, she watched him strip out of his briefs from heavy-lidded eyes. The last time they'd been together, the room had been dark and she hadn't fully seen him. But now…*wow.* Her center throbbed at the sight of those washboard abs, his muscular biceps, his perfect thighs…

And his arousal—it was large and impressive.

Aaron Burke was the perfect specimen of a man. And he was going to rock her world again.

He lowered himself onto her and settled between her thighs. And the next instant, he was filling her. Melissa gripped his back as the sweetest sensations thrilled her body. Aaron groaned as he thrust into her, slowly and deeply. And then he went still, his eyes connecting with hers.

Melissa stared back unabashedly, her chest rising and falling with ragged breaths, something stirring in her soul. She wanted this to be about satisfying a sexual need, the most base of human desires, but she was feeling something else. Something that injected fear into this world of excitement.

She liked Aaron. As much as she didn't want to care about him at all, she liked him. And she knew in her heart that it would be easy to spend more time with him, make love to him over and over again.

And then what? He would destroy her again?

If he was the kind of man who kept his true feelings bottled up, it would always cause problems in a relationship.

Aaron lowered his head and captured her mouth with his. And as he thrust deeply inside her while moving his lips slowly over hers, Melissa stopped thinking negatively. She stopped thinking about anything other than the here and now, and how incredible she felt in Aaron's arms.

Each of his gentle thrusts was punctuated by soft sighs falling from Melissa's lips. She looped her arms around his neck and pulled him close, opening her mouth wide for him. She flicked the tip of her tongue over his, again and again, before locking her lips with his and kissing him deeply.

Aaron's hands tightened on her hips and he plunged into her swiftly, burrowing his shaft inside her. Melissa cried out, gripping him tighter. His body inside hers felt so good, so right. Aaron's body fit with hers perfectly, as though they were made for each other.

She pushed her hips up against his, urging him to go faster. He did. Together, the tempo of their lovemaking increased, until Melissa was crying out his name on a stream of erratic breaths. He kissed her jaw, her cheek, her earlobe, all of those actions adding to the exquisite sensations her body was experiencing.

Slowing the pace, Aaron eased his head back to look at her, and again, Melissa felt a charge. A sexual charge, yes, but something else, too. Something deeper.

It was as though the feelings she'd had for him, which had been buried for so long, were starting to escape the locked box in her heart.

"I've been thinking about this every day since I last saw you," Aaron whispered. "Of you and me, naked like this. All night."

"All night?" Melissa asked breathlessly.

"And all day. That's how much I love making love to you. For as long as we both need it. But I don't think I can ever get enough of this."

His words turned her on. Made her feel more desired than she'd ever felt.

Melissa wrapped her legs around him, holding him tightly against her. Oh, how easily she could make love to Aaron all day and all night. How much she wanted to.

And then he was kissing her again, his deep thrusts pushing her closer and closer to the edge. He trailed his fingers against the side of her breast, swept his tongue deeply into her mouth and burrowed himself inside her. The sweetest sensations began to build in her, and each

stroke of his member, each taste of his tongue stoked not
only her physical desire but something deeper.

Something emotional.

"Look at me, baby," Aaron said.

She did. Stared into his eyes and laid her soul bare. He
held her gaze, and in that moment, she believed that there
was something deeper between her and Aaron than just
the physical act of making love.

She climaxed then, vaulting into that sweet abyss. Aaron
kissed her as raw pleasure consumed her body and warmth
filled her heart.

Chapter 20

Melissa's eyelids popped open. The room was dark, but she knew immediately that it was unfamiliar.

As was the arm draped across her naked torso.

Everything came back to her in an instant. The Waldorf Astoria. Aaron. Making love as if their lives depended on it.

They had barely been able to get enough of each other, sheer exhaustion the only thing forcing them to finally get some sleep.

A smile crept onto Melissa's face. The night had been incredible.

She angled her head, glancing at Aaron in the darkened room. She could make out his features, see his slightly parted lips, hear the soft inhalations of his breath. He seemed content.

And how easily she could be content in his arms. But there was that niggling fear.

Did he like her?

As soon as that question came into her mind, Melissa turned away from Aaron and frowned. Why was she contemplating whether or not he liked her? It didn't matter. She had spent these two nights with Aaron for one reason only—to scratch an itch. That had been the plan. Whether or not he liked her was of zero significance.

In fact, the goal was to forget about him once and for all. Clearly, she had a fierce attraction to him, but it was okay to be a hot-blooded female with desires. The time she'd spent with Aaron had reminded her that she was missing intimacy in her life. Why had she not yet set up a profile on an online dating site?

As for Aaron, hopefully after last night, she could purge whatever this was inside her that found him attractive and irresistible.

She glanced at him again, and desire spread through her body. The temptation to slip onto his body and wake him up with kisses under his jawline was seriously intense. Her mind and her body weren't on the same page. Her mind told her that enough was enough; it was time to be done with Aaron already. Her body, on the other hand, enjoyed every moment that he touched her, kissed her, made love to her—and wanted more.

And then there was her heart. It was telling her that what she was experiencing with Aaron was more than just sex.

The way Aaron held her, kissed her, the way he looked at her during the act of sex…it all felt amazingly intimate. Not like two people simply getting together to fill a physical need.

Don't go there, she told herself. Melissa couldn't get caught up in those feelings. She couldn't allow herself to believe that sex with Aaron was more than what it was. Obviously, a man like Aaron was used to having lots of sex with lots of women. He found her attractive; that was a given. And men like Aaron pursued attractive women and could have sex without letting emotions complicate things.

For Melissa to even begin to entertain any fanciful feelings that sex was more than just sex with him would be stupid.

He'd broken her heart once, hadn't he? She didn't want to give him the power to do that again.

She glanced at him again, thought of just how attentive he had been to her in and out of the bedroom, how great he'd been with the kids at the group home, and how much he cared about the Nunez family. He was a good man, one she could easily fall for again. But she had to remember that he had issues he hadn't dealt with, issues that caused him to shut down his emotions and walk away from her. He could easily do that again.

Melissa cared easily. She wanted to love without reservation. Give her body to a man who loved her from the depths of his soul. If she compromised on what she needed from a man, she would have to deal with the devastating consequences when she got hurt. She needed a man who was going to be open and vulnerable with her.

Even lying in bed with Aaron like this was entirely too comfortable, entirely the kind of thing that made her long for something more. She eased out from under his arm and slowly got off the bed. She was stuck in the past.

Because she'd never truly had closure on her relationship with Aaron.

She shook her head as she started to pad across the room, disappointed with the direction of her thoughts. She didn't need closure. She was over Aaron Burke. She'd gotten over him years ago.

Her dress was on the living room floor, where it had been quickly discarded when Aaron was desperate to get her naked. She wished she had something else to wear out of here, but the dress was her only option.

"Where are you going?" Aaron asked.

Melissa froze, surprised that he was awake.

She looked over her shoulder at him. "I was just going to use the bathroom and look for my clothes."

"And sneak off again?" Aaron asked, but there was a hint of humor in his voice.

"I probably do need to get back. I've got work."

"On a Saturday?"

"I typically go in on Saturday afternoons. I have some reports to do."

"We should have time for breakfast before you leave, then."

Did she want to extend her time with him? No. She wanted to flee. Even looking at him in the bed, his gorgeous body stretched out and the bedsheet carelessly strewn across his midsection, she felt her womb tighten with desire.

She wanted to stay here with him, make love to him over and over again, and forget the rest of the world existed.

Surely this wasn't normal.

"And maybe we could…one more time…" Aaron said, giving her a wink.

Her center throbbed. He hadn't spelled out the words, but it was obvious what he wanted. And good Lord, she wanted that, too.

Why was he so hard to resist? Shouldn't she be telling him now that this was the last time they could be together, that it had been fun while it lasted, but now she was going to get back to her real life in the real world and—

"Come here," he said, patting the spot she'd vacated beside him.

Melissa's pulse quickened. Then she did as he'd asked and made her way over to him. She eased her bottom down onto the bed, and he leaned forward and gave her lips a peck. "You standing there, naked, teasing me…it should be a crime. You know that?" He snaked an arm around her waist. "I can't get enough of you. Damn, girl, what have you done to me?"

Melissa swallowed. She wanted more than anything to believe that he'd never felt this kind of attraction for any-one else, that there was something special about her. That the sex between them was the best he'd ever had.

But she knew that was foolish.

She also knew that right now, she wanted nothing more than to have that one more roll in the hay with him. Before she went back to New Jersey and her life without him, she needed him one last time.

After making love once again, Melissa and Aaron had a breakfast of fruit, yogurt and granola while lazing around in bed. Melissa tried to keep a happy disposition, but every-thing felt bittersweet.

Soon she would be leaving Aaron, and this time she planned never to see him again.

But her heart was hurting a little over that fact. Their last time making love had been the most emotional of all their times together—slow, sensual and seemingly filled with meaning. Or maybe Melissa had felt more emotional intensity because she knew that she would soon be saying goodbye to Aaron forever.

There was no other way. She knew that. And yet, the idea that she was closing the door on him and what she'd once believed was possible made her a little bit sad.

Even more so because the sexual chemistry with Aaron had been all she could ever want with a partner. He brought her body to heights she'd never experienced. She missed kissing, making love, lying in bed with someone.

But she wanted that with someone in the context of a relationship—a real one. Not with someone who was good at scratching an itch, but not good at committing.

There was too much baggage between her and Aaron for her to believe he could possibly be the man she needed, even if on some level, somewhere deep inside her, she wished that he could be.

They'd had their chance, hadn't they? And Aaron had blown it. They hadn't talked over the years. Melissa had always believed that once a relationship was over, there was no going back to it.

She gazed at Aaron, who looked so darn tempting wearing only his boxer briefs, sitting on the bed beside her. She was wearing one of his T-shirts, which was huge on her. This was nice...and she would enjoy these last few minutes with him, then move on.

"I'd better get changed," Melissa said. Just as Aaron tried to reach for her, she slid off the bed, giggling.

Honestly, she knew that if she weren't leaving, she and

Aaron would spend the day here naked, making a love den out of this suite at the Waldorf Astoria.

Thankfully, Aaron had had the foresight to have her bag with her regular clothes sent up to the room, so Melissa didn't have to leave the hotel all decked out in her stunning gown. She was glad not to have to do that walk of shame. And the staff was nice enough to get her a hanger and a plastic dress bag to carry her gown with her.

A short while later, she was dressed and ready to leave. Aaron took her garment bag, and together they left the room, neither of them saying a word.

But once they were in the elevator, Aaron used his free hand to pull her against his body. He gave her a soft kiss on the lips. "I wish you didn't have to leave yet."

"You're insatiable," Melissa teased.

"You weren't complaining last night." He gave her another kiss. "Nor this morning."

She looked up at him, giving him a bashful smile. She hadn't been complaining, not in the least.

The elevator pinged, alerting them of their arrival on the main floor. With a groan, Aaron released her.

He adjusted the hanger with Melissa's gown at the back of his shoulder as the elevator doors opened. He took her hand and they strolled through the lobby. Melissa felt as though all eyes were on her.

The memory of Aaron's body tangled with hers caused a hot rush to pass through her body. Their time together had been spectacular.

Melissa glanced down at their joined hands, something she liked and hated at the same time. The hand-holding spoke of a level of intimacy between them, made her think that at least he didn't regard her as a woman he could just bed and throw aside. And she liked that.

But she almost wished that he *didn't* exhibit any signs

of caring where she was concerned. Because it would be that much harder to forget him.

They exited the front doors and walked out onto the street. Aaron walked her to the Maybach and opened the back door. He hung her dress inside, then dipped his head and gave her a soft, lingering kiss on the lips. "I had a great time last night," he whispered.

"Me too," Melissa admitted with a bashful smile.

"Maybe we can get together next weekend."

Melissa's heart spasmed. Next weekend? He wanted to see her again?

Before she had time to think, much less respond, he kissed her again, this time stroking her face as well. Tingles of delight spread through her.

Aaron groaned slightly, then released her. "Let me know you got home safely."

"Sure." Melissa got into the vehicle, a mix of conflicting emotions flowing through her.

She knew that seeing Aaron again would be crazy, and yet as the limo driver pulled away, she turned to look at him. He stepped into the road to get a better view of the disappearing car.

He waved. Melissa waved back.

This was goodbye. It had to be.

Chapter 21

"Well, well, well," Teresa said in a singsong voice, a huge smile on her face. "Someone had a great night."

"I *just* walked through the door."

"Yeah, and even your walk is different. Come on, tell me how it was!"

"Where are Mike and Ed?" Melissa asked, referring to the other counselors who were working today.

"It's a beautiful day. They took the boys to the park. I should have gone…but I figured this would be the only chance we had to talk. So come on, tell me *everything*!"

Melissa's face instantly flamed. She hoped her friend couldn't see the extent of her embarrassment.

But why should she be embarrassed? She'd had the best night of her life, hands down.

"All right. Let's talk in my office."

Teresa squealed and hurried behind Melissa into the office. Her friend's excitement had Melissa flushing hotly with the memory of last night. Every delicious detail flooded her mind…and a wave of sensations washed over her. Aaron kissing her, the way his fingers and tongue explored her body…

"Tell me!" Teresa said. "Because I can see it in your eyes. You're remembering some of the dirty details right now, aren't you?"

Melissa slumped into her chair with a satisfied sigh. "I had a great time," she said. "It was spectacular."

"I haven't heard you use those words about a night with a guy…*ever*."

Melissa remembered Aaron's tongue on her earlobe, and she had to make a concerted effort to push the image out of her mind in order to keep speaking. "I needed last night," Melissa admitted. "He's gorgeous. The evening itself was fun and meaningful. The fund-raiser had me totally emotional. It was such a wonderful gesture for the Nunez family."

"Hopefully that little girl survives and does well."

"From your lips to God's ears." Melissa paused. "Honestly, I thought I was going to be in a room with a bunch of snooty people. People with money to burn who show up and pretend to care just to be seen on Page Six. But honestly, I couldn't have been more wrong. They were sweet. And they really did care. I was moved. A lot of money was raised, and it was a wonderful thing to see these athletes giving back as opposed to being selfish."

"More points for Aaron Burke," Teresa said.

Melissa's pulse tripped. She wondered again if she had judged him too harshly. After all, he had been wonderful to her, hadn't he? But she didn't want to allow herself to go there.

Teresa's eyes were dancing with excitement. "I am so thrilled for you. When are you seeing him again?"

"I'm not sure that I am."

"What?" The look of shock that passed over Teresa's face could not have been more intense. "Why not?"

"First of all, we live in different cities. That's the biggest hindrance."

"He lives in your hometown?"

"Yeah."

"So? He can travel, can't he? Obviously he's got the financial resources. If he wants to see you, I'm sure you two can make it happen."

"I'm not trying to plan out this crazy life of fitting in sex with a guy between work and my other obligations."

"What other obligations? Stressing over the headaches that happen here? If anyone could use a steady romantic partner, it's you. Have you looked in a mirror? You look like a changed woman."

And how nice it would be to have Aaron as a steady romantic partner. Melissa could get used to spending nights with him. Enjoying breakfast in bed. But that was a fantasy life, a fantasy in her mind. It wasn't reality.

"Because I had a bit of fun, which was just what I needed," Melissa explained. "But that's all it was...fun."

Teresa frowned. "Why can't it be more?"

"Because," Melissa said succinctly, then sighed. "Listen, there's a lot you don't know about him. We used to date years back, when I was a teenager. And...he hurt me. We were young, I get it. Still, you know?"

"No, I don't know. I can't make sense of anything you're saying to me right now."

"He married my nemesis from high school. He knew how much of a headache this girl was in my life. And he married her. The one person who thought she was better than every other girl. The prettiest, the sexiest, the best, period. Aaron married her."

"But they're obviously not together anymore...because you wouldn't have slept with him. Right?"

Melissa made a face at her friend. "Obviously not. I would never get involved with him if he were still married to Ella or anyone else."

"So what's the problem?"

"I guess what I'm saying is we have baggage. Stuff I'm not sure I can fully overlook."

"Are you serious?" Teresa asked. "You used to date, what? Twelve, thirteen years ago?"

"Twelve. But the last time we talked before the wedding was eleven years, nine months and some-odd days ago," Melissa admitted in a soft voice.

"Wait a second," Teresa said, her eyes widening. "If you're still upset about a breakup from nearly twelve years ago, that means you never really forgot him."

"It means I don't want to make the same mistake twice. Aaron has a way of making you feel wonderful—but when he shuts down, it's awful. I don't know what I did wrong, if he suddenly thought I wasn't good enough for him—or if something else was going on. But he shut down, refused to talk to me and broke my heart." Melissa shrugged. "Some men never let you in, and I don't want to deal with that again. Besides, now he's famous and used to women throwing themselves at him. He'd probably grow bored of me."

"I doubt it."

"But do I want to take that chance?"

"Well, you seem to have put a lot of thought into this. I wonder why."

Melissa's stomach lurched at the question from her friend. Why, indeed?

"Because… I don't want to be a fool. I can be a modern woman and have a lover and not need a relationship."

"So you want him as a lover, then?"

"That's not what I said. I already had my fun. It's time to move on."

Teresa's lips twisted in a scowl. "If you say so."

When Aaron's phone trilled, indicating he had a text message, he quickly scooped it up and retrieved it.

Seeing Melissa's name on his screen, he smiled.

I meant to text you earlier. I got home safely but had to hustle to get into work, which is where I am now. Thanks again for a great night…

Aaron had hoped that she would call him, but seeing this message from her nonetheless lifted his spirits. At least she wasn't cutting him off like she had after the first time they'd spent the night together.

Though if she did, she'd be in for a surprise. He wasn't about to let her walk out of his life, no questions asked.

Not after the undeniable chemistry between them.

Aaron was well versed in the art of the chase, but he was starting to wonder if he was losing his touch.

He'd headed back to Sheridan Falls, leaving a full day between Melissa's text and him reaching out to her again. He called, but she didn't answer.

Aaron gave it a few more hours, and he called again. Again, she didn't answer. After that, he sent a text asking her to call him when she got the chance.

Two full days passed before she sent a text.

Sorry I haven't gotten back to you. I've been very busy. Hope all is well in your world.

Aaron frowned when he read it. This was all she had to say to him? His excitement over the idea that he and Melissa had been rekindling something quickly faded into confusion and disappointment.

Had she faked her attraction to him in the bedroom? No, that didn't make sense. What would be the purpose in doing that?

Besides, he'd been there. Nothing about her interaction with him had been faked.

In fact, the explosive sexual attraction between them was on a level he hadn't experienced with any other woman. Years ago, Aaron hadn't been ready for a relationship with her, but now they were both older, both more mature.

And he knew what he wanted.

Melissa.

He wasn't about to give up on her without a fight.

Which meant he would just have to up his game.

Chapter 22

"Come on, come on. Where's that paperwork?"

Melissa clicked through the various folders on her laptop, searching for the report from the probation officer. Why couldn't she find it?

"This is ridiculous," she muttered.

Teresa entered the office and drew up short. "Everything okay?"

"No. I can't seem to find the probation officer's report for Marcus. Did I misname the file?"

"It's got to be there somewhere."

Melissa pushed her chair back and stood. She blew out a frazzled breath. Why was she this upset? All day she'd felt a sense of irritation, and she didn't know why. Every request from the boys or her coworkers annoyed her today. And the argument between Tyler and Marcus earlier had really gotten on her last nerve. She'd yelled at the boys, and she rarely yelled.

On her desk, her cell phone rang. Melissa shot it a glance, saw that it was a private caller and decided to ignore it.

"Well, this might perk you up," Teresa said.

"What?"

"That was a delivery man at the door. He dropped off an envelope. It was addressed to the house, so I took the liberty of opening it. There are tickets to a New York Red Bulls soccer game."

"What?" Melissa asked, not understanding.

"There's a note from Aaron. He wrote, 'Since the boys are big soccer fans, I figured I'd get them tickets for a game. Enjoy. Aaron.'"

"Aaron sent tickets?" Melissa asked, and in that moment, she felt the chill on her heart melting slightly. A part of her wanted to smile. Had her irritation been caused by the fact that she and Aaron hadn't been in touch?

How crazy would that be, since she was the one who'd sent him a brief, carefully worded message, hoping he would understand that she didn't want to keep communicating with him?

And he'd given her what she'd wanted. For two whole days, there'd been nothing from him.

And now this...

God, why was her irritation fading away?

Melissa's phone rang again. Again with the unknown number.

Anyone who wanted to reach her for business would be calling her on the work phone. She let it ring.

"Can I see that?" Melissa asked Teresa.

Teresa passed her the manila envelope, plus the note from Aaron. Melissa was reaching into the envelope when her cell phone rang again. This time she saw her sister's number.

She quickly snatched up her phone, a bad feeling gripping her gut. "Arlene, is everything okay?"

"No, it's not okay," Arlene sobbed. "Raven and Dad... they're in the hospital!"

"What?" Her sister's words didn't make sense.

"Dad was driving, he had Raven in the car, and the police think he had a heart attack. Oh, God..."

Dread filled Melissa's stomach. "*What?* Is Dad...are they..." She swallowed. "Are they okay?"

"Dad's in critical condition, and Raven..." Arlene sobbed.

"What about Raven?" Melissa asked, her heart seizing.

"She's not seriously injured, and for now she seems okay. But Dad...you have to come home. Right now. We need you."

"I'm on my way."

* * *

Melissa had dropped everything and taken a taxi to the airport as soon as possible. Once she was there, she had been lucky enough to get a seat on a plane that was heading to Buffalo an hour later. From the Buffalo airport, she took a cab directly to the hospital. It took her just over four hours from the time she'd gotten the call from her sister to get to Sheridan Falls.

Four hours in which she had been terrified, her heart unable to deal with the reality that the worst might happen. While she hadn't spoken with her sister again—Arlene had been too much of a wreck—she had received texts from her letting her know that for the time being, nothing had changed.

As the taxi neared the hospital, Melissa's cell phone rang. She let out a strangled cry, then looked at her phone, praying her sister wasn't calling with more bad news.

Her shoulders slumped with relief when she saw that Aaron was the one calling. Not her sister or mother with bad news.

She swiped to answer her phone. "Hello?" she said, her voice sounding frazzled to her own ears.

"I just heard," Aaron said. "Where are you?"

"I'm in a taxi. I'm almost at the hospital."

"Okay, good. I'm almost there, too. Is there anything you need?"

"I just need to know that my father and my niece are okay," Melissa answered, her voice cracking. Though Arlene had said that Raven hadn't been seriously injured, internal injuries weren't always immediately obvious. What if she was bleeding internally and the doctors didn't know it yet?

"They will be," Aaron assured her. "I'll see you in a few minutes."

Melissa swiped to end the call and pressed the phone

against her chest. She prayed that Aaron was right—that her father and niece would pull through.

The moment Melissa stepped into the hospital's emergency waiting room and saw her sister with Raven on her lap, she burst into tears. Then she saw her mother, and Mrs. Winston, her mother's best friend, sitting beside Arlene and Raven. Melissa hurried through the waiting room and threw her arms around her mother when she jumped to her feet.

"Oh, sweetheart," her mother said and began sobbing.

"How's Daddy?" Melissa asked, reverting to calling her father by the name she had when she'd been a little girl.

"He's in surgery, sweetheart. He had a heart attack, plus he got injured during the crash. We're all praying."

"I've been praying for the last four hours," Melissa said, hoping that God had heard her. She couldn't lose her father.

"At least Raven is okay," her mother said and glanced at her granddaughter. "Thank God for that."

Melissa released her mother and moved over to Arlene, who had gotten to her feet and was still holding Raven in her arms. Melissa needed to see for herself that her niece was all right.

"Hey," Melissa said softly, and gently fingered the bandage on Raven's forehead. "You're okay, sweetheart?"

Raven nodded slowly. "But I have a boo-boo."

"I see that. Does it hurt?"

"Only a little." Raven's little face suddenly fell, and her eyes filled with tears. "But Grandpa didn't wake up. Is he going to die?"

"We're all praying for him," Melissa said, not wanting to lie to her niece. "We're going to keep praying, very hard. Can you do that, too?"

Raven nodded.

Melissa wiped Raven's tears, then turned her attention

to her sister. As their eyes met, Arlene started to cry. Melissa pulled her into her arms and hugged her long and hard.

"There's no word on how badly Dad was hurt?" Melissa asked.

"He's having open-heart surgery right now," Arlene answered before a wave of fresh tears fell down her cheeks.

Oh, God. This was worse than Melissa thought. The accident hadn't killed her father, but his heart might give out on the operating table.

"Melissa."

At the sound of Aaron's voice, Melissa's knees buckled. She turned, emotion washing over her when she saw him standing in the waiting room. He was like an anchor in a stormy sea.

"Aaron!" She rushed to him and threw her arms around him. He cradled her head as emotion poured out of her.

"Do you know how long your father's been in surgery?" he asked.

As Melissa shook her head, Arlene answered. "About three hours. That's too long, isn't it? They should have finished with him by now, right?"

Still holding Melissa, Aaron faced Arlene. "We have some of the greatest doctors in the country right here in Sheridan Falls. I know they're doing their best to save him."

His words seemed to comfort Arlene, and his mere presence was making Melissa feel marginally better.

But the fact still remained: her father wasn't out of the woods.

Please God, don't let him die.

Though Melissa told Aaron that she couldn't possibly eat anything, he left to go the cafeteria, promising to return with coffee and snacks. Melissa was pacing the floor, her sister sitting and cradling Raven, not wanting to let her go, her mother and Mrs. Winston holding hands as they prayed quietly.

Suddenly, it seemed as though all the air had been sucked out of the room. All heads raised in unison, looking beyond Melissa. She saw the look on her sister's face, the way her jaw tightened and fear flashed in her eyes. She pulled Raven closer to her body.

Melissa quickly turned, following her sister's line of sight. Her heart slammed against her rib cage when she saw Craig, her former brother-in-law, storming into the hospital waiting room like a man possessed. He was marching right toward them.

Arlene tightened her arms around Raven, a clearly protective gesture.

"Is she okay?" Craig demanded.

"She's fine," Arlene retorted.

"But she could have been killed," he shot back, the accusation in his tone clear.

"Please don't tell me you came here to pick a fight, Craig," Arlene said.

"Because of you, Raven was nearly killed."

"You need to leave," Arlene told him.

"Not without my daughter," Craig said.

Raven started to fuss. Melissa quickly stepped in front of Craig in an effort to keep her sister and former brother-in-law apart. "What are you doing?" Melissa asked him.

"Stay out of this." He glared at her, and Melissa was so shocked by the venomous look in his eyes that she reeled backward slightly.

"Craig, this is a *hospital*," Arlene said in a hushed tone. "You can't behave like this."

He took a step toward her, and Arlene quickly got to her feet and moved several feet away from Craig. He followed her. Melissa followed them both, again putting herself between Craig and her sister. "Craig," Melissa began, "I don't know what you're doing, but you need to leave."

"If you can't raise our daughter without always leaving her with your parents, then I will happily take her. With what happened today, I'm sure the judge will hear my petition for revised custody. I knew this was going to happen."

"You knew that my father was going to have a heart attack while he was driving?" Melissa asked, sarcasm dripping from her tone.

"He's an old man. And the point is, if Arlene were doing her job as a parent and not relying on your family so much, this wouldn't have happened."

"How dare you?" Melissa's mother said. She was on her feet now, her red-rimmed eyes flashing fire.

"You're being unreasonable," Melissa said.

Raven was crying now, full-out bawling. "Everyone's staring," Arlene said. "Craig, think about what you're doing."

"Give me my daughter." His words were slow, deliberate, his teeth clenched. "Or I'm about to give everyone here a show they won't soon forget."

Chapter 23

The moment Aaron rounded the corner toward the waiting room with two trays of coffee and a bag of muffins, he heard the commotion. His face narrowed in confusion. What the heck was going on?

And then he saw. Melissa, Arlene and Valerie were on their feet facing Craig, whose posture said he was enraged.

Aaron quickly placed the trays of coffee and the food onto the nurses' station and charged toward them. He immediately got in front of Craig, who was much shorter than Aaron. "Hey, hey. What are you doing, man?"

Craig scowled at him. "This is between me and my wife."

"*Ex*-wife," Arlene clarified. She was swaying her body from side to side, trying to calm Raven.

"Look how you're scaring your daughter," Melissa said. "You're out of control."

"You need to leave," Aaron said firmly. "I don't know what you're trying to accomplish, but this isn't the way."

"You think everyone has to listen to you because you're a Burke?" Craig spat out.

"I won't tell you again," Aaron said, and the resolve in his voice was unmistakable. It told Craig—and anyone within earshot—that he meant business. If Craig was here to do anything stupid, he was going to live to regret it.

"You'll be hearing from my lawyer," Craig said to Arlene, then turned and started to walk away.

"I already have primary custody," Arlene said. "And everyone here can see why."

Craig stopped in his tracks and whirled around, but Aaron was there, stepping into his path. "You're going to want to keep going," he said.

Aaron glanced at Melissa then, saw her looking at him with awe and appreciation. He gave her a little nod, letting her know that she could depend on him to handle the situation. Craig wasn't going to do anything crazy—not while he was here.

Surprisingly, Craig stood his ground, even though a security guard had just appeared in the waiting room. Aaron raised his hand in the man's direction, letting him know he had the situation under control. Then he narrowed his eyes at Craig. "I'll give you one chance to rethink your decision and turn around right now."

Craig looked up at him, then at the security guard. Finally, he gritted his teeth. But it didn't take more than a few seconds for him to turn around and stalk down the hallway toward the hospital's exit. Clearly he knew that if he stayed and continued to cause trouble, he would end up arrested.

"Why is Daddy being so mean?" Raven asked, her big eyes wet with tears.

"Sometimes Daddy gets too angry," Arlene explained, stroking Raven's hair. "But he's gone now. He won't be yelling at anyone anymore."

Once Craig was gone, Aaron asked, "What was that about?"

"Do you want to go get ice cream?" Mrs. Conwell asked, approaching Raven with her arms outstretched.

"Mmm-hmm." Raven nodded exuberantly, then went into her grandmother's arms.

"And maybe we can also stop by the gift shop and pick up a toy," Mrs. Conwell went on.

As grandmother and granddaughter headed down the hallway, Arlene faced Aaron. "I don't know why Craig feels he can behave that way in front of our daughter. Doesn't he realize that he scares her?" She blew out a frazzled breath. "He's angry because I got primary custody. And he's been making my life hell because of it. Anything I do, he finds fault with. Apparently it's my fault that my father had a heart attack while driving, and I should have known that would happen. He's angry that Raven was in the car instead of grateful that she wasn't seriously hurt."

"If memory serves, Sean Callahan was his lawyer," Aaron said, more to himself.

"Yes," Arlene said. "Word is, he gave Sean a hard time during our custody proceedings. He felt Sean was failing him somehow."

"That's no surprise." Given Craig's behavior minutes ago, he could imagine the man being belligerent with his lawyer when things didn't go his way. "Listen, Arlene. If Craig does anything that frightens you, anything at all, don't hesitate to call the police. In the meantime, I'm going to have a chat with his lawyer."

"You don't need to get involved," Arlene said. "I can take care of Craig."

"Still, I'll probably give Sean a call. See if I can gauge if he knows what Craig's frame of mind is. I don't like how he seems. Like he's off his hinges."

"I can't disagree with that," Arlene said.

"And you should alert the police to what happened here today," Aaron said.

Arlene made a face. "Oh, I don't know about that."

"He's right," Melissa said, coming to stand beside Aaron. "You need to make sure there's a record of what happened today. Maybe a visit from the police about his behavior is the wake-up call Craig needs."

Slowly, Arlene nodded. "All right. I'll call them."

When Arlene headed back over to her seat and slumped into the chair, Aaron put his hands on Melissa's shoulders. "Don't worry," he said to her. "I'll help take care of this. My dad knows the best legal people in the city and the state. Just make sure that your sister contacts the police. Craig needs to hear from them that he can't behave like this."

"You really want to help us, don't you?"

"Why do you seem so surprised?" Aaron asked her.

"I don't know." She offered him a small smile, and there was that look of wonder again. Was she surprised that he cared about her?

"I've known your family since I was a little boy. Of course I want to help. I don't want to see any of you hurt."

"I got the tickets you sent for the boys," Melissa said. "The package arrived just before I got the news. The kids will be thrilled." She exhaled a shaky breath, her expression twisting. "I'm so scared about my father."

"Hey," Aaron said, placing a finger beneath her chin and angling her face upward. "Have faith. The best team of cardiac surgeons is working on him. He's going to pull through."

And then Melissa laid her head against his chest, and he gently held it there. He wished more than anything that he could take this pain and fear away from her.

The best he could do was be by her side to help her through this. And that's exactly where he would be.

An hour later, one of the surgeons came out to the waiting room. Melissa, her sister and her mother gripped hands, waiting to hear the news.

"He pulled through the surgery," the doctor said, smiling. "We had to stop the internal bleeding from the accident, then do a coronary bypass to improve blood supply to his heart. He's very lucky."

"Can we see him?" Melissa's mother asked.

"Not yet. He's in recovery. But we'll let you know the moment you can visit."

The news was a relief, but Melissa knew that her mother wouldn't feel better until she was able to see her husband. Melissa felt the same way. She needed to see her father to truly believe that he was okay.

The neighbors had started arriving before the doctor had come out to speak to them, bringing cards and flowers and food. Even though there was a cafeteria in the hospital, the food kept coming. Casseroles, sandwiches, meat loaves and even some desserts. As one of the older residents of the town said, "You need real food, not that horrible stuff they serve in this place. When my Gerald was here for his operation, he complained every day that the food was going to kill him before the cancer."

Melissa was amazed—and touched. She hadn't lived in Sheridan Falls for years and had forgotten how the residents would rally around someone in trouble. She'd remembered the nosy ones, the busybodies, but she had forgotten the good hearts of the people in this small-town community.

They had brought enough food for a house party—and promised more. They wanted to ease the burden on Melissa's family so that they could concentrate all their energy on her father.

"This is so much food," Melissa's mother commented, looking around at the trays occupying the tables in the waiting room. "And I can't even eat much more than a bite. Not until I get to see your father."

Aaron had remained at the hospital with the family, a source of comfort for Melissa as well as her mother and sister. He seemed to realize that Melissa didn't want to talk. The stress of her father's situation had her silent and introspective, and he was respecting that.

Melissa looked around at the waiting room, filled to capacity with people. Some were eating the sandwiches and brownies, and they were chatting and laughing. It was all so surreal, as if they were here for a social call.

"I think I need to get out of here," she mumbled.

"Why don't we take some of this food to your parents' house?" Aaron suggested.

Melissa looked up at him. He glanced around the room, then back at her, and she realized that he'd heard her comment.

"Um, yeah," she said. "That's a good idea."

"We'll just grab what we can."

Melissa took two trays of fruit and sandwiches in her arms. "Mom, we're going to take some of this food home. I'll be back soon."

A short while later, they were in Aaron's car and en route to Melissa's parents' home. They were silent during the drive, but Melissa noticed that Aaron would occasionally glance at her. He was allowing her silence, though, and she appreciated that.

Twenty minutes later, the food was packed into the fridge and Melissa and Aaron were back in his car. When he didn't start the engine, Melissa looked at him.

"What are you doing?"

"Why do you keep running from me?" Aaron asked.

"I'm not running."

"Like hell you're not," Aaron said. "You've barely looked at me since I got to the hospital. I know it's a tough day, but it's more than that. I've reached out to you, and you've ignored me. I'd like to know why."

"You really think this is the time?"

"I don't like this...tension. I like you."

"You like a lot of women," Melissa found herself saying, not even thinking the words through before they fell from her lips.

Aaron made a face. "So that's the problem. You think I'm a player?"

"You owe me nothing, no explanation."

"Then you shouldn't be upset with me," Aaron said. "Yet you've been hot and cold."

Melissa's face flushed, thinking of how hot they'd been between the sheets. "This is...awkward. Honestly, I'm not really good at one-night stands."

"Well, it was two nights," Aaron said with a small shrug. "You think that was my interest in you? A casual fling?"

"I'm thinking that maybe you…you have a fear of commitment. You end things when you get too close."

His eyes narrowed as he stared at her. "Fear of commitment? I got married, remember?"

Melissa didn't need any reminding. She pressed on. "What happened with Chantelle…maybe you fear getting close to people. So you end things before you lose them."

"You're psychoanalyzing me now?" Aaron asked, one of his eyebrows shooting up. "Because from where I sit, you're the one who seems afraid to get close to me."

"How can I get close to you if you won't let me in? What happened with Chantelle could explain a lot. Why you've had so many women."

"So you're telling me that you're the type to listen to rumor and speculation. And now you've come up with some analysis to explain my bad behavior? Without even knowing if it's true?"

Melissa sighed softly. She didn't want to be doing this. She didn't want to entertain any conversation about Aaron and his past, especially right now.

"Not that I want to discuss this now, but I saw that interview Ella did on television about your marriage troubles. She said you were incapable of being faithful. Why would she say that?"

"Because Ella is Ella," Aaron said simply. Then he sighed softly. "But why did you sleep with me if that was your concern?"

Melissa said nothing. She didn't have an answer.

"This isn't the time to talk," Aaron said, "but I would like to talk. Whenever things settle down on your end. I'll be here."

Melissa nodded. "All right."

Aaron started to drive. "The tabloids said a lot of things about me, none of which were true. I want you to keep that in mind."

"Okay," Melissa said. She wanted to ask him why it mattered so much, but she didn't. Because she was afraid of the answer.

Players lied. That's what they did best. If she let herself believe the sweet things he might say, she would end up devastated. Especially if deep in his heart, he didn't believe that he deserved love. Aaron might never be able to give her what she needed.

Three minutes into the drive back to the hospital, Melissa's phone started to ring. She dug her cell out of her purse and saw her sister's face on her screen.

"Hello?" Melissa said.

"How far away are you?" Arlene asked.

"Not too far."

"Great," Arlene said, and Melissa could hear a smile in her voice. "Dad's awake."

Melissa ended the call and beamed at Aaron. "Hurry. My dad's awake."

Chapter 24

The next few days were busy and happy, with a steady stream of visitors making sure the Conwells knew they were loved. Melissa's father would survive, and for that she was extremely grateful. Her father, doing much better than anticipated, was discharged from the hospital and allowed to go home.

Aaron had been around, as had many other Sheridan Falls neighbors, but Melissa had avoided having any serious conversation with him. It was too much to handle with everything else that was going on.

A couple of days after her father was home and settled, Melissa headed back to New Jersey. She needed to get back to work and deal with some issues before she could return to Sheridan Falls.

She was in her office two days after returning to Newark when she saw her sister's number and face flashing on her cell phone. She answered right away. "Hello?"

"I don't know what Aaron did, but Craig is singing a different tune. I spoke to my lawyer, who spoke to his lawyer, who said that the police also spoke to Craig. He's apologized, and he's backing off. In fact, the judge is imposing a few months of lost visitation rights altogether."

"You're serious?" Melissa asked.

"Yes. I don't know what happened, but I'm so relieved. I did tell Craig that I won't keep him from seeing Raven. We had a family talk, and he apologized to Raven and told her that he was sorry for scaring her. Because she really was terrified. I don't know, Mel, but I'm cautiously optimistic. For the time being, at least, it does seem as though Craig has done an about-face."

"Wow." Melissa was shocked. Pleasantly so. "Well, I'm happy. I'm cautiously optimistic as well."

"My lawyer did tell me that it was made clear to Craig that if he messed up, acted like an idiot or threatened me in any way, there would be dire consequences for him in court. I'm not really sure what was going on with him, but he seems to have gotten the point."

Wonders never ceased. Melissa was curious as to how Craig had been so easily persuaded to do the right thing after the way he'd behaved at the hospital.

"I'm so happy for you, sis. How's Dad?"

"He's good. But he's asking for you. When will you be back?"

"In a couple of days."

"Good. It's been nice having you here."

"It's been nice seeing you guys more regularly, too, even if the situation right now is not ideal."

"At least Dad's pulling through."

"Definitely," Melissa agreed.

Learning that Craig had done a 180 in terms of his behavior, Melissa wanted to talk to Aaron. He'd promised to deal with the situation, and it appeared he had. She wanted to know the details.

So she sent him a text and asked if he could meet her when she got to Sheridan Falls the next evening. He agreed.

That night, Melissa got into town a little earlier than she'd planned, so she went inside the café to wait for him.

As she strolled toward the counter to place an order, she locked eyes with the attractive woman sitting at a booth.

Ella.

Melissa stopped midstride, wondering if she should turn and flee. The last thing she wanted was to have this meeting here with Aaron while Ella was present. Not having seen her high school nemesis in years, she wasn't keen on being under the same roof as her.

So she went up to the counter and ordered a coffee, then

took a seat on the opposite side of the café near the window so she could watch for Aaron's arrival.

Two minutes later, she sensed the person coming up to her table before she saw her. "Melissa," came the soft voice.

Her heart beginning to pound, Melissa turned her head. And there was Ella, standing beside her table.

"Ella," Melissa said with difficulty. "Hello."

"I heard what happened to your father," she said. "I'm glad to hear he's okay."

"Thank you."

Without asking, Ella pulled out the chair opposite Melissa's and took a seat. Melissa looked at her curiously.

"I hear you've been seeing Aaron."

Melissa's heart stopped. "Excuse me?"

"It's a small town. Word travels."

For a moment, Melissa didn't know what to say. Finally, she found her voice. "From what I understand, you and Aaron split over a year ago."

"After he disrespected me in every way possible," Ella said. "He was unfaithful, he mistreated me. He didn't care about my happiness."

Melissa glanced outside, uncomfortable. Then she looked at Ella and asked, "Why are you telling me this?"

"I know we weren't close when we were young, but that doesn't mean I want to see you get hurt. Aaron is very good at the chase. He's very good at smooth talking women, and of course it helps that he's gorgeous. Before you get too serious, you need to know that bedding women is a game for him."

Melissa raised her cup to her lips and took a hurried sip, scorching her tongue. She lowered the mug. "I can take care of myself."

"Can you?" Ella asked and gave her a pitying look. "I thought the same thing. I thought he loved me. But nothing I did was good enough. And the other women...oh, how you want to believe that Aaron will only have eyes for you, but you soon learn differently. The thing is, I always felt sympathy for him. I think I knew that all his womanizing was about his sister, Chantelle. He was always so racked with guilt over her death, it seems he did everything he could to sabotage the positive in his life. Including our relationship."

Melissa swallowed with difficulty. The mention of Chantelle was like a kick in her gut. Suddenly, Melissa couldn't discount Ella's words. Because this was exactly what she had worried about where Aaron was concerned—that he would never let himself truly love because he could never forgive himself for the tragedy that had cost him his sister.

"I thought having a baby would save our marriage," Ella went on.

Melissa's eyes bulged. "You—you were pregnant?"

Ella sighed sadly. "I was. He wasn't happy. The stress over knowing he didn't want our child…" Her voice trailed off, and she closed her eyes pensively. Then she glanced outside and promptly got to her feet.

Melissa followed Ella's line of sight to where Aaron was exiting his Mercedes.

"What happened to the baby?" Melissa asked.

"I think he knew he wasn't loved. I lost him. Aaron—he's great at making you believe the fairy tale. And then you're left with a broken heart when he's ready to move on." Ella threw a quick glance outside, then hurriedly said, "Think about what I said. I don't want you to get hurt."

And with that, Ella spun around and quickly headed to the door. Melissa watched her leave, then looked in Aaron's direction. He had just exited the vehicle, and the sight of him in jeans and a white dress shirt had her heart fluttering.

Would she ever be able to look at him and not have this reaction?

She doubted it.

Oh, how you want to believe that Aaron will only have eyes for you, but you soon learn differently.

Aaron saw Ella hurrying away, then looked toward the coffee shop with narrowed eyes. When he saw Melissa through the glass, his lips curled in a smile—and darn it, her reaction to him was instantaneous. Her skin felt flushed; she could imagine him kissing her, touching her...

But then Ella's comments got into her head. She had voiced everything that Melissa feared.

The door chimes sang as Aaron entered the coffee shop and headed straight toward her. His smile grew. "Have you been here long?" he asked.

"Just about ten minutes," she said. She got to her feet, and he hugged her. "But that's okay. I was early."

"I see you already have a drink," Aaron began, "but would you like something to eat? Maybe a muffin, or a sandwich?"

Melissa glanced in the direction of the menu on the wall behind the counter. "I'll have the lemon pound cake. That's always been my favorite thing on the menu here."

"All right. Sit tight. I'll be right back."

He made his way to the counter, and Melissa watched him. He oozed an easy sexuality. It didn't matter what he was wearing; he always looked as though he had stepped off the cover of a magazine.

Melissa noticed that other women in the café were also gazing in Aaron's direction. It was hard *not* to look at him.

And of course it helps that he's gorgeous...

Ella's words sounded in her mind, and Melissa glanced away. She thought about how easily he'd seduced her and wondered how many other women he had gotten into his bed just as easily.

A few minutes later, Aaron was back. He placed a plastic cup filled with iced tea on the table, followed by two plates, each with a slice of lemon pound cake.

Melissa dragged one of the plates toward her. "Thank you."

Aaron offered her a smile as he sat across from her. "My pleasure."

Melissa broke off a piece of the lemon cake, stuffed it in her mouth and rolled her eyes heavenward. "Oh, this is good. How can something so simple taste so fabulous?"

"I know. It's my favorite, too." He paused. "I'm glad you called. I've been hoping we could finally talk."

Melissa nodded. "Whatever you did to help my sister out, I wanted to say thanks. It sounds like Craig is really backing off, and that's exactly what she needs. What we all need."

"I'm glad I could help."

Melissa looked at him, frowning slightly. "What *did* you do? I mean, how could you so effectively have Craig changing his tune? I don't imagine you took him into a dark alley and beat some sense into him," she said, her voice trailing off with a chuckle. Then she asked, mostly in jest, "Did you?"

"Nothing like that," Aaron told her. "But let's just say I was aware of some issues that Craig had. It gave me some leverage to give to Arlene's lawyer."

"Oh?" Melissa sipped her tea, waiting for him to continue.

"Although this is a small town, some things do remain secret. The woman that Craig got involved with…well, she made some unsavory allegations. I know because a friend's sister was very close to Craig's secretary. The allegations had to do with a bad real estate investment, missing funds and Craig's possible culpability. The secretary moved out of town, but I was able to talk to her. She's willing to testify against Craig if need be. Craig was made aware of this, and he knows that if he plays unfair with Arlene and Raven, this allegation can lead to a charge. Which is the last thing he wants. So he's going to behave, knowing that the moment he steps out of line, it'll mean trouble for him."

"Wow," Melissa said. "That's crazy."

"Craig's the kind of guy who's been a bully all his life, gotten away with things, blamed everyone else for his problems. But he couldn't bully his way out of this one, and with actual leverage against him, he was singing a different tune."

"He certainly wasn't the best husband to Arlene. Sweet and charming at first—then he became a different person."

Aaron is very good at the chase. He's very good at smooth talking women... Melissa's stomach suddenly roiled.

"I'd appreciate it if you didn't say anything to Arlene about this. She doesn't know the specific details, just that Craig changed his mind. This being a small town and all, I don't want word getting out. But if Craig does misbehave in the future, there's a recourse. I'm pretty sure he doesn't want to face jail time."

"It's funny how self-serving people are when it comes to that," Melissa said. She took another bite of the cake and washed it down with the tea.

"Well, enough about Craig," Aaron said. "It's good to see you."

Melissa's heart fluttered. "It's good to see you, too."

"We never did get to finish our conversation," he told her. "About whether or not you believe every negative thing you've heard and read about me."

Melissa's stomach was tightening abruptly. She felt nauseous, unsettled. Ella's words were weighing heavily on her.

She glanced around the coffee shop, knowing that in a town like this, ears were always open for gossip. "I'm not sure that this is the time or the place."

"Then come back to my place with me."

Melissa's eyes bulged at the suggestion, then she whipped her head left and right, certain people had heard what he'd said. Soon, phone lines would be ringing, word would be spreading.

Hadn't it already? Given what Ella had said, and she hadn't even been at the wedding.

Hastily, Melissa pushed her chair back and stood. "I really ought to get going. I'd like to see my father."

She started to walk away. She needed to be away from Aaron to keep her head clear. She didn't want to be lured back into his bed—

"Melissa!" Aaron called, but she kept walking.

By the time she made it outside the café, Aaron was hot on her tail. "Melissa, hey. What's going on?" He moved to stand in front of her, blocking her path. "We were having a decent conversation, and now you're running again?"

"I just need to see my dad." She placed a hand on her belly. "And I feel a little nauseous." She closed her eyes as the wave passed.

"Are you okay?" Aaron asked.

"I don't know," Melissa said. "Maybe I haven't had enough to eat. I had too much coffee before I left Newark for the long drive here, I guess. I just… I just really need to get to my parents' place."

"All right," Aaron said, not pushing the issue, but looking at her with concern. "You're okay to drive?"

"Yeah, I'll be fine."

"Call me tomorrow," Aaron said.

"Sure," Melissa agreed. Then she quickly made her way to her car without looking back at Aaron.

Aaron stared at Melissa as she hurried off, his chest tightening. He hated the uneasy tension between them. His feelings for her had deepened more than he'd ever anticipated. He wanted to tell her, but every time they took steps forward, they hit a wall. Melissa seemed nervous, on edge, and he didn't want to scare her into running.

Did she not realize how much he cared? Heck, the last time they'd made love, he hadn't even used a condom. He'd gotten caught up in the moment, yes, but there'd been something else. A primal urge to make something real with her. He hadn't been consciously thinking about pregnancy, but he hadn't been afraid of the idea. He knew that Melissa wouldn't be like Ella, she wouldn't use a baby as a ploy.

There was something different about Melissa. Something innately good and honest and wonderful. She was the kind of woman he could settle down with. The kind who would be a good mother.

With what he'd been through, he should be terrified of the thought. But something inside of him that he couldn't describe told him that he and Melissa were destined to have it all. A life together, a family.

It was something he'd known in his soul when they'd first started dating.

He knew he had his work cut out for him, but he had to make her believe that, too.

Chapter 25

The next morning, Melissa got up and went downstairs into the kitchen. Her mother was frying eggs, and as the smell hit her, she had the sudden urge to vomit.

She clamped a hand over her mouth, holding her breath until the wave of nausea passed.

God, why was the smell getting to her?

"Good morning." Her mother looked over her shoulder and smiled brightly at her.

"Morning," Melissa returned, taking a seat at the table.

"I'm making your favorite," her mother said. "Sausages and scrambled eggs."

Just hearing the words made Melissa's stomach roil. Maybe she was coming down with something.

"I don't know, I'm not feeling that hungry. I think I'll have some toast. I don't quite feel myself."

Her mother looked at her with concern. "Oh?"

"I haven't been getting a lot of rest. There was a crisis at the group home, plus my long drive yesterday. I guess I'm not taking care of myself too well."

Her mother waved the egg-covered spatula at her. "What have I told you about taking care of yourself? If you're not healthy, nothing else matters. Look at your father. He didn't heed the doctor's advice, and he went and gave himself a heart attack."

"I know, Mom." Melissa rose and walked over to her mother, then hugged her around her waist from behind. "I love that you care."

"I'll always care. I'm your mother. A mother's job is never done."

As the smell of the food wafted into Melissa's nose, she once again felt that rush of nausea. She had to step back. "Excuse me."

She'd been planning to sit back down, but instead she headed straight for the bathroom. Her mouth began to water, that awful sensation that told her she was going to vomit.

And vomit she did. She threw up, retching painfully as what she'd eaten the night before came right back up and into the toilet.

When her heaving was done, she rose, ran the water at the faucet and drank some, then washed her face. She placed her palm on her forehead. Was she coming down with a fever? Had she picked up a bug? Or maybe gotten food poisoning?

Feeling better, she headed back into the kitchen. "Mom, is the kettle on?"

"Yes. You know I always have a cup of tea to start the day."

"Good. Any peppermint tea here? I feel like I need that."

"Your stomach really is unsettled, isn't it? I was like that when I was pregnant with you. When I felt sick, I craved peppermint tea. Certain smells got to me, too."

Melissa's hand stilled on the tea cupboard. Her mother's words suddenly dawned on her, as did a horrific possibility.

Pregnant? Oh, God, could it be?

No…it couldn't be. She and Aaron had only had sex a couple of times. Well, a lot more than a couple, technically, but still.

But still nothing, she told herself. *You know how babies are made. Of course you could be pregnant.*

They'd used protection only the first time that first night, going with the passionate flow the subsequent times. Melissa hadn't been thinking rationally; she'd been feeling.

Oh, God…

With that, another wave of nausea hit her, but this time it wasn't because of her stomach. It was because of the idea that she might be carrying Aaron's baby.

"I think it must be the flu," Melissa said, more for her

benefit than for her mother's. "Or maybe food poisoning. I had the leftover fish last night. You never know."

Her mother made a face. "I had the fish, too. I feel fine."

"Who knows what it could be?" Melissa commented.

"Sweetheart," her mother began, worry in her eyes. "You don't look too good. Maybe you should go back to bed and lie down."

"Maybe I should."

"I'll bring you the peppermint tea and toast."

"That would be great," Melissa told her. She turned on her heel and headed back through the house and upstairs to her bedroom. All the while, her mind was whirring a mile a minute.

Could she possibly be pregnant?

Aaron was starting to wonder what it was going to take for Melissa to get back to him on a regular basis. It always seemed as though they made great strides, only for her to pull back.

He'd made it clear that he wanted to talk to her about his marriage, clear the air. She told him she was okay with that. And then she never got back to him. He'd called her last night—no answer. His better judgment had kicked in before he decided to go over to her parents' house and knock on the door and demand to see her. Her father was sick, recovering. She had a lot on her plate. She'd come to town to see her family, after all. Not him. But he wanted to know that she was the least bit interested in seeing him and spending some more time together.

Aaron frowned. What had gotten into him? Whenever a woman had given him the hot-and-cold act in the past, he'd been able to walk away. But something about Melissa kept him wanting to bridge the gap between them.

Aaron drove to the center of town. He parked in front of the café where he and Melissa had met just two nights earlier. It was his favorite spot, as it was for most of the locals. He enjoyed starting his day with a bagel and coffee. Today he was back for a late-afternoon snack.

He put his hand on the car door's handle, looking out at the street to make sure it was safe to open it. That's when he noticed Melissa entering the drugstore across the street. He opened the door, about to call out to her, but she hustled inside the store as though on a mission.

Aaron decided to forgo the sandwich and iced tea for the time being and head over to the drugstore to say hello to Melissa. Maybe they could find a place to talk after she was finished buying whatever she'd gone in there for.

He jogged across the street and went into the pharmacy. He didn't immediately see Melissa down the main aisle, so he took a few steps to the right and glanced down the next aisle to see if she was there.

He spotted her several feet away, her back to him. His eyes ventured upward—right to the huge sign that read Family Planning.

Family planning? Suddenly, Aaron's stomach tensed. Moments ago, he'd been about to approach Melissa. But now he couldn't help wondering what she was doing in the family planning aisle.

He didn't imagine she was buying condoms.

Aaron made his way down the opposite aisle, which he could easily see over because of his height. Melissa's back was still turned to him, so she didn't know he was there. He watched, his eyes growing wide, as she put down one pregnancy test package and lifted another one.

Pregnant? Melissa was pregnant?

With *his* child?

Aaron ducked backward when Melissa promptly headed for the pharmacy-specific cash register at the back of the store. He heard only Mr. Baxter, the pharmacist, conversing as he rang up Melissa's purchase.

"Beautiful day, isn't it? How's your father doing?"

If Melissa responded, Aaron didn't hear it. About a minute later, he saw her quickly snatch up her bagged purchase and all but run out of the store.

Melissa glanced around as she exited the drugstore with the white paper bag clutched in her fingers. She felt paranoid, but there was no need to be, was there? She hadn't noticed anyone she knew in the store, which meant that no one had seen her pick up a pregnancy test. She hoped that Mr. Baxter wouldn't call anyone to share the news of what she'd bought, though she didn't imagine the older man would be so inclined. Besides, Melissa was sure that it would be against an ethical code for him to do so, anyway. But this was a small town, and word spread like wildfire.

Still, Melissa walked quickly to the corner and turned left to where she'd parked her car. She used the remote on the key to unlock it, and the headlights flashed. She rounded the car to the driver's side and opened the door.

And that's when her heart slammed against her rib cage. Because striding toward her car was Aaron.

For a moment she couldn't breathe. What was Aaron doing here?

She offered him a tentative smile. He didn't return the friendly gesture. Instead, as he got closer, she noticed that his lips were pressed tightly together. Something was wrong.

"Aaron," she said feebly. "Hi."

Aaron headed straight toward her, not breaking stride. Was he upset because she hadn't yet called him as she'd promised?

"I'm sorry, I meant to call you to set up a time to meet. It's just…well, my dad. I'm spending as much time with him as I can, obviously. And… I had to come out and pick something up for him." Holding up the bag, she smiled uneasily, hoping that he wouldn't question her little white lie. After all, her father was recovering from major surgery, and medication would be par for the course.

When Aaron still didn't crack a smile, Melissa wondered what was happening. He soon filled her in.

"Are you pregnant?" Aaron's eyes bored into hers. "With my child?"

Chapter 26

All the blood drained from Melissa's head. Feeling instantly faint, she swayed unsteadily on her feet. Good Lord, why had he asked her that?

As Aaron's unwavering gaze held hers, Melissa didn't know what to say. She finally sputtered, "Y-you were *spying* on me?"

"I saw you going to the store," he said. "I went in after you to say hello. Imagine my surprise when I saw you picking out a pregnancy test."

Oh, God...

"Are you pregnant?"

How could Melissa get out of this one? This was the last thing she wanted to talk about with Aaron, and now here he was, demanding an answer.

"I assume it would be mine," he said.

"Of course it would be yours," she replied, thinking only of defending her honor. "I told you I hadn't had sex for several months." Then, realizing what she'd said, she tried to backtrack. "I'm not saying I'm pregnant. I think... I'm probably being super paranoid. I'm just a little bit sick today."

Aaron's eyes lit up, as though something suddenly made sense to him. "And in the café yesterday, too. You said you were leaving because your stomach was bothering you."

"I'm sure it's just a touch of something. Maybe I ate something that didn't agree with me, or I'm coming down with the flu, or—"

"You obviously think it's more than a touch of something or you wouldn't have bought a pregnancy test." Aaron paused. "That is what's in the bag, isn't it?"

This was a nightmare. She could lie to him, yet what

would be the point? He already knew. He was just asking to see if she would be honest.

This was the worst possible thing that could have happened.

"I'm gonna take the test, just to be certain. But I'm ninety percent positive I'm not pregnant," she said, chuckling nervously to give the impression that she wasn't worried.

Aaron didn't blink—and she could tell that he didn't believe her.

How could she blame him? People didn't buy pregnancy tests unless they thought they were pregnant, for crying out loud.

"And if you *are* carrying my child?" Aaron asked.

Carrying his child…just phrasing it that way made the situation even more real. *His* child. They would be tethered together forever.

"If I am…" Melissa swallowed, the very idea terrifying. She couldn't deal with this right now.

"Were you even planning to tell me?"

"Aaron, you're jumping the gun."

"And yet you're the one holding a pregnancy test."

This was too much. Him demanding answers, her barely able to deal with the fact that she might actually be carrying his child…

"I'm not trying to pressure you or anything," he said, his tone a little softer now. "I was just…it was like a kick to the solar plexus when I saw you picking up a pregnancy test."

"This is a shock to me, too. But I'm probably overreacting. I'm used to thinking about the worst-case scenario."

"So carrying my baby is the worst thing that could happen?" Aaron asked, narrowing his eyes.

She didn't need him scrutinizing every word she said. "I'm not saying that. I just…let me take the test first."

"You'll keep the baby, right?" Aaron asked.

"If I am pregnant, it's going to be my decision what to do."

Something flashed across Aaron's face, something Melissa couldn't quite read. Then he said, "Would you actually consider terminating the pregnancy?"

"It's very early, but I know that you understand I have to make the decision that's right for my life. I won't be forced to do something I'm not ready for."

"You can't terminate the pregnancy," Aaron said, his voice leaving absolutely no room for discussion.

Why was he saying this? Guilt? Ella had made it clear that Aaron didn't want children.

"Aaron, I'm not going to have this conversation on the street. I'm also not going to have you telling me what I can and can't do." Defiance crept into her tone, and she was glad for it. She needed some anger to help her stay focused. She and Aaron didn't have a relationship, and yet here he was expecting her to have his child if she were pregnant?

Perhaps he would feel an obligation to his child and want visitation on the weekends, summers with his son or daughter. She would constantly have to deal with a man who was not her partner... Or worse, he might try to force a relationship because of the baby, but how long would that last?

Oh, Melissa had done her best to tell herself that she could sleep with Aaron and not get emotionally involved, but she knew now that she'd been lying to herself. He'd always been the man she had wanted, but did she dare to trust him with her heart again? She had been crushed when their relationship fell apart the first time. If she allowed herself to fall for him again and it didn't work out, then what? Especially with a child in the mix. She didn't want Aaron to want her only because of the baby.

"...consult me," Aaron was saying.

Melissa realized that she wasn't fully paying attention to him. Her pulse was thundering between her ears.

"I'd like to go home now," she said.

Aaron was silent for a long moment as he regarded her.

"Aaron, please. I feel so overwhelmed right now."

After a moment, he nodded. "All right. But we're in this together, so I need you to call me." When Melissa said nothing, Aaron went on. "Are you hearing me? I need you to call me and let me know if you're pregnant or not."

"I doubt it, but—"

"Call me regardless," Aaron said.

She opened her car and quickly got behind the wheel. The moment she closed the door, Aaron tapped on the window. She didn't roll it down; she needed to get away. Aaron frowned, then mimed a phone call.

Melissa looked ahead and drove her car into traffic, not acknowledging Aaron's request.

Good Lord, she'd hoped to find out if she were pregnant and deal with the news on her own. Now Aaron knew it was a possibility. He was going to be waiting to hear back from her.

And he expected her to keep the child, no matter how it might affect her life.

Well, she wasn't going to have him tell her what to do. This was the twenty-first century. A woman was entitled to make pregnancy decisions for herself. And she intended to make that decision without any interference from a man who was incapable of committing.

Melissa couldn't bring herself to take the test until several hours later. Arlene had come to pick up their parents and take them to a park for a change of pace. Melissa had begged off, claiming that she wasn't feeling well.

Which wasn't a lie. Although now, besides the nausea, she also had a pounding headache. The reality that she could be pregnant was too much to contemplate.

With the house quiet, this was the time to finally take the test. Waiting wasn't going to change the result.

She withdrew the test stick and followed the instructions. And then she sat on the edge of the bathtub and waited.

The seconds that passed seemed like hours. Was the line going to appear telling her that she was pregnant or not?

Melissa closed her eyes and kept them shut for probably a minute before she reopened them, reached for the stick on the bathroom counter and held it in front of her. As she looked at it, her stomach sank.

Positive.

Oh, God, the worst had happened.

She was pregnant.

With Aaron's baby.

What was she going to do?

Aaron didn't sleep a wink.

He had expected a phone call from Melissa hours ago, but midnight had come and gone and there had been no call.

He was trying to bide his time and be patient, not aggressively tell her what she should or shouldn't do. Even though he knew that there was only one acceptable action if she were pregnant.

To keep the baby.

Something inside him had perked up when he'd realized there was a possibility that he might become a father. He didn't even know how Melissa felt about him, and yet the idea of becoming a father had excitement filling his heart. It was something he'd wanted for years, a little boy or girl to call his own.

Sure, the situation wasn't ideal, but if he and Melissa had conceived a child, he would see it as a sign from God—that God had forgiven him for what had happened to Chantelle.

Aaron swallowed at the thought of his sister and how he'd lost her. When would the pain truly heal?

He had to convince Melissa to keep the baby. She had

to know that he would accept all responsibility for their child without reservation.

He had the means to take care of a child. And it wasn't like they were two teenagers. He would give the baby all the love in the world.

Enough love to make up for his one fatal mistake.

And yet, Melissa hadn't called him.

Aaron realized when he felt the pain in his jaw that he was clenching his teeth. He drew in a deep breath and then let it out slowly. He turned onto his side and glanced at the bedside clock—5:14 a.m.

Given Melissa's track record of disappearing, she could very well be heading back to Newark today. Before she left, he needed to know. He would give her the morning to get back to him, but she had to know that if she didn't call him, he was going to go and find her.

He had to know one way or another if she was carrying his child.

Melissa's feet felt like lead as she swung them off the bed. She sat there for several seconds. Her hands sank into the mattress, and she squeezed hard.

She wished she had just woken up from a dream, but she hadn't. The dawn of another day didn't change her reality.

She was pregnant.

Every time she thought about the positive pregnancy test, she felt such disbelief that she could hardly accept it. She needed to do another test. But not in this town. Getting one here had been bad enough, and she wouldn't put herself through that again.

When she got back to New Jersey, she would verify the test. False positives happened every day, didn't they? Taking another test before accepting the first result was the smart thing to do.

She couldn't stay in her bedroom all day, so she got up

and made her way into the kitchen. Her mother was sitting at the small table, as was her father. They had teacups in front of them, and they both smiled when they looked up at her.

Melissa returned the smile, trying to forget her own dilemma. It was good to see her father sitting up and smiling. He looked so much better than he had right after the heart attack.

"You look good, Dad."

"I feel better, too," he said. "Almost like my old self."

"That's because he's finally eating the veggies I made for him. This morning, he had steamed veggies and some roasted potatoes. He didn't even complain when I didn't give him any bacon."

Melissa looked at her father in awe. "Wow. That's progress."

"I'm getting used to it," he said. "This low-fat diet nonsense. I guess it won't kill me."

"It's meant to keep you alive, actually."

Her mother gave her husband a pointed look. "See? I'm not the only one who knows what's best for you."

Melissa smiled and wandered over to the counter. She reached for a single-serve coffee pod, but her hand stilled in the air. She'd done some research on the topic of coffee and pregnancy, and the experts said pregnant women should limit coffee consumption to one cup a day. But why not cut it out altogether to be safe? She would have peppermint tea instead.

The thought made her realize something. If she were indeed pregnant, she wanted this baby. Very much.

"I didn't know what to make for you," her mother said. "But there are some potatoes and veggies left, if you're okay with that."

The potato idea sounded heavenly. Melissa needed as much starch as her stomach could take.

"Sounds perfect," she told her mother.

She ate, and the potatoes did seem to do the trick. Although she'd felt a wave of nausea earlier, she was able to keep her food down. Maybe whatever she'd been feeling wasn't due to pregnancy after all. Maybe her stress over her father's accident and Aaron had led to a false positive. The only thing she knew for sure was that she needed to have a proper test with a doctor to verify whether or not she was indeed pregnant.

She would do that as soon as she got back to Newark.

A few hours later, Melissa was packed and ready to head out. "Dad, please stick to the new diet the doctor prescribed for you. I want to see you around for a long, long time."

"Exactly," her mother said. "He needs to be here for the grandchildren you're going to give us."

Melissa stiffened, a chill slithering down her spine. Why had her mother just said that?

But as she looked in her mother's direction and saw that she was smiling at her father, she knew her mother hadn't had some psychic revelation; she'd merely said the kind of encouraging thing a person would say when one's partner was facing a life-threatening illness. *Stick around so that you can see your future grandchildren.* There was nothing suspicious about her mother's words.

But still, the comment held far more meaning now than it would have just last week.

Melissa drew in a breath to steady her nerves, then made her way to the sofa and leaned down and gave her father a hug and a kiss. Then she did the same with her mother. "All right, I'll be in touch when I get home."

"You sure you can't stay a couple more days?" her mother asked.

Suddenly, Melissa started crying. Her mother got to her feet and put her arms around her. "Oh, sweetheart. I didn't mean to pressure you. I know you'll come back as soon as you can."

"I need to take care of some things," Melissa said, trying to contain her soft sobbing. Good Lord, what was wrong with her? "I'll be back before you know it."

Her sudden outburst was proof that she needed to get to Newark and her doctor's office immediately. She was an emotional basket case.

She hoped that when she returned to Sheridan Falls, this burden would be lifted from her shoulders. That she would know, once and for all, that she *wasn't* pregnant.

Chapter 27

Melissa felt a modicum of guilt as she exited her parents' home and brought her bags to the car. She'd promised Aaron that she would be in touch. And now she was leaving without speaking to him.

She sat behind the wheel of her car and decided to send him a text.

I need to go to the doctor to get a proper pregnancy test. That's the smartest thing to do.

And then she backed out of her parents' driveway and onto the street.

About a minute later, she glanced in her rearview mirror. And her heart spasmed. Was that…*Aaron*?

It didn't take more than five seconds for her to realize that it was him. The Mercedes pulled out from behind and sped up alongside her. She glanced to her left and cringed. He put the window down and gestured for her to pull over.

She turned her attention back to the road, not wanting to stop. Had he already received her text? Had he been lying in wait for her?

Aaron continued to gesture at her, but she didn't engage. And then he sped up and pulled in front of her. Melissa gasped. She feared he was going to stop the car, but of course that didn't make sense. Several seconds later, the traffic light changed to red, and he stopped. She was forced to stop behind him, trapped.

Aaron quickly exited his car and walked toward her. He rapped on the window, and she put it down. What else could she do?

"Turn into the next plaza. We need to talk."

Darn it, there was no avoiding this. She could run now,

but he would track her down. And the truth was, she did owe him an answer. Perhaps he hadn't slept all night, just as she hadn't.

She pulled into the next driveway behind him, which led into a strip mall plaza. Aaron drove to the far end of the parking lot and parked his car. Melissa pulled up alongside him.

He glanced through his window at her. She looked back. Then he got out of his car, came to her passenger door and pulled on it.

It was locked, and Melissa quickly unlocked it so that he could gain access to her car. As Aaron got into the passenger seat beside her, his disappointment was clear. "You were supposed to call me."

"I sent you a text."

"I just saw that. You didn't give me an answer about the pregnancy test."

"I think it's best that I go to the doctor to have a proper test done."

Aaron was silent, his eyes scrutinizing her. "Does that mean that the test was positive?" he surmised. "Because if it wasn't, you wouldn't go to the doctor to double-check, would you?"

When Melissa said nothing, he nodded, convinced of his own assessment. "Yeah, that makes sense. You got a positive result, now you're panicking. And you were gonna leave town without telling me what was going on."

"Aaron, this is all so overwhelming. I need time to digest this. Time to…deal."

"You mean *we*," he said. "You didn't get pregnant by yourself."

"But I might not be pregnant. There's definitely a chance that the test was wrong. I think it makes perfect sense for me to want to validate it first before you and I have this conversation."

"Please tell me you're not considering terminating the pregnancy."

"I need time to figure out what's best."

"What's best is keeping the baby."

"Do you even want a baby?" Melissa asked. "You're a jet-setter. You've retired from playing, but you might end up coaching in Europe or God knows where. A child would cramp your style."

"That's what you think?"

Melissa sighed softly. "Look, maybe I shouldn't mention this, but the day we met in the coffee shop, Ella was there."

"Yes, I saw her leaving."

"Well, she told me a bit about your marriage. Specifically that you didn't want kids."

Melissa saw rage fill Aaron's eyes. "That's what she said?"

"She also said that you sabotage relationships because of your guilt over Chantelle."

Melissa saw the way Aaron's jaw flinched. But he said nothing.

"You're still not going to talk about your sister?"

"Chantelle has nothing to do with why my marriage to Ella ended."

"Doesn't it?" Melissa challenged. "It makes sense that you ended our relationship because you didn't think you deserved love—"

"I don't want to talk about Chantelle," Aaron said through gritted teeth.

"Ella said you didn't want the baby, and that you cheated because your guilt led you to destroy everything good in your life. If she hadn't mentioned Chantelle, I would have dismissed everything she said. But I know how much guilt you carried over your sister."

"It seems you've let everyone else talk to you about my marriage without giving me the chance. It's about time you hear my side."

"Okay," Melissa said softly. "I'm listening."

"I know it can be hard to ignore the crap you hear people gossiping about, or the stuff that's in the tabloids. But I'm not this playboy that the world thinks I am. Yes, I've dated my share of women. *Dated*, not slept with. But I've had a lot more women chasing me. It comes with the territory when you're a sports star. They all want something superficial. Bragging rights. A sugar daddy who will wine and dine them." He paused. "And that includes Ella. She lied to me from the very beginning."

"You must have loved her if you married her." Just saying the words left Melissa with a bad taste in her mouth.

"She told me she was pregnant." Aaron held her gaze, let that sink in. "Before we were married. We met up one time when I was in town, hung out a few times, and one thing led to another. I thought she loved me. But she had an agenda."

Melissa stared at Aaron, waiting for him to continue.

"One day she tells me she's pregnant. Far from what she told you, I was excited. A baby…it felt like a blessing. Like forgiveness for what had happened with Chantelle. I was determined to be the best dad ever. To spoil the baby and never let any harm come to him or her. So I did the right thing. I married her. It was quick. I was happy. Only after we got married, I noticed that she wasn't developing. Her stomach wasn't growing. She wasn't having any morning sickness. I asked her if we could go to the doctor, check on the baby's progress. Well, the very next day she came home crying, telling me that she'd had a miscarriage. Said she'd been to the hospital and the baby was gone. I asked why she never called me, and she didn't have a good reason, except to say everything happened so fast. I found that odd, but I figured it could have happened that way. Mostly I was upset she hadn't called me. I wanted to be there for her. Anyway, several months later I ran into her doctor. I talked to him about the miscarriage, and he was confused. In fact, he was confused by the claim of pregnancy altogether. And that's when I found out she'd been lying. She was never pregnant."

Melissa gasped. All this time, she had assumed that Aaron had fallen for Ella's looks and sex appeal. Instead, he had tried to do the right thing by her, only to find out he'd been deceived.

"You have no clue how much that hurt me," he said, shaking his head as his jaw tightened. "I thought she was having my child. I was excited about that. When she lost the baby… I felt her devastation, and I was devastated, too. Then I wondered if I hadn't done enough for her. Maybe if I'd gotten the help she'd wanted, this wouldn't have happened. The guilt I felt over Chantelle was back full force. I felt as though I'd failed Ella."

"Aaron, I'm so sorry."

"She wanted the status of having me as her husband and wanted all the best things money could buy. I gave her almost everything she wanted, especially after she lost the baby, because I felt guilty over what happened. Plus, she was so depressed and needed pampering. A trip to Venice with her best friend would perk her up. Or a shopping spree in Miami. Honestly, I felt like a fool. Once I learned the truth, I left her. That's when she started her smear campaign, so I didn't file for divorce right away. I wanted things to die down."

"You never said anything."

"Because I didn't want to lower myself to dragging her name through the mud. I always thought my character would show who I really was. But it appears I was wrong."

He held her gaze. Melissa's lips parted. "For the record, I never could wrap my mind around the rumors I'd heard about you—at least not that you would be callous with your indiscretions."

"There *were* no indiscretions," Aaron said. "I didn't cheat on Ella."

"What I'm trying to say is that I slept with you because… because on some level, I knew you weren't some heartless jerk."

"Marry me."

Melissa's eyes bulged. "What?"

"Marry me. I'll be there for you and the baby."

Was Melissa losing her mind? Certainly Aaron hadn't just said what it sounded like.

"There's no need for you to consider adoption, or God forbid, abortion…"

"I can't marry you," Melissa said.

"Why not?" Aaron asked, and the expression on his face said that he was genuinely perplexed.

"Because…you just got finished telling me that you wanted to the right thing with Ella, and how that turned into a big mistake. Now you're proposing marriage to me?"

Hadn't he learned his lesson? Marrying someone for altruistic reasons was doomed to fail. "I know you want to do the right thing, and I appreciate that."

"Are you saying there's nothing between us? Because this isn't like with Ella. We never had a meaningful relationship. I never cared about her the way I should have."

"And we have a meaningful relationship?" Melissa asked. Her pulse began to race. Part of her—a very big part of her—wanted to believe that they did. But the wall around her heart was so high, and she didn't want to get her hopes up.

"Definitely, we could."

Melissa's hope fizzled. "It has to be more than *could*. We can't just do something because I'm pregnant. This can't be about Chantelle."

As she looked at him, she also knew that he was proposing marriage not just to do the right thing, but because he didn't want her to terminate the pregnancy or give the baby up for adoption. She sensed that the loss of this baby would be as devastating as losing Chantelle. "Look, I promise you that I won't terminate the pregnancy. That's not something I ever really considered. It's not who I am."

"But adoption? You'd give away our baby?" The question sounded like an accusation.

"And your option is for us to enter a loveless marriage?"

He looked stricken then, and Melissa couldn't understand why. They didn't love each other. A wave of sadness washed over her with that thought. Her feelings for him had deepened. No doubt about it. Sex had clouded her emotions.

"I liked how things were developing between us," Aaron said softly.

"But we don't really have a relationship," Melissa countered.

"Because you keep pushing me away. When are you going to realize that I keep coming back?"

"For how long?" Melissa asked. "Because if you won't deal with the pain from your past, how long before you run?"

"How do you think I'm supposed to deal with losing my sister? I'm just supposed to forget?"

"That's not what I'm saying. But you have to let go of your guilt."

Aaron expelled a heavy breath. "I'm not going anywhere. I *want* to be a father."

"You're only suggesting marriage because I'm pregnant. I know we like each other, but it's nothing more than that."

"On your part," Aaron countered.

"Both of our parts." Aaron had never told her that he loved her or anything even remotely like that. He was only saying this now because he wanted her to keep the baby.

"We can make it work," Aaron said.

"I can't say yes to your proposal."

She swallowed, thinking just how surreal this was.

Years ago, she'd hoped that Aaron would propose to her. If things were different and Melissa believed that he loved her and this was a romantic proposal, she would say yes. In a heartbeat.

But this was a practical proposal. A solution to a problem.

"So you're not even going to consider it?"

"I know that we have sexual chemistry," Melissa said softly. "But love...?"

She looked into Aaron's eyes, searching for an answer. Perhaps he would refute what she was saying, prove her wrong. Instead, he looked away. She couldn't read what he was thinking, but she could see that his brain was working.

"Just a few weeks ago, marriage wasn't even a remote possibility for us," Melissa continued.

"I do have feelings for you. Very strong feelings. But every time I think we're making progress, you pull away."

Melissa sighed softly. She didn't doubt that he had feelings for her. Lust, attraction and, perhaps, respect. But love?

"I have a long drive ahead of me," she said. "I promise, when I get a test done at my doctor's, I'll let you know the result. But right now, I do have to go. Okay?"

Aaron looked at her long and hard. Then he finally nodded. "As long as you agree to consider what I said. I don't need an answer now or next week. Just...give it some thought."

Then he exited her car, and tears instantly filled Melissa's eyes. The only man she'd ever loved was offering her the one thing she'd always wanted—and she couldn't say yes.

Chapter 28

The next day, it was confirmed. Melissa was indeed pregnant.

She left the doctor's office and went to work, hoping she could escape to her office and stay there undisturbed. If she didn't have work to do, she would go home. She needed time to truly process this news.

When Melissa entered the Turning Tides group home, she could hear voices in the kitchen. She went straight to the office but caught a glimpse of Teresa in the hallway just before she closed the door.

Seconds later, Teresa was opening the door. "You sneak in like that without saying hi?"

Melissa burst into tears.

"Hey, what is it?" Teresa asked, gliding across the room and over to the desk. "Tell me."

Melissa wiped at her tears, then spoke. "I'm pregnant."

Teresa's eyes bulged. Seconds passed. "You're sure?"

"Yes. My doctor confirmed it."

"But you're not happy?" Teresa surmised.

"The whole thing is a mess. I wasn't supposed to get pregnant…how can I have a baby now? It's the wrong time."

"As a single mother, I can tell you that there's never a right time. You make plans, but life happens."

"I know," Melissa said. "And I really admire people like you who seem to be able to do it effortlessly without a partner. But this isn't what I wanted for myself."

"What does Aaron want?"

"He asked me to marry him."

Teresa looked confused. "But that's great…isn't it? I thought you had strong feelings for him."

Melissa scoffed. "It was fun, but it wasn't a relationship. He just wants to do the right thing."

"This is the twenty-first century. There's no need to get married just because you're pregnant."

"I don't want a man who wants to marry me just because I'm having a baby. I want a man who's crazy and passionately in love with me."

"Maybe you've been so busy running from Aaron out of fear that you're not seeing the truth."

"What would you know?"

"Look to your left."

"What?" Melissa asked, confused.

"Look to your left. On the wall."

Melissa did. And she gasped.

Because there on the wall was the painting she'd put a bid on at the charity auction. The one of the swan on a lake by Felix Virgo.

"What…when…how?" Melissa asked.

"This morning," Teresa answered. "The card's in the top drawer." A slow smile spread on her face. "It's from Aaron, isn't it?"

"Did you read the card?" Melissa asked.

"No. But who else would send it for you?"

Melissa quickly opened the envelope and pulled out the card. She opened it and read.

I hope this painting puts a smile on your face. You loved it so much, I made sure you'd be the one to have it.
Love, Aaron

"What?" Melissa asked, the word catching in her throat. When had he gotten this? They'd left the auction early, and she'd hoped to hear that her bid was enough. Now that she thought about it, had Aaron made sure to whisk her away to keep his winning the bid a surprise?

"You need to call him," Teresa said. "Stop being so afraid."

Teresa left and closed the door behind her. Melissa pulled her cell phone from her bag. She held it in her hands for several seconds before she finally made the call.

"Melissa," Aaron said without preamble. "What's the news?"

"I'm pregnant."

"You are? You're sure?" He sounded excited.

"The doctor confirmed it. So, here we are…"

"I'd like to come see you. So we can talk in person. When's a good time? Tomorrow? Friday, maybe?"

"Tomorrow I have to go to court. How about Friday?"

"Friday's good. I'll see you then."

"Aaron, wait. The painting. I…when did you get it? I don't understand."

"I bought it the night of the auction."

"You did?"

"I put down a bid that I was certain would win. I wanted to surprise you with it at the right time. Today seemed like that time."

"Aaron… I'm shocked. I… I love it. Thank you so much."

"You're welcome. I hope it gives you that sense of calm it did when you first saw it."

"Yes," Melissa said, surprised that Aaron remembered what she'd said about the painting. "It does. In fact, I can use a good dose of that calm right now."

"I don't want you worrying about the pregnancy, okay?"

"It's not just that. I have to go to a hearing with one of the boys tomorrow. I'm worried about him. I'm hoping the judge will have leniency on him and understand that his father not being around was a factor in him committing the crime. I'm hopeful, but I always worry. I know that Tyler has a big heart. He just made a mistake."

"I'm sure the judge will see that, too."

"I hope so." She sighed. "All right, so I'll see you Friday."

"Yep."

As Melissa ended the call, her eyes ventured to the painting. A smile touched her lips. She no longer felt as anxious as she had just an hour earlier.

Did Aaron actually care more for her than she wanted to let herself believe?

The next morning, Melissa was heading out of the house with Tyler and Mike, one of the other counselors, when she drew up short. She blinked, making sure that her eyes weren't playing tricks on her.

Indeed, they weren't. Aaron was standing outside a car in front of the house. When his eyes connected with hers, he smiled.

"Excuse me," she said to Mike and walked down the driveway toward Aaron. "Hey, what are you doing here? We said Friday, remember?"

"I know." He looked beyond her, toward Tyler, and waved. "I figured I'd come by and see if I could go to court with you. On Tyler's behalf. Speak up for him, tell the judge he's a great kid. That I'm happy to mentor him, if that's okay with you."

Melissa stared at him, unable to fathom what he'd just said. Then she glanced over her shoulder at Tyler, who was grinning from ear to ear. She faced Aaron again, confusion making her head swim. "You're saying you came here to go to court...for Tyler?"

"If that's okay," Aaron said.

A wave of emotion washed over Melissa. She couldn't believe it. He cared that much?

He must, because here he was, in Newark, prepared to go to court to support a boy he had met once.

"What you told me really got to me," Aaron said in a hushed voice. "A kid should have his dad in his corner. I can't understand anyone who would walk away from that responsibility."

His words hung between them, and Melissa knew that they were for her as much as they were about the situation with Tyler.

"I'm prepared to come back here…often. Not just because I want to see you, but because I'd happily spend more time with the kids. They're great. Every kid needs an opportunity to succeed. It's what we believed way back when, when we were counselors at that summer camp."

Indeed it was. A slow smile spread on Melissa's lips. This was the man she'd fallen in love with. The one who cared about others and was giving of his time.

The wall around her heart was crumbling. And she couldn't stop it.

"I'm sure Tyler will be elated. Just look at him." She glanced over her shoulder, saw that Tyler was still beaming. "I don't know if you'll be able to speak to the judge, but we'll play it by ear."

"If nothing else, I'll be there for him."

This wasn't grandstanding. This wasn't putting on some elaborate show just to get to her. What would be the point of that? To play with young Tyler's emotions to score some brownie points with her?

No, she didn't believe that.

"Tyler," Melissa called, turning to face him. "I've got something to tell you."

Considering Aaron had only met Tyler once, he wasn't allowed to speak on his behalf before the judge's ruling. But it didn't matter. The very fact that Aaron was here by Tyler's side had caused a marked difference in the boy. He looked confident and happy, like a totally different child. Perhaps that was why the judge decided to be lenient. Or maybe she'd already made that decision before today. Melissa would never know. What she did know was that Aaron being there for Tyler had changed something in the boy so profoundly that the difference brought tears to her eyes. It was as though finally Tyler knew somebody cared.

Yes, Aaron was a celebrity. But it was more than that. Tyler had held his hand and looked up at him with the eyes of a boy looking up to a hero.

To a father.

Melissa was deeply moved. She could tell that today marked a turning point in Tyler's life. Aaron being here meant the world to him.

The fact that the judge had been lenient was a bonus.

They left the courthouse, all of them excited about the news that Tyler would not have to go to juvenile detention. He would be able to return to the group home, and in a couple of weeks, he would go home.

"Aaron!" Tyler bounded out of Mike's car and toward Aaron as he exited Melissa's vehicle back at the group home. He threw his arms around his waist as though this was the first time he was seeing him.

Tears welled in Melissa's eyes.

"Are you coming inside?" Tyler asked.

"Sure. I'll come in for a little while. I can't stay too long."

"I want you to be with me when I tell everyone the good news," Tyler said.

"Absolutely," Aaron agreed.

"I'm gonna miss everybody when I go back to my real home," Tyler said.

"Sure you are, buddy. That's normal. But you know what's awesome? You can still visit."

"Are you going to visit me?"

"Tyler," Melissa began.

But Aaron cut her off. "I sure am. I'm gonna make sure you're keeping on track." Aaron affectionately rubbed the boy's head. "Is that okay?"

"It's awesome!"

They entered the house, and Tyler shared his exciting news with the other boys. Aaron was by his side the whole time. Melissa stood back, watching the very real bond between Aaron and Tyler, her heart filling with even more love.

"Hey, can we play a game of soccer in the backyard?" Tyler asked Aaron.

Aaron leaned over so that he was at eye level with Tyler. "Actually, I'll have to come back and we can do that later, okay? Right now, I need to talk privately with Ms. Conwell."

Tyler looked from Aaron to Melissa. "You like her, don't you?"

"Of course I do."

"You *really* like her," Tyler stressed.

Aaron chuckled softly. "Is it that obvious?"

Tyler nodded enthusiastically.

Aaron stood tall. "I'll see you later, okay?"

Chapter 29

"Where are you taking me?" Melissa asked.

"You'll see," Aaron told her.

"You were really awesome today," Melissa said. "Tyler was so happy. I've never seen him so genuinely excited and hopeful."

"I was happy to be there. And I meant what I said. I plan to come back and visit. I'd love to take the kids to that soccer game whenever works best."

Melissa noticed that they were heading in the direction of the beach. "Are we heading to Brighton Beach? I don't have a bathing suit."

"All will reveal itself in time."

Melissa sat back in the car, listening to the slow jams playing on the Bluetooth. Songs from twelve years ago, when she and Aaron were teens. She closed her eyes, getting caught up in the emotions that the words evoked.

And then he reached across the seat and took her hand.

They stayed that way as they drove, the music taking Melissa down memory lane. Several minutes later, Aaron pulled up next to a walkway that led to a stretch of beach. It was out of the way, not at all on the popular portion of the beach that people frequented. To the right was an older wooden house that looked like it needed a lot of fixing up.

Aaron put the car into Park and got out. Melissa looked around, wondering what on earth they were doing here as he made his way around to her side of the car and opened the door.

"What are we doing here, Aaron?" Melissa asked as he offered her a hand to help her out of the car.

"You'll see."

So she let him take her hand and lead her down the path to the beach. It was hard to walk in the sand with her heels, so she kicked them off and scooped them up. As they passed the tall thicket of grass, she noticed a dock come into view.

"I don't understand," Melissa said.

The house in front of the dock had been partially obscured by all the brush and the large wooden fence. Now she could see that the yard was filled with tall, unkempt grass. The house definitely looked abandoned. Certainly he wasn't taking her here.

The dock reminded Melissa of the one on Sheridan Lake where she and Aaron used to sneak off and kiss at night.

Was that what this was?

He took the first tentative step onto the dock, and, determining that it was secure, extended a hand to her and helped her onto it as well. He walked all the way to the end and peered out over at the water. Melissa followed him. When she reached his side, he slipped an arm around her waist and held her close.

"I remember everything about that summer," he said.

So that *was* why he brought her here.

"I remember how we always snuck out on the dock at night." He looked at her, trailed a fingertip along her cheek. "How we used to steal kisses under the moonlight."

Melissa's heart began to pound. She thought for sure that he would have forgotten all about that. It was so long ago.

Aaron released her and bent to roll up the cuffs of his pants, then he sat down and dangled his feet over the edge. He looked up at Melissa, shading his eyes from the sun. "Join me."

Melissa carefully held her skirt around her thighs and then lowered herself down onto her bottom. She slipped her bare feet over the edge as well, let them hang above the dark water.

"I don't want this baby just because I want to be a dad. Although, I admit, that's something I've wanted for a long time. But I want this baby because I want *you*." He took her hand in his. "Because I love you."

A shuddery breath escaped Melissa's lips. The wall around her heart had already come down when Aaron showed up this morning to support Tyler, and hearing him say he loved her caused a thrill to rush through her body.

"I know we never really discussed the past, and what happened. Why I let you walk out of my life. I hoped you would realize that I was a different person now, but you kept running." He paused. "I was young and dumb. I was afraid of what I felt for you at the time. I know that's not a great excuse, but then there was my soccer scholarship, and me wondering if things could really work out between us…"

"I would have done anything to make it work between us," Melissa said. "I loved you so much. But when you shut me out, I felt like you never cared about me at all."

Aaron stroked her cheek. "I did. I fell for you, too, Melissa. How could I not?"

"And yet you could walk away?"

"I have something to show you. Actually, come back to the car with me."

Melissa stared at him with curiosity. They'd just gotten here and started to talk, and now he wanted to go back to the car?

"Bad planning on my part, but you'll understand in a moment."

Aaron hopped to his feet, then helped her up. They walked the short distance back to the car, where Aaron opened the trunk. Melissa sidled up beside him.

"What do you want to show me?"

Inside the trunk was a large rectangular box. Aaron took out the box, closed the trunk, then opened the box on the trunk's smooth surface.

Inside the box, Aaron pushed aside wads of tissue paper,

and the edge of a painting came into view. "Take a look," Aaron said.

Melissa did. It was beautiful. The painting depicted a night sky with a full moon. The moon's rays were shimmering on the water below. There was a dock on the lake and two people sat at the edge, with their feet entwined as they hung over the edge.

Melissa's lips parted as she fully checked out the picture. It was a young couple, African American, their bodies angled toward each other. Even without being able to make out their faces, Melissa's beating heart told her what the picture was.

"Is that us?" she asked.

"Yeah."

Then her eyes widened as she saw the signature. "Wait a minute—is that a Felix Virgo painting?"

Aaron nodded, a smile on his face.

Melissa's heart slammed against her rib cage. She stepped fully in front of the picture, holding it up in the box to better inspect it. The familiar brushstrokes, the unique way that Felix put color on a canvas. The feeling of calm his paintings evoked.

But this was *them*. This looked like the lake in Sheridan Falls. This couldn't have been a random picture that Aaron picked up.

"Are you saying that…you had this painting *commissioned*?" she asked, her tone full of disbelief.

"You love the artist. So I found him. Asked him to recreate this picture for me. For us."

Melissa was so shocked that she couldn't even find her voice. Aaron must have done this before he learned she was pregnant. Tears sprang to her eyes.

"Like I said, I remember everything about that summer. The way you used to smile at me under the moonlight. The taste of your lips. The feel of your skin against mine. The way we used to tangle our feet together."

Melissa's blood was rushing through her veins at warp speed. This was…incredible.

"Look at the moon," Aaron told her.

Melissa had to wipe the tears from her eyes in order to focus fully on the picture again. She saw now that there was a small object in the moon. She looked closer, and realized it was a little angel. As she stared at the angel more fully, she saw that it had a little girl's face.

She looked up at Aaron, not understanding.

"Why did I let you go? You were right when you said that guilt affected my relationships. I didn't believe that I deserved happiness. I didn't come to realize that until years later, when I did some serious soul searching. But it was more than that. I was also afraid, Melissa. Afraid of losing anything I loved. That angel is my baby sister," he explained. "I asked Felix to include her in there, because…well, Chantelle is a big part of the reason I fell in love with you."

Chantelle, his sister who had drowned.

"That summer, I shared with you my deepest pain. My sister drowned. On my watch. I'd been in the house, and somehow she got outside. She got into the pool. When I finally found her…" He grimaced. "Well, it destroyed me. And for a long time, I blamed myself. I was able to lose myself in the world of soccer. It helped me to escape my guilt. But when it came to love…" His voice trailed off, and he shrugged. "Why would a guy who let his sister die deserve love?"

Melissa put the painting down in the box and turned to Aaron. She stroked his cheek. "Oh, Aaron. Of course you deserve love. What happened to Chantelle wasn't your fault."

"At the time, I didn't think I did. I blamed myself for Chantelle's death, and you were the only one I opened up to about what I was going through. You understood my pain, you understood my heart. The night when I told you, you hugged me and cried with me and told me everything would be okay...that's the night I fell in love with you."

A sense of awe and love and bittersweet emotions spiraled through Melissa. She remembered that night vividly. Aaron's body folded against hers, his heavy breaths, his broken heart. She remembered it so much because it was the night she had fallen in love with him, too.

"Did you really fall in love with me that night?" she asked.

"How could I not?"

"I fell in love with you that night, too."

It was that night that they had left the lake and made love on the shore. With all the campers sleeping, they'd found a secluded spot and consummated their relationship. For Melissa, it had been the most profound and wonderful experience of her life.

"Then you shut me out," she said. "You let me go."

"Because what I felt for you scared me to death. It was something I'd never experienced before. Something so powerful it scared me. And I doubted it. I questioned whether or not I even deserved it. Did I deserve someone as special as you? So yeah, a stupid young guy unable to deal with his guilt pushed away a girl he loved. But it was never because I fell out of love with you."

Aaron was staring into her eyes now; she could see into his soul. Good Lord, he was telling her the truth. All this time, she felt that their relationship hadn't meant as much to him, but it had. And she'd been so devastated by her broken heart that she had kept her walls up this time, not truly allowing him in.

Until now.

"Oh, Aaron."

"I'm sorry," he said. "I never meant to hurt you. But... I didn't know how to deal with everything I was feeling. You were the one good thing that came into my life after

Chantelle, and I ran. Seeing you again at the wedding, everything came flooding back. All of it. But I realized you had shut down emotionally where I was concerned. And when you asked me about Chantelle, it opened up old wounds and feelings I'd tried to keep buried. You accused me of still not opening up to you, and you were right. I've kind of been at war with myself over the past several weeks because of what you said to me. I wanted you, but I knew that meant I would have to finally deal with my guilt. Which meant admitting something I never told anyone about the day Chantelle died."

Melissa's eyes narrowed and her heart pounded. "What didn't you tell me?"

Aaron paused. Swallowed. "The day Chantelle died, the reason I wasn't paying as much attention to her as I should have been was because I was distracted by some girl. I was on the phone with a girl I liked, sweet-talking her, making plans for the weekend, while my sister got out of the house and into the pool."

"Aaron…" Melissa's heart broke for him.

"Now do you understand? Love and relationships for me were connected to how Chantelle died. I couldn't get past that."

"You can't live like this, blaming yourself for a mistake. It's not a crime to have been on the phone. It was an accident."

"I know that now. But in order to really forgive myself, I had to finally tell my parents the truth about that day. I told them a few days ago."

"And what did they say?" Melissa asked, regarding him tentatively.

Aaron's eyes misted. "That it was high time I forgave myself. That Chantelle is in a better place where she's happy. That they know she loves me with all of her heart and would never want me to be sad. And that one day, when I see her again, she'll tell me that herself."

"Aaron." Melissa's voice cracked. "That's the sweetest thing I've ever heard. Your parents really are wonderful people."

Aaron nodded. "They are. They never blamed me when it happened, and that's why the guilt was worse. Because I hadn't been totally honest with them. I couldn't bear to tell them the full truth at the time, but I knew I needed to tell them in order to finally forgive myself. That weight has now been lifted off my shoulders."

Melissa stroked his face. "I'm so glad."

A small smiled lifted Aaron's lips. "And now…" He put his hand on her belly. "You're carrying my baby. I want you, and this baby. Because I love you. I always have."

Tears streamed down her face now. No one had ever given her a gift as meaningful as the painting. Every doubt she had about him vanished. She believed, finally, that she meant more to him than she'd ever known.

She looped her arms around his neck. "Oh, Aaron. I love you, too. I didn't want to. But I think a part of me never stopped. I kept running from you because you'd hurt me so much…but now I'm through running."

Aaron swallowed, and Melissa saw his eyes mist. "I'll ask you again, sweetheart. Will you marry me? Make me the happiest man alive and be my wife?"

A smile burst onto Melissa's face, and happy tears spilled onto her cheeks. "Yes! Oh, Aaron, yes!"

And then he kissed her, one hand smoothing over her belly while the other one stroked her cheek. It was a slow and meaningful kiss that bridged the gap from the past, and paved the way to the future.

A future that would be filled with lots of happiness and love.

* * * * *

THE BILLIONAIRE'S PRIZE

REBECCA WINTERS

PROLOGUE

DEA CARACCIOLO STOOD inside the grand dining hall of the castle on Posso Island. She was ready to flee now that she'd done her part during the wedding ceremony of her twin sister, Alessandra, and Rinieri Montanari.

"Darling? Why are you here by the doors?"

Oh, no. She turned her head in surprise. "Mamma."

"I still need to be in line to greet the guests and would like you to go sit with Guido and his parents."

Dea didn't think she could bear it. "Please don't make me."

"But you're the maid of honor. Your father and I are depending on you to entertain the best man and his family. Alessandra says they love Rini, and Signor Rossano has spoken highly of you since the night you were a model in the fashion show on his yacht. Come on. I'll walk you over to their table."

The mention of the yacht increased her agony, but this was one situation Dea couldn't get out of. Somehow she would have to endure Guido's company for a few more minutes.

During the wedding ceremony they'd gone through

the motions to be civil to each other in order to carry out their duties, but he'd hardly looked at her and she knew why. He couldn't help but have a low opinion of her since that night on the yacht when she'd made the worst blunder of her life with Rini in front of Guido. He probably assumed she was still in love with her new brother-in-law.

The situation couldn't be uglier, but her mother expected her to be gracious for a little while longer. When they approached the table, Guido and his father got to their feet before inviting her to sit down.

Guido's mother was a lovely woman and Dea tried to concentrate on her once they started to eat. "My sister told me about your generous gift to her and Rini."

"We thought they should honeymoon on our yacht to get away from everyone else. Alessandra is perfectly charming, and Rini's a favorite of ours."

"So I've heard."

"I have to say, you looked so beautiful the night of the fashion show," Signora Rossano continued. "But tonight you're even more beautiful."

"Thank you," she whispered.

"It's only the truth," a smiling Signor Rossano interjected. "Don't you think so, Guido?"

His son put down his champagne glass. "Papà? As you well know, Signorina Caracciolo has most of the Italian male population at her feet."

His father nodded with satisfaction. "That is true."

To his parents' ears, Guido's comment must have sounded like a supreme compliment. But the choice of the word *most* let Dea know he didn't include himself in that particular population.

"Signor Rossano, the other models and I were amazed you would allow your yacht to be used for a fashion show backdrop. It was a great thrill for them and they're hoping you'll offer it again."

"I wouldn't count on it for another year," Guido murmured out of his father's hearing, sounding turned off by her comment. She hadn't meant that she included herself in those who hoped to wangle another invitation. But no doubt Guido had assumed as much. She shouldn't have said anything at all.

Feeling more and more uncomfortable, she almost gasped with relief when her aunt Fulvia came over to the table and asked her if she'd like to say goodbye to the Archbishop of Taranto, who'd married her sister and Rini. It was a great honor and Dea excused herself with as much grace as she could muster before clinging to her aunt's arm. Her mother's only sister had saved her from further embarrassment and she would always be grateful.

CHAPTER ONE

One year later

"Signora Parma is expecting you. Walk back through the doors to her workshop."

Dea Caracciolo thanked the receptionist and headed for the inner sanctum of the world-renowned Italian opera-costume designer. The only reason Dea had been given this privilege was because her aunt Fulvia and Juliana Parma were such close friends.

Though Dea had met Juliana and her husband on many occasions at her aunt's southern Italian *castello* in Taranto, this particular meeting wasn't social and the outcome—good or bad—would rest entirely on Dea's shoulders.

The sought-after redheaded designer in her late sixties stood surrounded by her staff, giving orders to one and all in her flamboyant style. When she saw Dea, she motioned her to come closer and clapped her hands.

"Everyone?" Their eyes fastened on Dea. "You've all known Dea Loti as Italy's leading fashion model.

She's actually Princess Dea of the Houses of Caracciolo and Taranto and the niece of my dear friend Princess Fulvia Taranto. But while she's here working with me during her spring-semester designer course at the Accademia Roma, you will call her Dea and accord her every courtesy."

Dea was so surprised she blurted, "You mean you're willing to take me on without talking to me about it first?"

"Of course. Fulvia has told me everything I need to know, so I called the head of your department and asked them to send you to me."

Dear Fulvia. Dea loved her so much. "I can hardly believe this is happening."

"Believe it! You're even more beautiful than the last time we were together. Imagine if you were a soprano in the opera too—you would have every tenor in the world dying of love for you."

Heat filled Dea's cheeks. "How awful." Once upon a time Dea would have liked to hear a compliment like that, but not since she'd been in therapy to help her get on the road to real happiness.

Juliana chuckled. "Come in my private office."

The others smiled as she followed the older woman into a small cluttered room that still managed to be tidy. Dea handed her a small bouquet of roses.

"What's this?"

"A token of my gratitude that you even agreed to meet with me."

"*Grazie*, Dea." She inhaled the perfume from the

flowers. "Heavenly. Fulvia must have told you how much I love pink roses."

"I remember your husband giving you some after the opera a year ago."

"You're a very sweet and observant young woman. You're going to go far in this business. I feel it in my bones."

Sweet? That wasn't a word one would apply to the Dea of the past. The old Dea was too self-absorbed. She'd learned a lot about herself in therapy. The new Dea was working on thinking about others.

Juliana put the flowers in a bowl and sank into the chair behind her desk. "Sit down, my dear." Dea did her bidding. "What's this news that you've given up modeling?"

"It's true. I did one show at the end of last semester, but my goal is to become a period costume designer for the opera, like you. As you know, I've loved costume design from the time I was a child. You have no idea how excited I am to work with an expert like you and learn all I can. It's a great privilege."

Juliana's brown eyes sparkled. "You're going to love the project I'm winding up now. It's the costuming for *Don Giovanni*, which will go into production the third week of May. I'd like to hear your comments on this new sketch for Donna Elvira." She thrust a rendering into Dea's hands.

Don Giovanni was one of Dea's favorite operas. But the second she saw the drawing, she shot Juliana a glance. "Don't you mean Donna Anna?"

A smile broke the corner of Juliana's mouth. "Bravo,

Dea. Nothing gets past you. This costume is indeed meant for a younger woman. I've always known you to have a discerning eye. In fact I remember the fashion shows you used to put on at the *castello* with your sister when you were little. They were delightful and, in some instances, brilliant!"

Brilliance was a quality one attributed to Alessandra, not Dea. The unexpected compliment sent a curl of warmth through her body. Juliana handed her another drawing from a pile on her desk. "*Here* is a first draft of the costume for Donna Elvira that she'll wear in the dark courtyard scene. One of the staff worked it up."

Dea studied it for a few minutes. Her brows formed a frown.

Juliana chuckled. "Don't be afraid to tell me exactly what you think. I've always admired your honesty."

Coming from Juliana, that kind of praise meant a great deal.

"In my mind this gown is too frivolous and doesn't reveal her true character. I see Donna Elvira as a mature woman who's ahead of her time. She's hurt and outraged with Don Giovanni for his abandoning her. I'd like to see her gown toned down to convey that she's anything but a fool. She's been on a mission to find him."

"I agree completely. Bring me your version by tomorrow at 11:00 a.m." She took back the drawing and rose to her feet. "That's all the time I can give you for now."

"Mille ringraziamenti, signora."

"Juliana, *per favore.*"

Dea rushed around the desk to give her a kiss on the cheek. "I'm more grateful than you know for this opportunity."

After saying those words, she left the building and took a taxi back to her apartment. Located in the heart of Rome, the elegant complex she lived in was in walking distance of the Pantheon and the Piazza Navona. It had been home to her for quite a while. She loved the ancient street, which was over five hundred years old, with its dozens of wonderful shops. On this particular Monday, the lovely April weather matched her lightened mood.

Once she'd eaten lunch she would get to work designing a gown already forming in her mind. But first she needed to make an important phone call to her aunt, who'd made this unexpected meeting with Juliana possible.

When the older woman answered, Dea said, "Zia Fulvia?"

"Dea, how wonderful to hear from you! Your mother is here with me. I'll put the phone on speaker so we can both talk to you."

"Mamma?"

"Darling. I've been anxious to hear from you."

Her heart pounded with excitement. "Guess what? Juliana called my department at the Accademia and has taken me on. I've been given my first assignment. And it's all thanks to you, Fulvia."

"Juliana wouldn't have offered to help you if she

didn't already think you could do the job. When you break out on your own one day, your résumé will be worth its weight in gold because you'll have worked under her tutelage."

"I know that and I'm so thrilled! It's all because of you that I'm finally going to fulfill my dream! Now I've got to prove myself."

"I have no doubt of it."

"Neither do I," her mother said. "I don't think I've heard you this happy in years!"

Tears stung Dea's eyes. "This is the beginning of my new life."

"Your father's going to be overjoyed with this news."

"You've both given me wonderful advice and told me my future is out there waiting for me. Being able to work with Juliana, I know I'm going to find it!"

"Good for you, darling."

"I love you and will call you later."

She hung up, eager to get started on a design that would convince Juliana she hadn't been wrong to do this enormous, unprecedented favor for Fulvia. Dea had meant it when she'd said this was the beginning of her new life.

While she'd been in therapy this last year, she'd been forced to dig deep into her psyche to understand what made her tick. She'd been given several assignments to work on: forget self, put other people first and be kind before blurting out something she'd regret, even if it was true.

But her assignment to let go of the pain of the past was easier said than done. She had to stop dwelling on the fact that her identical twin sister, Alessandra, had been the one to attract the gorgeous engineering magnate Rinieri Montanari, not Dea, in an incident that had brought on Dea's emotional crisis.

She'd met Rini and his best friend Guido Rossano on board the fabulous Rossano yacht during a modeling assignment in Naples. Though Dea had been the first to meet Rini and had fallen for him on the spot—even kissing him passionately in front of Guido before saying good-night—Rini hadn't been interested in her.

When she looked back on that now, she was mortified to imagine what Guido must have thought of her behavior. As for Rini, she'd never expected to see him again. But to her shock, he met Alessandra while he was on business in the south of Italy. That was all it took for the elusive bachelor to fall in love and marry her sister.

Dea had been crushed and her serious loss of confidence had required professional help. Through therapy it became clear that, among other things, she'd always been jealous of her sister's intelligence and scholastic success. Alessandra had already written and published an important factual historical book on their ancestor Queen Joanna.

But it was her aunt Fulvia's comment that had brought her up short and made her realize she needed help.

Dea Caracciolo, do you want to conquer every man you meet? What would you do with all of them? It's not natural.

Her aunt had been right. It wasn't natural. Despite Dea's attempt to flirt with Rinieri, he hadn't been drawn to her. Period.

Following her conversation with Fulvia and her mother, Dea had gotten counseling and had been going through a difficult, painful period of self-evaluation and remembered mistakes. Her darkest memory had involved Alessandra's first love years earlier.

He'd pursued Dea. Part of her had felt guilty, yet another part had been flattered when he'd followed her back to Rome, where she was modeling at the time. But he'd turned out to be a man incapable of being faithful to any woman. A torturous time had followed for her and Alessandra. Only in the last year had they finally put the pain of that experience behind them and had become close in a new, honest way.

Still, trying to find one's self was not an easy journey. Though being a top fashion model had initially brought her excitement and a lot of interest from men, in time Dea hadn't found the fulfillment she craved in a career she'd always known couldn't last forever.

As was brought out in therapy, those deep longings for inner contentment had eluded her. She knew she would have to change her focus if she was going to have a happy life like her parents, or like Alessandra, who was now ecstatically married and a new mother. Because of a soccer injury, Rini hadn't been able to give her children, so they'd adopted little Brazzo. Dea couldn't be happier for them.

After serious thought, she'd chosen to follow her

natural inclination and make her way in a new direction that used her brain and God-given talents rather than her looks, but she was still filled with anxiety.

Forget self.

That's what her brilliant underwater-archaeologist sister had done. In the process, she'd won a wonderful man and already had a family.

Somewhere out there, Dea's prince existed. As her wise mother had promised her, "One day he'll find *you*. In the meantime, work on finding yourself, darling."

Friday afternoon Guido paused at the door of the soccer store adjoining his suite of offices in the Stadio Emanuele soccer stadium in Rome. "I'm leaving now, Sergio. As usual I'll be back Sunday morning before the big game. Have a good weekend."

"You too, boss." His administrative assistant smiled because he thought he knew why, when he could, Guido spent every Friday night and Saturday away from Rome, unable to be reached by anyone. But Sergio would be dead wrong about the reason.

Guido eyed his spectacular soccer mate from the past, whose serious leg injury at the height of his game prevented him from ever competing again. Now that Guido was the owner of a minor national soccer team, he'd recruited Sergio to do a little of everything.

The man knew more about the ins and outs of the national soccer league than anyone. He not only ran their business and ticket sales with meticulous care, but he kept the museum and their soccer store stocked and profitable. On top of that, he handled the phones and kept out unexpected visitors unless they made appointments.

"How come you haven't left already, Sergio? You work too hard. As far as I know you haven't taken a break in months." The man screened Guido's incoming phone calls from the media, but most important, those from Guido's hovering parents.

Being an only child, Guido realized they'd had a hard time accepting that he'd taken a year off from the Leonides Rossano Shipping Company to pursue an old soccer dream. Guido loved them and stayed in touch, but he'd felt smothered and enjoyed the freedom his new career was giving him away from the family business.

"Work saves me from my demons," Sergio commented. Guido could relate to that. "Don't you know there are tons of women calling here all the time after hours, or wanting to order stuff online? You're still a poster hero with those who remember you winning those past championships."

"Even after ten years?" Guido smiled wearily. "I leave all the fans to you. As I see it, you've been divorced long enough and need to find someone who can accept your passion for the sport. You had a big female following of your own."

He scoffed. "That all ended after my marriage. I don't think there is such a woman."

Neither did Guido, but he kept that comment to himself. "Try to enjoy yourself this weekend."

"I know *you* will," Sergio fired back. "Go ahead

and keep it to yourself, but you can't tell me you don't have a woman somewhere."

Conversation over. "Ciao, Sergio," he called to his friend before shutting the door.

There'd never been a lack of women for Guido. In his late teens he'd gotten into a serious relationship with one of the most popular girls at school, Carla, but over time he discovered she loved his celebrity status, not him. From that point on, he was wary of women.

The shock of learning she didn't truly love him changed his perspective on the dating experience. After that, Guido continued to enjoy women, but he didn't get into any more serious relationships. His soccer life had been so full, he'd put the idea of settling down out of his mind.

However, there'd been one woman over the last year who'd taken his breath and was still unforgettable. Dea Loti. Italy's most famous model. Her lesser-known name was Dea Caracciolo.

He'd met her aboard his father's yacht during a fashion show taped for television. It had been galling to realize she'd looked right through him in order to pursue his lifelong friend Rinieri Montanari, and it had aroused Guido's jealousy.

That emotion was something that had never happened to Guido before. He'd tried to put it away because Rini was the best, but it still haunted him.

Guido left the stadium in his Lamborghini and headed straight for the airport. By dinnertime his private jet, with the logo of Scatto Roma—the name of his soccer team, which meant *surge* in Italian—

landed at a private runway just outside Metaponto in Southern Italy. Rini would be waiting on the tarmac for him in the Jeep. They had a lot to catch up on.

Through a quirk of fate, his best friend had married Alessandra Caracciolo, Dea's identical twin sister. Since the wedding, the couple had been spending part of the time at Rini's villa in Positano and the rest of it at her family's island *castello*.

Montanari Engineering, located in Naples, was now drilling for oil on Caracciolo land in Southern Italy, thus the reason for meeting Rini here on the island.

After learning his friend had become a father, Guido had invited Rini for a meal at his apartment in Rome. But this would be the first time Guido had been back to the island since Rini's wedding to Alessandra when he'd been best man. They'd issued him many invitations to come, but Guido had turned them down, using business as the excuse. In reality, he didn't want to take the chance of seeing Dea again.

By now it shouldn't bother him that the woman who'd been so fascinated by Rini while they were on the Rossano yacht was none other than Alessandra's sister. Dea had been her maid of honor. After the wedding ceremony, she'd sat down to dinner with Guido and his parents. While she talked to them, all he could see was her kissing Rini before saying good-night to him on board the yacht.

But that was a year ago. Time had passed and he knew her modeling career took her all over Italy. He was certain she wouldn't be here at the castle. If Rini had mentioned otherwise, Guido wouldn't have accepted the invitation.

As he exited the plane he could see Rini.

"Your team name is perfect," his friend called out the window of the Jeep on the tarmac. "You *are* surging. Bravo."

"Grazie."

When Guido climbed in the Jeep, his first sight of his dark-haired friend said it all. "Fatherhood agrees with you. How is *piccolo* Brazzo?"

"He's going to be a soccer player for sure."

"I can't wait to see him."

"I'm sorry. Not this visit. He's staying with my family at the villa in Positano so Alessandra and I can have our first weekend alone."

"Lucky you."

Rini had found great happiness in his marriage. Guido would give anything to feel that fulfilled. As he sat there, it came to him that he was envious of the happy-ever-after his friend Rini had achieved, a happy-ever-after Guido hadn't thought he'd wanted himself all these years.

He stared at his friend. A spirit of contentment radiated off Rini as they drove across the causeway to the Caracciolo *castello* on Posso Island that jutted into the Ionian Sea.

Only sand surrounded the ancient structure, no grass or trees. In Guido's mind, it was Italy's answer to Mont-Saint-Michel of French fame, with a benign appeal in good weather like this. But he imagined it could look quite daunting during a storm.

Guido found it fascinating to think the beautiful twin princesses of Count Onorato di Caracciolo were born and raised here, away from civilization. From this convent-like place had emerged Italy's most beautiful supermodel. One fashion cover had called Dea Loti "Italy's own Helen of Troy."

The face that launched a thousand ships had done something to Guido...

He'd been so stunned after meeting her in person that he hadn't been able to get her out of his mind. It probably wasn't a good idea to meet Rini here after all because it brought back the memory from the wedding when he'd been watching Dea, who'd been watching Rini. Was she still hungering for him? But it was too late to think about that now or wish he hadn't come. *Get a grip, Rossano.*

"You're being unusually quiet," Rini murmured as he pulled the Jeep up to the front of the castle. "I expected to see you overjoyed with your success so far."

"I am pleased," Guido muttered, "but the season isn't over yet. We've had one loss and still have some tough games to face."

Rini shut off the engine. "You've already brought your team to new heights. I'm proud of what you've done so far."

"Spoken like my best friend," Guido murmured.

He could feel Rini's eyes on him. "How is it going with your parents?"

Guido sighed. "The same. Papà is praying I'll give up this madness and come back to the company."

"Surely not right now."

"Of course not, but he fears I'll stay away from the business for good."

Rini's brow lifted. "Do *you* think you've left the shipping business for good?"

"I don't have an answer to that yet."

"Well, I'm glad you were able to break away and come. Tomorrow we'll go out on the cruiser and do some fishing. I've got some business ideas I want your opinion on. But tonight Alessandra has arranged dinner for us with one of your favorite fish dishes."

To his chagrin, Guido had a problem he couldn't talk over with Rini. How could he tell him that Rini *himself* was the problem? "I'm already salivating."

Filled with shame over his own flawed character, he jumped out of the Jeep and grabbed his gym bag that contained all he needed for this weekend visit. They walked to the front entry. When Rini opened the door, they were greeted by a marmalade cat Guido had played with at the wedding.

"Well, hello, Alfredo."

The housekeeper's pet rubbed against Guido's jean-clad leg. He put the bag down and picked him up, remembering that the cat was getting old and needed to be carried up and down stairs. "Did you know I was coming?"

Rini grinned. "He remembers you—otherwise he wouldn't let you hold him."

"I'm honored."

"Let's go up to your old room." Rini grabbed Guido's bag and they climbed the grand staircase two steps at a time past the enormous painting of

Queen Joanna to the third floor. The windows in the bedroom looked out on the sea. He'd stayed in here before the wedding. "Go ahead and freshen up, then come down to the dining room."

"I'll be right there." Still holding Alfredo, he said, "Thanks for inviting me."

Rini headed for the entry. "I've missed our talks," he said over his shoulder.

Guido watched him disappear out the door. *What in the hell is wrong with you, Rossano? No bear hug for your best friend? What has Rini ever done to you?*

He put the cat on the bed and slipped into the bathroom. When he came out, he opened his gym bag and pulled out two presents. One was a small gift he'd bought for Alessandra in Florence after a match. The other was a baby toy he'd seen in a store near his apartment. A little purple octopus with bells on the tentacles.

"We'd better not keep everyone waiting, Alfredo." He gathered the cat in his arms along with the gifts and went down the staircase to the dining room. The second he walked in, the cat took one look at Alessandra and wanted to get down. Guido lowered him to the parquet floor.

Her gaze darted to Guido and she beamed. "So that's where the cat has been! You're one of his favorite people." She rushed over to hug Guido. He hugged her back and gave her his gifts.

"You want me to open them now?"

"I think I do."

She removed the paper from the smaller box and

lifted the lid. Inside was a small enamel painting of Queen Joanna framed in gold filigree, probably three by four inches. He heard her gasp. "Oh, Guido—"

"I saw it in Florence at the House of Gold and couldn't resist. Consider it a gift to celebrate the publication of your book."

Just then Rini came in the room. *"Caro—"* she cried and rushed over to show her husband.

His friend flashed him a warm glance. "You knew exactly what she'd love."

"I read the book and was so impressed by your knowledge I had to do something to honor you."

"I'm glad you liked it. This is exquisite. I'll treasure it forever." She laid it on the hunt board and undid the large gift. "Oh, how adorable! A purple octopus! Brazzo will love it!" She gave Guido a kiss on the cheek. "Come and sit down. We want to hear all about the team and how things are going."

"First I want to hear about Brazzo."

"He's gorgeous! We'll show you videos later."

No sooner did they get settled and start to eat than Guido heard the helicopter overhead.

"That'll be my parents," Alessandra murmured as they enjoyed their meal. "They've been in Milan."

"For another of Dea's fashion shows?" Damn if the question wasn't out before he could recall it.

"Oh—I guess you didn't know that she has given up her modeling career."

Guido's fork dropped on his plate. *No more modeling?* He couldn't comprehend it. "Since when?"

"Quite a while now. She realized the life of most

supermodels fades after twenty-five years of age and it's past time for her. Dea went back to her true passion and this last year has been finishing her degree at the Accademia Roma. This is her last semester."

Her true passion? Guido blinked. He didn't know she'd ever gone to college. "I had no idea. What is she studying?"

"Period costume fashion design. I'm so thrilled for her. She has an extraordinary gift in that area."

Before Guido could think, he heard voices at the entry. Alessandra's parents walked in the room, but he only had eyes for the gorgeous woman behind them. His heart thundered.

Dea!

She wore her long hair back in a chignon, a style he hadn't seen her in. All that glossy brown hair with streaks of sunlight was hidden. The oval of her face with less makeup than he'd ever noticed before caused him to stare. With those dark burgundy eyes—like the color in a stained glass window—she was beautiful in a brand-new way.

Guido stood up and greeted the three of them. Alessandra begged her parents to join them for dinner, but they said they'd already eaten and were going upstairs.

"What about you, Dea?"

"I'd love some dinner, but first I want to see the baby. I brought Brazzo a present. I hope he doesn't have a bear yet. This one speaks!" She handed it to Alessandra, who opened it and pressed the button. They all listened and laughed.

"Brazzo will love this, but we left him with Rini's father and family. They wanted to give us a break."

"I'm sure you're thrilled, but I'm horribly disappointed."

"There'll be plenty of other times for the rest of our lives."

"You're right, of course." She sat down at the table. "I left work without grabbing a bite and now I'm starving. This dinner looks wonderful. Baked halibut and vegetables with feta cheese. How perfect!"

She was wearing a simple white blouse and a print skirt. Her outfit was so unexpectedly casual that Guido was still trying to make sense of everything when she sat down next to him.

For the rest of the meal Guido was amazed to watch her dig into her food and eat everything. Where was the woman who never ate anything that wasn't on her special diet? Come to think of it, she looked like she'd gained some becoming weight since the last time he'd seen her at the wedding.

Over a glass of wine she turned to Guido. He noticed she no longer wore her fingernails long and painted. "There's a girl at the shop named Gina. She and her fiancé, Aldo, went to the soccer game at the Stadio Emanuele last weekend."

Where was this leading?

"Aldo came in to pick Gina up and she told him I knew the owner. He fell all over me." Guido could believe that. "According to him, you were the greatest soccer player he'd ever seen and he desperately wants to meet you in person sometime, hopefully with my help."

Dea had discussed him with her coworker? He couldn't believe it.

She kept talking. "According to Aldo, the Scatto Roma team is going to win the championship this year. He was a soccer player himself, not on your level, of course. He thinks you walk on water already for lifting the B team to top-tier status."

"Thank you, Dea," he said, attempting to take it all in, but he couldn't understand her interest. "Have you ever been to a soccer match?"

"Never," she confessed without shame. "I've never even watched it on TV. You must think I'm terrible. I had no idea you'd won so many championships for Italy. Aldo said you were everyone's favorite player and the women were crazy about you."

"They were," Rini inserted with a grin.

She hadn't talked to Guido like this at the wedding reception, where she had seemed very stiff. This was something else. He decided to change the subject.

"I understand you're no longer modeling."

"Not for the last year."

"Where do you work?"

"I started at the shop of Juliana Parma ten days ago. She's *the* costume designer for the opera. I've been permitted to shadow her. My aunt Fulvia made it possible. You remember her from the wedding?"

"Of course." The woman had taken Dea away from the table before the wedding cake had been served.

"They're best friends and Juliana took me on as

a favor to my aunt. But now that I'm working there, I'm on my own and I'm terrified."

"How could you possibly be that when you've been Italy's top model?"

"That period of my life is over, and modeling modern-day fashions has nothing to do with being a period costume designer for the opera." Guido still had a hard time believing she had changed her whole life in the last year. To his mind, she was more beautiful than ever. "I have to prove myself in a whole new field. I'm not like you."

"What do you mean?"

"Alessandra said that when you bought that floundering soccer team, you had the satisfaction of being one of the greatest soccer players ever to compete in Italy. With your knowledge and confidence, you've been able to turn your team around. I'm very impressed."

"He's done that, all right," Rini concurred. "So I have an idea. Why don't the four of us go out behind the castle and play a little soccer before it gets dark? Two against two. It works even if we don't have a whole bunch of guys around. Since Brazzo was born, Alessandra and I haven't had a weekend to enjoy like this. Let's team up."

"That sounds fun!" Alessandra chimed in with enthusiasm that sounded real. "I like soccer, but I'd love to learn more about it since Rini is determined our son will be a great player like you, Guido. What do you say, Dea?"

"I'm hopeless when it comes to sports and would hate making a fool of myself, but I'll do it this once."

So she was willing to toss him a bone after she'd just admitted she'd never even seen a soccer game?

"Let me run upstairs to put on my trainers."

Alessandra patted her husband's arm. "I'll find mine too."

Rini got to his feet. "My soccer ball is around here somewhere. We'll all meet in the foyer in a few minutes."

Everyone took off except for Guido, who stood there in a funk. Since Rini's marriage, they hadn't had time to kick a ball around. And now he wanted them to play with the women?

He'd go along with this, but before he went to bed, he intended to have a talk with Rini about what was going on.

CHAPTER TWO

DEA RACED UP the stairs to her bedroom. Rini had no idea how petrified she was when it came to participating in sports. Alessandra was the one who did everything well: tennis, golf, swimming and scuba diving. But Dea didn't dare say no to his suggestion in front of Guido.

The tall, attractive dark blond was not only a recognized national celebrity in the sports field; he was Rini's best friend. Dea didn't want to be a drama queen and create a scene. Those days were relegated to the past. She'd turned over a new leaf and was embracing a different life that meant accepting challenges she'd avoided before now.

She changed out of her skirt into jeans and put on her trainers. No doubt she would fall flat on her face repeatedly for being out of her element, but at least she would be prepared. If Rini allowed her to be on his team, then she'd wouldn't feel so terrible when she let him down. Alessandra would be a much better fit for Guido when it came to sports.

How strange that today of all days Dea's folks had

come to the shop and begged her to fly home with them after work for the weekend. None of them had known that Rini and Alessandra had invited Guido. It had come as a shock to see the three of them at the dining room table.

Both on the yacht and at the wedding, Dea had only seen him dressed in a tuxedo. This evening Guido was wearing a blue polo shirt that emphasized his well-defined chest, which combined with tight jeans made it impossible to look anywhere else. Soccer kept him in the sun. His bronzed complexion accentuated the midnight blue of his dark-fringed eyes.

She could understand why female soccer fans would have gone crazy over him. Guido might not be playing soccer now, but it didn't matter. He was an incredibly appealing man.

After the fashion show on the yacht, Guido's father had sought her out. At the time she'd taken an instant dislike to the renowned shipping-company CEO. He was so full of himself that he was quite unbearable. Dea's modest father was a completely different type and so easy to be around. Meeting the puffed-up man's son was the last thing Dea and her friend Daphne, who had modeled with her, had wanted to do, but she knew she had to be gracious.

Prepared not to like his son, who was probably an obnoxious replica of his father, she'd been shocked to meet his best friend, Rini Montanari, the dark-haired handsome prince standing next to him. At that moment everything else had left her mind. He wasn't a real prince, but he'd seemed to have stepped right out

of her childhood dreams. But Rini hadn't responded
to her as she'd hoped and her world had fallen apart.
Of course, that was ages ago...

Tonight she felt she was truly seeing Guido for the
first time and not just as Rini's best friend. It had been
unfair to judge him because of his father. This was
important to Rini and Alessandra. For that reason she
made up her mind to be a good sport and act friendly.
Why not? If nothing else, she might be able to talk
him into meeting Gina's fiancé after a game, or giving Aldo an autographed team poster or something.

Dea left the bedroom and hurried down to the
foyer, where the others had congregated. Rini glanced
at her. "While we were waiting, we flipped a coin.
You're on Guido's team." He smiled broadly. "My
wife is on mine."

"Hmm. I wonder how that happened. Sorry, Guido."
Dea rolled her eyes at him. "You got the bad end of
this deal."

"Why don't I show you a few moves before we
start." He was holding the soccer ball. "Who knows
what can happen?"

She chuckled. "I'm game if you are. Let's go."

They left the castle and walked around to the back,
where the cruiser was pulled up to the dock in the
distance. Rini and Alessandra had moved on to draw
boundary lines in the sand.

While Guido explained the basic rudiments of the
sport to her, there was no chitchat. He was all business.
No doubt the players on his team held him in awe.

"The whole point of the game is to prevent the

other team from driving the ball forward and scoring. One of the first basic moves is to take a big side step and pull the ball with you to put space between you and the enemy."

"Show me."

"It goes like this."

Dea watched his hard-muscled body and legs do the move with sheer masculine grace and speed. Whoa. She smiled. "Do that again."

He did it five more times. No matter how she anticipated what he was going to do, she couldn't react fast enough to stop him.

"Again!"

This time she was desperate to succeed. Refusing to let him elude her, she made a flying leap and tackled him with all her strength. They both went down. She turned over to look at him, trying to catch her breath, but laughter kept bubbling out of her. "I'm sorry."

"No, you're not." He lay there looking at her before bursting into laughter himself. Their faces were so close she could tell his incredible blue eyes were smiling. Guido Rossano was a sensational-looking man. How could she not have noticed before today?

His gaze continued to play over her features. "For a first soccer lesson, you did well. You'd make an excellent player in American football—tackling is what they do in their football games. Tackling isn't what we do in soccer. Who would have thought?"

"Forgive me. I got so frustrated I didn't know what else to do."

"You've got all the right instincts, but you need to refine your technique to soccer or you'll get thrown out of the game."

"Hey, you two?" Rini called from a distance. "Are we going to play, or what?"

"I need to show her a few more moves before we start," Guido shouted back.

Guilt swept over her as he helped her to her feet. Conscious of their clasped hands, she eased hers from his grip. As his eyes focused on hers, her heart skipped a beat for no good reason. "We'll start with the lift, step and go." He put the ball on the ground. "Use your foot to push it toward me and watch."

Dea was loving this. She started moving the ball toward him. He lifted his foot as if to do a sideward motion. But it was a fake move. He stepped forward and drove the ball away from her. She groaned.

"Let's do that again."

She pushed the ball three more times, but he evaded her every time. "You're amazing!"

"Not amazing. I've been doing this move since childhood."

"No wonder Aldo idolizes you." After four tries she got the hang of it.

"Okay. Now what's the next move called?"

"You're not tired yet?"

"No, but maybe *you* are."

His hard jaw rose a fraction and he put his hands on his hips in a totally male stance. "This one is called the chip shot. Come toward me, moving the ball with your feet."

She did his bidding and thought he would push the ball forward, but he chipped it instead so it flipped up, catching her off guard.

"Oh! I *like* that move. I want to try it." But with her next effort, she used too much force and fell on her derriere. He chuckled and helped her to her feet.

"Try once more."

Dea did her best and stayed upright.

"Bravo. You're ready. Let's try out those moves on them before they decide they want to go home."

"You think I can do it?"

"We're about to find out." The way he smiled made him look like a devilishly handsome blond pirate with a wicked gleam in his eyes. How odd that she'd never dreamed of a tall blond pirate prince before...

The guys played goalie so the girls could battle it out. Guido hadn't had so much fun in years and was silently betting on Dea to outplay Alessandra.

Right away it became clear that Rini hadn't taught Alessandra any special moves. She could run and scrap, but Dea pulled a few moves on her with an expertise that shocked Guido. In the end, Team Scatto Roma took the honors over Team Montanari. Again he was surprised she'd caught on so quickly and he discovered he was proud of her.

Alessandra eyed the three of them. "Now it's the men's turn. You and I will play goalie, Dea."

"I'm ready."

"It's too dark out," Rini protested.

His wife smiled. "Since when has that ever stopped you? I'm counting on you to win for our side."

Guido turned to his friend. "Come on. Let's show the girls how the game is played."

"You're on."

Before they spread out, Guido took Dea aside. "Try not to let the ball get past you. Do whatever you need to do."

"I'm afraid Rini will kick it so hard I won't stand a chance, but I'll try."

He squeezed her elbow. "No one can ask for more than that."

In a minute play commenced. Rini gave as good as he got, but Guido's competitive spirit had kicked in. That's when he realized he was fighting a demon from the past and taking it out on his friend. The score was two to two. Rini went all out for the last play. He gave the ball a kick as fierce as the expression on his face. Dea didn't stand a chance. Or so Guido thought until he saw her catch it midair.

"I did it!" she cried out in unfeigned excitement. Forgetting everything, he ran toward her and swung her around. "Keep this up and I'll sign you on to my team." Before he lowered her warm beautiful body to the ground, there was a breathless moment when even in the semidark her cognac eyes seemed to sparkle. He wanted badly to taste her mouth, but they had an audience and she would probably slap his face.

Alessandra ran up to Dea and hugged her. "I thought you said you've never done sports. What's happened?"

Dea flicked Guido a glance. "I had a good teacher."

"I'll say you did. Come on. Let's go in."

Rini kissed his wife. "We'll catch up with you two in a minute."

As the women walked off, Guido sucked in his breath. The time for the talk with Rini had come. His friend stared him down. "Do you want to tell me what's going on with you? Everything has been different since Alessandra and I have been married, so I'll make this easier for you and start. Why haven't you wanted to get together like we used to do?"

He rubbed the back of his neck. "You really don't know?"

"Guido—" The bleak expression on his face spoke volumes and made Guido feel guiltier than ever. "Talk to me! If I've done something wrong, I'll fix it if I can."

"You can't."

"Why?"

It was hard to swallow. "I'm ashamed to tell you."

"Why?" he demanded again.

Just tell him, Rossano, and get it over with.

"It's ever since that night on the yacht. I'd never known jealousy in my life until then. But I did the moment I met Dea and she took one look at you and fell head over heels."

Rini's black brows formed a line above his dark eyes. "Way back then *you* were jealous of *that*?"

"The force of it hit me like a blow to my gut."

"Are you telling me you were interested in Dea?" He shook his head in total bewilderment. "I thought you'd never met her before that night."

"I hadn't, but her face was continually in the news. Seeing her on deck did something visceral to me. But before I could do anything about it, she walked right into your arms."

Rini shook his head. "I don't know what to say."

"You don't have to say anything. You couldn't help that she was attracted to you. The fact that I knew you weren't attracted to her didn't help me. I've suffered ever since that night because I've held something against you that couldn't possibly have been your fault. You have every right to tell me to go to hell and stay there."

Rini came closer. "That's the last thing I want to do. All this time you've been suffering…"

"And I've made *you* suffer. I'm so sorry, Rini."

To his shock, his friend smiled. "If I don't miss my guess, I believe cupid shot an arrow into your heart when you laid eyes on Dea. The same thing happened to me when I met Alessandra."

"You're right," he murmured.

"*Paisano*—you've been smitten since the night your father brought Dea and her friend over to meet us after the fashion show. After your experience with Carla, I've wondered for years when love would hit you. Little does your *papà* know his endless machinations to find you a wife finally worked!"

Guido threw his head back. "They did."

"Now that I know your secret, I understand what happened out here on the sand just now. You swung Dea around with more energy than I've ever seen in you. I guess her flying tackle earlier had something to do with your reaction."

"I've never been so surprised in my life."

Rini grinned. "Contact sports can be fun, especially when it was Dea who initiated that move. You must be doing something right or she wouldn't have allowed herself to get in *your* arms."

No one ever had a better friend. Guido cocked his head. "You don't despise me for being a total fool this last year?"

"It's forgotten." He gripped Guido's shoulder. "Listen—I'm going to tell you a secret and I hope you can handle it. You have no idea the number of times I envied you for all the women who threw themselves at you. I didn't have that experience growing up and feared I'd never meet the right woman for me.

"Need I remind you of Arianna, who was so crazy about you she came to every game and hung around you for weeks? I might as well have been invisible. She was gorgeous and I was jealous as hell."

"You're kidding—"

"No. Don't you remember my telling you that I wouldn't have minded if she'd come after me, but it didn't happen? And then there was Carla." Guido preferred not to think about her. "Let's be honest. You could have had any woman you ever wanted."

"Except Dea…who wanted you."

His dark brows lifted. "Dea didn't want me. We talked about it. Growing up in a castle together, she and Alessandra had this idea of marrying a tall, dark-haired prince. My image filled the bill. But that's all it was. The image vanished. If you're asking me if she still sees me as her prince, the answer is a definite no. Surely you could tell that at the wedding. I'm now her irritating brother-in-law."

"She seemed to be in a world of her own that day," Guido said.

"That's because she was going through a major life crisis, another thing you're going through yourself taking on a soccer team. In many ways, you and Dea are a lot alike. You had your pick of women over the years but didn't settle. She always had her pick of men, yet didn't end up with any of them. One day she's going to fall so hard that'll be it. Lucky will be the man who captures her heart."

"Wouldn't it be funny if it turned out to be me," he muttered.

Rini shot him a piercing glance. "You and I both know that no matter how bad it looks, you never leave the stadium until the game is over. Astounding surprises happen in the last second."

"True." Guido couldn't argue with that kind of logic. Nor could he doubt that Rini had given him all the truth inside him.

His friend picked up the ball. "Come on. Let's get back to the *castello*. How soon do you have to return to Rome?"

"I have to fly out early Sunday morning for the game."

"I happen to know Dea will be around until then too. Alessandra had planned a day out on the cruiser for the three of us tomorrow. But with Dea still here, it'll be even more fun. Maybe you can teach her how to water ski. She gave up after trying it the first time."

"She hasn't done any water sports?" Guido was incredulous.

"A little swimming. That's it. But the way she got into the soccer match proves to me she's not only game, she's a fast learner. I only have one question. Are *you* game?"

Until their talk a few minutes ago Guido would have said no.

They returned to the castle, where the girls had dessert and coffee waiting for them in the dining room. Guido enjoyed the snack while they chuckled about Dea's tackle, then he excused himself to go up to bed.

"Don't forget tomorrow," Rini called after him. "Once we've eaten breakfast, we'll go out on the cruiser."

"Sounds good." With a smile for the three of them, he left the room.

Alessandra came to Dea's bedroom the next morning in order to French-braid her hair before breakfast.

"Thanks for doing this for me. I can't do it right. Now it won't get in my face."

"As you know, I had mine cut short years ago because I spent so much time in the water scuba diving."

"I'm thinking I might get mine cut too, after I get back to Rome."

"Oh, no, Dea. Your gorgeous long hair? Are you sure?"

"It drives me insane while I'm working. I used to wonder why Juliana wore her hair short. Now I know. Hair gets in the way when you're kneeling in front of a mannequin to work on a hem. We're constantly bending over to examine a drawing or a cut of fabric. All you need is an irritating strand to fall at a critical moment."

"Well, it's your call," Alessandra murmured. "Now let's hurry down to breakfast before the guys eat everything in sight."

"I just hope Guido's forgiven me for tackling him. I don't know what came over me."

"I do. It's called frustration beyond bearing! They're both so good at everything it can drive you crazy! I'm sure no one ever did such a thing to Guido before."

"That's what has me worried."

"Rini laughed about it after we went to bed. He's sure you're the only woman who ever got the best of Guido."

"Now I'm worried he'll pull something on *me* today."

Alessandra's eyes sparkled. "Just don't let your guard down." Her warning excited Dea.

After her sister left the bedroom, she dressed in shorts and a yellow top worn over her orange-and-white-striped bikini. Once ready, she grabbed her tote bag and flew down the stairs in sandals to the dining room. At the entrance, a pair of inky-blue eyes met hers across the room, causing her pulse to race.

"*Buongiorno*, Dea." His deep voice curled through to her insides.

This morning Guido had put on a white T-shirt

and cargo pants that couldn't hide his powerful legs. He held a mug of coffee and looked so sensational she was taken back. A nervous smile broke out on her face. "I hope you didn't wake up with any aches or pains."

"I'm managing to survive," he mocked gently.

Uh-oh. "Where is everyone?"

"Alessandra grabbed a jam *cornetto* and went out to help Rini load the cruiser. Come and join me before we head out."

Since Guido was still here, maybe it meant he'd been waiting for her. Her heart flipped over again.

"Cook makes the best cappuccino in the world."

"I agree," he murmured over the rim of his cup.

Aware of his scrutiny, she walked over to the hunt board and reached for a pastry. After pouring herself coffee, she moved to the table to eat. Once he joined her, she couldn't resist asking, "Are you a champion water-skier too? Alessandra said Rini can't wait to get out on the water and ski double with you."

He sat back in the chair, studying her through shuttered eyes. "I've done a little of everything."

"But soccer is your passion."

"One of them."

A shiver of excitement ran through her. The intimation of what his other passions might be brought heat to her cheeks. With his dark blond hair slightly disheveled, she discovered he had a potent male appeal no woman could possibly ignore. His girlfriends must be legion.

Once they'd finished breakfast, they left the castle for the dock around the back. During their short walk she thought about him and Rini being such close friends since childhood. They were so different, *except* in two major ways. Their masculine charisma was lethal and they both had an air of authority that seemed to be part of their natures.

Dea had met many men over the years, but none of them possessed those extraordinary qualities. She might have known that Rini's best man would be someone who stood out from all the rest too. He wasn't anything like his father. At least she didn't think so, but what did she know?

Maybe if she'd stayed at the table the night of the wedding reception and had gotten better acquainted with the head of Rossano Shipping Lines, she'd have seen similarities that hadn't been apparent at first. Guido was his son after all.

In the past Dea had had a problem with making snap judgments about people. It came from a fear that people saw her as only a superficial narcissist—an unfair label given to models in general. Her mother had pointed out that she put up a defensive shield because part of her felt insecure. Dea had had to learn to give everyone a chance.

Since she'd gone back to school, she'd been making a conscious effort to get along with people. While she and Gina had been at the shop discussing one of the designs that wasn't working, she'd learned the other woman loved the theater. Dea would never have guessed that—all Gina seemed to talk about was Aldo, who lived in her apartment building.

He worked in a garage and wasn't happy because he couldn't make good money. The last thing he'd do was spend the little he had on going to watch a play he had no interest in. Soccer was a different story. Dea had offered to go to the theater with Gina, who was delighted. They planned to see *Othello* at the Silvano Toti Globe in Rome the next weekend. It would give them a chance to study the costuming while they enjoyed Shakespeare.

"Hey, you two," Rini called to them.

When they reached the cabin cruiser, Dea climbed over the side first. After stowing her tote bag below deck, she came back up and slipped on the life belt Alessandra handed her.

Rini took the wheel and signaled to Guido, who untied the ropes. Dea drew in a deep breath, filled with a sense of anticipation that was new to her. She wouldn't lie to herself. Guido's presence was the reason for this feeling, plus a warm sun that portended a perfect day to be out on the water.

Except for a few freighters way off in the distance, they had the sea to themselves. Five minutes later Rini cut the engine. He shot Guido a glance. The other man had already removed his T-shirt. The sight of his hard-muscled body changed the tenor of Dea's breathing.

"Ready to give the girls a show?"

Guido fastened his life belt. "Whenever you are."

The guys tossed two slalom skis in the water and dove off the transom like porpoises. Alessandra turned to Dea. "While I drive, you get in the back.

Keep an eye on the ropes while they're uncoiling. When the guys are up, spot them. In case they get into any trouble, tell me and I'll cut the engine."

With a legitimate excuse to feast her eyes on Guido, she knelt on the banquette and watched them fasten their skis. Then she heard Rini yell, "Hit it!" Alessandra increased the speed and a minute later both men were out of the water like professionals who'd been doing this for years.

They moved in wide arcs and displayed an expertise on one ski Dea marveled over. How would it be to ski like that? "They're fabulous!" she called to Alessandra. "Have you gotten up on one ski yet?"

"No. It's hard."

I want to learn.

Several minutes went by before she saw Rini lift his free arm. "I think they want to stop," she shouted.

"Okay! Start reeling in the ropes and coil them."

Dea did as she asked and wound the rope. Alessandra brought the cruiser around and cut the engine in order to reach for the skis and put them on the transom. With masculine dexterity, the men heaved themselves aboard. Dea couldn't take her eyes off Guido. The sun bathed him in light. He looked like a golden god as he reached for a towel.

"Bravo," she told both of them.

Rini flicked her a glance. "Think you want to do it?"

She finished coiling the second rope. "I'd like to try, but it won't be on one ski. Can you do it on your feet?"

Deep laughter came out of Guido. "I'm afraid it hurts too much."

"Even though you were a soccer player?"

"Even though. Want to go now?"

No…but she *had* to. That was her new rule. Don't hang back. She'd given up before when she'd gone skiing with Alessandra, but her sister was so good at it that Dea had decided not to try anymore. Thank goodness she'd worked out in a gym close to her apartment all these years in order to stay in shape.

"Sure."

"Good for you. There's very little wind right now. It's the best time."

Rini nodded. "I'll drive and Alessandra will spot you."

"Okay," she said on a jerky breath. *Here goes nothing.* Dea undid the belt in order to remove her clothes, then refastened it.

Guido told her to walk over so he could fit her feet in the skis and adjust them. While he hunkered down, she put a hand on his solid shoulder to steady herself. The warmth from his skin crept into her body. Then she stepped out of the skis with his help.

"I'll go first." He jumped in the water and she handed him the skis. Then it was her turn. Once her head surfaced she felt Guido's hands steady her from behind while Rini started the cruiser and slowly pulled away from them. Alessandra let out the rope.

"Grasp it in your hand while I put the skis on you." Guido did everything with ease. "Now I want you to lie back in my arms and brace your legs so they're ready to come out of the water straight. Don't be frightened. When I call out, 'Hit it,' you'll be pulled right up. Just hold on to the rope with both hands. Let the boat do the rest and don't look down. I'll be right here in case you fall."

"Thank you." Saying a little prayer, she watched until the rope was all the way out. Suddenly she heard Guido's voice and the cruiser leaped forward. To her shock she rose right up on top of the water and was skimming across the placid surface.

Dea couldn't believe she was actually water-skiing again, but she was moving fast and made the mistake of doing the one thing Guido had told her not to do. That's when she lost her balance and let go of the rope. The boat swung around and came alongside her. In a second Guido was there and pulled her back against his chest.

"You were terrific."

"No. I blew it because I looked down."

Her sister smiled at her from the boat. "I didn't get up until four tries."

"Let's do it again," Guido urged her. "Your skis are still on. Throw her the rope, Alessandra, and we'll have another go."

Uh-oh. But she refused to reveal weakness in front of Guido.

Once again Rini sat at the wheel and started the engine while Guido put her in the same position as before. He tugged her braid. "Did you know you have a lethal weapon here?"

"I'm sorry if it flipped you."

"I'll live."

His comment brought a giggle out of her, but it was

lost in a cry when she felt the cruiser take off and pull her on top of the water. More used to the sensation, she stayed up rather inelegantly for over a minute, but her legs were tired because she wasn't used to this.

She lifted her arm and immediately Rini cut the engine. This time when she sank in the water, she didn't panic like before. The belt helped her stay afloat. This was fun. So much fun she couldn't believe she'd lived twenty-eight years without knowing the thrill.

CHAPTER THREE

DEA HAD HEARD the others talking about planning a scuba diving trip. She didn't know if she could ever gird up her courage to take lessons and try it, but she wouldn't say no if she got the chance. That was because she had an excellent teacher in Guido, who was fast approaching. The glint of admiration in those dark blue eyes mesmerized her.

"We'll have you on one ski before the day is out."

"Not now. Two are all I can handle, but one day I plan to get there."

After Guido removed her skis, Rini helped her onto the transom and Alessandra was there to hand her a towel.

Now it was Alessandra's turn to ski while Guido spotted her. Dea let out the rope and watched her sister come out of the water on two skis like a champion.

No longer envious of her sister, she admired her. Once Alessandra had done a four-minute run, they brought her in. Dea praised her sister. As for the adoring look in Rini's eyes, it was something to behold. To be loved like that...

For the next hour they enjoyed an alfresco lunch and spent the rest of the day swimming around the boat and fishing with different lures. Dea had gone trolling with her parents many times in the past, so this wasn't new to her. But the company made it an experience she didn't want to end. Guido and Rini exchanged fishing stories and past shenanigans that had the girls roaring with laughter.

They arrived back at the castle having caught a lot of sun and enough cod to feed everyone, including their parents. The cook grilled it for their dinner. Alessandra and Dea helped in the kitchen to speed up the process for all of them, and they sat down to a delicious meal.

In time they retreated to the dayroom, where her father got out the family movies and turned on the TV screen. "First we'll watch the latest videos of Brazzo."

Alfredo wandered in and climbed on her lap. She hugged the cat to her.

The videos of the baby were adorable. Then her father put in another video.

"This shows you girls playing house with your own play castle when you were six."

Dea had forgotten about that one. They used to set it up in the living room with all kinds of props, dolls and clothes. She and Alessandra wore long make-shift costumes and performed as if they were doing a documentary.

"This is where Dea's dream to become a costume designer began," her father informed them. "She was the one to decide what they would wear."

"I was so bossy it's embarrassing."

Her father smiled. "If you'll notice, Alessandra was much more interested in the boat outside the castle she moved around and around."

Everyone laughed, but Dea was mortified. She hoped the videos would end soon. Dea's prayers were answered when her father finally shut off the TV and her parents went to bed. Then Rini and Alessandra said good-night, leaving her alone with Guido. Her heart beat fast.

"I've enjoyed getting to know you today, Dea. Since we're both working in Rome, I'd like to spend time with you again."

"I had a fun time too, and would like that."

"Then I'll call you later in the week. Much as I'd love to stay up and talk to you longer, I've got to get to bed. I have a big game tomorrow and have to be up early."

"Of course. Good luck. I'm counting on your team to win."

"Thank you. So am I." He got to his feet. Alfredo leaped off her lap to follow him.

"No, no, Alfredo." She jumped up and grabbed him. "You have to go to your own bed." Dea lifted her head to look at Guido. "Good night."

His eyes pierced hers. *"Buonanotte."*

Dea took the cat back to the housekeeper's suite, then went upstairs.

After a luxurious shower, she reached for the laptop and climbed into bed to search for the Scatto Roma website. A world of revelation met her eyes.

For the next hour she was entranced and read every bit of information about the history of the team, the new owner, the players, schedules, stats, the soccer museum and the online store.

When she typed in Guido's name, dozens of references came up. There were galleries of his pictures from when he'd been the sensational soccer player of the day. They called him *Cuor di Leone*, the Lionhearted. The explanation stated that it wasn't in honor of Richard the Lionheart but for Guido's father, Leonides Rossano, who was known as Naples's business lion.

Every picture of the striking, fierce competitor took her breath. Guido had worn his hair longer then. In some pictures it resembled a lion's coloring. She went back to the online shop and picked out two large signed posters of him to be sent to her. One was for Gina to give Aldo.

The other poster she'd keep in the bedroom at her apartment. Dea had never been a typical teen who worshipped boys and musical groups. She'd never had posters on her bedroom walls. This would be her first one.

Because of her insecurities, Dea had never handled boys right at school. Since becoming a model, she could never trust the men she dated to see past her looks. Therapy had taught her she hadn't given them a chance. There'd probably been several great guys she might have fallen in love with if she'd understood herself better.

With a deep sigh, she put the laptop on the floor

and got under the covers, but she didn't fall asleep for a long time. Her mind relived those moments in the water when Guido had cradled her in his arms. He smelled wonderful and made her feel safe and confident enough to move beyond the tight boundaries she'd drawn for herself years ago. She'd see him at breakfast before he left. Morning couldn't come soon enough.

At eight the next day she went down to the dining room and found her parents eating. "*Buongiorno*, darling."

She kissed their cheeks. "Where's everyone else?"

"Your sister and Rini drove Guido to the airport two hours ago."

"Two hours ago?" Dea was shocked.

"He had to get back early for the game. The two of them will be back later."

With the disappointing news that he'd already gone, the bottom fell out of her day. "I have to get back to Rome too."

"But your flight won't leave until three. Sit down and eat breakfast with us. We know we're lucky you would come home with us this weekend. Have you had a good time so far?"

"It's been great." That was the truth.

She poured herself some coffee. Guido had told her he'd phone her. She hoped he meant it. There'd been moments this weekend when she'd thought he was attracted to her, but she'd learned from her sister that Guido had enjoyed his share of girlfriends.

He was her brother-in-law's age, thirty-two, yet

still not engaged or married. Maybe he was this way around all women, making them feel special in the moment without having deeper feelings for them. He couldn't have known she'd be coming to the *castello*. Was he glad to discover she'd come? Would he forget about calling her once he was back in Rome?

A tiny moan escaped. There she went again, making this whole situation about her. He'd said he would phone. But until he did, she had work to do. Her mind cast back to what her mother had told her when she was at her lowest ebb. *One day your prince will find you. In the meantime, work on finding yourself.*

Good advice. *Keep remembering it, Dea. Hit the gym before work and concentrate on the fabulous opportunity of learning from the great Juliana.*

Guido waited until Wednesday morning to phone Rini and Alessandra to thank them for the great weekend.

"Are you telling me you had a better time than you'd imagined?"

"You could say that." Thoughts of Dea had been on his mind ever since. "Before I went to bed that night, I told Dea I'd call her, but I don't have her cell phone number."

"I've got it."

Guido wrote it down. "Thanks for that."

"You're welcome. Congratulations on another win on Sunday. Your name is all over the sports news."

"We're on a roll right now. Here's hoping it lasts."

"I have no doubt of it."

"Thanks again for everything. Talk to you soon."

"Ciao."

At noon Guido phoned Dea, but his call was put through to her voice mail. He wanted to meet her for lunch on Thursday if she was available and asked her to call him back. Later in the day Dea rang back. They decided on a little bistro around the corner near her work. She'd meet him there tomorrow at twelve thirty. With the opera's opening coming up in May, they were swamped with work.

Thursday finally arrived. Guido had been living for it. Even in jeans and a top with her hair pulled back in a chignon, Dea was a standout beauty. She drew the attention of everyone when she walked in the foyer, but no one more than Guido, who'd arrived ten minutes ahead of time to wait for her.

A smile lit up her face. "Hi, Guido! I hope I'm not too late."

"I'm early," he explained. "Shall we eat outside?"

"I'd love it. The workrooms tend to suffocate you when we're all in there running around for this and that."

The waiter showed them to a table and they sat down while he took their order. "I'm glad I called ahead for a table. This place is crowded."

She nodded. "It's so popular I've only been here once. And that time we had to wait in line for a half hour, which made us late for work."

"Us?"

"My friend Gina, who works at the shop too. I told you about her. By the way, congratulations on your win last Sunday. You must be feeling on top of the world."

"That feeling lasted until Monday morning."

She chuckled. "So your fears are working up to a frenzy again for this coming Sunday?"

"*Frenzy* is the right word."

Their pasta arrived. "While the waiter is here, would you like some wine?"

"Not during my workday, thank you. Just coffee."

"You're no fun."

"It wouldn't be so funny if I designed the skinny pants for the baritone and they ended up being for the fat tenor, who couldn't pull them on."

Guido burst into laughter. "I see where you're going with this. You've made your case."

Dea was working her charm on him and it made him nervous as hell, but he couldn't identify the reason why until after she'd told him she had to get right back to work. He followed her through the restaurant to the front door.

"Thanks for lunch, Guido. I enjoyed this break with you."

"So did I. I'll phone you again."

"Good. Ciao."

He watched her walk off. So did every other male in sight, many of whom had probably recognized the famous supermodel.

On the drive back to his apartment, he figured out what was wrong with him. Dea wasn't just any woman. She had the title of princess, if she ever wanted to use it, but he couldn't see her doing that.

What worried him was that she'd become his addiction since their unexpected time at the castle. He knew he wanted a serious relationship with her, but would a princess consider what he did for a living to be something suitable?

Guido's father had always been very negative about soccer being a proper career. The comments he had made in the past were never very far from the surface, and they came back to haunt Guido now. For the next few days he let that concern prevent him from calling Dea again.

On Saturday afternoon Guido was getting ready to leave the stadium and found Sergio in the mail room. "How come you're still here?"

"I've had to stay open until the suppliers delivered this week's inventory. A few more orders need to get mailed out before I go to my sister's place for a party."

"That sounds fun. Before I leave, tell me, what's selling the most?"

"Besides T-shirts, our signed soccer balls and autographed posters of our team's stars, of course. We can't keep in enough of the ones of Drago and Dante."

That figured. The two forwards were the current rage. Guido's brows lifted. "How many requests came in for posters of you?"

"Give it up, Guido. None this week, but last weekend someone ordered two posters of you. They picked the one of you making the point that won our game against Team Lancio. I blinked when I saw the name."

"Why?"

"How many women do you know with the name

Dea? You know who I'm talking about. Italy's own Helen of Troy."

Guido's heartbeat skidded off the charts. "I imagine there are hundreds of Deas living in Italy," he muttered in a gravelly voice. Sergio knew nothing about Guido's private life.

"You're probably right."

"Don't keep your family waiting. I'll see you tomorrow before the game."

"Ciao, boss."

He left the stadium and went out to the parking lot for his car. Tonight his parents had invited him for dinner at the family villa in Naples. He'd take the helicopter from the airport.

During the flight he couldn't stop thinking about Dea. It had to be a coincidence that someone with the same name had ordered from the store. Much as he wished he could forget it, he remained preoccupied throughout the evening with his parents. It was good to see them, but he was anxious to get back to Rome before it grew too late.

After his return, he had every intention of driving straight to his apartment. But at the last second he turned off the main route and headed for the stadium. He wouldn't be able to sleep until he knew who had ordered those posters.

The night watchman nodded to him before he let himself inside the store. Once on the computer, he found the week's invoices and scrolled down until he saw a name and address near the bottom that stood out like a flashing red light. *Dea Caracciolo, Via Giustiniani 2, Roma, Italia.*

She'd ordered them the previous Saturday night.

The breath Guido had been holding escaped. That exclusive, pricey address was near the Pantheon, not far from the soccer stadium. She'd ordered two posters of him. He remembered her telling him about her friend Gina, whose fiancé, Aldo, wanted to meet him. Maybe Dea had decided to buy her a signed poster of Guido to give to him. But why had she ordered two?

Guido walked through to the mail room. No tubes or packaged soccer balls were in the out basket. That meant Sergio had taken all the mail to the post office on his way home. She would have received them by now.

The worry he'd felt since their lunch was suddenly replaced by a flicker of hope that his job didn't turn her off. But ordering some posters from the store could mean anything. Guido would be a fool to jump to conclusions until he saw her again.

If he hadn't stopped in to talk to Sergio for a minute, he would never have known she'd ordered something from the store. Every Italian male was halfway in love with Dea's image. It was no surprise his business partner had picked up on her name immediately.

Preoccupied with thoughts of her, he locked up and drove home to his apartment. Morning would come early—he would be meeting with the team and the coaches then. The game against Genoa tomorrow would be critical. Granted, his team had been riding a wave since last November with only one loss, but that could change. A defeat at this stage would tell the soccer world that Team Scatto Roma wasn't ready to compete at A-tier status.

Five more games to go. The season would be over at the end of May. Tonight his father had asked him if he intended to continue for a second season. Guido couldn't give him an answer, but he'd promised to work part-time at the shipping office during June and July. That was as much as he could agree to and still run summer-camp training sessions with the team.

There were other businessmen who would love to buy him out if the team won the national B championship at the end of May. But the decision to sell was still a long way off. Going back to the shipping firm full-time meant signing on as CEO. Guido wasn't ready for that. At the moment he loved the work he was doing. Whether that translated into being fully involved in the soccer world for the rest of his life was a question he couldn't answer yet.

When he'd made the decision to buy a failing team, some element in his life had been missing. It was still missing. The more he thought about it, the more he feared that no matter what path he took, his life would go on to be unfulfilling without the right woman.

Now that he'd spent some time with a Dea he hadn't known existed, the truth of that statement stood out as nothing else could have. He'd lived with her image for a long time, but with that tackle, she'd gotten under his skin in a brand-new way. There was a fire in her he wanted, needed to explore.

Guido fell into bed experiencing alternate waves of

anxiety and excitement at the thought of being with her again. He needed to call her but couldn't handle falling so hard for her only to meet with eventual rejection because his choice of career didn't meet her expectations.

If those posters had been ordered for her friend only, then he didn't want to know about it.

Stadio Emanuele held seventy thousand fans. Dea had researched everything on the website before hiring a taxi to drop her off Sunday afternoon. Tickets for the game against the soccer team from Genoa were still available, but she had to get to the ticket office two hours before the match started.

She'd never been to a sporting event. Men, women, children of all ages made up the massive crowd. They were fired up and so noisy already she could hardly hear herself think. This was sheer craziness.

After standing in line for twenty minutes, it was her turn. She asked for the best ticket on the long side—as if she knew what she was talking about— and was charged 130 euros. Before she went to her seat, she wanted to visit the soccer museum, but she found out it would be open for only fifteen more minutes.

She had to wait to get inside, but by the time she reached the doors, the person in charge announced the museum was closing. If people wanted to see pictures and videos of the all-time best Italian soccer greats, they would have to come another day. People filed out.

Dea stood aside until the last one had gone. "Signor? When will you be open again?"

"Tomorrow afternoon."

"Until how late?"

"Seven o'clock."

"I'll come after I get off work." She wanted to see videos of Guido that couldn't be viewed anywhere else.

The attractive Italian in charge gave her a long look of male admiration and approached her. He'd probably been a soccer player himself, but she noticed he had a very slight limp. "I've seen you before, signorina. You're Dea the model, aren't you?"

Uh-oh. "How did you know?"

He let out a hearty laugh. "Surely you are joking." His hand went over his heart. "Your pictures are on the inside of half the locker doors in the gym here at the stadium."

Heat rushed to her cheeks. "I think you're full of it, but thank you for the compliment. Now I'd better get going and find my seat before the match begins, but I'll be back."

"You're here alone?"

"Yes."

"Is this your first time at the stadium?"

"Yes."

"Be careful. It can get rowdy out there during a game."

"I've heard, but I can take care of myself."

He grinned. "I'll look for you tomorrow."

She thanked him, then left the store to make her way through the crowds to her seat.

The next two hours felt like being on a giant roller-coaster ride, taking her emotions up and down. She'd never sat through anything so riveting. Many times she saw those few moves Guido had taught her. They helped her understand the game a little because she'd been taught by a master. Her admiration for him grew seeing his team play like this.

To her chagrin, the score remained tied until the last few seconds, when Guido's team had a break-through by the crowd favorite Dante. When his kick got past the goalie, the crowd let out a deafening roar. Everyone went wild over the two–one score, scream-ing, "Dante! Dante!"

Dea was elated for Guido, but she barely escaped the pandemonium inside the stadium with her life. Thank goodness she'd arranged for a taxi ahead of time to meet her outside. Otherwise she would have been forced to walk blocks.

She asked the driver to stop at a deli so she could take food home to eat. Later, after getting comfort-able on the couch, she watched the ten o'clock news. The sports segment featured a clip of the soccer game. She heard the announcer praise the rise of the Scatto Roma team and pictures of Dante were flashed on the screen. Guido had to be so proud.

After working up some new costume sketches for tomorrow, she went to bed and got up early to go to the gym before reporting to the shop for work. The costumes for *Don Giovanni* were shaping up. She worked hard and didn't lift her head until five thirty.

Though she'd planned to go to the stadium museum after work this evening, she changed her mind. If she ran into Guido by mistake, he wouldn't believe it was a mistake.

The man who worked at the soccer museum had recognized her on Sunday, and she realized he had to be a friend of Guido's. She should have disguised herself. If he happened to mention that she'd been in the museum, Guido would suspect she'd been looking for him.

Because he hadn't phoned her since their lunch, that was the last thing she wanted him to think. *Let your prince find you.*

By Thursday she was totally deflated that Guido hadn't tried to reach her. At the end of work she found Gina and handed her a tube. "I have a present for Aldo."

"What?"

"Open the end and see."

Gina did her bidding and pulled out the signed poster of a twenty-year-old Guido caught in action midair with the banner *Cuor di Leone*. "Oh, Dea—" She lifted shining eyes to her. "Aldo's going to be thrilled when I give him this."

Dea had been just as thrilled when she opened her own tube and spread the poster on her bed. It now graced her bedroom wall. How she would have loved to meet the dashing athlete back then!

"I'm sorry it was already signed when it was printed."

"That doesn't matter. Isn't he gorgeous? Of course, I don't dare tell Aldo that."

"That might be wise." No man compared to Guido.

"You're fantastic, Dea!" She put the poster down and hugged her so hard she almost knocked her over. "How much do I owe you?"

"Nothing. I wanted to do this for you."

"Ooh." She squealed. "I'm so glad work is over. I'm going to drive by the garage and surprise him with it. You're the best friend I ever had."

Dea watched her run out of the shop. It had made her glad to see her new friend this happy. While she was cleaning up a few minutes later, the middle-aged receptionist came in the back room.

"Dea? There's a man here to see you."

Her heartbeat picked up. She lifted her head. "Did he give you his name?"

"He only said he'd come from the museum at the Stadio Emanuele."

Museum? How had the man running it found out she worked here? "Please tell him I'll be right out."

Most everyone had left already. She hurried into the ladies' room to freshen up and make sure the clip holding her chignon in place was still secure. Her uniform was a pair of sneakers, jeans and a top. Today she'd worn a simple red tee with short sleeves.

She went back in the room for her purse and made her way through the shop past all the racks of costumes to the reception area. Her footsteps slowed. Instead of the dark-haired man from the museum, she spied the dark blond male who'd been haunting her dreams. He stood in front of a dozen framed photographs of Juliana taken at various operas.

Dressed in beige chinos and a silky black shirt with an open collar and short sleeves, his tall, well-honed physique captured her gaze. She couldn't look anywhere else. "Guido?" she asked in a breathless voice. Dea had feared he might never call her again.

He turned to her. Those midnight blue eyes raked over her from head to toe, spilling warmth through her body. "I'm glad I caught you before you left," he said in his deep voice. "My business partner and former soccer buddy Sergio Colombo told me you were going to come by the museum on Monday. When you didn't show, I'm afraid he was very disappointed."

Her brows met in a delicate frown. "I don't understand."

"When an order for two posters came in online, he was the one who sent them out to a Dea Caracciolo. As soon as you walked in the museum, he recognized you as the famous model and made the connection. You're all he could talk about. Surely you know you made a conquest of him?"

After being in therapy, she didn't like that word anymore. Was this all about Sergio? "He was very nice and warned me to be careful in case the crowd got too boisterous."

"He is nice, but he's become supersensitive since his divorce. Why didn't you come?"

"Please tell him I had to work later than planned." Guido probably saw through her lie, but she wasn't about to tell him the truth.

He moved closer with his hands on his hips. The tension was thick between them. "Did you enjoy the soccer match Sunday?"

"I loved it, actually. Even with the few moves you taught me, I was able to understand some of it and enjoy it. Congratulations on your win. My ears rang with Dante's name all the way home in the taxi."

A glimmer of a smile hovered at one corner of his compelling mouth. He cocked his head. "I was in the dugout. But if I'd known you wanted to see a match, you could have sat in my suite to watch it."

"I should think the last thing the owner of the team would want is to worry about entertaining a guest while you're invested in an important game like that one."

"It depends on the guest. Why didn't you just call and ask me to send you a couple of posters?"

She sucked in her breath. "I didn't want to impose on you. It was easy enough to go online. They were for my friend."

"So I gathered. Now that we have matters clarified, the reason I'm here is to ask you out to dinner. If you come with me, you'll win my forgiveness for being ignominiously tackled. You owe me that much."

Another rush of heat swept through her. Looking at his virile physique now, she couldn't believe she'd done such a thing. "I'll never live it down."

"I won't hold it against you forever," he drawled in a seductive tone. "Do you have plans for this evening?"

"No," she answered honestly. "I intended to go

home for a meal and watch a little television before going to bed."

"You like TV?"

"A good film is one of my guilty pleasures."

"Can you give it a miss long enough to spend the evening with me?"

Thump, thump went her heart. The last time she'd seen him was at the bistro. But her fear that she'd never see him again had vanished because he was standing right here in front of her. Dea wanted to get to know him better and this was her chance.

"I'd like that very much, but I'll need to go home first and change."

"*Bene.* I'll drive you."

"I have my own car."

"Then I'll follow and wait for you in front of your apartment."

At this point he probably knew exactly where she lived. "My car is parked in the alley around the corner. It won't take me long."

"That's good. Plan to wear whatever you like."

Dea felt feverish with anticipation as she drove to her apartment. In the rearview mirror she could see Guido behind the wheel of a sleek black Lamborghini.

She pulled into the private parking area and hurried up to her apartment. Since he wore casual attire, she didn't want to be overdressed. After a quick shower, she put on a silky thin-striped shirtdress in tan and cream with a drawstring at the waist and a curved shirttail hem. The sleeves fell to the elbow, a classic look. She teamed a pearl clip that held her hair in place with a small pair of pearl earrings.

Once she'd slipped on tan heels, she applied lipstick and felt ready. When she left the apartment and approached his car waiting at the entrance, she trembled to think this fabulous man wanted to be with her this evening.

He levered himself from the driver's seat and opened the door for her. She felt his gaze play over her as she got inside. "You look stunning," he murmured near her cheek. His breath sent rivulets of delight through her.

Dea had heard compliments like that for years. But for those words to come from him meant more to her than he would ever know.

"You look great out of uniform too."

Her daring comment caused him to laugh out loud before he closed the door and went around to get behind the wheel. She loved hearing his deep chuckle before he pulled onto the main road. The scent of the soap he used filled the interior. He drove with expertise, maneuvering through Rome's hectic evening traffic with ease.

To her surprise, they ended up at the heliport at the airport. She turned to him. "Where are we headed?"

"It's a surprise. We'll be at our destination within a half hour."

She took a deep breath. "That sounds exciting." Where on earth were they going?

"I hope it will be. Come on. The pilot is waiting for us."

Within minutes they'd climbed aboard the helicopter. She sat in the back while he took the copilot's seat. Dea was no stranger to flights in helicopters. Seeing Rome from the air was an experience she was very familiar with, but right now she couldn't focus on anything but the striking male seated in front of her.

The scenery changed and after a little while the helicopter dipped. She glimpsed Mount Vesuvius in the distance. Her breath quickened as they descended and suddenly the pilot set them down on a helipad. She looked out the windows and realized they'd landed on a *ship*.

Not just any ship.

He opened the door and put out his hand to help her down into the balmy night air. She turned to him in bewilderment. "You've brought us to the yacht."

Guido's jaw tightened perceptibly. Something was going on inside him she didn't understand. He drew her away from the helicopter. "Let's start again, Signorina Loti. Welcome to Naples."

Time stood still while Guido's words sank in. Dea's thoughts flew back to that night on the yacht when she'd been introduced to him. But in her mind, she hadn't been able to see him because his best friend had stood next to him and taken her breath.

"When you look back on that night, do you even remember me?" he asked in a teasing voice.

She swallowed hard. What did he want her to say? Dea needed help. "Rini turned and asked me to dance. I never had a chance to talk to you again."

"Would it surprise you if you knew *I'd* wanted to

be the one to dance with you first? But Rini stood closer to you."

Oh, no… "I had no idea. Your fath—"

"My father forced us on you and your model friend," he interrupted her. "But let's admit Rini was your choice. You couldn't take your eyes off him and I didn't stand a chance."

CHAPTER FOUR

DEA STARTED TO TREMBLE. She thought she'd put the memory of that night behind her, but Guido had brought it up because it had obviously been painful for him too. She'd heard it in his voice. "I—I'm sorry," she stammered.

"Don't be. It wasn't anyone's fault and it happened over a year ago. I brought you here in the hope that tonight I could wine and dine you with no other distractions."

He meant Rini.

This was the time for honesty no matter how frightened she was to discuss such a sensitive issue for both of them. "I admit I was attracted to Rini, but it was one-sided."

She heard him take a quick breath. "Are you over him?"

Guido knew how to go for the jugular. It was part of his makeup. She bit her lip. Rini was his best friend. The answer to Guido's loaded question could spell life or death for a future relationship with him. If he wanted one. She lifted her eyes to him.

"His looks filled an image I'd carried in my mind since I was a girl, but it had no substance. I was never into Rini, because he was a figment of my imagination. Amazingly, Alessandra carried that same image in her mind. We're not twins for nothing. But the moment she met Rini, that image took on substance for her and she fell hard.

"The beauty is, he fell hard for her too and pursued her. As you know, they're madly in love and terribly happy. Believe me when I tell you I'm beyond happy for them. I hope that answers your question. Please tell me it does," she pleaded with him.

After a long silence, he said, "Your honesty has blown me away." To her relief, he broke into a smile that melted her bones. "You're good at doing that."

"Am I never to hear the end of it?" she teased.

"I don't know. Come on." He cupped her elbow and walked her over to the covered dining area on the top deck. "Are you seeing another man right now, Dea?"

"No. What about you? Is there a woman in your life at the moment?"

"Only you."

One table had been set for them with candles and flowers. Guido helped her sit down, then poured some wine for both of them.

"I take it we're alone."

"I told you there'd be no distractions tonight."

The steward brought their food to the table and removed the covers. A wonderful aroma of fish with lemon and rosemary wafted in the night air.

She smiled. "In other words, your parents won't show up."

"Not tonight." His eyes searched hers. "Tell me—did they say or do something that made you uncomfortable at the wedding reception?"

"Not at all, Guido. I'm afraid I wasn't myself that day and am sorry if it showed."

But she could tell he wouldn't let it go when he asked, "Was it my father making you uncomfortable? What did he say when he talked to you and your friend after the fashion show?"

She put down her fork. "Nothing. He simply wanted us to meet you and your best friend before we left the yacht."

"Papà came on strong, didn't he?" Dea averted her eyes. "I knew it. There are times when he can be unbearable."

"That's because he loves you so much and is proud of you."

"You were probably afraid I was made in his image."

Guido was so intuitive it was scary. "You and your father bear a physical resemblance. Was he an outstanding soccer player too?"

"He had no interest in the sport."

"But he came to all your games."

"Yes."

"Lucky you."

"He's a hunter."

She took another bite of fish. "Do you hunt too?"

"Maybe once a year when I go with him, but I prefer fly-fishing. What about your father?"

Dea smiled. "Dad would rather camp out with our family."

"That's something else I'm crazy about," he informed her.

"It's so fun."

After the steward brought them a pastry dessert, Guido changed the subject. "What are you doing Saturday night?"

She got a fluttery feeling in her chest. "Gina and I are going to see *Othello*. We made arrangements for it last week."

"Then getting together with you this weekend is out since I have another match on Sunday in Bologna."

He'd be out of town. Maybe he was as disappointed as she was. "When will you be back?"

"Monday."

Dea wanted to see him again too. "What's your Monday evening like?"

A flicker lit up his eyes. "What do you have in mind?"

"After work I'll pick up some groceries and fix us dinner at my apartment."

"She cooks too?"

The warmth of his smile invaded her insides. "I spent years in the *castello* kitchen after school watching and learning from the cook. When she did her shopping in Metaponto on the weekends, I often went with her."

"But you don't have to cook for me."

"I'd like to. It's fun now that I can eat things I long for. The only drawback is cooking for one."

"I know what you mean. I normally eat out."

"So—" she rolled her eyes "—you chip, drop, kick, sweep and cook too?"

The corners of his arresting male mouth turned up. "Tell you what. After you get home from work on Monday, call me and I'll pick you up. We'll go shopping and spend a culinary evening together."

"Be sure to bring a video of your game against Bologna. I'd like to see at least a part of it."

"If we lose, I won't bother to bring it."

She studied him over the rim of her wineglass. "You *won't* lose."

"How do you know?" he whispered.

"Your team played its heart out last Sunday. I imagine they'll do it again and again."

"That's the kind of faith that helps me push them. On that positive note, I'll get us back to Rome."

"This was a long way to come, Guido. We could have gone anywhere to eat."

His features grew serious. "True. But it was important to me that I erase the bad memory of that night from my mind by doing this again."

She moaned inwardly. "I never meant t—"

"I know you didn't," he broke in. "We'll never talk about it again. Thank you for coming with me." He stood up and helped her from the table. They walked toward the helipad at the other end of the yacht with his arm at the back of her waist. The Bay of Naples glittered with lights, making a glorious sight. To be with Guido like this thrilled her.

"Please thank the steward and the cook. The food was delicious," she said before climbing in the helicopter.

"I'll tell them." She felt his hands squeeze her hips gently before she moved all the way inside. He shouldn't have touched her like that. It sent a voluptuous curl of heat through her body.

For Guido to bring her all the way here to clear up something so vital meant his attraction to her was more than skin-deep. Guido was a man of great substance. But he'd been hurt; otherwise he wouldn't have asked if she was over Rini. To embark on a relationship with him, they had to build total trust between them.

His sensitive nature had picked up on her pain at the wedding. If she got the chance, she'd explain to him that she'd been going through her own personal crisis that had nothing to do with his parents or anyone else.

Dea shivered. The whole issue with Rini was hard to explain, but it was long since over. Much as she was dying to get to know Guido better, she realized there were things he was holding back from her about himself. She would work on getting him to tell her what was wrong.

The flight from Bologna touched down at the airport at one on Monday afternoon. Their one–nil win had made the whole team giddy. After a training session at the stadium with the players and coaches, Guido drove home on fire for the evening planned with Dea.

It seemed like months instead of days since their dinner on Thursday night.

He watched the video of the game and made notes. But he kept waiting for the phone to ring and lost his concentration. When it finally rang and he saw the caller ID, he picked right up.

"Dea?"

"Are you back?"

"I've been at the apartment several hours. How are you?"

"Relieved to know you made it home safely." He liked hearing that. "Your win was all over the news last night. You must be ecstatic."

He was ecstatic all right, but she was the underlying reason for this joie de vivre he'd never felt before. "What time should I pick you up?"

"If you'll give me an hour, I'll be ready. But why don't we walk to the market at the Via della Pace? It's close and they'll have everything we need."

"I'll be outside the entrance waiting for you. *A presto*, Dea."

Guido showered and shaved. As he was finding out, anytime he was with Dea, surprising things happened. To go grocery shopping with her would no doubt be an adventure, followed by a casual night at home. It was exactly what he needed after the stressful weekend when once again he thought the team wouldn't win until the last few seconds.

He pulled on a sport shirt and jeans, grabbed the

disc with the video and left. Once he'd found a parking space near her apartment, he walked to the entrance expecting to have to wait. Instead she was outside drawing the interest of every male in the vicinity.

Why not? She was wearing taupe-colored trousers topped with a sheer flutter blouse in a pale blue. The hem fell to her waist, emphasizing the feminine curves of her body. A mesh shopping bag hung from her fingers.

Her long, sparkling brown hair with its gold highlights was tied at the nape with a thin pale blue ribbon. Her natural beauty staggered him. When she saw him, she broke into a smile that lit up her eyes. He moved closer, already feeling out of breath. "I've been looking forward to this evening."

"Me too. Are you hungry?"

She should know better than to ask him a question like that. "Starving. I skipped lunch in anticipation of tonight."

"Good. I plan to feed you well. We only need to buy a few items. It's just a short walk after we reach the corner."

"I want the exercise. It helps me unwind."

"I know what you mean."

Exhilarated to be with her, he headed down the street with her. "What's on the menu for tonight?"

"Chicken Tetrazzini. I thought it would be a nice change from fish."

"I like anything."

"Sounds like you're an easy man to please. Lucky

for me." They rounded the corner and soon arrived at the market. "Help me find chicken breasts, white mushrooms and linguine. I'll gather the rest."

"Like what?"

"Parmesan cheese, fresh garlic, onions, parsley and thyme, and cream."

"We'll need a good wine too."

"Why don't you pick it out."

He knew a Tuscan Chianti that would go well with their dinner. They worked together. She reached for some herb focaccia bread and he found a couple of *baba al limoncello* pastries.

Guido paid for the groceries and carried the bag home. It was bursting at the seams. He slanted her a glance. "Just a few items," he ribbed her.

"I guess I'm a typical woman after all. Sorry if it's heavier than a soccer ball…"

"I'm relieved your apartment is only a couple more steps away. I just might make it."

"Let's hope there's no reporter hanging around trying to take a picture of the famous soccer player in your sad condition." Her comments continually amused him. "Tell you what. Once we're inside, you can stretch out on the couch and watch the game while I cook."

"I thought *you* wanted to watch it."

"I do. I'll come in and out of the kitchen."

"That won't work. We'll cook together, then eat while we watch. I want to hear your commentary."

"It won't be worth much."

"Let me be the judge of that."

"The bathroom is down that hall if you'd like to freshen up."

"Thank you."

Her elegant apartment reminded him she was a woman who had the title of Princess Caracciolo and Taranto. But the way she behaved, you'd never know she came from a long line of aristocrats. She'd worked her way around the market picking out what she wanted and taking her time like any Italian housewife. Surely he'd never seen a more beautiful one.

As he came out of the bathroom, he passed her bedroom, then backtracked in slow motion. On the wall next to the window was a poster. To his shock, it was the one of a younger Guido. She'd kept this one for herself. The sight of it gave him a heart attack.

He checked his breathing before going back to the living room. Within a half hour delicious aromas filled the apartment. She made a place on her coffee table in front of the television. He poured the wine while she went back to the kitchen for their plates.

Guido could see doing this for the rest of his life. Never had he been with a woman who caused his thoughts to expand as far as marriage. Since he'd taken her to the yacht, part of him was alarmed by the depth of his feelings for her because he didn't know if he trusted everything she'd told him concerning Rini.

He had no doubt she'd spoken the truth as much as she could admit. But he sensed there was more she was holding back from him. Since it involved his best friend, he couldn't be satisfied with a half confession any more than he could a half loaf of bread, especially not now, when he knew what was hanging on the wall in her bedroom. The poster's presence had to mean something vital.

He would have to go on seeing her to learn the whole truth. Maybe that would involve digging it out of her soul. Until then he would spend as much time as possible with her because he couldn't help himself. At this point she was on his mind day and night.

They watched part of the game, but she fired questions at him that suggested she really wanted to understand. He was only too happy to oblige.

"Are your players trained into the ground?"

His lips twitched. "Maybe not into the ground. On an individual basis they train by working out hard, running a lot, eating right, practicing skills. If you have a love for it, it isn't so hard."

She sat back against the cushion of the couch. "So what part do you play as the owner?"

"I'm like one of the coaches and get right in there. When we're not out on the field, the players work out in the gym. I work on them to focus on abs and quads. They need to increase their agility and endurance."

A glint of amusement entered her marvelous eyes. "Do they hate to see you coming?"

"Always. When the other coaches are through, I usually make the team run a variety of drills and practice plays. I force them to concentrate on being as fit as possible by combining sprints with long runs."

"Well, it's certainly paying off. You've only lost one game this year."

"True, but we barely won yesterday's. That's got me nervous. I don't want the team to get comfortable."

She took another sip of wine. "Do you have a motto?"

He nodded. "Discipline yourself so others don't!"

"What a great slogan! It makes perfect sense."

"I'm glad you approve."

"Are you kidding? Let's watch the end of the game and see if your team has taken your words to heart."

After fifteen minutes it was over. She wanted to know how many players were on a team, their positions and tactical skills. "How did you train when you were high school age?"

"I started soccer at seven."

"I should have remembered that."

Even if she was being polite, it flattered him that she would show this much interest in the game.

"During the summers, when I had no guidance, I'd start by running hills with my friends. Later on I'd work on sprints and sudden bursts of speed. Then again, I always had to have a ball at my feet so I wouldn't lose touch until soccer practice started.

"I went to as many matches as I could attend and played every position, including defender, goalie and midfield. But my favorite position was forward."

"The position you excelled at until you became the epic champion."

His brows lifted. "Epic?"

"That's you. I'm truly in awe of you, Guido."

"It's past history."

"But that excellence is living on in your team. Are you happy you left the shipping company to do this?"

"Yes, but whether I decide to own and manage a soccer team for the rest of my life isn't a question I can answer yet."

"I bet your father wants you back."

"Yes, but I won't do it unless I can embrace it a hundred percent. Let me ask you a question. Are you happy your modeling career is behind you?"

A shadow entered her eyes. "You want to know the truth?"

"What do you think?"

"I went to college to study fashion design, something I'd always been interested in. But by the time I was halfway through, I couldn't seem to produce something that wasn't mediocre. I felt like Salieri in the film *Amadeus*."

Guido would have laughed if he didn't know how serious this was. "You're referring to the Italian composer at the time of Mozart."

"Yes. As someone put it, you have to squint your ears and listen for the magic. If you can sense a supernatural beauty within, you know it's Mozart. If it's just music, it's not Mozart and probably someone like Salieri."

"You were awfully hard on yourself."

"I know. Halfway through school I was approached by the agency that hired me to model for them. I thought I'd take a year off school and try it."

Guido was fascinated. "Did you love it?"

"*Love* is a strong word. I enjoyed the first year

very much, but after that I sensed a lot was lacking in my life. The problem was, I felt it was too soon to give it up. I knew I could go back to school, but what if I failed to find my true calling? The owners of the agency put a lot of pressure on me to remain with them."

"You made a lot of money for them."

"Money runs the world." She didn't sound happy about it. For once he'd met a woman who wasn't impressed by the Rossano name and fortune.

"So tell me how you came to work for Juliana Parma now."

She shook her head. "I don't want to bore you."

"You mean the way I've bored you for the last two hours?"

A small laugh escaped her throat. She looked at him. "Throughout my life, my parents and aunt and uncle have taken me to the opera. I'd sit in my seat and envy the singers whose voices could bring such pleasure to people, to me. I cried through every opera. I thought if God had given me a great voice, I would go on singing forever."

His throat thickened with emotion. "God gave you another gift, Dea. You've thrilled a lot of people modeling the clothes of famous fashion designers."

She sat forward. "That's the point. It was the designers who created all the haute couture fashions. I envied their brilliance. All I did was walk around to display them."

"But those designers needed a woman like you to carry them off to the greatest advantage."

"Thank you for trying to build me up. In time I realized that the only thing that could make me truly happy was to create something of my own, something that came from me. That's probably how you feel about soccer. It comes from *you*, no one else."

Dea got that right. "When I saw you and Alessandra in that video, even at your young age your father acknowledged that you had an aptitude for design."

"That's because I wasn't good at anything else."

"I could argue with you, but I'm afraid you wouldn't listen. Go on and tell me about Juliana."

"Many times our family went backstage to talk to her. I saw how much she loved her work and I could understand because her creations brought life to the singers on the stage. The richness of the sets and clothes makes the opera so fantastic.

"When you watch them perform in street clothes, it's so different from casting them into their parts with all the trappings. It's a kind of magic she creates.

"After I went back to finish school, I knew I wanted to do what she did." Tears filled her eyes. "My aunt made it possible for me to work under her this semester. You'll never know what a great honor that is."

"I think I do. I've attended many operas in my life. What you've admitted helps me understand why I've enjoyed it so much."

"She designs for the theater too. The other night Gina and I were engrossed in the costuming for *Othello*. Bringing in the Moorish elements made it very exciting. In the future I hope I can be a part of such a project."

"With a drive like yours, I have no doubts." It was getting late and he knew she had work early in the morning. The last thing he wanted to do was overstay his welcome, but he needed to do this right. He sensed in his gut this woman could change his life. "Let me help with the dishes before I leave."

"Those are my department tonight."

"Your food was fabulous. I hope you know that."

"Thank you." He reached for the disc and she walked him to the door. "I'm so glad you came over tonight."

"We'll have to do it again. I'll be in touch."

She opened the door. "I'd like that."

Much as he wanted to crush her in his arms and kiss the daylights out of her, he didn't dare. He was a greedy man. The poster on her wall still wasn't enough. He wanted to hear her bare her soul to him.

Like Carla, who'd hovered in the recesses of his mind because she'd judged him lacking, was Rini still lurking somewhere in her psyche because he hadn't wanted her? That's what he needed to find out. But that kind of deeply buried secret would take time to emerge—he'd have to get the whole truth from her. He couldn't be with her much longer and not find out.

"Thank you for tonight." He cupped the side of her lovely face with his hand before walking down the hall to the elevator. The warmth of her skin stayed with him all the way out to his car for the drive home.

CHAPTER FIVE

THURSDAY EVENING AT the close of work, Gina and her fiancé, Aldo, were waiting for Dea at the front entrance. After introductions were made, the cute auburn-haired mechanic shook her hand.

"Thanks for the poster. Since you won't take any money for it, let us buy you dinner."

"That's very nice of you, but I have a better idea. How would you like to see the soccer game on Sunday?"

"I can only afford seats behind the goalie."

"I know a better place to sit and have a friend who'll lower the price for you."

He squinted at her. "Are you serious?"

"Yes. Follow me to the stadium and we'll buy them now. You can tour the museum at the same time. It doesn't close until seven." Now Dea had a great excuse to see the videos of Guido without his thinking she was chasing after him.

"That would be wonderful!" Gina hugged her.

"I must be dreaming," Aldo murmured. "I've heard this game is already a sellout."

"One thing I've learned—they always have tickets. I'll get my car."

She hurried off. Before long the three of them arrived at the stadium and parked near the suite of offices. There was a long line of people waiting to buy tickets. "Why don't you get in line while I go in the museum. I'll only be a minute."

When she went inside, she saw that another man was in charge. She went up to him. "Is there any way I can talk to Sergio if he's here?"

His eyes swept over her. "You're the famous model!"

"Past tense. Could you get in touch with him?"

"He's running the ticket booth. Maybe I can help."

"Thank you, but no. He's the one I have to talk to."

"Just a minute." He pulled out his phone and made a call. After a minute Sergio walked in the rear door. She ran over to him.

"I'm sorry to bother you, but I need a favor. There's a couple at the back of the ticket line. He has dark red hair. Give him the very best seats you can for Sunday's game, but only charge him the cheapest price. I'll make up the rest." She opened her wallet and pulled out enough euros to cover it.

"I'll be happy to. Don't go away."

"I won't. After they get the tickets, we're going to spend time in here. Maybe you can give him the royal tour. It would mean everything to him and a lot to me."

"Sure thing."

He left through the same door. Dea thanked the other man and went outside to find Gina. Fifteen min-

utes later they'd bought their tickets. It wasn't until
they headed for the museum that Aldo cried, "Do you
know who that guy was who sold me the tickets? Sergio Colombo! He's only the greatest soccer player in
Italy next to Guido Rossano. And these are the best
seats in the stadium!"

Gina flashed Dea a smile of such gratitude it warmed
her clear through.

"Now that you're set, let's take a tour before it
closes."

Some moments in life were precious. Sergio gave
them a personalized visit with anecdotes about Guido
she'd never forget. The videos thrilled her to the core.
When they thanked him and turned to leave, the man
who stole her breath every time she saw him stood
in the doorway.

"Guido…"

He moved toward her. "Why don't you introduce
me to your friends."

Sergio must have told him she was here. If he'd
still been in his office, then he'd had to come only a
few steps. Before she could say a word, Aldo walked
toward them. "I can't believe it. Guido Rossano. I've
idolized you for years. Gina—" he drew her along
"—this is the legend."

"It's an honor to meet you at last." She shook his
hand. "Thanks to Dea, this day has come."

"Have you been well taken care of?" No one could
be more charming or dashing than Guido.

Aldo beamed. "This is about the best day of my
life!"

Dea was touched to see a grown man so happy to meet a boyhood idol.

"They'll be at the match on Sunday," Dea informed him.

"Why don't you two pick a poster before you leave and I'll sign it."

"You mean it?" Aldo's eyes widened. "How about the one at the national championship."

Sergio pulled it out of the bin and put it on the counter. He handed Guido a felt-tip pen. Gina looked at Sergio. "We'd like a signed poster of you too. I'll pay for it."

"No, no. It's on the house."

A minute later Dea saw two people ready to leave the store looking like they'd been given all their Christmases at once. She turned to the first man running the museum, then Sergio and Guido. "Thank you all." But as she started to follow her friends out the door, Guido said, "Where do you think you're going?"

Dea looked around. "Home."

"Do you have to drive them?"

"No. We came in our own cars."

"Good. That saves me a trip. Come to my office with me first."

"All right." After taking a breath, she turned and called to Gina, "I'll see you tomorrow." They waved back.

To her surprise, Guido put an arm around her shoulders in front of the other men and swept her through the back doorway, a shortcut to his inner sanctum. "I don't want the guys thinking they have a chance with you."

She blushed. "They were both so nice."

He took her inside his office and shut the door. "If you want to know the truth, it's not every day the ravishing Dea makes an appearance at a soccer stadium not once, but twice. One more time and their hearts might not be able to take it."

"You idiot." She pushed against his chest playfully and was rewarded by being crushed against him.

His eyes pierced hers. "You really don't have any idea what you do to a man, do you? I'm going to kiss you so you'll find out." Guido's intensity shook her before his head descended and his mouth closed over hers. Enveloped in heat, she felt his hands roam over her back and hips, urging her closer so she could feel every hard muscle and sinew in his body.

Though Dea had been with a few men who'd wanted to kiss her passionately, she hadn't fully reciprocated. Something had always held her back... until now.

This was different. Guido was different.

The feel of his mouth slowly devouring hers created such divine sensations that she felt like she'd been born for this moment and couldn't get enough. "Guido," she gasped in pleasure as he drew her into a wine-dark rapture. She clung to him, and they moved and breathed like they were a part of each other. Emotions greater than she could describe took over now that Guido had swept her into his arms.

She was already crazy about the man, but the sheer

physical feeling at this moment was all consuming, burning everything in its path so there was no room for anything else. Mind, body and soul were on fire for one man who answered the question of her existence.

"My office is no place for this. Come home with me, Dea," he whispered against her lips, swollen from the refined savagery of his kisses. "I need to be with you more than you can imagine," he confessed in a ragged voice.

I want that too, Guido. I'm in love with you. I know I am. But if you only need me, and aren't in love with me, then I can't let this go any further.

After one more long, hungry kiss, he opened the door. She was so dazed she would have fallen if he hadn't helped her to her car.

"I—I don't think I can drive." Her voice faltered.

"Let me. My car is in the private parking area. I'll come back for it tomorrow."

She shook her head. No matter how much she wanted to go home with him and throw away the key, she didn't plan to spend the night with him. "You mustn't leave yours here. I'll follow you."

Guido kept Dea in his sights for the short drive to his apartment. Once she'd pulled alongside him in his private parking garage, they took the elevator to the second floor. It wasn't until they'd entered his apartment that he realized he'd never brought a woman here before.

He turned on the lights. "Forgive my generic apartment that has no personality."

"Oh, yes, it does. You can tell in an instant that a bachelor lives here."

He flicked her an amused glance. "That bad, huh?"

Her eyes smiled. "It tells me you're a practical man. No nonsense about you. You certainly don't have to make excuses to me."

"Nevertheless, I want to explain that the convenience of the location to the stadium makes it ideal, and it serves as my base for eating and sleeping while I'm living in Rome."

"Where did you live before?"

"Naples. But I sold that apartment when I moved here. It would have been pointless to keep it. I'm afraid it didn't have any personality, either." She laughed quietly.

Guido studied her features. "Is that what you really think about me? No nonsense?"

One brow lifted. "When you were teaching me some soccer moves behind the castle, you were all business. But on second thought, maybe the Lamborghini doesn't quite match the profile of the down-and-out bachelor who doesn't need more than a roof over his head."

"Do you know something, Dea Caracciolo? I've never laughed as much with anyone else."

"You should do it more often. It's very attractive."

His pulse raced. If he got started on Dea's attributes, he'd never stop. After those moments in his office he still hadn't recovered from being set on fire. His desire for her was off the charts.

If she was worried he was about to carry her straight to the bedroom, she ought to be. He'd already broken his own rule about not rushing things with her. He hadn't been able to help it. *Slow down, Rossano.* "Have you had dinner?"

"Not yet. Gina and Aldo surprised me as I was leaving work this evening. They wanted to take me for a meal to thank me for the poster. I told him to save his money for soccer tickets and we went straight to the stadium. You and your staff were so nice to them."

"It was our pleasure." Holding on to his last vestige of self-control, he said, "The restroom is down that hall if you'd like to freshen up first."

"I'd love it. Thank you."

"I'll be in the kitchen. I know I saw eggs and cheese in there this morning and will whip something up for us."

"Perfect."

Guido headed there and made tasty omelets they ate at the kitchen table. He produced some oranges to go with their meal.

"Hmm. These are gorgeous." He watched her finish the last section of her fruit and thought he'd never seen or tasted such a luscious mouth. "So were the eggs. You're a terrific cook."

"Thank you."

"Having lived on your own for so long, you're probably a great chef and don't know it."

He chuckled. "What I am is a nervous wreck now that the soccer season is coming to an end. Three more games now that it's May."

"How many at home?"

"One. The others will be in Cagliari and Siena."

She sat back in the chair drinking her coffee. "Has owning this team been fulfilling for you? Can you see doing this for years and years?"

Her interest sounded genuine. If he had his heart's desire, he could see doing just about anything. "I don't know. My father's not getting any younger. His emotional pull on me to come back to the shipping lines is strong."

"You're his only son. That puts you in a vulnerable position."

He nodded. "But Papà has two brothers and they have three sons who also sit on the board. And there's my grandfather. At ninety-five, he still wields influence with my father."

She cocked her head. "I understand from Alessandra that you're the light of your grandfather's life. He believes you're the one in the family to take Rossano Shipping Lines in a new direction."

"But that's my father's decision, no one else's." Guido swallowed the rest of his coffee. Here they were talking in his kitchen instead of picking up where they'd left off in his office. He feared she was thankful for the breathing room between them effectively lowering the heat.

"If you're through eating, let's go in the living

room. I want to talk to you about something important."

Those fabulous orbs narrowed. "I thought that's what we're doing."

Until he learned everything hiding inside her, he knew he would never have peace. "It's more comfortable in there."

She averted her eyes, a subtle sign of nervousness. "First I'll just clear our dishes."

"Not tonight. Remember your rule? It applies at my house in reverse. After you."

Resigned to do Guido's bidding, Dea went through to the living room and sat on one of the chairs near the couch. He'd followed her, but the tension radiating from him let her know something was wrong. "What is it?"

In a surprise move Guido leaned over her and put his hands on the arms of the chair, virtually trapping her. With his lips so close to hers, she couldn't think, let alone breathe.

"We entered deeper waters this evening. Though I want to carry you to my bedroom and make love to you all night, we need to talk before we can no longer feel the sand beneath our feet. I won't be able to go on seeing you until I have all the honesty in you," his voice rasped.

All her honesty? "What do you mean?"

"If you're holding anything back where your feelings for Rini are concerned, I need to know."

After those words he gave her a long, lingering

kiss that left her trembling before he released her and sat on the couch across from her with his hands clasped between his legs.

His eyes had taken on a haunted look, as if he couldn't make up his mind about her. Sickness swept through her.

"I've told you everything! I don't know why you don't believe me. I think what you meant to say is, you need to hear all the dishonesty in me. The problem is, I'm not sure I *could* identify all of it and agree that to go on seeing each other would be a waste of time."

Either Rini or Alessandra had betrayed her and told Guido every ugly detail about her past. One of them had undoubtedly gone so far as to reveal the details of that tumultuous period in the past when Alessandra's boyfriend had betrayed her and chased after Dea. No other explanation would explain why the earth had suddenly tilted.

Now that Guido knew her history, it didn't surprise her that he wanted to understand her behavior from her own lips. If he was hoping it was all a lie, Dea couldn't help him out.

She'd thought she'd put all the misery behind her and was endeavoring to become a better person who had faith in herself. But there'd be no convincing Guido of anything. The damage was too great for her to fight for him.

What a fool she'd been to let her guard down. Now she'd fallen in love with him, and she knew this was the one fatal mistake in life she'd never recover from.

There was no one like Guido, but he was beyond reach.

On unsteady legs she got to her feet and reached for her purse on the coffee table. "There's nothing more for me to say. Goodbye, Guido."

Before Dea broke down and dissolved into tears, she left the apartment and hurried to the parking garage for her car. She could hear him call out to her, but she didn't stop. When she backed around, he stood in her way looking fierce and so handsome it hurt.

"You're not going anywhere."

Her breath caught. "You worded that wrong. *We're* not going anywhere. All the family secrets are out. It could never work for you and me. Please move aside. It's late and I have to be up early in the morning."

In the dim light of the garage his face seemed to have lost color. "I can't let you go until we talk this out. You've obviously misunderstood me."

"No, I haven't," she fired back. "You were crystal clear."

Her words rang in the air. He finally stepped aside so she could drive out to the street. Her last glimpse of him through the mirror reflected a man wearing a mask so bleak she hardly recognized him.

Dea drove to her own apartment. When she walked inside, she was aware that the recent joy she'd been experiencing had left her soul. Before going to bed, she removed the poster of Guido from the wall. Unable to throw it away yet, she rolled it up and put it in the closet.

Once under the covers, she buried her face in the

pillow until it was wet. *No prince is going to find you, Dea.* From here on out it was work and more work to get through this life.

Friday morning after sleeping poorly, she got dressed, skipped breakfast and worked out in the gym. One of the guys on duty there, who was a big flirt, came over to bother her. He couldn't be a day over twenty-four.

"When are you going to let me take you out?"

"Never."

"Ooh. That was brutal."

Dea was in a brutal mood. Even if it was her fault, her experiences with men had brought her nothing but misery. "I can see three women in here at least five years younger than I am. I'm sure they'd love your attention."

"They're not you."

"Lucky them."

Her comment got rid of him for the moment. She took advantage of the time to slip back out and grab a cappuccino on her way to the shop. Today they were having a meeting to discuss a few of the men's costumes for *Don Giovanni*.

She welcomed the busy day so she wouldn't give in to her agony over losing Guido.

There was no one she could confide in about this, not even her aunt. It saddened her because she'd been getting along with her whole family for a long time. The next time her mom let her know Rini and Alessandra had gone back to Positano for a while, she'd fly home to visit her parents. Her parents could always fly here. That was the only way to avoid more pain.

At quitting time Gina came over to her table, her face beaming. "I'll never be able to thank you enough for what you've done. Aldo's a different person. Are you going to be at the game on Sunday with Guido?"

"I plan to," she lied without compunction. She didn't want to talk about him, not ever again. While their heads were together, the receptionist came in the room and approached her.

"Some flowers arrived for you, Dea. At first I thought they must be for Juliana until I saw the card with your name. They're out in the reception room on my desk." Her brows lifted. "Three dozen red roses! Someone's in love."

Dea's heart did a double kick. "I'll be out in a minute. Thank you."

Gina nudged her. "Guido Rossano is absolutely crazy about you. If I didn't like you so much, I'd be horribly envious."

"You've got Aldo."

"Yeah. I do, but there's no one quite like the *Cuor di Leone.*"

Her eyes closed. Gina was right. Guido was unique in so many ways she could hardly breathe just thinking about him. Why did he bother to send her anything? He could have no idea how painful this was for her.

"Well, come on," Gina urged her. "It's time to go home. If you're not dying to look at them, I am."

Dea took a quick breath. "Okay." She grabbed her purse and followed her friend. The second they reached the foyer, the heavy perfume from the roses assailed her. They both gasped as she walked over to the enormous spray and reached for the card perched in a little plastic pick. *You have to forgive me. I said everything wrong and want to start over.*

Tears stung her eyelids. She pressed the card to her heart. They couldn't start over.

Gina stood behind her. "If you'll bring your car around, I'll help you put these flowers in the backseat so you can take them home."

Before the flowers could be placed inside the car, Dea and Gina had to tip the vase to pour out the water. Somehow they managed. "Thank you," she said to her friend before driving home.

After parking in her space, Dea had some difficulty taking the roses out of the car so the heads wouldn't get broken off.

"Let me help," sounded a deep, familiar male voice behind her.

She started to tremble. "Guido—"

"I've waited here wondering if you'd bring them home or throw them away at work. I have my answer."

Dea should have tossed them. Now she'd been caught in the act.

"I'll bring them in. You go ahead and open the door for me."

Guido had left her no choice. When they reached her apartment, he carried them out to the kitchen to fill the vase with water. He darted her a glance. "I meant what I said on the card. I need to start over with you by taking you for a drive in the country.

We'll stop at some spot for dinner and talk. Please don't deny me this."

"You already know everything there is to know about me. There's no need for more talk."

"We haven't even started," he came back. His dark blue eyes glittered. "Let's get something straight. We may have been the closest of friends all our lives, but I swear before God that Rini has *never* discussed you with me. Neither has Alessandra, so you can put that misconception out of your head once and for all."

Was he speaking the truth? Dea wanted to believe him.

No matter how hard she fought it, the force of his words and personality cut through her defenses like a sharp knife. Not only that, he was wearing a dusky blue jacket over a cream shirt open at the throat and beige trousers. His masculine beauty melted her on the spot. It wasn't fair. She could feel herself weakening.

"I—I need to shower first," she stammered.

"While you do that, I'll carry these roses into the living room and put them on the coffee table. I want you to see my apology every time you enter your apartment."

Oh, Guido…

Dea hurried to her room and got ready. She chose a dressy peach blouse and skirt. After brushing out her hair and leaving it loose, she joined him in the living room. The red roses had already filled it with their fragrance.

She was probably a fool to go with him, but she'd

promised herself not to make snap judgments anymore. Tonight she would hear him out one last time, but this was it.

Quiet reigned as Guido drove them a short distance from Rome to Lake Nemi, which was set in the crater of an ancient volcano. He turned on some music. Neither of them felt the need to talk. That suited Dea, who was waiting for an explanation from him when he was ready.

She sat back to enjoy the landscape, especially since she'd never been here before. The lush nature preserve surrounding the lake came as a pleasant surprise. He took them to a charming restaurant bordering the water and asked for them to be seated in an isolated area. The waiter led them to a candlelit table for two separated by ornamental trees.

Guido ordered their meal. Wine and *cacio e pepe*, a dish of Pecorino Romano cheese and pasta to die for. Halfway through their meal she eyed him frankly. "This is delicious. The flowers were lovely too, but I'm still waiting for you to tell me why you don't think I've been totally honest with you. That hurt, you know? More than you can imagine."

He leaned forward. "I believe you've told me the truth, but—"

"But what?" she cried softly.

"Maybe you're still in denial over deep feelings you don't realize are there?"

"I take it you're talking about Rini, the proverbial elephant in the room." His sustained silence confirmed her suspicions. "You're still afraid I'm in love with my brother-in-law, and you want chapter and verse, is that it?" She put her napkin on the table. "Sorry I can't change history to make it more palatable for you, Guido."

His brows furrowed. "I'm not asking for that," he insisted.

"No? It sounds to me like you're asking for blood, so now you're going to get it. Long before that night, I'd been floundering emotionally when it came to men. Since childhood the image of the perfect man had lived in my imagination, but no man ever thrilled me to the point that I wanted to marry him."

"Until Rini," he grated.

"Yes. I took one look at him and no one else existed for me. The fact that there was no substance to back up that feeling—only a girl's dream—didn't stop me from throwing myself at him. When I say *throw*, I mean I slid my hands up his chest and kissed him with hunger. I'd never done such a thing in my life and assumed he had to feel the same way, but he didn't kiss me back. In truth, he couldn't get rid of me fast enough."

Even with his tan, Guido's complexion had gone ashen. "Stop, Dea—"

"No! I haven't finished. You wanted the unvarnished truth? Well, here it is. I suggested we get together the next evening, but he said he wouldn't be in town. After thanking me for the dance, he walked away without saying anything about seeing me again. I left the yacht in shock."

Guido's grim expression couldn't prevent her from

getting everything off her chest. "He was the second man in my life to do real damage."

"What do you mean, the second?"

"Rini didn't share that with you?"

"I told you. You were never a topic of conversation between us."

"I see. Well, years ago Alessandra's fiancé made a play for me and followed me to Rome. I never encouraged him. He swore he was in love with me, but the minute he got there, he went off with another model. The incident not only put me off taking any man seriously, but made me feel horrible for my sister and it drove a knife in her heart. Both of us had been so hurt it took us years to become friends again."

"You don't have to say another word." Clearly uncomfortable over the direction of the conversation, Guido got to his feet. After leaving some bills on the table, he walked around to her chair. "Come on. Let's go out to the car."

Still fired up, she walked quickly without letting him touch her. The second they got in the Lamborghini, she turned to him. "I know you don't like hearing this, but you wanted *all* of my truth."

"I never meant to cause you this kind of pain."

"Maybe not," she admitted, but Dea was too far gone now. At a glance, his profile resembled chiseled stone, but that didn't stop her from telling him everything.

"Simply put, Rini's rejection put me in the blackest hole of my life. Who could imagine a greater irony than the one where he met my sister and fell madly in love with her? They say lightning doesn't strike twice in the same place, but it did with me. I needed help. If it hadn't been for my family and my therapist, who pulled me out of that abyss, I don't know what would have happened."

"Please don't say any more."

"I have to. You wanted an answer. After many talks I began to figure out my life. Alessandra and I are now closer than we ever were throughout our childhood and have come to a perfect understanding.

"She knows that Rini represented the figment of my imagination that had lived inside me for years. He didn't know me from Adam and had no interest in me. So for me to feel rejected by him tells you the precarious state of my mental health."

Traffic was light entering Rome. It didn't take long to reach her apartment and drive to her parking level on the third floor.

"In time I worked through my humiliation. Rini was very kind and told me to forget it. Whatever he chose to tell Alessandra is their business, but she knows the whole truth. At her wedding I realized any amorous feelings for him had been wiped clean from my heart. Soon after that I gave up modeling and went back to college."

Without saying anything, Guido turned off the car and reached for the door handle. She told him not to bother. "I don't want you to see me inside my apartment. In fact I don't want to see you again. You have a trust issue with me that will never go away. I understand where you're coming from, but I can't be with a man who won't ever be free of his suspicions. Something, someone, has robbed you of your ability to trust."

Dea let herself out of the car. Before she shut the door, she said, "Let me leave you with this thought, which you can choose to believe or not. If you or your parents felt slighted by me at the reception, it wasn't intentional. What you sensed was my shame because you were his best friend and had witnessed my brazen behavior that night on the yacht.

"No one could expect you to forget that. But please be assured of one thing. I've loved getting to know the former *Cuor di Leone.*"

"Dea—"

"*Adio per sempre*, Guido."

"Goodbye forever?" he ground out.

"Just what I said." She shut the door. Wild with pain, she hurried toward the entrance leading to her apartment.

CHAPTER SIX

"YOU'RE NOT RUNNING away from me again." Guido caught up to Dea and wrapped his strong arms around her from behind so she was trapped. His breathing was as ragged as hers. "I'm not letting you go until you agree to spend all day tomorrow with me."

She moved her head from side to side. "There's no point."

"Of course there is! You're right about me. I do have trust issues and need you. I want to show you the real me. I know in my gut you and I are good for each other. Give me tomorrow to turn this around, Dea. You can't mean things to end this way. I couldn't take it." He held her tighter, sounding frantic.

Once again she could feel herself giving in to him. "You have a game this weekend."

"On Sunday. Tomorrow is Saturday. I'll be here in the morning at seven thirty. Where we're going, it will be sunny and you'll want to wear something casual. We'll be gone the whole day and won't be home until late. Promise me you'll be ready when I come for you."

His body was actually trembling like hers. Feel-

ing the strength of his emotions made it impossible
to deny him. "I…promise."

"Grazie a Dio."

"Buonanotte, Guido." Before he tried to kiss her,
she reached for the door handle and hurried inside
the building.

Once in her apartment, Dea dashed to her bedroom and pulled out her cell phone. There was only
one person she could talk to about how she was feeling. She needed her twin. The two of them had suffered through so much. Alessandra, now a married
woman with a child, would understand Dea's pain
and fear as no one else could.

Her sister answered on the third ring. "Dea?"

"I know it's late, but I need some advice. If Rini
is right there, maybe you could call me back later?"

"No, no. I'm back in Positano. He's still with our
parents working, but will be home tomorrow."

Dea was glad she hadn't disturbed them. "How's
Brazzo?"

"Thriving. I put him to bed several hours ago."

"Then you don't mind if we talk?"

"Are you kidding? I've been dying to know if you've
seen or heard from Guido since that weekend when
we were all together. But in case nothing came of it, I
was afraid to ask any questions."

Her eyes closed tightly. "Quite a lot has gone on,
actually."

"Oh, Dea—that's the best news!" She heard pure
happiness in her sister's voice. "I just love Guido. He's
a fantastic man. You two seemed so great together I

couldn't believe it. Rini thought the same thing. To quote him, you were 'like two halves of the same incredible whole.'"

It had felt that way to Dea. "We've been out several times. He's been by Juliana's office and sent me roses. Tomorrow we're spending a whole day together."

"Meraviglioso!"

"I don't know, Alessandra. That's why I'm calling."

"What's wrong?"

"He's been relentless in getting me to bare my soul to him. Now that I have, he—he's afraid I'll always have feelings for Rini," she stammered. "I don't know what more I can say or do to convince him otherwise."

"From what Rini has told me, Guido has always been as closed up as my husband when it comes to the personal. He's a deep one."

Dea shivered. "I've already learned that about him. I'm frightened to spend any more time with him."

"Because you feel doomed to love a man who isn't sure of you, right?"

"Exactly." Dea knew her sister would understand. "I can't think of anything worse than having to prove myself to him over and over."

"I can think of one thing."

"What's that?"

"Never seeing him again."

She gripped the phone tighter. "You're right. The thought of his being gone out of my life is anathema to me."

"He's exciting, all right. Something must have hap-

pened over the years that has made him so distrust-
ful. If you want my advice, do to him what he did to
you. Stick to him like glue until you uncover *his* secrets. When that day comes, he'll get the point that
he's the only male in your universe."

Was that possible?

"Thanks for talking to me, Alessandra. I'll do what
you said, but I'm so nervous."

"So was I when I flew to Positano to surprise Rini
long before we were married. It was a bad time for us
and I was terrified he'd tell me to go home and never
darken his doorstep again."

"You knew he wouldn't say that to you."

"No. Not then I didn't. There's no man more for-
bidding than Rini when he's upset. All I can say is,
I'm thrilled to hear Guido hasn't left you alone. Just
keep doing the unexpected."

"We'll see." But it took courage she didn't have
a lot of. "Give the baby hugs for me until I can see
him again."

"I will. And when you're with Guido tomorrow,
tell him Brazzo adores the purple octopus. Between
the color and the bells, I'm positive it's his favorite
toy."

"I'll relay the message. I'm sure it will please him."

"Dea? Do me one more favor. Keep me informed.
I'll be dying until I hear from you again."

"I promise. Love you."

"Love you too."

She clicked off. It was hard to believe that after

so many years of pain, the two of them were close again in a brand-new way.

At seven twenty in the morning Guido parked his car in front of Dea's apartment building and hurried inside to ring her on the foyer phone.

"There's no need for you to come up, Guido. I'll be right down and meet you at the car."

Elated that she was ready, he went back outside to wait for her. Though it was semicloudy in Rome, there'd be full sunshine where they were going.

Every time he saw her, she wore something different. Five foot seven and beautifully built, she could wear anything and look fabulous. This morning she'd put on white jeans with cuffs at the ankles and strappy beige sandals. On top she wore a round-necked three-quarter-sleeve cotton sweater in a soft hyacinth color. She left her freshly washed hair loose. It sparkled in the light. Best not to eat her up until they were alone.

"Buongiorno, bellissima." He opened the car door and helped her inside before going around to get behind the wheel. "I hope you haven't had breakfast yet."

"Just coffee."

"Good. We'll eat on the plane." He pulled into the traffic and headed for the airport.

She glanced at him from eyes the color of vintage Burgundy. "Are we flying to Naples again?"

"Si, signorina. But we won't be visiting the yacht."

"Are you going to take me on a sightseeing tour of your childhood haunts?" The question intrigued him.

"Would you like that?"

"I'd love to see the places that helped shape you into the person you are."

"We'll do that another day. Today I don't want to think about the past."

Her brows furrowed. "Why would you say that? Is it so painful?"

"That was an interesting choice of words."

"But the right one obviously. Otherwise you wouldn't question my asking."

He was glad they'd reached the airport so he could avoid an answer until they were on board the plane eating breakfast.

"Before we land in Naples, I'll try to explain myself. I grew up an only child. Since you were a twin, you can't possibly comprehend what it was like for me. My parents couldn't have more children and my father refused to adopt. He wanted a child from his blood. My mother was eager for more children, but it didn't happen."

"I'm sorry for all your sakes."

"My parents' marriage suffered because of my father's refusal to make my mother happy. His intransigence broke her heart. Ever since he said no to the idea of adoption, Papà has been paying for the damage he did to their union."

"So you became the golden child who had to meet your father's every expectation."

Guido nodded. "From the time I could comprehend pressure, I felt like I had to be perfect in his eyes to make him happy. I knew he expected me to follow in his footsteps. But I loved playing soccer and saw the disappointment in his eyes when I had to leave for practice or another game. He warned me that a life of sports wouldn't give me stability."

"That couldn't have been pleasant for you."

"No, but what made it worse was the fact that he was right."

"What do you mean?"

"In my late teens I had a serious girlfriend named Carla."

"You did?" At last he was revealing something vital about himself.

"I imagined us getting married one day after I'd had my run at soccer. But after I gave it up to go back to work for my father, she went off with another soccer player. When I realized it was the celebrity status of being the wife of a high-profile athlete she wanted, not me, I became wary of women."

Her eyes looked wounded as they played over him. "I'm sure that hurt a great deal."

"It made me angry. I did go back to work for my father, but I wasn't happy. The rest you know. Last year I left the company to buy a minor team. Not only have I turned out to be a great disappointment to Papà by leaving the business for a time, I'm a thirty-two-year-old bachelor.

"For the last five years he's been pushing me to get married. I know what's motivating his overzealous methods of throwing women at me. He wants me to provide grandchildren, hoping it will ease my mother's pain."

"So *that* was why he allowed the fashion show to take place on board the yacht."

"Of course. He planned it to coincide with my birthday because he wanted us to meet. Since nothing else had worked over the years, why not introduce me to the supermodel who's been the talk of Italy? With his reasoning, no real man could resist you, certainly not his own son.

"For once in his life, my father was right. Rini and I had been talking when Papà brought you and your friend over to your table. I'd seen your pictures everywhere, but meeting you in the flesh was something else."

Dea moaned. "When you and I were at the wedding reception, I was afraid I'd offended you when I made the remark about my friends hoping to do another fashion show on the yacht."

"I think you know by now that didn't offend me."

She nodded. "I'm afraid I've jumped to too many conclusions."

"So have I. I don't know how much you know about Rini and me. We met at seven years of age and attended the same schools together until college. The two of us went through every good and bad time together. I'll never forget when he learned that his soccer injury left him without the ability to have children."

"That had to have been so terrible for him."

Guido nodded. "When you met him on the yacht

and danced with him, I thought he was the luckiest man alive to meet you after what he'd been through. I also believed he deserved to find an amazing woman like you. But deep inside me I wanted you for myself and was appalled at my feelings of jealousy."

"Oh, Guido—"

"*Oh, Guido* is right! You have to understand that I was at a vulnerable point in my life because I'd decided to buy the soccer team and leave the company for a while. Nothing was a sure thing and I risked alienating my father in a way that might ruin our relationship for good. You talk about floundering while you were at Rini and Alessandra's wedding— so was I."

Before anything more could be said, the Fasten Seat Belt light went on.

"Come on. Let's get back to our seats. We'll resume this talk later."

Dea had wanted secrets from him and she finally had the truth. Now that she knew about his girlfriend from the past and her rejection of him to chase after another celebrity, she understood the war going on inside him where his father was concerned.

When they touched down and got off the plane, he led her to the waiting helicopter and helped her on board. "I promise our flight won't last longer than ten minutes."

Once they were in the air, he used the mic to talk to her. "We're headed for Ischia Island. Have you been there?"

She shook her head. "In my teens Papà drove us past it and the other islands off Naples in the old cruiser, but we never went ashore."

"Then you're in for a treat. We'll be putting down near Serrara Fontana in the mountainous southwest part."

"Does this island have special significance for you?"

"I'll explain in a few minutes," was all he would tell her.

The pilot made a beeline for the highest summit on the island and descended toward an isolated piece of property partially hidden by the vegetation. Soon a helipad appeared and they made a gentle landing.

Guido thanked the pilot before helping Dea to climb out. He grasped her hand and walked her along a path through the grove of chestnut trees. The sound of the rotors grew faint. As they came out the other side to a terraced garden of palms and flowers, he heard Dea's soft gasp.

Her eyes had taken in the two-story pastel-pink villa above the garden with its pool. The ornamental parapets of the balconies overflowed with bougain-villea and hibiscus. "This all looks like something out of a dream." The marvel in her voice told him everything he wanted to know.

He threaded his fingers through hers. "It wasn't like this when I first saw the place sixteen years ago with Rini. We were through diving for the day and decided to explore on rental bikes. After we swam in one of the many hot springs throughout the island, we arrived up here at the top. That's when I saw this wreck of what was clearly once a magnificent villa overlooking the sea, closed up and isolated. Its beauty haunted me."

"You were young to be so affected."

"I agree. Living in Naples all my life, I'd been surrounded by beauty and had traveled to many exotic places in the world. But this spot had such a strong pull on me, I eventually made inquiries of the locals."

"What did they tell you?"

"The original owners had lost their money and were forced to sell. The second owner bought it as an investment but only visited it a few times. Little by little the place fell into more disrepair, and a small portion part of the villa suffered fire damage."

She shook her head, causing her fabulous hair to float around her shoulders. "That's so sad."

He took a deep breath. "Over the years I flew here often. The worse it looked, the more I wanted it. The day it went up for sale again, I bought it and the first thing I did was clear a space for a helipad. Once that was done, I spent all my weekends here restoring the garden and making renovations. To get out of the Naples office and come here to work in the soil was therapeutic for me."

"You did all this by yourself?" She sounded incredulous.

"Most of it, though I did hire locals from time to time."

"When was that?"

"I took possession three years ago."

Her eyes were smiling. "So you could transform it."

"That's one way of putting it."

"Just as you decided to turn a grade-B soccer team into a national champion. I see a pattern here."

He chuckled and drew her into his arms. "But I don't know the outcome of either transformation yet."

"Why not?"

"For the obvious reason that our last three games of the season haven't been played yet. As for the other..." Her mouth was a temptation he couldn't resist. After kissing her long and hard, Guido put his arm around her shoulders and walked her up to the villa. "See for yourself."

He unlocked the main door and drew her inside the large foyer with a curving staircase rising to the next floor and rooms extending on both sides.

Dea walked around the interior, which was devoid of anything but the prepared drywall. She turned to him. "From the outside of the villa, you would never guess this is all unfinished."

He nodded. "It's ready for the right person to take over and create an ambiance of beauty from the flooring to the ceiling."

She eyed him for a moment. "Why not yourself?"

"You've seen my apartment, and I've told you about the one in Naples. This is no bachelor pad and needs the eye of someone with exquisite taste."

"Have you found that person?"

Guido moved closer and put his hands on her shoulders. "How would you like the job?"

Maybe it was a trick of light but he thought her face lost a little color. "Please don't joke about something like that."

"I would never joke about anything this personal. The first time I visited your apartment, I saw a reflection of the real you in everything and loved being there."

"Zia Fulvia helped me decorate when I moved in."

He tightened his fingers around her upper arms and shook her gently. "Why don't you ever take credit for your own genius? Don't you know how wonderful you are?"

"Guido—" Her cheeks filled with color and she pulled away from him.

"It's true. When you were telling me about the opera and how vital the costumes and settings were to making it come alive, I felt *you* come alive. That's the moment I knew I wanted you to see this villa and tell me what needs to be done. I'm sick of apartments and plan to live here for the rest of my life."

"You don't require anyone's help. You've created a masterpiece outside."

"I'm glad you think so, but the real task still awaits me. Come on. After you see the whole house, we'll drive down to the village for lunch and you can tell me what you think."

Not giving her a chance to argue, he grasped her hand and led her up the stairs to see the four bedrooms and bathrooms. The superb view of the Tyrrhenian Sea from the master suite held her gaze for a long time.

A tour of the downstairs included a library and a separate den off the living room. The large kitchen and dining room on the other side of the house produced more cries of delight. He could hear her mind working and knew her imagination had taken over.

A detached garage in the same Mediterranean style with a tiled roof stood behind the villa. Along with the gardening equipment, Guido kept a truck and his Alfa Romeo Spider convertible locked up there. He helped her get in his vintage sports car and they took off down the winding road. The smell of roses and jasmine hung heavy in the air. The woman seated next to him had no clue what she meant to him. Not yet...

I'm sick of apartments and plan to live here for the rest of my life. This is no bachelor pad and needs the eye of someone with exquisite taste. How would you like the job?

"We're coming into Sant'Angelo, an old fishing village." Guido's deep male voice curled through Dea's insides. "My sailboat is moored there in the harbor. One day I'll take you out and we'll sail around the island."

"Which one is it?"

"The white and blue one, which isn't much help, since so many boats are the same."

She laughed. "This little town is a panoply of white, blue and ochre houses all pressed together in a symphony of color. I've lived by the water all my life, but our family's island has no color, just a dark stone castle."

He threw her a glance. "The severity has a beauty all its own."

"I agree, but this paradise dazzles the eye. The impossible yellows and pinks of the flowers make me think you live in heaven."

"Today I'm there."

She felt the same way as he slowed down and parked the car in a tiny space only someone as daring as Guido would have tried to navigate. He levered himself from the driver's side and came around to open her door. "In a few minutes you're going to taste pasta *arrabbiata* with a spicy kick that is out of this world. Emanuela's is right here on the beach."

For a little while Dea let go of her fear that he couldn't trust her feelings for him and inhaled the experience of being with Guido like this, a man whose background she was only beginning to understand, a man she already loved with all her heart and soul.

The food and wine turned out to be divine. Throughout their meal, his dark blue eyes wandered over her, causing every nerve in her body to throb with desire.

Following a tasty treat of raspberry gelato, they walked back to the car and took a drive around the island on the main road.

Traveling to the quaint, picturesque villages filled her with delight. He was better than any tour director or history teacher. He talked about the local legend of the giant living in the volcanic rock and the tufa lime-stone deposits built up around the fumaroles and spas.

Dea learned the island was shaped like a trapezoid and housed sixty-two thousand people. The larger towns sold everything imaginable. In Casamicciola she bought some small ceramic tiles of Ischia for her mother and sister. It was after five when Guido drove through the hamlet of Ciglio, close to the villa. They bought sausage rolls in puff pastry and fruit tarts to take with them.

After arriving back at the villa, Guido parked the car in the garage. Then he led her to a wrought iron bench by the pool, where they ate their picnic. The helicopter would be coming shortly, but Dea didn't want to think about that yet.

"Do you know one of the meanings of *alfresco*?" His eyes gleamed with mischief.

"Besides eating outside?" She smiled. "This garden is no prison. You know very well you've created a work of art out here."

"Then will you do me a favor and think about my proposition? While you're getting the costumes ready for *Don Giovanni*, will you picture the villa in your mind and tell me what kind of floors you envision here? A color scheme? Would you work up a rough draft that will point me in the right direction?"

She swallowed the rest of her pastry. *Stick to him like glue*, Alessandra had advised her. She had to prove to him how important he was to her.

"I'm flattered that you want my opinion. Let me think about it and I'll get back to you."

A look of relief crossed over his striking features. "That's all I ask. I'd like to fly you here again next Friday night after work if you don't have other plans. We can stay over in Ciglio, then spend Saturday here. I'll have to get back to Rome Saturday night because the team is flying to Siena first thing Sunday morning."

"I'll try to get off on the dot of five. Maybe I can drive to the airport from work and meet you at the plane to save time. As it is, we won't get here until nightfall."

They both heard the helicopter coming. Her disappointment that they had to leave this paradise was killing her.

"I'll be counting the hours until we can be here together again, Dea." He cupped her face with both hands and kissed her mouth. "Umm. I can still taste the cherries on your lips."

He kissed her thoroughly before they walked through the trees to board the helicopter. As it rose in the air, she felt like her heart had been wrenched from her body. The villa got smaller until she could see the island where she'd known such great happiness. Dea couldn't bear to go back to her apartment. But she needed to get hold of herself so he wouldn't know how much this day had meant to her.

On the flight back to Rome, she told him one of her ideas for decorating the villa while they were seated in the club compartment of the plane. "When we were in Casamicciola, we passed a store with the most wonderful ceramic floor tiles in various shades from white to cream."

"You noticed all that?"

"Well, you *did* ask me to think about it. I couldn't help but see your main floor and walls as an extension of the outdoors where light sweeps through the interior, even up the staircase.

"One of the bedroom floors upstairs could contain a soft pink pigment to reflect the exterior of the villa. Maybe another bedroom could be done in a subtle gray-blue. Your kitchen would be gorgeous with hints of a lemon motif in the wall tiles to reflect the astounding yellow of the flowers on the island."

His brows lifted. "Wall tiles... You've already envisioned that in your mind?"

She smiled. "You'd be surprised what's going on in there." Dea had already designed a nursery for his children. Her thoughts wouldn't stop. "It's your fault, you know."

A low laugh came out of him. He sounded happy, in fact happier than she'd ever known him to be. This blissful state continued until they landed in Rome and he drove them to her apartment.

"Just pull up in front and let me out. I know you have a game tomorrow and I don't want to keep you."

"You're sure?"

That one question threw her for a loop. Dea had thought he would insist on seeing her inside so he could kiss her senseless. He'd spoiled her today. Now she was a mess, wanting so much more. *You're being selfish again.* He had a huge day ahead of him.

"Good luck tomorrow, Guido." She undid her seat belt to kiss his cheek before getting out of the car with her small souvenirs.

"I'll call you tomorrow night if it isn't too late."

"Don't worry about that." Dea shut the door and hurried inside the building to her apartment. He hadn't asked her if she wanted to attend the soccer match. What did that mean?

Once she'd showered and climbed into bed, she lay there wide-awake reliving her incredible day. Was it another test to see if she cared about him enough to show up uninvited? Should she do the unexpected, as Alessandra had suggested?

Dea wrestled with that question for a long time. Finally she concluded that since he'd asked her advice on how to decorate the villa, she'd take her chances and go to the match. She had to see him again or she wouldn't be able to make it to Monday when she had to go to work.

Guido, Guido. I love you so much I'm in pain.

CHAPTER SEVEN

GUIDO AND SERGIO sat in his private suite next to the press box to watch the game. Maybe thirty minutes had gone by when he heard his phone ring. When he saw the caller ID, he picked up.

"What's going on, Mario?"

"This is important. Someone has asked to be let into your suite, but it has to be all right with you."

He could only think of one person he wanted with him today, but that was a dream that wouldn't happen. "If you're referring to Rinieri Montanari or his wife, Alessandra, you know they always have an automatic entrée."

"I'm talking about the gorgeous supermodel who was here last week with friends."

"You're serious—"

"*Sì*. I swear she's here at the ticket booth."

Guido's breath caught in his throat. He hadn't expected her to show up today.

Last night he'd been tempted to ask her to come to the game and spend the rest of the night with him, but he'd held back, waiting for her to suggest it. When she didn't, he'd suffered disappointment.

As he and Sergio had discussed many times, few women—barring those who played the game or had a family member on the team—could get into soccer in a big way. But Dea had been supportive from day one. Maybe she was different.

"Boss? Shall I bring her up?"

"Please," he said when he could find his voice.

Sergio stared at him after he clicked off. "What's wrong? Is Dante's leg still bothering him?"

He hoped not. "We're about to have an unexpected visitor."

"I thought you said your father would never come to the stadium to watch a game."

"You've got the wrong gender."

"Your mother?"

"Wrong again." He got to his feet.

"Ah… Then it must be your secret woman."

Sergio never let up. Guido moved to the door and opened it to watch for her. In a moment he saw her walking in the corridor alongside Mario.

The dark blue short-sleeved dress with small red poppies Dea was wearing hugged her figure, then flared from the waist to the knee. With every step, the material danced around her beautiful legs, imitating the flounce of her hair, which she wore down, the way he liked it. Talk about his heart failing him!

"Dea—"

Her searching gaze fused with his. "I hope it's all

right." The slight tremor in her voice betrayed her fear that she wasn't welcome. If she only knew...

"You've had an open invitation since we met." Nodding his thanks to Mario, he put his arm around her shoulders and drew her inside the suite. Sergio slipped out of the room and closed the door so they could be alone.

He slid his hands into her hair. "You're the most beautiful sight this man has ever seen." With uncontrolled hunger he lowered his mouth to hers and began to devour her. Over the announcer's voice and the roar of the crowd, he heard her little moans of pleasure as their bodies merged and they drank deeply.

When she swayed in his arms, he half carried her over to the couch, where they could give in to their frenzied needs. She smelled heavenly. One kiss grew into another until she became his entire world. He'd never known a feeling like this and lost track of time and place.

"Do you know what you do to me?" he whispered against her lips with feverish intensity.

"I came for the same reason."

Her admission pulled him all the way under. Once in a while the roar of the crowd filled the room, but that didn't stop him from twining his legs with hers. He desired a closeness they couldn't achieve as long as their clothes separated them.

"I want you, *bellissima*. I want you all night long. Do you understand what I'm saying?"

Before he heard her answer, the noise from the crowd became earsplitting. Within a minute someone unlocked the door and burst in. "Boss? I've been trying to reach you. Though we won the game, Dante's leg may be broken. You're needed in the locker room. *Viene subito!*"

Dante... The game was over... For the last hour he'd been so caught up with Dea he hadn't noticed the passing of time.

After being jerked back from rapture he hadn't thought possible, his brain was slow to digest what Sergio had just told him.

Dea had more presence of mind. She eased herself out of his arms and got to her feet before he did. He stood there for a minute, raking one hand through his ruffled hair. "What happened?"

"He fell hard on his sore leg after getting kicked."

Dea put a comforting hand on his arm. "Go to him, Guido. If you can, come to my apartment later. If not, call me." In the next breath, she ran out the door before he could detain her.

Much as he wanted to go after her, he knew his duty was to Dante. Dea hadn't wanted to leave him; otherwise she wouldn't have told him to come to her place later. Loving her for her consideration, he started down the hall. By now the team doctor would have looked their star player over.

It wasn't until he was on his way into the locker room and saw Dante's family that he realized those hours with Dea had swept him away to a different world where nothing else had mattered. Not even his team. After she'd arrived, he hadn't watched a second of the game. Worse, he hadn't known of their victory until Sergio barged in.

It would all have been taped for Guido, but the news was bittersweet. Only two more matches before the end of the season. They'd have to play them without their star, Dante. For Sergio this had to be déjà vu. Ten years ago he'd suffered an injury that had knocked him out of competition for good. Guido had to pray Dante would heal well enough to play again.

This was the downside of being a team owner. His job was to encourage the rest of the team to carry on to a national victory. Realizing what he had to do tonight, he knew he wouldn't be able to get over to Dea's until long after she went to bed.

After he watched the ambulance take Dante to the hospital, he congratulated the team and had a short pep talk with them. Once the guys left, he phoned Dea. She answered on the second ring.

"Guido. How is Dante?"

"He's gone to the hospital. I'll know more by tomorrow morning."

"You sound exhausted. Don't come over tonight. It's late. Go home to bed and if you can, concentrate on your latest win. You're almost there."

"I don't know. Without Dante, our strength has been reduced."

"I don't think that's true. You have other players who will step up. One of them will realize this is their opportunity to become a new star for the team. Sometimes wonderful things come out of tragedy."

If she was speaking from experience, then she'd

learned a great deal about life. Her fighting spirit was exactly what he needed right now. "Thank you for those words. They mean more than you could know."

"I'm happy you said that. Here I was afraid that my arrival during the game prevented you from watching the rest of it and you resented me."

He let out an exasperated sigh. "What I resented was having to let you go at all. May I have a rain check for tomorrow evening? I'll bring takeout to your apartment after work and we'll watch the game we missed. How does that sound?"

"I'd love it, but tomorrow evening my aunt will be in Rome and we're going out to dinner with Juliana." He had to swallow the bad news that they wouldn't be able to see each other as soon as he'd wanted. "Maybe the next night? I'll show you some of my ideas for your villa. They bombarded me all night long. Where do you keep all your trophies?"

Her mind leaped around and fascinated him so much that laughter escaped his lips despite his disappointment. "My parents' villa."

"How many do you have?"

Guido shook his head. "I don't know."

"Enough to fill a room?"

"Why?"

"You know that little nook off the den? It would be a great place to keep them. Kind of like your own museum. I can see a wallpaper motif of a real lion head with the words *Cuor di Leone* above it. On one side could be family pictures of your parents. On the

other, pictures of you at different ages to immortal-
ize the Rossano name.

"I can hear what you're thinking," she added, "so
here's the plan. You could have double doors hung
that locked and couldn't be opened unless you used
a remote. I know how modest you are, so if you don't
want anyone else to see it, then there's no problem."

He was so touched by her words he had trouble
finding the right response. "I can see you think bigger than life."

"It comes from living in a castle with the enormous
painting of Queen Joanna dominating the foyer. We
Caracciolos can't think any other way."

His throat had swelled with emotion. "I'll call you
Tuesday and we'll make plans. Miss me, Dea." He
hung up and headed to his car. The next time he was
with her, he was going to have the most important
discussion of his life with her.

Miss me, Dea.

She'd heard the huskiness in his tone. Didn't he
know she wouldn't be able to breathe until they were
together again?

Luckily Dea was kept so busy at work the time
flew until she went out for an enjoyable dinner with
her aunt and Juliana Monday evening. During the
meal her mentor praised Dea's work. She also announced that they'd be working at the opera house
for the next three evenings while rehearsals for *Don
Giovanni* were going on. The opera would open the
following week.

Exciting as that prospect would be in the professional sense, it meant Dea wouldn't be able to see Guido until Friday. When his phone call came Tuesday afternoon, she had to tell him news that was hard on her too. "But I promise that nothing will keep me from meeting you at the airport on Friday at four thirty."

A full half minute of silence met her ears before he said, "I don't know if I can last that long."

"I feel the same way," she admitted, but something else was bothering him, evidenced by some nuance in his voice. "How's Dante?"

"He's out for the season."

"I'm so sorry."

"He received flowers at the hospital, among them some roses with a card that was signed by Dea Loti and said, 'A fan who is wishing you back to health as soon as possible.' Do you have any idea how honored he felt?"

"Good. He got them!"

"All the guys have come in and out of his room and read your card. Now his celebrity status has shot through the roof. Sergio and Mario are green with envy."

"Guido...those flowers were meant to cheer you up too."

"You succeeded. How am I supposed to wait until Friday?"

"The same way I am. Work, work, work."

"There's steel beneath all that beauty."

"And a warrior lives inside you! Your team is

going to be superb at their next match, all because of their legendary owner."

"The things you say," he whispered. "If you were with me right now…"

"We'll be together on Friday. I'm staying positive for you. *A presto*, Guido." She hung up before blurting that she loved him, but that day was coming soon.

At four fifteen on Friday, Dea arrived at the airport by taxi, so eager to see Guido her cheeks were flushed and she thought she might be running a temperature. She hurried out on the tarmac to the section for the private planes. In the distance she saw the Scatto Roma jet. The door was open and the staircase had been placed against it.

He was here! She ran all the way with her overnight bag and raced up the steps straight into his arms. Guido put her bag down and buried his face in her hair. "I saw you coming. Thank heaven you're early. I couldn't have stood to wait another minute."

"Neither could I!" She pressed her mouth to his, kissing him so hungrily she almost knocked him over like she had playing soccer with him. Dea was no longer the same person. This man Guido—the love of her life—was eating her alive while he carried her all the way to his bedroom. For the next while she lost cognizance of her world. Overwhelmed with the pleasure he gave her, she hardly realized a voice had sounded over the plane's PA system.

"Signor Rossano? Do you wish to take off now?"

On a groan, Guido lifted his head and pulled out his phone. "We're ready."

"Bene."

His blue eyes were glazed with desire as he looked down at her. "We have to go to the club compartment."

"You shouldn't have brought me back here."

"I couldn't do anything else." He snatched another kiss from her lips and helped her to stand. Her hair was a complete mess and her lipstick had long since disappeared. She felt herself wobble on the way to the front of the jet, where they strapped themselves in their seats.

His eyes never left hers as the plane taxied out to the runway. Soon the engines screamed and they lifted off into the early evening sun. Once they'd achieved cruising speed, the steward brought them dinner.

"To shorten the time we're in the air, we're flying directly to Ischia and will drive a rental car to our hotel in Ciglio. How does that sound?"

She finished munching on some bruschetta. "I think you already know."

"Tell me how things are going at the opera."

"It's a whole other world. You can't imagine how exciting it is to see the singers get dressed in their costumes. All our hard work is on display, but I have to tell you one funny thing. Gina wasn't given the right dimensions for Leporello's jacket. When he tried it on, his considerable belly prevented it from closing. Gina and I tried not to explode from laughter."

Guido flashed her a broad smile.

"Juliana saved the day by finding a red scarf that she wrapped around him so the front edges would lie flat. When he reached for notes, we were all afraid the scarf would burst, but it didn't. Her ability to innovate at the last second makes her the queen of costume designers."

"I'm looking forward to seeing the opera performed."

"Me too. It starts next week."

"You'll have to show me the costumes you designed."

"I only helped."

"Now who's being modest?"

She finished her coffee. "Do you think your team is ready for the game in Siena?"

His brows furrowed. "They're going to have to be, but Drago can only do so much."

"One of the other players will step up. Have no fear."

"You really believe that, don't you?"

Heavens—in chinos and a sport shirt, the man was so incredibly attractive with that dark blond hair that she couldn't help staring. "Yes. They want you to be proud of them. You're their hero."

He made a protesting sound. "You don't know that."

"Oh, yes, I do. I'll never forget the look of worship in Aldo's eyes when he met you in person. Your team's feelings for you have to be a hundred times stronger."

"Did I ever tell you how good you are for me?"

"I don't know how you can say that when I caused you to miss watching an hour of the game last Sunday evening."

"There's a lot more I want to say on that subject, but I'll wait until we're completely alone."

How wonderful that sounded. A minute later the steward removed their trays and told them they'd be landing soon. Dea sat back, aching to get Guido all to herself. Within three minutes the Fasten Seat Belt sign flicked on and they began their descent. In the dying rays of the sun, Ischia rose up to greet them.

A rental car was waiting on the tarmac. Guido loaded them inside and drove them out to the main road. Guido pampered her to the point she felt sorry for every woman who would never know what it was like to be with a fabulous man like him.

It soon became clear that the island was overrun with tourists. She wished they didn't have to stay at a crowded hotel tonight, no matter how charming it might be. "We should have brought sleeping bags we could put down at the villa."

"On those hard subfloors? Not exactly my idea of comfort, but I'm living for the day when it's ready for occupation."

Dea eyed him covertly. "There's still your sailboat. We could pick up some goodies in the village and sleep on board."

She heard a harsh intake of breath. "You must have been reading my mind. I wanted to take you there in the first place, but it's intimate. Contrary to what you've probably heard about me, I'm not the kind of man who sleeps with every woman I fancy. I would never treat you that way."

"You thought I'd feel more comfortable staying at a hotel with adjoining rooms?"

"I'm trying hard to be a gentleman with you."

"Please try harder not to be."

His deep unexpected laughter filled the car's interior. "There's no other woman in the world like you, Dea. How did I get so lucky?"

"I've been saying that to myself about you ever since our own little soccer game." She ached with love for him. "I'm afraid I'm not known for my subtlety. To be honest, I've never been to bed with a man."

"That's what I thought."

"Does it show so much? Is that why you haven't tried to take advantage of me?"

"A woman who knows her value is more desirable than you can imagine."

"Well, I hate to ruin that image you have of me because it's all I can think about when I'm with you."

"Now she tells me."

His teasing was driving her crazy. "Surely at this point you must realize that if I thought you were a true playboy out to use me, we would never have made it this far."

"I think that's a compliment of sorts. But in case you've got the entirely wrong opinion about me, I'll be honest too. Over the years I've had a few very short-term intimate relationships with women. None since my birthday last year, however."

The birthday on the yacht… "That night changed history for both of us, Guido."

"You're right. That was the night my world underwent an upheaval from which I've never recovered and don't want to." He reached over and put a hand on her thigh. Through the fabric of her cotton pants, she felt his touch electrify her body. "If you really want to spend the night on the boat, there's nothing I want more. We'll head straight to Sant'Angelo now."

"I'd love it," she answered in a trembling voice. "But if you've already made reservations, I—"

"Don't worry about it. I'll cancel them now."

To her delight he pulled out his cell phone and made the call, ensuring a perfect night. All week she'd imagined them alone and away from other people with no pressure. It looked like she was going to get her heart's desire, and she preened like Alfredo when he found a spot in the sun.

Within an hour they'd picked up food and had walked over to the pier. They planned to go sailing in the morning. Dea had brought her bikini in case they decided to swim and sunbathe. But they would stay right here for tonight.

Guido led her to his one-man sailboat moored in its own slip. When she saw the name of it painted on the side, she let out a cry and stared at him. "The *Bona Dea*?"

He nodded. "The *Good Goddess*."

Her eyes rounded. "How long have you owned this boat?"

"I bought it off a fisherman two years ago. He'd

owned it for fifteen years and had named it for the ancient Roman goddess of fertility, *your* namesake, as it turns out."

"I don't believe it!"

"Truth is stranger than fiction. I was in love with your name long before we met. It just took meeting you in the flesh to complete my entrancement."

CHAPTER EIGHT

DEA BLUSHED AND climbed on board. It was no surprise to Guido she knew her way around a boat. She'd lived by the water all her life, even if she hadn't learned to water ski until he'd helped her.

Together they went below with their overnight bags and freshened up. She helped him make the bed with clean sheets and a blanket from the cupboard. After pulling out an extra quilt, he took it and the pillows up on deck so they could be comfortable.

"Come here." He propped himself against them and drew her down so she lay against him on the padded side of the boat. It rocked gently in the water. Once he'd covered them with the quilt, they enjoyed some of the nuts and chocolate they'd bought.

The lights of the village reflected in her eyes. "It's like looking at wonderland, Guido."

He kissed her temple. "You like this place?"

Dea nestled closer. "What a question."

"I've spent many nights right here on the water."

"I can see why."

"Can you imagine yourself living here?"

"That's not a trick question. Or is it?" She lifted her head to look at him. Her glossy hair drifted across his cheek. "What are you saying?"

He kissed every part of her face. "Do I really have to answer that?"

"Guido—" By now she was sitting up. Her body had gone taut with emotion. "Please don't tease me. Not about this. I couldn't take it."

His expression grew serious. "I'm in love with you, Dea. So in love that I never want to be apart from you."

"You are?" she asked in a shaky voice. Tears glistened in her eyes.

"Do you really need convincing, my love? I want to marry you right away and spend the rest of my life on this island with you. I want so many things. I'm bursting with the need to tell you. Forgive me if I'm moving too fast, but I can't help it. I've loved you for too long believing there was no hope."

She put her hands on his shoulders. "I've been waiting, dying for you to tell me. I was afraid I might never hear the words. I'm madly in love with you, Guido."

"I thought maybe I had a chance with you when I saw a poster of me in your bedroom at the apartment."

"You *saw* it?"

He nodded. "I knew you'd bought two posters. The evidence gave me hope, something I badly needed."

"Oh, darling. After our day on the water with Alessandra and Rini, I knew I was truly falling in love for the first time in my life."

"It happened to me when you tackled me."

"But *I* didn't know that! You left the castle that morning before I could say a final goodbye to you."

"You know why. I knew it was too soon to ask for all your passion."

"And all my truth," she reminded him. "You think I didn't want the same thing?" Dea gave him another fervent kiss and shook him gently. "When I discovered you'd already gone that Sunday morning, I felt such pain go through me that I knew you'd taken my heart with you. What if I never saw you again? I was terrified until you called me to go to lunch."

"*Adorata*, I've lived in terror since that night on the yacht. If I couldn't have you, I didn't want another woman. For a while I was out of my mind fearing I would never be able to have my heart's desire."

She kissed him hard. "No more talk about the past. I want to be your wife, Guido. I've already designed our whole villa, complete with the most adorable nursery you ever saw in your life. We're going to have children to keep both sets of grandparents busy. Is this your official proposal?"

The lovelight in her eyes blinded him. "It's official, *bellissima*." He reached in his pocket and put a diamond solitaire on her ring finger.

"It fits perfectly!" She squealed. "Oh, Guido— you've had this all along?" She hugged him around the neck with the same strength she'd shown playing soccer. "It's gorgeous! *You're* gorgeous!"

"So are you. I love you." He covered her mouth with his own, hardly able to believe that she was going to be his wife after he'd lived through so much agony. Later, when he let her up for breath, she said, "Let's go below so I can show you how much you mean to me."

"Dea, before we both lose complete control, we need to talk about our future." He grasped her hands and kissed the palms. "You've made me the happiest man alive. To know I'm going to be your husband is such a privilege. I want to do everything right."

"What do you mean?"

"Just that I want our wedding night to be the first time we make love. After what you've told me, it's my way of honoring you."

"But—"

"No buts." He pressed another kiss to her lips. "I want to be worthy of you."

"Guido, of course you're worthy! We *love* each other. I don't understand."

"I need you to love me always and be proud of me. Especially of what I'll be doing in the future."

Her brows knit together. "I *am* proud of you and whatever you do. You have to know that!"

"You say that now, and I love you for being so supportive of me. But the owner of a soccer team isn't a befitting profession for the husband of Count Caracciolo's princess daughter."

"What?"

"You know it isn't! Hear me out, *squisita*. I couldn't sleep thinking about you last night. I couldn't wait for us to be together so I could ask you to marry me. The fact that you've said yes changes everything."

"In what way?"

"I'm no prospect at the moment. Certainly no father's idea of the right kind of son-in-law. My father never liked it that I fell in love with soccer."

"But that doesn't mean he doesn't love you with all his heart and support whatever decision you make. Where is all this insecurity coming from? Are you afraid I'll leave you if you stick with soccer? I can see that I'm right."

He shook his head. "Whatever the reason, this comes from wanting to take care of you the best way I can and be an example to the children we'll have. So I've decided to sell the team at the end of the season whether we're victorious or not. It's only two weeks away. Sergio and Mario have always been interested in buying me out if I chose not to go on."

"You don't mean it! You love the soccer world!"

"Not the way I love you and the children I want to have with you. Tomorrow I'll inform my father and grandfather that I'm coming back to work for the company. They'll be ecstatic."

"I'm sure they will, but it's you I'm worried about. You left the company last year because you felt stifled and needed to do something of your very own. We've already talked about this. I thought we were going sailing tomorrow and talking more about plans for the villa. I was thinking we could put in an herb garden at the side of the house."

"I love all your ideas, Dea, and want to do everything with you. But this is too important to put off.

If you don't mind, I want us to go back to Rome in the morning."

"Stop, Guido. Can't you hear what you're saying? You haven't worked for the company in almost a year. How can you be sure it's what you want to do?"

"I'm very sure now that I know I'm going to have a loving wife to take care of for the rest of our lives. Nothing's more important to me than you."

"Being CEO won't give you the freedom you've had as a soccer-team owner. Think about the way you felt when you decided to leave the company and do something that made you feel alive."

He crushed her to him. "I didn't have you in my life then. I want our lives to have stability."

"But you have that being the owner of Scatto Roma."

"It's not the same thing. Trust me."

"If your team wins the national championship, you might feel very differently about things then. Give it a little more time, darling. How can you think about all this when you're flying to Siena Sunday morning to play an important match?"

"I'll be able to fit everything in." He pulled her down next to him again. "After we get back to Rome, I'll fly to Naples. My father will be so elated he'll plan to call a meeting of the board and things will be put into motion to make me CEO. I want all that in play before we tell either of our parents that we're getting married."

She lay against him, much quieter than before. "Then I'd better not wear this engagement ring around anyone yet."

He kissed her neck. "It'll be our secret for two more weeks, then we can shout it to the world. For now I'll know you have it and that you've promised to be my wife."

"Tell me what it is you'll do as CEO."

"Find new markets for new ships. The business is constantly evolving."

"How do you go about doing that?"

"Right now I'd rather talk about you and your work. When do you graduate?"

"In June. My internship with Juliana will be over."

"Do you think she'll let you go on working with her?"

"I wouldn't dream of asking her. I need to prove myself and will have to apply elsewhere. It may take time to find a company that will hire me. One day I hope to build a reputation for myself."

"You don't have to wait to do that. I'll set you up in your own business and opera companies will flock to you."

"That's very generous of you, darling, but this I have to do myself. Gina is in the same boat. We're both watching out for each other. While I wait for a bite, I'll be helping you work on the villa."

"Before that we'll be planning our wedding. I already know where you want to be married."

"Since you're an only child, maybe your parents would love to see you married in Naples at your church."

"You're going to be the bride, Dea. It'll be your day and your choice."

"You mean that?"

He drew her closer. "How can you even ask me that question?"

"Then I think it would be lovely to let them give you the wedding of their dreams. They don't have a daughter. My parents have twin girls and they've already had the joy of helping Alessandra plan her wedding."

"It was magnificent," he murmured. "The Archbishop of Taranto even officiated."

"You've told me of your mother's sorrow and your father's pain because he knew she'd wanted more children. When you tell him his plan worked to find you a wife, I have a feeling your parents will get a new lease on life and plan something magnificent too."

Guido looked into her eyes. "You don't have a selfish bone in your delectable body. More than ever I know I don't deserve you, but I'm going to try from here on out to be all the things you want me to be. *Ti amo*, Dea. *Ti amo*."

With Guido's declaration of love, he'd sent Dea the message she'd been waiting for all her life, and eventually she fell asleep. But in the middle of the night she awakened disoriented. It took her a minute to realize she was on the sailboat with him.

Careful not to disturb this man she loved to distraction, she eased out of his arms and got to her feet. The moonlight picked out his striking features and caught the facets of her diamond. Tonight he'd asked her to marry him. On her finger was the proof, yet during her sleep something had bothered her so badly she'd come wide-awake.

She needed another talk with her sister, but that couldn't happen until they flew back to Rome. The night was cool so she went downstairs and slept under the blanket until she heard Guido call to her.

"I'm right here, darling!" She slid off the bed and started up the stairs. They met halfway and Guido swept her in his arms. His kiss was to die for.

"Where did you go?" He sounded alarmed.

Dea rubbed his hard jaw. "Umm. You have a beard."

"Don't change the subject."

"I guess I'm so excited at the thought of marrying you I woke up during the night. You were sleeping peacefully. I didn't want to disturb you, so I came down here and went back to sleep."

"When I couldn't find you, I—"

She hushed the rest of his sentence with her mouth. "It's going to be fun getting to know all the fascinating little things about each other."

He cupped her face. "Except when you scare the daylights out of me."

"What did you think happened?" Dea wanted to understand him.

Guido held her close. "You don't want to know. I feared someone might have come by and tried to drag you off."

"Oh, darling, I'm so sorry."

"No. *I* am for not insisting we go downstairs last night, where we could be totally private and I could better protect you. If you'll gather your things, we'll get going. We can shower on the plane and have breakfast."

She smiled. "Don't shave. I like your five o'clock shadow."

His eyes darkened with emotion. "I don't know if I can wait to marry you."

"You're going to be exciting to live with. Already I know you're an impatient man. It will be a challenge to keep up with you. Come on. Let's get going. I can tell you're hungry. I think there are a few more nuts left on deck to tide you over."

She gave him a kiss on the cheek, then hurried back down to the bathroom to gather her things and straighten the blanket on the bed. Guido brought the quilt and pillows downstairs and put them in the cupboard.

"Pretty soon we'll be getting a lot of use out of that," he said, glancing at the bed.

Her heart raced. "Don't make promises you can't keep." On that bold note she dashed out of the room and up the stairs with her overnight case. His deep laughter preceded him on deck.

Before they got in the rental car, she took off her ring and slipped it in her purse. It wouldn't do if the steward or the pilot saw her wearing it. Secrets always had a way of getting out. Word would somehow get back to Guido's family.

On the way to the airport she brushed her hair and put on lipstick. Guido watched her out of the corner of his eye. "You're going to be my wife, but I still can't believe I'm marrying my fantasy."

"I love you so much. It seems too wonderful to be true."

His hands tightened on the steering wheel. "I'd like to take you to Naples with me. I hope you understand why I need to go alone first."

"I do."

"I probably won't get back to Rome until midnight and then I'll have to be up at dawn."

"Guido? How would you feel if I flew to Siena to watch the game with you?"

"Much as I'd love it, when we're the visiting team I can't see to your needs or make you comfortable."

She could tell what he was trying to do. He had no idea how much this was hurting her. To her grief, there was no dissuading him from his plans. "Then I'll watch it on TV."

"As soon as it's over, I'll phone you and we'll make plans to spend Monday night together."

Once they boarded the plane and were in the air, Guido disappeared long enough to shower and change so he'd be able to fly directly to Naples from the airport in Rome. Dea decided to wait until she got home to her apartment to shower and wash her hair.

The steward served them a delicious breakfast. Guido asked her to show him some of her drawings for the villa. She got them out of her case and they pored over everything. He had his own ideas, of course, but loved most everything she'd suggested except for the *Cuor di Leone* motif.

"That's too over the top, *bellissima*." He squeezed her hand across the table. "Have I hurt your feelings?"

"Yes, but I'll find a way to live with it. In fact I'll put that poster of you on the door of our new walk-in closet, where I can indulge my fantasy about you."

Too soon the seat belt light flashed. They were getting ready to land. This would be their first separation as an engaged couple, but she could tell Guido's mind was in a dozen different places. He was a man on a mission. The wrong one, as far as she was concerned.

When they'd taxied to a stop, Guido walked her out of the plane and down the steps to a waiting limo he'd arranged for her. He helped her in the back with her case and told the driver where to take her.

"The next time we're together, we'll plan our wedding. One more game a week from Sunday, and then we'll tell our families. *Miss me*." He planted a fierce kiss on her mouth before shutting the door.

That was the second time he'd said that to her. Did he honestly think she wouldn't? Didn't he know yet what he meant to her?

She gave him a little wave. The limo drove away before he could see moisture bathing her cheeks. It didn't take long for Dea to get into her apartment. She hoped no one had seen her tear-ravaged face.

The minute she was safely inside, she opened her purse and put the ring in her jewelry case. With that done, she pulled out her phone and flung herself on the bed to call Alessandra.

Please be home. Please answer.

Five rings and her voice mail came on. Of course it

did. On a Saturday she and Rini had to be out somewhere with the baby. Dea asked her to phone her back when she could without leaving a reason for the call.

This ought to have been the happiest day of her life, but as it wore on, her pain grew heavier. A trip to work out in the gym didn't relieve it. All she could think about was Guido's reason for flying to Naples today.

She came back to the apartment to shower and wash her hair. The rest of the day was taken up when Daphne Butelli, the friend who she'd modeled with, phoned. Daphne wanted to meet up, so they decided to see a film and get dinner after. The distraction didn't help her mental state. She came back to the apartment still filled with anxiety.

While she was watching the news on TV, her phone rang. *At last*, she thought when she saw the caller ID.

"Alessandra?"

"Hi, Dea. I'm so sorry not to have gotten back to you until now. We spent the day with Rini's father in Naples. It was his birthday. Carlo and his family came too. As usual we had to take so much stuff for Brazzo I forgot my phone. Until we got back home tonight, I didn't realize you'd called me this morning."

"Please don't apologize. Is Rini close by?"

"No. He's in the den taking care of business he didn't get done today. Are you all right?"

"Yes."

"No, you're not. I can hear it in your voice."

"I'm afraid Rini will walk in on our conversation."

"This is about Guido, right?"

A sad laugh escaped. "Who else?" The tears started again.

"We're safe for a while. Talk to me."

"I'll make this short. In case Rini surprises you, please don't react to what I'm going to tell you and don't tell him anything after you hang up. Make something up. This is for your ears only."

"I promise."

"We spent the night on his sailboat in Ischia. He asked me to marry him and gave me a beautiful diamond ring. But he doesn't want anyone to know we're engaged yet. He plans to sell his soccer team after his last game a week from tomorrow.

"In the meantime, he flew to Naples today to tell his father he's going back to the shipping lines and will accept the position as CEO. When all that is accomplished, then we'll announce our wedding plans."

"What you've just told me has me jumping out of my skin for joy, so why are you so unhappy?"

Dea sank down on the side of the bed. "Because when I see Guido on Monday night, I'm giving back the ring."

A long silence followed. "What am I missing?"

"Guido's afraid I'll leave him."

"I'm not following."

"Maybe this will help." She told her sister about Guido's insecurity where his father was concerned. "He said that the owner of a soccer team isn't a befitting profession for the husband of Count Caracciolo's princess daughter."

"He actually *said* that?"

"Oh, yes."

She heard her sister groan. "I can't believe it."

"Neither can I. Deep in his psyche he thinks he has to work for his father to prove his own worth."

"Oh, Dea, I don't know what to say."

"You're not alone. A year ago he left the shipping business to buy the soccer team. He loves what he does *now*. There's excitement in him. I'm afraid he'll lose all that by giving it up. He's only doing it because of me, Alessandra, and what he thinks his father expects of him. I can't live with him knowing he's giving up what he loves most."

"No. I couldn't, either."

"I'm glad you agree with me." Given the turbulent, painful history between Dea and her sister, only Alessandra could understand her reasoning. "If I return the ring on Monday night, no harm will have been done. No one will ever have to know he proposed and it will all be over before any decisions he's made are final. Then he'll be free to do what he really wants."

"But he wants you."

"He won't want me, not when he knows why I can't keep the ring. And I've made another decision."

"What's that?"

"Tomorrow I'm going to send out résumés over the internet to places needing period costume designers for either the opera or the theater. If it means moving to England or France for a time, I know it will be a good thing. My career is important to me and I'm not going to let this set me back."

"I love you, Dea, and I'm behind you a thousand percent."

"Thank you for listening. I needed to say it out loud." She appreciated her sister not trying to reason with her or talk her out of anything. "I love you too. Take care. Good night."

CHAPTER NINE

I‍T WAS TEN to twelve Sunday night when Guido arrived back at his apartment. The fabulous game results were in. Team Scatto Roma: 2—Siena: 0

A forward on the opposition side had developed a bad case of stomach flu and couldn't play. Fate was with Guido's team despite Dante's fractured leg. One more win next Sunday and the national championship would be theirs.

Guido quickly phoned Dea. He had so much to tell her, he couldn't wait to hear her voice. But disappointment flooded him when his call went to her voice mail. He'd have to wait until tomorrow to talk to her.

Exhausted from virtually no sleep in the last twenty-four hours, he passed out the minute his head hit the pillow. He woke up at eight and checked his phone. Dea still hadn't responded. Guido left another message, but no results. After showering and getting dressed, he grabbed a quick bite and left for his office at the stadium to do a follow-up after the game.

As the day wore on he called her several times. No phone calls from Dea proved something was wrong.

After telling Sergio he was leaving, he drove straight to her work only to discover she'd already left for home. By now he was feeling close to frantic. He parked and entered her apartment foyer to ring her. If he couldn't reach her, he would call her parents.

Relief swamped him when he heard the buzz that let him inside. He took the stairs two at a time to the third floor. She'd left the door open for him, but instead of running into his arms, she stood in the living room dressed in her workout clothes. He moved inside and shut the door, struggling for the right words.

"What's going on, Dea?" he rasped. "Why in heaven's name haven't you returned my calls?"

"First let me say welcome back and congratulations on another win."

He rubbed the back of his neck, completely bewildered. "What's happened to you since we kissed goodbye at the airport?"

"If you'll sit down, I'll tell you."

"I'd rather stand."

"Guido, I haven't intentionally tried to be cruel by not answering the phone." Her sincerity smote him. "The truth is, I've needed this much time to gather my thoughts before we spoke again. I had to be sure that you'll understand perfectly what I'm about to tell you."

He felt like he'd been slugged in the gut. "You've decided you don't want to marry me after all."

Her unmistakable nod caused such excruciating pain he couldn't breathe. While he stood there in shock, she walked over to the end table and put the ring down.

"More than anything in the world, I want to marry you and be your wife. But I don't want my husband to give up the career he loves for me."

Her first salvo found its target, crippling him.

"I want the Guido I met, who was full of life and excitement, who's still young and has an extraordinary gift that can't be bought. That man has the ability to motivate thousands of younger men who need a hero to model themselves after. A man like that only comes along once in several lifetimes.

"I fell in love with that man, not the man who's going back to a job he'll still be able to do years from now, a job that doesn't fulfill him, a job that squeezes the life out of him.

"Guido Rossano? You're worried you'll never live up to your father's expectations if you don't go back to the company. *I'm* worried you'll never be happy again if you do, so we need our engagement to end."

Zing. Another salvo to finish him off. He broke out in a cold sweat.

She moved to the doorway. "You're welcome to stay here as long as you want. I'm off to the gym."

In the next instant she was gone, leaving her words ringing in his ears. *I don't want my husband to give up the career he loves for me.*

Little did Dea know he'd already come to his senses and she'd been preaching to the converted. But she hadn't given him the chance to talk.

Galvanized into action, he raced out the door to

stop her. But when he reached her parking space, he discovered her car was still there. She had to have taken the staircase to escape him. Where in the hell was the gym? But even if he could find her, the gym wasn't the place to continue their conversation.

Guido went back to her apartment. After locking the door, he pocketed the ring. A quick examination of the kitchen revealed she had enough food for him to make them a meal. But she didn't come home and he ended up putting the food away.

He sat on the couch to watch the evening news and the sports. At five after eleven he heard her key in the lock and she opened the door. Her eyes collided with his across the expanse. She looked drawn and pale. Her hair had been tied at her nape with a band. "Guido! What are you doing here?"

"What do you think? You disappeared on me before I had a chance to talk to you about anything."

She closed the door. "I can smell garlic and basil."

"I made us a meal. If you're hungry, I'll warm it up."

"I ate dinner earlier."

"By yourself?"

"No. With Gina. We met at the gym first."

He'd been lounging back on the couch with his legs extended. "You told me I could stay as long as I wanted, so I took you at your word. If you're too tired to hear what I have to say right now, I'll still be here in the morning."

Her features wooden, she came closer and sank down on one of the chairs.

"Go ahead."

Guido sat forward. "After I flew to Naples to surprise my family, I discovered they were away for the day with friends in Salerno. I was the one surprised and ended up visiting with my grandfather and his nurse. He mostly talked about the war years and his hard life when he was young."

Her head lifted. "You didn't talk business?"

"No. He told me he always wanted to go to sea and travel the world. But he revered his strict father too much and stuck with the shipping company like a dutiful son. He looked me in the eyes and said, 'My life was successful. I had a loving wife and family, but my great regret was that I wasn't happy in my career. Good for you for doing what makes you happy.' With those words he said he was tired and told me to kiss him before he went to bed."

She rubbed her hands over her knees. "That must have been a very emotional experience for you."

"I heard a side of my grandfather I didn't know existed. Yesterday in Siena I underwent another shock when my parents showed up to be with me at the game."

She looked startled. "They actually came?"

"Yes. I knew it was my grandfather's doing, but the fact that they made the effort was a revelation. My mother had always been on my side and would have come to all my games if she hadn't felt it was disloyal to my father. It was an added bonus for them to see that my team won the game."

"I heard the score on the news," she murmured.

"When I saw them off at the airport and thanked them for coming, I told them I loved owning the team. So much in fact that I wasn't planning to go back to the company for a few years. But to sweeten the bad news, I told them you and I were getting married and wanted him and Mamma to help us plan everything."

Dea's eyes went suspiciously bright.

"I thanked him for never giving up on me and finding me the love of my life."

"You did?" She sounded incredulous.

"Do you know he wept? So did my mother, but I've never seen my father break down like that. Before he had a chance to say another word, I promised him that God willing, we'd give them grandchildren. I also invited them to fly to Ischia with us soon so they can see where we're going to live. We'll let them choose the room they'd like to have when they stay with us."

"Oh, Guido—" Suddenly Dea had launched herself into his arms and broke down sobbing. "Forgive me for the things I said to you, darling. You have to forgive me for doubting you."

He crushed her against him, burying his face in her hair. "I can understand why you said what you did. To be honest, when I was talking to you on the sailboat, I was thinking of my own father, not yours."

"I know that now." She half sobbed the words.

"I've always been afraid he didn't think soccer was a worthy job for a son of his."

"I understand it all. I get it, but you have to know he doesn't feel that way."

"You're right."

She covered his face with kisses. "I never meant to hurt you. Where's my ring?"

"Right here." He reached in his trouser pocket and put it on her finger.

"I swear I'll never take it off again."

Their mouths met hungrily. When he finally lifted his head, he said, "Do you think it's too late to call your parents and tell them our news?"

"Yes, but they'd never forgive me if I didn't waken them anyway. And then I want to phone Alessandra and Rini. She loves you and has wanted this marriage since the day we went out on the cruiser together."

"You made that up."

"No. What you don't know is that she and I have had several talks about you, all my doing. Rini's going to be so happy for us too. Now the *four* of us will be joined at the hip forever."

Guido burst into laughter. Heavens, how he loved this woman! What was it Rini had said that evening at the castle when he'd confided in him about Dea?

You and I both know that no matter how bad it looks, you never leave the stadium until the game is over. Astounding surprises happen in the last second.

Astounding was right. At the last second all Guido's dreams had come true. He stretched out on the couch and started to pull her on top of him, but she held back. "If we don't make the call now, it'll be too late."

"You're right."

She went over by the chair to get her purse and pulled out her phone. He sat up and she rejoined him on the couch. Guido wrapped his arm around her and held her close while she punched the programmed number. "I've got it on speakerphone."

"Dea?" her mother cried after picking up on the third ring. "What's wrong, *tesoro*?"

"Not a thing, Mamma. Can you put your phone on speaker so Papà can hear this too?"

"Just a minute. Okay. Go ahead. We're both listening."

Guido squeezed her hip.

"Do you remember the day you told me to concentrate on finding myself? If I did that, my prince would find me?"

"Prince?" he whispered in her ear.

"Of course I do."

"Well, you're full of wisdom. My blond pirate prince has asked me to marry him."

Pirate?

"Grazie a Dio!" her father said in a booming voice.

"Oh—*tesoro*, we've been praying for this day since your sister's wedding."

She stared at Guido. "You have?"

"We weren't the only ones, either."

"What do you mean?"

"When you and Guido stood at the front of the cathedral as maid of honor and best man, Guido's parents smiled at your father and me. We were all thinking the same thing—that our beautiful son and daughter were meant to be together, but you didn't know it then. I'm so happy for you. Guido? Are you there? Do your parents know yet?"

Dea handed him the phone.

"They know, and they think I'm the luckiest man alive, which I am."

"Welcome to the family, Guido." This from Dea's father.

He felt a thickening in his throat. "I'm thrilled to become a part of it. I don't know if Dea told you, but my father arranged for that fashion show on the yacht so I could meet the breathtaking Dea Loti. He thought she would make me the perfect wife. I took one look at her and knew she would."

"That's very touching," Dea's mother said in a tear-filled voice.

"Mamma? How would you and Papà feel about our getting married in the Rossanos' church in Naples?"

"We don't care where you take your vows as long as we're there," her father asserted.

"Darling? Have you picked a date?"

Dea kissed Guido's lips. "Maybe three weeks? A month? By then I will have graduated and the soccer season will be over. We don't want to wait any longer than that."

"Does Alessandra know?"

"We're going to phone them right now."

"You do that and we'll talk more tomorrow. Fulvia will be overjoyed."

"She will! I guess I don't have to tell you that I have the best parents on earth. *Dormi bene.*"

"Ooh!" Dea threw her arms around him, almost knocking him over. "I'm so happy I can't breathe."

"You have to breathe to live, *adorata*. Come on.

Let's get this call to your sister over with. You and I have things to do."

She kissed one corner of his mouth. "Are you going to make us wait a whole month?"

"Yes, you gorgeous witch. Keeping the fires burning will add infinite pleasure to our wedding night and all the nights destiny allows us from then on."

Dea grasped his hands and kissed the tips of his fingers. "So—" she rolled her eyes at him "—you chip, drop, kick, sweep, cook and are an incredible romantic too. What did I ever do to deserve you?"

June 30, fourteenth-century church of San Giovanni, Carbonara, Naples

"There are so many photographers here you'll be late for your own wedding."

Dea clung to her father's arm, trembling with excitement as she carried a sheaf of white roses tied with a white satin ribbon. "I love you, Papà."

His eyes glazed over with love. "You know how I feel about my daughter."

She did. "I don't know what I'd do without you." People had thronged from everywhere to watch, but all she could think about was Guido, who stood inside the church waiting for her. She couldn't get to him fast enough.

"Juliana outdid herself when she designed your wedding dress. Her gift to you is almost as magnificent as you are, my darling girl."

The exquisite lace covering her arms and shoulders

hugged her white princess-style wedding dress. She wore a shoulder-length veil of the same lace and had left her hair long. Guido asked that she never cut it. Since he felt that strongly, she wanted to please him.

Organ music filled the vestibule where Alessandra and Rini were waiting for them dressed in their wedding finery. Her twin's smiling gaze fused with Dea's. They heard the chords of the wedding march at the same time. This wasn't like the pretend weddings they'd staged in their play castle when they were little. This was really going to happen.

Two friends of the Rossano family opened the doors and Dea began the long walk to the front of the church with her handsome father. Alessandra and Rini followed them down the aisle. The church overflowed with guests from both their families. With every step closer to Guido and the priest who would marry them, her heart thudded harder and harder.

Out of the corner of her eye she saw some friends from the college and the models she'd worked with over the years. With another step, she spotted Gina and Aldo and realized everyone from Juliana's shop, including her staff, had come.

Farther on, she saw Sergio and the other men and coaches who worked with Guido. Many of the players on his team had come to honor him. Still others from Rossano Shipping Lines had come en masse.

Closer to the altar she saw the Montanari family, including Valentina and Giovanni, Rini's sister- and brother-in-law. They sat on one side of the aisle. On the other sat her loving mother and aunt Fulvia, plus the staff from the castle. Juliana and her husband sat behind them. The older woman beamed. Dea owed her so much.

Suddenly her father walked her to Guido's side and lifted the roses to hand to her sister. Dea turned toward her fiancé, but she couldn't prevent the slight gasp of awe that escaped her lips.

With his tall superb physique and dark blond hair, he looked so splendid she almost fainted. A white rose decorated the lapel of his wedding suit, the same midnight blue color as his eyes. Guido wore his jacket buttoned over a matching vest with a stark white shirt and pastel gray-blue tie. He flashed her a haunting smile that took her breath away.

"Bellissima," he whispered in a husky tone and grasped her hand. *"Grazie a Dio* you're no longer a figment of my imagination. If you had any idea how long I've been waiting for this moment…"

She *did*, actually, because she'd been in the same pain.

As the ceremony began, she feared the Rossanos' family priest performing the rites could hear her heart resounding throughout the nave. Very little registered until they'd repeated their vows to love and honor each other.

"I now pronounce you man and wife and ask that you remain faithful to each other. May God bless this union. In the name of the Father and the Son." He made the sign of the cross. "Amen."

Guido didn't wait for any prompting. He reached for her shoulders and lowered his mouth to hers, giving her what she would always remember…the divine kiss of life from her new husband. Unspeakable joy filled her heart.

For three days and nights they stayed in their suite at the villa on Ischia, the only area aside from the bathroom that had been furnished in time for their honeymoon.

This morning Guido had left her arms long enough to go down to the village for more food. So far they'd subsisted on love and little else.

Dea's hungry eyes played over his hard-muscled body as he put some sacks on the table. He was the most gorgeous man on earth, whether in shorts and a T-shirt like he was wearing, or nothing at all.

"I brought you something that will interest you."

"I thought by now you'd figured out that you are my only interest."

A smile of satisfaction lit up his handsome face. He drew a newspaper out of one of the bags and handed it to her. "Look on page two. No doubt my father had a great deal to do with the half-page article and picture in the *Corriere della Sera*."

She smiled up at him. "The paper with the largest circulation in Italy? Of course he did. He's the proud *papà*."

Dea propped herself against the pillows. The second she opened to the article, she let out a cry. There she was in her flowing white wedding gown and veil coming out of the church with Guido in a formal dark suit hugging her waist. The happiness on their faces brought tears to her eyes as she read the article.

On June 30, Signor and Signora Guido Ernesto Fortunati Rossano were married in the fourteenth-century church of San Giovanni a Carbonara in Naples. A reception followed at the Rossano villa. The island of Ischia will be home to the famous couple.

The bride, gorgeous former supermodel now turned opera-wardrobe designer Dea Caracciolo, is the twenty-eight-year-old daughter of Count Onorato Caracciolo and Princess Taranto of Southern Italy.

The groom, thirty-two-year-old Guido, the son of prominent shipping magnate Leonides Rossano and Isabella Fortunati, and the grandson of Ernesto Rossano, is the former national soccer champion of Italy known as the *Cuor di Leone*. At present he is the new owner of the fast-rising soccer team Scatto Roma. The team is tied for first place with Team Venezia, and the two will compete in a play-off for the national championship July 3 at the Emanuele Soccer Stadium in Rome.

Dea put down the newspaper. "I think the reporter got it all in and then some."

"Do you mind? You know Papà."

"Darling, I love him. He's your father and I love

his son so terribly that if you don't get in bed and love me this instant, I won't survive another minute."

"Well, we can't have that." He removed his clothes with startling speed and slid beneath the quilt to roll her on her back. "Dea," he whispered, looking down at her. "I keep thinking we're in a dream and I'm going to wake up. We aren't dreaming, are we?"

"I don't think so, and I'm afraid you're stuck with a wanton for good."

"If every man were stuck with a passionate woman like you, we'd all be in permanent heaven."

"Honestly? H-has it been good for you?" Her voice faltered.

He shook his dark blond head. "Can't you tell what you do to me? For three days I haven't let you leave my arms. You're so beautiful, I'm constantly out of breath. If you could see the way you look with your hair spread out on the pillow, and the way your eyes darken with emotion, maybe you'd understand. But you're not a man."

"Thank heaven for that. You make me thankful I'm a woman." Her eyes filled with tears. "I wish we'd met ten years ago. When I think of the time we've wasted."

"I try not to think about it. What matters is now. You've made me happier than I could ever have imagined. Love me again, *squisita*." He lowered his mouth to hers and began to make love to her with a new ferocity. For the next few hours Dea was shaken by a passion she'd never known.

Her amazing husband had been so wise to insist

they wait until they were married to become intimate lovers. To experience the wonder of lovemaking like this without knowing you belonged to each other first would take away this ultimate joy.

They finally fell asleep again. Later he wakened her with a hungry kiss. "How would you like to sleep on the boat tonight? I thought it was time we christened that bedroom too."

She chuckled. "I agree. Why don't we eat and then go sailing?"

"Are you saying that for my sake?"

Dea gave him an impish grin. "Yes! Because I can tell you're suddenly restless. The game on Sunday is on your mind. I'm thinking about it too. Tomorrow we'll be flying back to Rome. Before we leave, I want to spend our last night on the *Bona Dea*. She *is* the goddess of fertility."

His blue eyes flickered with emotion. "Would you really like to start a family right away?"

"Yes, if we can. But if you don't feel that way…"

He kissed her deeply. "I want it all with you as fast as possible."

"I'm so glad you said that. We're not getting any younger. It would be so nice if we had a baby soon who would become friends with Brazzo. They're planning on adopting another baby one of these days."

"I know. Rini told me."

"When did he tell you that?"

"Yesterday evening while you were in the shower, he left me a message that they were negotiating for another baby. According to Alessandra, it will be the closest thing to having twins. He said he hoped I was doing my own form of negotiation in order to get the job done too. He ended with, 'Hurry.'"

She sat straight up. "He didn't!"

"Oh, yes, he did. Do you want to see my phone?"

"No. You two are incorrigible. Alessandra would have a cow if she knew he'd written that to you."

"A cow?"

"It's an American expression Gina picked up from Aldo's New York friend and she passed it on to me."

He grabbed her hand and pressed it against his heart. "I swear I'll keep it a secret from my new sister-in-law." In the next breath he threw off the quilt. She screamed, provoking his laughter.

"Come on, Aphrodite. Even your lover, who can never get enough of you, has to renew his energy, and I'm starving!"

October 10, Posso Island, Southern Italy

The sun had just fallen into the water. "There they are!" Dea had glimpsed the Jeep behind the castle as the helicopter dipped closer. "This is so exciting to be having a reunion here at last!"

Once they landed, Guido hugged her hips before helping her down. Every time he touched her, her legs turned to jelly. She hurried toward the Jeep and saw that her sister had brought Brazzo with them. He was seated on her lap playing with his purple octopus, tugging on one of the belled tentacles.

Their dark-haired fourteen-month-old toddler was

so adorable Dea could hardly stand it. With coloring like that and olive skin, you'd never know he wasn't their birth son.

"Oh, you cute little thing." She kissed his cheeks and then her sister's cheek before climbing in the back.

"What? No kiss for me?" Rini teased.

"How about a hug instead?" She wrapped her arm around his neck from behind. Guido followed her into the backseat with their luggage.

"It's about time you lovebirds left the nest." This from Rini. Dea saw the secret look the two men flashed each other.

"We've been busy decorating the house," Guido explained.

"Sure you have. Excuses, excuses." Rini kept up the banter.

Alessandra laughed. "I hope you're hungry. Dinner is waiting."

Dea reached forward to tousle Brazzo's curls. "I'm starving. Someone should have warned me that getting married makes you hungry. Are Mamma and Papà here?"

"They will be later." Alessandra looked over her shoulder at Guido. "How does the team look to you for this new season?"

"It's good. They've recovered from the loss in July and are working harder than ever. Dante's back with us and suiting up. Another month and the doctor will clear him to play."

"That's wonderful news."

Rini drove them around to the entrance of the castle. Dea got out behind Alessandra and trailed her into the foyer, where Alfredo was waiting. "Oh, my buddy." She scooped him up. "Have you missed me?"

But at this point Brazzo was toddling around and the cat squirmed to get down. "Well, I just got my question answered. This fickle cat has a new playmate. Look at you walking, Brazzo!"

The men had just come inside with the bags. They all watched in amusement as the precious boy chased after the housekeeper's pet.

"Come on, you two." Rini started for the stairs. "We've put you in the same bedroom Guido has used when he's stayed here."

"Brazzo and I will be in the dining room, won't we, sweetheart. Hurry back down."

Dea hugged her sister, then followed the men upstairs. Excitement rippled through her body to think she'd be sleeping with Guido in her old home.

Rini left them alone while they freshened up. Guido grabbed her from behind while she was looking out the window. "You have no idea how I longed to drag you up here after our soccer match on the sand. The dreams I had about you would make your face turn crimson."

She wheeled around and threw her arms around his neck. "I had my own dreams that night. The thought of sneaking into your bedroom in the middle of the night never left my mind. I guess I don't have to wonder what you would have done. You would have been the total gentleman and escorted me back to the hall-way."

"Don't be so sure. I was on fire for you that night."

"So on fire you didn't even say goodbye to me."

"You know why, my love. Come on. We'll have all night to finish this conversation. In the meantime, our hosts are waiting."

They clasped hands and went downstairs to the dining room. Brazzo was sitting in his high chair at the corner of the table between Rini and Alessandra. He banged the tray with a spoon.

Dea chuckled and sat across from them with Guido. "Umm. I can see the cook has outdone herself with my favorite salmon and eggplant."

"She knew you were coming and remembered."

"I'll go out to the kitchen later and thank her."

"Now that we're all here, Rini and I have an an-nouncement." Dea eyed Guido while they waited for Alessandra's news. "We had to be certain to make sure everything was going right, but we have just been told to expect our next baby in a month!"

"I knew it!" Dea squealed in delight.

"It's a girl this time." Rini's smile lit up his dark eyes.

"There couldn't be better news, *paisano*," Guido said.

"I agree, but do you think you can stand a little more?" Dea reached in the pocket of her pleated pants for a picture. "We've got a little news of our own."

The shocked look on Guido's face was worth all

the trouble she'd taken to keep her secret to herself. "Dea?" he whispered huskily.

"It's Rini's fault."

Everyone looked shocked at her comment, especially her brother-in-law. "You did send my husband a text four months ago. I'll quote it for everyone.

"'We're negotiating for another baby. According to Alessandra, it will be the closest thing to having twins. I hope you're doing your own form of negotiation in order to get the job done too.' Your postscript said, 'Hurry.'"

While quiet reigned, she handed Guido the picture. "Take a look and see what you did, darling."

Her husband looked down at the sonogram like he was in a trance.

"If you'll notice, there are two babies in there."

"Dea!" Alessandra's cry of joy reverberated in the dining room and probably the whole castle. She shot out of her chair and hurried around to look at it over Guido's shoulder.

"There *are* two."

"One is a girl. The doctor couldn't tell the gender of the other one yet. I'm four months along."

"Then our daughters will be less than six months apart. That's so perfect! We'll get out the play castle when they're old enough."

"It'll be déjà vu."

"Wait till our parents hear about this—"

Guido was still processing the information in a daze. He turned to Dea. "I thought you'd been putting on weight recently, but I didn't want to say anything."

"I knew you had to have noticed." She leaned over and kissed him on the mouth. "Sorry if I worried you about that."

"I wasn't worried, Dea."

"Liar. I love you more than ever for not giving me grief about it."

He got to his feet. "Are you all right?" When he put his hands on her upper arms, he was trembling. "Is everything going the way it should?"

"The doctor has given me a clean bill of health."

Alessandra ran the picture around to show Rini. While everyone was occupied, their parents walked in. "What's going on?" their father wanted to know.

Dea smiled at him. "We all have news, Papà. You go first, Alessandra."

Once her sister told them that they would be getting a girl within the month, she ran back around to give Dea the picture. "Now it's your turn."

The moment was surreal as she handed her mother the sonogram. She watched her parents study it.

Suddenly her mother pressed a hand over her heart. "Twins... You're going to have twins."

Her dad smiled broadly. "Well, what do you know. Fulvia said twins ran in the Taranto side of the family. Thanks to the Montanari side of the family, we're going to have a set of twins before another set comes along."

Dea loved her father intensely for making Rini feel included in a very real way.

"Let's break out the champagne, but you won't be able to drink it, Dea. No alcohol until after the babies are born," her father informed her. "Your mother and I know every rule."

Dea lifted shining eyes to Alessandra. "But you, my dear sister, can have all you want."

Rini hugged her. "I'm afraid it's wasted on my wife."

"Dea?" Guido whispered in her ear. "I need to be alone with you. Can we go upstairs soon?"

She nodded and kissed his jaw. He'd just found out he was going to be the father of twins. That had to be staggering news for any man. Perhaps even as staggering as it had been for the woman who carried them.

Her mother seemed to understand what was going on. "Dea, honey, you look tired. I think you should go up to bed. We'll celebrate in the morning."

Bless you, Mamma.

"Bed does sound good. It's been a long day."

Now that the evening had come to an end, everyone said good-night. Guido put his arm around her waist as they climbed the stairs to the bedroom on the third floor. "Oh, I forgot the picture."

"We'll get it in the morning. Right now I want to take care of you."

She hadn't realized that having to keep her news a secret from Guido had drained her. Suddenly she felt relaxed and couldn't wait to drift off with his arms around her.

As soon as she brushed her teeth and undressed,

she fell into bed. "I know you want your parents to know. Why don't you give them a call? Then I'll answer every question. I'm sorry I didn't tell you before now, but when the doctor detected two heartbeats, I wanted to wait until he could take a picture and make sure the babies were healthy. I couldn't see worrying you until I had to."

"I'm not upset with you, Dea. If anything, I'm glad I didn't know before now. We've had to deal with the villa and work, your graduation. But now that I know, I'm going to make certain you take perfect care of yourself. We have two precious babies growing inside you. It's a thrill I still haven't fully comprehended yet."

"That's the way I felt when the doctor first told me. Go on and phone your parents. They'll be ecstatic."

He put the covers over her and sat on the edge of the bed to call his family. The joy in their voices rang out through the phone. Dea reached for it. "We don't know if there's a boy or another girl in there. Maybe by the next appointment the doctor will be able to tell us."

"You're going to need help," his mother said through the tears.

"We'll need a lot of it," Dea assured her and meant it. "I'm so thankful we already have your room ready at the villa. Here's Guido back."

She waited while he finished talking to his parents. By the time he'd hung up and gotten into bed, she was half gone.

"You know that song…he had the whole world in his arms… Those words were written for me."

Dea turned into him, loving his hard, solid strength. "It works both ways. She had the whole world in her arms… You're my whole world, Guido Rossano.

"My whole glorious world. *Ti amo*."

* * * * *

A BABY TO HEAL
THEIR HEARTS

KATE HARDY

To C. C. Coburn and Cathleen Ross – hope
you enjoy Herod!

CHAPTER ONE

'SHE'S A BONNY LASS, our Bailey,' Archie said.

Jared's heart sank at the expression on the coach's face. Clearly Archie had taken a fancy to the researcher. And Jared had a nasty feeling that this might be a case of the coach's libido taking over from his common sense.

Allegedly, this 'bonny lass' researcher had a system that could reduce soft-tissue injuries among the players. So far, so good—but the figures being bandied about were crazy. In Jared's experience, when something sounded too good to be true, it usually was. And he could really do without some pretty, flaky girl distracting the players and getting in the way when he needed to treat them. Especially when he'd only just started his new job as the doctor to the youth team of a premiership division football club.

He'd been here before, when a manager's or player's head had been turned by a pretty girl, and the outcome was always messy. Worse still, it tended to have an impact on the rest of the team. With a bunch of teenage lads, this could get very messy indeed.

But he kept his thoughts to himself and gave the coach a polite smile. 'That's nice.'

Hopefully this Bailey woman would get bored quickly, or her system would be debunked, and they could go back to a more sensible way of preventing soft-tissue injuries—like sport-specific training, after he'd assessed each of the players and taken a proper medical history.

In the meantime, he'd have to grit his teeth and be as polite and as neutral as possible.

'Bailey—oh, good, you're here. Come and meet Jared Fraser, the new team doctor,' Archie McLennan called over from the side of the football pitch as Bailey walked through the players' tunnel.

Bailey smiled at the youth team's coach, but she made sure that she stood just far enough away so that Archie couldn't put his arm round her shoulders. She liked him very much as a colleague—he was at least prepared to listen to new ideas and he'd been more than fair with her on the research project so far—but she really wasn't in the market for a relationship.

Particularly with someone who was recently divorced and with a lifestyle that really didn't work for her; that was just setting things up to fail. And Bailey had failed quite enough in her relationships, thank you very much. She wanted life to be simple in the future—full of her family, her friends and her work, and that was enough for her. She didn't need anything more.

'Jared, this is Bailey Randall—the doctor whose research project I was telling you about,' Archie said.

For a moment, Jared looked as if he'd seen a ghost. Then he seemed to pull himself together and gave her a brief nod of acknowledgement. 'Dr Randall.'

But he didn't smile at her. Did he not approve of women being involved with a football team? Was he not good at social skills? Or—given that his accent was quite distinctive—was he just living up to the stereotype of the slightly dour, strong-and-silent Scotsman?

It was a shame, because he had the most gorgeous eyes. A deep, intense blue—the colour of a bluebell carpet. If he smiled, she'd just bet his eyes would have an irresistible twinkle.

Which was crazy. Since when did she think so fancifully? Bluebells, indeed.

'Pleased to meet you,' she said, giving him her brightest smile, and held her hand out for him to shake.

He gave another brief inclination of his head and shook her hand. His grip was firm, brief and very businesslike. He still didn't smile, though. Or say any kind of social pleasantry.

Oh, well. It wasn't as if she'd need to have that much to do with him, was it? Her project—to test a monitoring system to see if it could help to reduce the number of soft-tissue injuries in the team—had been agreed by the football club's chair of directors. She'd been working with Archie, the youth team coach, at training sessions and on match days when they played at home, and so far the system's results were proving very interesting indeed.

'Hey, Bailey.' John, one of the players, came over to the side and high-fived her.

'Hey, John. How's the ankle?' she asked.

'It's holding up, thanks to you,' he said with a smile.

'And you're still wearing that support?'

He nodded. 'And I'm doing the wobble-board exercises, like you showed me last time,' he said.

'Good.'

'Bailey helped out on a couple of sessions when she was here and your predecessor called in sick,' Archie told Jared. 'John sprained his ankle a few weeks back.'

'Sprained ankles are the most common injury in football,' Bailey said, just so Jared Fraser would know that she did actually understand the situation—maybe he was the dinosaur kind of man who thought that women knew next to nothing about sport. 'He was running when he hit a bump in the field, the sole of his foot rolled under and the movement damaged the ligaments on the outside of his ankle.' She shrugged. 'The wobble-board training we've been doing reduces the risk of him damaging his ankle again.'

Jared gave her another of those brief nods, but otherwise he was completely impassive.

Oh, great. How on earth was he going to connect with the players? Or maybe he was better at communicating when he was in work mode, being a doctor. She certainly hoped so, because the boys were still young enough to need encouragement and support; they weren't likely to respond to dourness.

'I ought to give you each other's mobile phone numbers and email addresses and what have you—in case you need to discuss anything,' Archie said.

'I doubt we will,' Jared said, 'but fine.'

Oh, what was *the guy's problem?* She itched to shake him, but that wouldn't be professional. Particularly in front of the youth team. Doctors, coaches and managers were supposed to present a united front. OK, so strictly speaking she didn't work for the football club—she was here purely as a researcher—but she still needed to be professional. 'Give me your number,' she said, 'and I'll text you with my email address so you have all my details.'

Once that was sorted out, she took her laptop out of its case. 'OK, guys, you know the drill. Let's go.' As the players lined up, she switched on her laptop, then called each team member by name and handed him a monitor with a chest strap, checking each one in with the laptop as she went.

'So what exactly is this system?' Jared asked when the players had filed onto the field to warm up. 'Some kind of glorified pedometer, like those expensive wristband gadgets that tell people they woke up three times during the night, but don't actually tell them why they woke up or what they can do about it?'

He sounded downright hostile. *What was his problem?* she thought again. But she gritted her teeth and tried her best to be polite. 'It does measure the number of steps the players take, yes,' she said, 'but it also monitors their average speed, the average steps they take per game, their heart rate average and maximum, and their VO2.' VO2 measured the amount of oxygen used by the body to convert the energy from food into adenosine triphosphate; the higher the VO2 max, the higher the athlete's level of fitness.

He scoffed. 'How on earth can you measure VO2 properly without hooking someone up to a system with a mask?'

'It's an estimate,' she admitted, 'but this system is a lot more than just a "glorified pedometer".' She put exaggerated quotes round the phrase with her fingers, just to make the point that she wasn't impressed by his assessment. Sure, once he knew what the system did and how it worked, she'd be happy to listen to him and to any suggestions he might have for improving it. But right now he was speaking from a position of being totally uninformed, so how could his opinion be in the least bit valid?

'The point is,' she said, 'to look at reducing the number of soft-tissue injuries. That means the players get more time to train and play, and they spend less time recovering from injuries. This particular system has been tested with a rugby team and it reduced their soft-tissue injury rate by seventy per cent, and my boss thinks it's worth giving it a try on other sports.' She gave him a grim smile. 'Just so you know, I'm not trying to put you out of a job. If anything, I'm trying to make your life easier by taking out the small, time-consuming stuff.'

'And you're actually a qualified doctor?' he asked, sounding sceptical.

Give me strength, Bailey thought, but she gave him another polite smile. 'Remind me to bring my degree certificate in with me next time,' she said. 'Or you can look me up on the Internet, if you're that fussed. I run sports medicine clinics three days a week at the London Victoria, so you'll find me listed in the department there, and I spend the other two working days each week on a research project.'

'So you're using this system of yours with other teams as well?' he asked.

'No—this is the only team I'm working with, and I only do one research project at a time. My last one was preventative medicine,' she explained. 'Basically I worked with patients who had high blood pressure.

The aim was to help them to lose weight and maintain lean muscle mass, and that reduced both their blood pressure and their risk of cardiovascular incidents.' She couldn't resist adding, 'And by that I mean heart attacks and strokes.'

'Right.' Jared stared at Bailey. Archie had called her a 'bonny lass', but she was so much more than that. She was truly beautiful, with a heart-shaped face and huge brown eyes—emphasised by her elfin crop. She looked more like some glamorous Mediterranean princess than a doctor.

But, in Jared's experience, beautiful women spelled trouble and heartache. His ex, Sasha, had used her stunning looks to get her own way—and Jared had fallen for it hard enough to get very badly burned. Nowadays he was pretty much impervious to huge eyes and winsome smiles. But he'd already seen how Archie was following Bailey round like a lapdog; he had a nasty feeling that Bailey Randall had used her looks to get her own way with her ridiculous bit of computerised kit, the way Sasha always used her looks.

Still, at least this system of hers wasn't something that would actually hurt the players. It wouldn't be of much real use—like the pricey fitness wristbands he'd referred to earlier, it wouldn't give enough information about what was actually wrong or how to fix it—but it wouldn't do any real harm, either.

Jared spent the session on the side of the pitch, ready in case any of the players had an injury that needed treating. But there were no strains, sprains or anything more serious; and, at the other end of the scale, there wasn't even a bruise or a contusion.

Half a lifetime ago, he'd been one of them, he thought wryly. A young hopeful, planning a career in the sport and dreaming of playing for his country. He'd actually made it and played for the England under-nineteen squad, scoring several goals in international matches. But Bailey Randall's bit of kit wouldn't have done anything to save him from the knee injury in his final game—the tackle that had stopped his football career in its tracks. Jared had ended up pursuing his original plans instead, studying for his A-levels and following in the family tradition by taking a degree in medicine.

The lure of football had drawn Jared to work with a club as their team doctor, rather than working in a hospital or his parents' general practice. And he still enjoyed the highs and lows of the game, the camaraderie among the players and hearing the supporters roar their approval when a goal was scored.

At the end of the training session, Archie turned to Bailey. 'Over to you.'

Jared watched in sheer disbelief as Bailey proceeded to take the youth team through a series of yoga stretches and then breathing exercises.

What place did yoga have on a football pitch? In his experience, the players would do far better working on sport-specific training. As well as ball control, they needed to focus on muscular endurance and lower-body strength, and also work on explosive acceleration and short bursts of speed. If Archie wanted him to do it, Jared could design a training programme easily enough—either a warm-up routine that would work for the whole team, or some player-specific programmes to help deal with each player's weak spots—and it would do a lot more for the players' overall neuromuscular co-ordination than yoga would.

But having a go at Bailey Randall in front of the team wouldn't be professional, so Jared kept his mouth shut until the lads had gone for a shower and she was doing things on her laptop. Then he walked over to her and said, 'Can we have a quick word?'

She looked up from her laptop with an expression of surprise, but nodded. 'Sure.'

'What *exactly* does your box of tricks tell us?' he asked.

'It analyses each player's performance. For each player, I can show you a graph of his average performance over the last ten matches or training sessions, and how today's performance compares against that average.'

So far, so good. 'Which tells us what?'

'The system will pick up if a player is underperforming,' she said. 'Maybe he's coming down with a cold but isn't showing any symptoms yet—and if he's sick he's more at risk of sustaining injury and shouldn't be playing.'

He gave her a sceptical look. 'So you're telling me you can predict if a player's going to get a cough or a cold?'

'No, but I can predict the likelihood of the player sustaining an injury in his next match, based on his performance today and measured against an average of his last ten sessions.'

'Right.' Jared still wasn't totally convinced. And

then he tackled the subject that bothered him most about today's antics. 'And the yoga?'

'As a football team doctor—someone who's clearly specialised in sports medicine—you'd already know that dynamic stretches are more useful than static stretches.' She held his gaze. 'But if you want me to spell it out to prove that I know what I'm talking about, dynamic stretches means continuous movement. That promotes blood flow, strength and stability. It also means you can work on more than one muscle group at a time—so it's more functional, because it mimics what happens with everyday movements. And you only hold the stretch for a short period of time, so the muscle releases more effectively and you get a better range of movement with each repetition.' She raised her eyebrows, as if challenging him to call her on it. 'Happy?'

He nodded. She did at least know her stuff, then. Even if she was a bit misguided about the computer programme. 'So you're a qualified yoga teacher?'

'No. But a qualified teacher—the one who's taught me for the last five years—helped me put the routine together.'

'Right. And the breathing?'

She put her hands on her hips and gave him a hard stare. 'Oh, for goodness' sake! Are you going to quiz me on every aspect of this? Look, the project's already been approved by Mr Fincham.' The chairman of the club's board of directors. 'If you have a problem with it, then maybe you need to speak to him about it.'

'I just don't see what use yoga is going to be to a bunch of lads who need sport-specific training,' he said.

'"Lads" being the operative word,' she said. 'They're sixteen, seventeen—technically they're not quite adults, and most of their peers are either still in education or starting some kind of apprenticeship. I won't insult them by calling them children, because they're not, but they still have quite a lot of growing up to do. And, in the profession they've chosen, they're all very much in the public eye. The media hounds are just waiting to tear into the behaviour of overpaid footballers, whipping up a frenzy among their readers about how badly the boys behave.'

'That's true,' he said, 'but I still don't get what it has to do with yoga.'

'Discipline,' she said crisply.

'They already have the discipline of turning up for training and doing what Archie tells them to do.'

'Holding the yoga poses also takes discipline, and so does the breathing. So it's good practice and it helps to underline what Archie does with them. Plus it's good for helping to deal with stress,' she said.

That was the bit Jared really didn't buy into.

She clearly saw the scepticism in his expression, because she sighed. 'Look, if they get hassled by photographers or journalists or even just someone else in a club when they're out—someone who wants to prove himself as a big hero who can challenge a footballer and beat him up—then all they have to do is remember to breathe and it'll help them to take everything down a notch.'

'Hmm,' he said, still not convinced.

She threw her hands up in apparent disgust. 'You know what? You can think what you like, Dr Fraser. It's not going to make any difference to my research.

If you've got some good ideas for how the data can be used, or about different measurements that would be useful in analysing the team's performance, then I'd be very happy to listen. But if all you're going to do is moan and bitch, then please just go and find someone else to annoy, because I'm busy. Excuse me.'

Bailey Randall clearly didn't like it when someone actually questioned her. And she still hadn't convinced him of the benefits of her project. 'Of course you are,' he said, knowing how nasty it sounded but right at that moment not caring.

As he walked away, he was sure he heard her mutter, 'What an ass.'

She was entitled to her opinion. He wasn't very impressed by her, either. But they'd just have to make the best of it, for as long as it took for Archie and the team director to realise that her 'research' was all a load of hokum.

CHAPTER TWO

'HE'S IMPOSSIBLE. TALK about blinkered. And narrow-minded. And—and— Arrgh!' Bailey stabbed her fork into her cake in utter frustration.

To her dismay, Joni just laughed.

'You're my best friend,' Bailey reminded her. 'You're supposed to be supportive.'

'I am. Of course I am,' Joni soothed. 'But you're the queen of endorphins. You always see the best in people, and to see you having a hissy fit about some-one—well, he's obviously made quite an impression on you.'

'And not a good one.' Bailey ate a forkful of cake and then rolled her eyes at the plate. 'Oh, come on. If I'm going to eat this stuff, it could at least reward me with a sugar rush.'

'Maybe it just makes you grumpy.'

Bailey narrowed her eyes at her best friend. 'Now you're laughing at me.'

Joni reached over the table and hugged her. 'I love you, and you're in an almighty strop. Which doesn't happen very often. This Jared Fraser guy has really rattled you.'

Bailey glowered. 'Honestly. He quizzed me on every single aspect of my project.'

'Which is better than just dismissing it.'

'He *did* dismiss it, actually. He thinks the players should be doing sport-specific training.'

Joni coughed. 'You're the sports medicine doctor, not me. And I seem to remember you saying something about sport-specific training being the most effective.'

'But it's not the only kind of training they should be doing,' Bailey said. 'Yoga means dynamic stretches, which are more effective than static ones. And there's the discipline of holding the pose and doing the breathing. It's really good for the boys, and it helps them to focus.'

'Maybe you should make Jared do the stuff with the boys,' Joni suggested. 'And you can make him do extra planks.'

'Don't tempt me.' Bailey ate more cake. 'Actually, Joni, that might be a good idea. He needs to chill out a bit. Downward dog and breathing—that would do the trick.'

'I'd love to be a fly on the wall when you suggest it to him,' Joni said.

'No, you wouldn't. You hate people fighting—and he really doesn't like me.'

'You don't like him, either,' Joni pointed out.

'Well, no. Because he's rude, arrogant and narrow-minded. With men like him around, I'm more than happy to stay single.'

They both knew that wasn't the real reason why Bailey was resolutely single. After her life had imploded two and a half years ago, her marriage had cracked beyond repair. And Bailey still wasn't ready to risk trying another relationship. She didn't know if she ever would be.

'I don't know what to say,' Joni said, giving her another hug, 'except I love you and I believe in you.'

'You, too,' Bailey said.

'And I worry about you. That you're lonely.'

'That's because you're all loved up. Which is just as it should be,' Bailey said, 'given that it's just under two months until you get married to Aaron. And he's a sweetie.'

'Even so, I worry about you, Bailey.'

'I'm fine,' Bailey said, forcing herself to smile. 'Just grumpy tonight. And don't breathe a word of this to my mum, or she'll say that I'm attracted to Jared Fraser and I'm in denial about it.'

'Are you?' Joni asked.

Bailey blew out a breath. 'You're about the only person who could get away with asking that. No. He might be nice looking if he smiled,' she said, 'and to be fair he does have nice eyes. The colour of bluebells. But even if he was as sweet as Aaron, I still wouldn't be interested. I'm fine exactly as I am. I don't need anyone to complicate my life.'

Her words were slightly hollow, and she was pretty sure that Joni would pick up on that. But to her relief Joni didn't push it any further, or comment on that stupid remark she'd made about bluebells.

She wasn't attracted to Jared Fraser. She wanted to give him a good shake and tell him to open his mind a bit.

And bluebells were out of the question.

* * *

Before the next match, Bailey had a meeting with Archie to discuss the latest results from her software. As she'd half expected, Jared was there. Still playing dour, strong and silent. Well, that was his problem. She had a job to do.

'Travis is underperforming,' she said, showing them the graph on her laptop screen. 'It might be that he's had too many late nights over the last week, or it might be that he's coming down with something—but I'd recommend that he doesn't play as part of the team today.'

'I've already assessed the squad this morning, and they're all perfectly fit,' Jared said.

'A player who's underperforming is at a greater risk of soft-tissue injury,' she reminded him.

'According to your theory. Which has yet to be proven, because if you pull a player off every time they do a few steps less per game, then of course he won't get a soft-tissue injury, because he won't actually be playing. And if you follow that through every time, you'll end up with a really tiny pool of players. And the rest of them won't have had enough practice to help them improve their skills.'

'If they're off for weeks with an injury, that's not going to help them improve their skills, either,' she pointed out.

'Travis is fine.' He folded his arms. 'You're making a fuss over nothing.'

'Travis *isn't* fine.' She mirrored his defensive stance. 'But it isn't our call. It's Archie's.'

'Fine,' Jared said.

Archie looked at them both and sighed. 'I'll have a word with the lad.'

Clearly Travis was desperate to play, because Archie came back to tell them that the boy was in the team.

If Jared said 'Told you so', she might just punch him.

He didn't. But it was written all over his face.

Cross, Bailey sat on the bench at the side of the pitch and texted her best friend: Jared Fraser has to be the most smug, self-satisfied man in the universe.

A few seconds later, her phone beeped. She glanced at the screen, expecting Joni to have sent her a chin-up-and-rise-above-it type of message, and was surprised to see that the message was from Jared Fraser. Why would he be texting her? He was sitting less than six feet away from her. He could lean across and talk to her. He didn't need to resort to texting.

Curious, she opened the message. Herod?

What?

Don't understand, she texted back. Ridiculous man. What was he on about?

Her phone beeped a few seconds later. Your message: <<Herod Fraser has to be the most smug, self-satisfied man in the universe.>>

Then she realised exactly what had just happened.

Oh, no.

She'd been typing so fast that she obviously hadn't noticed her phone autocorrecting 'Jared' to 'Herod'. And Jared's name was right next to Joni's in her phone book. When Bailey had tapped on the recipient box, she'd clearly pressed the wrong name on the screen.

So now Jared Fraser knew exactly what she thought about him.

Which could make life very awkward indeed.

Sorry, she typed back. Not that she was apologising for what she'd said. She stood by every word of that—well, bar the autocorrected name. She was only apologising for her mistake.

Didn't mean to send that to you.

I'd already worked that one out for myself.

She sneaked a glance at him to see if she could work out how much he was going to make her pay for that little error, and was shocked to realise that he was actually smiling. He wasn't angry or even irritated; he was amused.

There was a sudden rush of feeling in her stomach, as if champagne was fizzing through her veins instead of blood. Totally ridiculous. But when the man smiled, it changed him totally. Rather than being the dour, hard-faced, slightly intimidating man she'd instinctively disliked, he was beautiful.

Oh, help. She really couldn't afford to let her thoughts go in that direction. For all she knew, he could be married or at least involved with someone. She knew nothing about the man, other than that he was the new youth team doctor and he didn't believe in her research at all.

'Sir, are you *the* Jared Fraser?' Billy, one of the substitutes, asked, coming over to sit in the pointedly large gap on the bench between Bailey and Jared.

The Jared Fraser? Why would there be something special about a football team's doctor? Bailey wondered.

'How do you mean?' Jared asked.

'Me and the lads—we saw it on the Internet. We weren't sure if it was you. But if it is—you were one of the youngest players ever to score a goal in the England under-nineteen team. And on your debut match,' Billy added breathlessly. 'And you scored that goal in the championship, the one that won the match.'

'It was a long time ago now. I haven't played in years,' Jared said.

Bailey couldn't quite work this out. Jared had been a star football player as a teenager? Then how come he was a doctor now? He didn't look that much older than she was—five years at the most, she reckoned—so surely he could still play football. Or, if he'd retired from football, it was more likely that he would have become a coach or a manager. Footballer to medic was quite a career change. Especially given that you needed four years at university followed by two years' foundation training, and then you had to work your way up the ranks. To be experienced enough to have a job as a football team doctor, Jared must have been working in medicine for at least ten years. Maybe more. So why had he switched careers?

Feeling slightly guilty about being so nosy—but she could hardly ask the man himself, given how grumpy and impossible he was—she flicked onto the Internet on her phone and looked up 'Jared Fraser footballer England team' in a search engine.

The photograph was eighteen years old now, but the teenager was still recognisable as the man she knew. Jared Fraser had indeed been a footballer. One of the youngest players to score a goal for his country, at the age of seventeen. He'd played in several international matches and had scored the winning goal in a championship game. All the pundits had been tipping him to be one of the greatest players ever. But then, according to the online biography she was reading, he'd been involved in a bad tackle. One that had given him an anterior cruciate ligament injury that had ended his playing days.

So his dreams had been taken from him and he'd ended up in a totally different career. Poor guy. It would, perhaps, explain the dourness. She'd be pretty grumpy, too, if she was no longer able to do her dream job.

Maybe she'd give Jared Fraser just a little bit of slack in future.

Though not from pity. She remembered what it felt like, being an object of pity. It was one of the reasons why she'd moved departments. She might've been able to stick it out, had it not been for the guilt— the knowledge that people felt they had to be careful around her instead of beaming their heads off about a piece of personal good news, the kind of joy everyone else would celebrate with. Because how did you tell someone you were expecting a baby when you knew they'd lost theirs, and in such a difficult way?

Yeah. Bailey Randall knew all about broken dreams. And how you just had to pick yourself up, dust yourself down and pretend that everything was absolutely fine. Because, if you did that, hopefully one day it *would* be just fine.

Halfway through the match, she noticed Travis

lying on the ground, clutching his leg. Jared was already on his feet and running towards the boy; play had stopped and Jared was examining the player as she joined them.

'What's wrong?' she asked.

'Let me finish the SALTAPS stuff,' Jared said.

'SALTAPS?' It was obviously some kind of mnemonic, but not one she'd come across before.

'Stop play, analyse, look for injury, touch the site, active movement, passive movement, stand up,' he explained swiftly. 'Travis, what happened?'

'I don't know—there's just this pain down the back of my left leg,' the boy said, his face pale with pain.

Gently, Jared examined him. 'Did you hear a pop or a crack before the pain started?'

'I'm not sure,' Travis admitted. 'I was focusing on the ball.'

'OK. Does it hurt when you move?'

Travis nodded.

'I want you to bend your knee. If it hurts, stop moving straight away and tell me.'

The young player followed Jared's instructions and winced. 'It really hurts.'

'OK. I'm not even going to try the last bit—getting you up on your feet. I think you've got a hamstring injury, though I need to check a couple more things before I treat you. Archie's going to need to substitute you.'

'No, he can't!' Travis looked devastated. 'I'll be all right in a second or two. I'll be able to keep playing.'

Jared shook his head. 'Play on when you're injured and you'll do even more damage. You need treatment.'

Bailey had been pretty sure it was a hamstring

injury, too, given Travis's symptoms. Hopefully it would be a partial rupture and wouldn't affect the whole muscle. 'Dr Fraser, you need to be on the pitch in case there's another injury,' she said. 'I'll take Travis to the dressing room and finish off the assessments for you.'

He looked at her and, for a moment, she thought he was going to refuse. Then he gave a brief nod. 'Thank you, Dr Randall. That would be helpful.'

'I'll talk to you when I've assessed him,' she said. Even though she was pretty sure that they'd recommend the same course of treatment, strictly speaking, Jared was in charge and Travis was his patient, and she was only here for research purposes. She didn't have the right to make decisions for Jared.

She supported Travis back to the dressing room. There was a wide, flat bench that would do nicely for her purposes; she gestured to it. 'OK. I want you to lie down here on your back, Travis, so I can go through the assessments and see how much damage you've done.'

'There's no need, really. I'll be all right in a few minutes,' Travis said, but she could see that his mouth was tight with pain.

'I still have to assess you, or Dr Fraser will have my guts for garters,' she said with a smile. 'OK. I'm going to raise your legs one at a time, keeping your knees straight. Tell me as soon as it hurts, OK? And I'll stop immediately.' She took him through a range of tests, noting his reactions.

'I'll put a compression bandage on—that'll stop the pain and the bleeding inside your ligament, which

causes the inflammation—and an ice pack,' she said
when she'd finished. 'And now I'm going to make
you a cup of tea, and I want you to sit there with your
leg up and the ice pack on the back of your thigh for
the next ten minutes or so, while I go and talk to Dr
Fraser, OK?'

'Yes, Doc.' He sighed. 'Am I going to be out of the
team for long?'

'For at least a couple of weeks,' she said. 'I know
it's hard and I know you want to play, but it's better
to let yourself recover fully now than to play on it
too soon and do more damage.' She finished making
the tea. 'Sugar?'

'No. You're all right.' He gave her a rueful smile.
'Thanks, Doc.'

'That's what I'm here for. And painkillers,' she
said. 'Are you allergic to anything, or taking any medication for anything?'

'No.'

'OK. I'll give you a couple of paracetamol for
now—you can take some more in another four
hours—and I'll see what else Dr Fraser suggests.'
She patted his shoulder. 'Chin up. It could be worse.'

'Could it?' Travis asked, looking miserable.

'Oh, yes. Imagine having an itch on your leg in
the middle of a really hot summer day—except your
leg's in a full cast and you can't reach the itchy bit.'

That earned her another wry smile. 'OK. That's
worse. Because I'd be off even longer with an actual
break, wouldn't I?'

'Yes. But you're young and fit, so you'll heal just
fine—as long as you do what Dr Fraser says.'

'I guess.'

She left him miserably sipping his mug of tea while she went to find Jared.

Jared knew the very moment that Bailey stepped out of the tunnel onto the field, even though his back was to her. The fact that he was so aware of her was slightly unnerving. They didn't even like each other—he'd known that even before she'd accidentally sent him that text saying exactly how she felt about him, in very unflattering terms. Dressed in a hooded sweat-shirt, baggy tracksuit pants and flat training shoes, Bailey Randall should've looked slightly scruffy and absolutely unsexy—the complete opposite to his über-groomed ex-wife.

The problem was, Bailey was gorgeous. And those unflattering baggy clothes just made him want to peel them off and see exactly what was underneath them.

Not good. He didn't want to be attracted to her. He didn't want to be attracted to anyone.

Work, he reminded himself. This is work. You have an injured player, and she's helped you out. Be nice. Be polite. Be professional. And stay detached.

'How's young Travis?' he asked when she reached him.

'Pretty miserable,' she said.

Yeah. He knew how it felt, being taken off the pitch with an injury when you were desperate to keep play-ing. And, even though Travis's injury was relatively minor and he'd make a full recovery, Jared knew that the inactivity would make the boy utterly despon-dent. He'd been there himself. 'So what's your ver-dict?' he asked.

'I got him to do a straight leg raise and resisted

knee flexion, then did a slump test and palpation,' she said. 'I'd say it's a grade two hamstring strain. I've put an ice pack on and a compression bandage for now and explained to him about standard RICE treatment. He's having a cup of tea while I'm talking to you and seeing what treatment you want him to have.'

'Thank you,' he said. He was impressed by the quiet, no-fuss way she'd examined the boy and reported back. There was no 'Told you so' or point-scoring against him, even though he probably deserved it; all her focus had been on making her patient comfortable. She'd also come to talk to him about a treatment plan instead of telling him how to treat his patient, despite the fact she was obviously more than capable of doing her own treatment plan, so she'd respected his position in the club, too. Maybe he'd been unfair to her about her project, because she'd been spot on about the actual medicine she'd discussed with him. If she was that competent, she was unlikely to be working on a project that had no merit.

'The poor lad's going to be gutted about missing training and matches, but he needs to do it properly or he'll end up with another tear in the muscle on top of this one, and it'll take even longer to heal,' she said.

Jared nodded. 'He needs cold therapy and compression every hour for the first day, and to keep his leg elevated while he's sitting, to reduce the swelling.'

'I gave him some paracetamol—he said he's not on any other medication and he's not allergic to anything.'

'Good. That'll help with the pain during the acute stage, over the next couple of days,' he said.

'I told him that you'd come up with a rehab programme,' she said, 'but if he was my patient I'd suggest a sports massage at the end of the first week, and strengthening exercises in the meantime—standing knee flexion, bridge and seated hamstring curls with a resistance band. Nothing too strenuous, and he has to stop as soon as it hurts.'

'Good plan,' he said. Exactly what he would have suggested. They might not get on, but in medical terms they were definitely on the same page. 'He can also do some gentle walking and swimming, then introduce running gradually. Though it'll be several weeks before he's ready to come back to full training.'

She nodded. 'Look, I know you don't believe in the stuff I'm doing, and I'm not going to rub your nose in it and say "I told you so". But I do want some time to talk you through what I'm doing and—well, I suppose I really want to get you on board with the project,' she admitted. 'Can we have a meeting to talk about it—I mean *really* talk?'

If he'd listened to her and supported her argument that Travis was underperforming, the boy might not be sitting in the dressing room right now with a hamstring injury. Guilt made him sharp. 'The only free time I have is before breakfast.'

He knew he was being obnoxious, but he couldn't seem to stop himself. What was it about Bailey Randall that made him behave like this? Something about her just knocked him off balance, and he liked things to be in perfect equilibrium nowadays.

'Before breakfast,' she mused. 'I normally train at the gym then—but OK. I guess I can skip my session in the gym for once.'

'Or we could train in the gym together.' The words

were out of his mouth before he could stop them. What on earth was wrong with him? Panic flooded through him. This was *such* a bad idea.

'Train together, and then talk about my project over breakfast? That works for me. As long as your partner doesn't mind,' she added quickly.

'No partner.' Though he appreciated that she'd tried to be considerate. In the world of football, there was a lot of jealousy. Sasha definitely wouldn't have been happy about him having a breakfast meeting with a female colleague. Then again, Sasha had had meetings of her own with his male colleagues. In hotel rooms. He pushed the thought away. 'Will yours mind?' He tried to extend the same courtesy to Bailey.

'I'm single,' she said, 'and I like it that way.'

Which sounded to him as if she'd been hurt, too.

Not that it was any of his business. And he wouldn't dream of asking for details.

'One last thing to sort—my gym or yours?' she asked.

'So you don't go to a women-only gym?' Oh, great. And now he was insulting her.

She smiled. 'I'm not intimidated by anyone, regardless of their gender or their age or how pretty they are. I go to a place that has equipment I like and staff who can push me harder if I want a one-to-one training session. And it happens to be reasonably close to the London Victoria, so I can train before work.' She paused. 'There's a café there, too. The coffee's not brilliant, but they do a pretty good Eggs Florentine—which they don't serve in the hospital canteen, or I'd suggest breakfast there because their coffee's slightly better.'

There was no way he could back out of this now. 'OK. Your gym, tomorrow. Let me know the address and what time.'

'Seven,' she said. 'And I'll text you the address.' And there was a tiny, tiny hint of mischief in her eyes as she added, 'Herod.'

CHAPTER THREE

AT FIVE TO SEVEN the next morning, Jared walked down the street towards Bailey's gym. She was already waiting outside for him, wearing another of her hooded sweatshirts and baggy tracksuit pants, and she raised her hand to let him know she'd seen him. He acknowledged her with a nod.

'Good morning,' she said as he walked up to her. 'Are you ready for this?'

'Bring it on,' he said, responding to the challenge in her gaze and trying not to think about how gorgeous her mouth was. This was a challenge of sorts, not a date. They were supposed to be discussing business. And the fact that they were meeting here right now was his own fault—for being deliberately awkward and not trying to fit their meeting into normal working hours.

They walked into the reception, where she signed him in as her guest, and took him through to the changing rooms. 'I need to put my stuff in my locker. Meet you back outside here in five?'

'Sure.'

'Oh—and do you have a pound coin for your own locker? I have change if you need it.'

'Thanks, but I'm good.'

It didn't take him long to stow his things in the locker.

When Bailey came out from the women's changing rooms, Jared's jaw almost dropped. Clearly she'd been wearing the hoodie and the tracksuit pants just for warmth outside, because now she was wearing form-fitting black leggings and a bright cerise racer-back crop top. And he was horribly aware of just how gorgeous she was. Curvy, yet with fabulous muscle definition. Bailey Randall was a woman who looked after herself. She was utterly beautiful and could easily have held her own with any of the glamorous WAGs he'd known at the football clubs he'd worked at. And yet he didn't think she'd be the sort to go to endless spa days and nail parlours.

This was beginning to feel like the most enormous mistake. They were supposed to be training together and then discussing her project over breakfast, and all he wanted to do right now was to scoop her up and carry her to his bed. Even though it was actually a Tube ride away.

It was obvious that, like Sasha, Bailey was aware of her effect on men. She was gorgeous. So was Bailey like his ex-wife in using her physical attributes to get her own way? The idea made him pull himself together. Just. 'So what's your normal workout routine?' he asked.

'Today is a weights day,' she said, 'so that means a quick cardio warm-up and then a resistance routine. You?'

He shrugged. 'I'll join you and adjust the weights to suit me. Just tell me what we're doing and when.'

She nodded. 'Any injuries I should know about?'

Jared had no idea whether Archie had told her anything about his past, but it was irrelevant now. 'A very old knee problem,' he said. 'But I know my limits and I'm certainly not going to be stupid about it.'

'Good. Then let's do this. How about using the elliptical as a warm-up, then through into the back room with the free weights?'

'Fine by me.'

Why on earth had she agreed to train with him? Bailey asked herself. Jared was wearing baggy tracksuit pants and a loose sleeveless vest, like all the other men in the gym. She barely took any notice of them other than to smile hello, acknowledging the fellow athletes in her time slot. But Jared Fraser was different. She was horribly aware of the hard musculature of his body. Particularly his biceps.

He was an ex-footballer. A sports team doctor. He shouldn't have biceps that beautiful and that well defined.

Worst of all, she had a real thing about biceps. Bailey always dragged Joni off to the cinema whenever her favourite actor had a new movie out—and Joni still teased Bailey about the time she'd said, 'Ohhh, just look at his biceps,' really loudly, in the middle of the cinema. The actor was incredibly handsome, perfectly built, but so was Jared Fraser.

She sneaked a sideways look. He was concentrating on putting the time and intensity settings into the elliptical machine, and right at that moment he looked incredibly sexy. It made her wonder what it would be like to have that brooding concentration completely focused on her, and she went hot all over. This training thing was a very bad move. She wished now that she hadn't challenged him. How on earth was she going to be able to concentrate on talking to him over breakfast? Even if he changed into something with long sleeves after his shower, she knew now that he had gorgeous biceps and that could seriously distract her. Right at that moment, she really wanted to reach over and touch him.

Well, she was going to have to make a lot more of an effort, because no way was she acting on that pull of attraction. She liked her life exactly as it was, with no complications—and Jared Fraser could be a real complication. If she let him. Which she really didn't intend to do.

When they'd finished warming up, Bailey talked him through her planned routine, the large compound movements that worked several muscle groups at once. 'I thought I'd do a full-body workout today, if that's OK with you, rather than an upper or lower split.'

'It's a good balance,' he said. 'I notice you're doing hams and then quads.'

'You need to balance them out properly or you'll end up with a back injury,' she said, 'and you wouldn't believe how many patients I have to explain that to.'

Funny how easy it was to talk to him when they were both concentrating on doing the right number of reps and keeping their form correct.

'What made you specialise in sports medicine?' he asked.

'I started off in emergency medicine,' she said, 'but then I found myself doing more of the sporting injuries, especially at the weekends or on Monday

mornings. I did think about maybe working in ortho-
paedics, but then again I like the preventative stuff,
too—it's great being able to make a difference. Then
I had the chance of a secondment in the new sports
medicine department. I liked my colleagues and I
liked the work, so I stayed.'

That was the brief version. She had no intention of
telling Jared the rest of it—how that secondment had
saved her sanity, just over two years ago, and given
her something else to concentrate on when she'd desperately needed an escape. OK, so in sports medicine
there wasn't the speed and pressure that could take
her mind off things as there was in the emergency
department; but she also didn't have to walk into her
department again after first-hand experience of being
treated there, knowing that everyone in the department knew exactly what had happened to her and trying to avoid the concern that shaded too far into pity.

'What about you?' she asked. 'Why did you become the doctor of a football team?'

She wondered if he was going to tell her about
his past as a footballer, but he merely said, 'I enjoy
working in sports medicine, and this job means I get
to travel a bit.'

Surely he must've guessed that she'd looked him
up and knew what had happened to his knee? Then
again, it had been a life-changing accident, and he was
on a completely different path now. She didn't blame
him for not wanting to talk about the injury that had
wrecked his career—just as she didn't want to talk
about the ectopic pregnancy that had shattered her
dreams and then cracked her marriage beyond repair.

No doubt he, too, knew what it felt like to be sick and tired of pity. They didn't have to discuss it.

'How did you get involved in this research project, or have you always been a football fan?' he asked.

'I ought to admit that I'd much rather do sport than watch it, and football isn't really top of my list,' she said. 'My boss was asked if someone on his team would work on the project, and he thought I'd enjoy it because...' She felt her face heat. 'Well, I like techie stuff,' she confessed. 'A lot.'

'You mean gadgets?' He zeroed in on exactly the thing she knew he'd pick up on. 'And would I be right in guessing that you've got one of those expensive wristband things?'

'Um, yes,' she admitted. 'I use it all the time in the gym. I didn't wear it today simply because I knew you'd be really rude about it.'

He burst out laughing. It was the first time she'd actually heard him laugh and it was gorgeous, rich and deep. Sexy, even. *Oh, help.*

'Oh, come off it—are you trying to tell me that you don't like game consoles and whatever?' she asked. 'My brothers are total addicts and so are Joni's—my best friend,' she explained.

'I'm not so much into game consoles,' he said, 'but I do like music—and that's where my techie stuff comes in. I bought one of those systems where the sound follows you through the house.' Then he looked surprised, as if he hadn't meant to tell her something so personal.

'What kind of music?' she asked.

'What do you think?' he parried.

She looked at him as she put the barbell down. 'I'd say either dinosaur rock or very highbrow classical.'

'The first,' he said.

She almost—*almost*—told him about Joni's brother's band and invited him along to their next gig. But that would be too much like asking him out on a date. She and Jared Fraser most definitely weren't on dating terms.

'I'm assuming you like the stuff you can sing along to,' he said.

'Musicals,' she said. 'I'm pretty much word perfect on the soundtracks to *Grease*, *Cats* and *Evita*.'

'Uh-huh.'

But there was a tiny hint of superciliousness in his expression, so she added, 'And Dean Martin. Nonno's favourite. He taught me all the famous songs when I was tiny—"That's Amore", "Volare" and "Sway".' Just in case Jared had any intention of mocking *that*, she said, 'And, actually, it's great stuff to salsa to. It's not old-fashioned at all.'

'Nonno?' he asked, looking confused.

'My grandfather in Milan. My mum is Italian,' she said.

'That explains it.'

'Explains what?' She narrowed her eyes at him.

'Why I thought you were a bit like a pampered Mediterranean princess when I first met you.' Then he looked really horrified, as if he hadn't meant to say that.

'A pampered princess,' she said, and glowered at him. 'You think I'm *spoiled*?'

He stretched out a foot and prodded the floor next

to the mats. 'Ah. The floor's obviously not going to open up and swallow me.'

It amused her, though at the same time she was a bit annoyed at what he was implying. 'Princess,' she said again in disgust.

'Hey. You called me Herod,' he pointed out.

'That was an autocorrect thing on my phone, and it wasn't meant for you in any case. You know what they say about eavesdroppers hearing no good of themselves,' she said loftily.

'You didn't actually take it back, though,' he reminded her.

'No, I didn't—I do think you have tyrant tendencies,' she said, 'given how you wouldn't even listen to what Archie or I said about the project.' She paused. 'And the fact that you could dismiss me as princessy just now, when you barely even know me. That's definitely Herod-like behaviour.'

'I think,' he said, 'we just got back onto the wrong foot with each other—and this morning's meant to be about listening to each other's point of view and finding a bit of common ground.'

He had a point. Maybe she should cut him some slack. 'So you're actually going to listen to what I say? And you'll admit that you were wrong about Travis?'

'*Possibly* wrong,' he corrected. 'That injury might still have happened to one of the other players—one who was performing around his normal average on your charts.'

It was much less likely, she thought. But at least he was admitting the possibility that he was wrong. That was a start. 'What about the yoga?' she challenged.

'No. I'm not convinced. At all,' he said.

'So you think yoga is easy?'

'It's simple stretching.'

Remembering the conversation she'd had with Joni, Bailey smiled. 'Right. So we can finish this session with a bit of yoga, then.'

He rolled his eyes, but muttered, 'If you must.'

When they'd finished the weights routine, she said, 'Yoga will be the cool down and stretch. Have you ever done any before?'

He stared at her. 'Do I look as if I do yoga?'

'Actually, there are a couple of men in our class. They recognise the importance of flexibility training as part of a balanced exercise programme,' she pointed out. 'But OK. I'll talk you through the poses.' First, she talked him through the downward dog. She noticed that he seemed reasonably flexible, and she was impressed that he managed both the warrior pose and the tree without any difficulty. He had a strong core, then.

'So far, so easy?' she asked.

'I can tell which muscle groups each one works,' he said.

'Good. Now for the plank,' she said, and showed him the position. She moved so she could see the clock. 'And we'll start in five. Hold it for as long as you can.' She counted them down, then they both assumed the position.

Jared managed to hold it for a minute before he flopped.

Bailey took it to three—even though that was pushing it, for her—just to make the point.

It looked effortless, though Jared could see Bailey's arms just beginning to shake and he knew that her muscles were right on the verge of giving in. But, when she stopped the pose, he knew he was going to have to be gracious about it—especially given that her performance had been so much better than his.

'OK,' he said, 'I admit that was hard. And clearly you've done that particular one a lot.'

She grinned. 'I have. That one usually shuts people up when they say yoga's an easy option. Though, actually, you did well. A lot of people cave after twenty seconds, or even before that.'

He appreciated the compliment, particularly as it sounded genuine and as if she was trying to meet him halfway.

'So you do a lot of yoga?' he asked.

'Every Monday night with my best friend. Any decent training regime needs flexibility work as well as resistance and cardio.'

He agreed with that. 'So what do you do for cardio?'

She actually blushed.

And he started to have all kinds of seriously impure thoughts about her. He really wished he hadn't started this discussion. The fact that she'd blushed meant she must be thinking something similar. So the attraction was mutual, then? Heat zinged through him. If she felt the same pull, what did that mean?

Then again, he didn't want to get involved with anyone. Sasha had hurt him badly—not just with the affair, but the bit she'd really lied to him about—and Jared wasn't sure he was ready to trust again.

'Cardio. I like dance-based classes,' she said. 'Also there's a salsa night at a local club. I quite often go to that. I like the music, and the dancing's fun. I'm a great believer in endorphins.'

For a moment Jared thought she was going to challenge him to go with her—and he wasn't sure if he was more relieved or disappointed when she didn't. He'd hated clubbing with Sasha in any case; a salsa club was probably just as much of a meat market as any other kind of dance club, and that didn't really appeal to him. Though the idea of dancing with Bailey Randall, up close, hot and sweaty, with her body pressed against his...

Focus, he told himself. Work, not sex.

'I assume you run?' she asked.

'Intervals,' he said, 'and rowing—it's more effective than hamster-wheel cardio. No offence to your warm-up today, because that was fine—it's just that it would bore me stupid if it lasted for more than ten minutes, even with a decent playlist to keep me going.'

'Each to their own,' she said. 'I don't mind doing a whole session on the elliptical if I have a good playlist. There are programmes on the machine that change the resistance and make it a bit more interesting.'

He just grimaced.

'So, rowing, hmm? That would explain your biceps.'

And then she blushed again.

Now he was really intrigued. She liked his biceps?

Well, he liked the muscles in her back. They had beautiful definition. And he really, really wanted to touch them. No. More than that. He wanted to kiss his way down her spine.

'Would that be proper rowing on a river, or machine?' she asked.

'Machine,' he admitted.

'And I assume you're careful with your knee.'

'I'm wearing a knee support under my tracksuit pants,' he said. 'I'm hardly going to nag my players about looking after themselves properly and then not take my own advice.'

'I guess.' She held out her hand to shake his, and his palm tingled where their skin touched. How long had it been since he'd been so aware of someone? 'That was a good session. I enjoyed working with you, Jared.'

'I enjoyed working with you,' he said, meaning it; he was surprised to realise just how much he'd enjoyed it.

'Let's hit the shower and have breakfast.'

He went hot all over again at the thought of sharing a shower with her. He knew perfectly well that wasn't what she'd meant, but now the idea was stuck in his head. And he was glad they had temperature settings on the showers in the male changing rooms, because he needed a blast of cold water to get his common sense back and the fantasies out of his mind.

When he met Bailey outside the changing rooms, he noticed that she was wearing a black tailored suit for work. This was yet another side of her; he'd seen the slightly scruffy scientist on the football pitch and the sculpted goddess in the gym, and now she was the calm, confident medical professional.

He wished that he was wearing something a bit more tailored, too—but then again he was off to work himself after this and that meant dressing appropriately. A sharp suit wasn't what you needed when you were working on a football pitch.

Clearly the staff knew Bailey well here, because the waitress didn't bat an eyelid when Bailey ordered Eggs Florentine without the hollandaise sauce. 'And a rich roast latte?' the waitress asked.

It was obviously Bailey's usual, because she smiled. 'That'd be lovely, thanks.'

He ordered porridge with blueberries and cinnamon, paired with a protein shake.

'Not a coffee fiend?' she asked.

'I had mine before my workout. It gets the best use out of the caffeine,' he said. 'I'm balancing my protein and my carbs now, post-workout.'

She nodded. 'Good point.'

'So, are you going to take me through this system of yours while we wait for breakfast to arrive?'

'Sure. The idea behind it is that you're more likely to end up with a soft-tissue injury if you play while you're under par. You'll be slower and your reactions won't be as fast. So if you look at your performance during training or a game and your VO2 is down, you're doing fewer steps, your resting heart rate is up and your average speed is down, either you've had a slow game—and that's where Archie comes in, to tell me if playing conditions on the field have been different and affected anyone's performance— or you're under par and you're more likely to be injured in your next game.'

He asked her various questions about the measurements she used, and he was impressed that she didn't have to look up a single answer. Bailey Randall wasn't the glib salesman type, able to put a spin on her answers; she really knew her stuff. And she clearly believed in her research project. He liked her enthusiasm; it was one of the reasons why he'd chosen to look after the youth team, because he loved the enthusiasm that young players brought to the job, unjaded by internal politics.

And he also liked the way Bailey talked with her hands, completely animated when she was caught up in the subject. Now he knew she was half-Italian, he could really see it. Everything from her classic bone structure, to the slightly olive colour of her skin, to the rich depths of her eyes. Naturally stylish, she was like an Italian Audrey Hepburn, with that gamine haircut and those huge eyes.

'OK,' he said. 'I still think those wristband things are ploys to extort money out of the gullible with too much disposable income and too little common sense, but the stuff you're doing has a point.'

'Thank you,' she said. 'So do you take it back about my system being a glorified pedometer?'

'I'll reserve judgement until I've seen a month of results,' he said, 'but I will agree that it's better than the wristband things. Especially because you do at least use a proper heart-rate monitor strap with your system.'

'And the yoga?'

He shook his head. 'Even though the plank was hard, I'm not convinced that yoga's going to do what you think it will. Not for a bunch of seventeen-year-old boys.'

'It's still worth a try.'

'Do you make them do the plank?'

She laughed. 'No. That was just to prove a point to you.'

He liked the fact that she'd admitted it.

And it worried him that he liked it. Now that he was getting to know her, he quite liked Bailey Randall. Which was a very dangerous position. He couldn't afford to think of her in terms of anything other than a colleague, but she seriously tempted him. To the point where he could actually imagine asking her out on a date.

Bad, bad move.

He had a feeling that he was going to have to resort to a lot of cold showers to keep his common sense in place. Dating Bailey Randall was absolutely not on the cards. He'd only just finished gluing the pieces of his heart back together, and he had no intention of putting himself back in a position where it could shatter again.

CHAPTER FOUR

OVER THE NEXT couple of weeks, working at the football club was easier, Bailey thought. Jared was at least showing some interest in her research project rather than being an insurmountable bulwark, and he'd even come up with a couple of suggestions that she was trying to incorporate into her data.

Then she noticed that he was favouring his right knee when he went onto the pitch to treat one of the players. She waited until he'd come back to sit next to her on the bench, and then asked, 'What did you do?'

'For Mitch?' He shrugged. 'It was just a flesh wound—some studs scraped against his shin, so I cleaned it and dressed it. He shouldn't have too much trouble with it.'

'No, I meant what did you do to your knee?'

He looked away. 'Nothing.'

'Jared, I'm a doctor, so don't try to flannel me. I could see you were favouring your right knee,' she said.

He sighed. 'It's an old injury. I guess I might have overdone the running a tad at the weekend.'

'Tsk. And you're a sports medicine doctor,' she said.

He gave her a crooked grin that made her libido sit up and beg. 'It'll be fine. It's strapped up.'

'So you didn't actually see anyone about it?'

'I didn't need to.'

She tutted. 'What a fine example to set the team—*not*. Let me have a look when they've gone, so they don't know what an idiot you are.'

He shook his head. 'It's fine. You don't have to do that.'

'You're my colleague. You'd do the same for me.'

Jared thought about it. Would he? Yes, probably. And he'd nag her if she was being stubborn about it, just as he'd nag Archie. Just as she was nagging him. 'I guess,' he admitted.

'Are you icing it? Because obviously you're not resting it or elevating it.'

'No. I'm taking painkillers,' he said. 'And not strong ones, either. Just normal ibuprofen to deal with the inflammation.'

'Hmm,' she said.

After the training session, Jared said to Archie, 'I'll lock up if you need to go. I want to discuss a couple of things with Dr Randall.'

'Cheers,' Archie said. 'It'll give me a few extra minutes to make myself beautiful for my date.'

'What, another one?' Bailey teased. 'I'm sure she'll think you look beautiful.' She blew him a kiss.

Archie grinned and sketched a bow.

'Why didn't you just tell him that your knee hurts?' Bailey asked quietly when Archie and the players had gone, and she and Jared were alone in the dressing room.

'Because it isn't relevant.'

'Of course it's relevant. If you have to kneel on the pitch to treat one of the players, it's going to hurt you.' She rolled her eyes. 'Men.'

'Women,' he sniped back.

'Just shut up and lose the tracksuit bottoms.'

Oh, help. The pictures that put into his head. To clear them, he drawled, 'Fabulous bedside manner, Dr Randall.'

Except that made it worse. Bed. Bailey. Two words he really shouldn't have put together inside his head, because now he could imagine her lying against his pillows and giving him a come-hither smile...

She just gave him a dry look. He shut up and removed his tracksuit bottoms. He knew she wasn't thinking of him in terms of a man right now, but in terms of a patient. What she saw wasn't six foot two of man; she saw a sore knee. An old injury playing up that needed to be looked at and soothed.

Gently she examined his knee. 'Tell me where it hurts, and don't be stubborn about it—because I can't help you if you're not honest with me.'

'Do you talk to all your patients like this?' he asked.

'Just the awkward ones.'

He guessed he deserved that. 'OK. It hurts there. And there.' He gave a sharp intake of breath. 'And there.'

'All righty.' She grabbed a towel and spread it across her lap. 'Leg. Here. Now.'

His bare leg astride her body.

Uh-oh. How on earth was he meant to stop his thoughts doing a happy dance?

'Yes, ma'am,' he drawled, hoping she didn't have a clue what was going through his head right now.

Her hands had been gentle when she'd examined his knee. Now they were firm. There wasn't anything remotely sexual about the way she touched him, and he had to grit his teeth on more than one occasion.

But when she'd finished the deep-tissue massage, he could move an awful lot more easily.

'You're very good at that,' he said when she'd finished and he'd put his tracksuit bottoms back on. 'Thank you.'

'Better?' she asked.

He nodded. 'Sorry for being snippy with you.'

She shrugged. 'You were in pain. Of course you were going to be snippy. It's forgotten.'

'Thanks. I owe you one,' he said lightly, expecting her to brush it aside.

To his surprise, she looked thoughtful. 'I wonder.'

'Wonder what?'

'I do need a favour, actually, and you'd be perfect.'

He still wasn't following this. 'For what?'

She took a deep breath. 'My best friend's getting married in three weeks' time. And I'm under a bit of pressure to take someone to the wedding with me. My family's convinced that I need someone in my life, and I can't get them to see that I'm perfectly happy just concentrating on my career.'

'You want me to go to a wedding with you?'

'Yes.'

'As your partner?'

She grimaced. 'I'm not asking you on a date, Jared. I'm asking you to do me a favour.'

'To be your pretend boyfriend.'

'For one day. And an evening,' she added.

Go with her to a wedding.

She'd just made his knee feel a lot better. And this would be payback.

But…a *wedding*.

Where people promised to love, honour and cherish, until death did them part.

Vows he'd taken himself, and had meant every single word—although it turned out that Sasha hadn't. For all he knew, Tom hadn't even been her first affair. He'd been so clueless, thinking that his wife was happy, when all the time she'd been looking for something else.

Sasha had broken every single one of her vows.

She'd lied, she'd cheated—and then she'd made a crucial decision without talking it over with him. A decision that had cut Jared to the quick because he really couldn't understand her reasoning and it was totally the opposite of what he'd wanted. Even *if* the baby hadn't been his, it would still have been hers. They could've worked something out.

Except she hadn't wanted to. The only person she'd thought about had been herself. Not him, not the baby, not the other man who also might've been the baby's father—as she'd been sleeping with them both, she'd had no idea who the father of her baby was.

To go and celebrate someone else making those same vows when he'd lost his faith in marriage…that would be hard.

'If it's a problem…' her voice was very cool '…then forget I asked.'

He didn't want to tell Bailey about the mess of his divorce, Sasha's betrayal and the termination. He didn't want her to pity him. Besides, he owed her for helping him with his knee. 'OK. I'll do it.'

He knew it sounded grudging, and her raised eyebrow confirmed it. He sighed. 'Sorry. I didn't mean to sound quite so—well—Herod-ish.'

That netted him the glimmer of a smile. 'Knee still hurting?' she asked.

It would be an easy excuse. But he thought she deserved the truth. 'Let's just say I've seen a lot of divorces.' He'd been through a messy one, too. Not that she needed to know that bit. 'So I guess my view of weddings is a bit dark.'

'This one,' Bailey said, 'is definitely going to work. My best friend used to be engaged to a total jerk, but thankfully she realised how miserable her life was going to be with him, and she called it off.'

Interesting. So Bailey was a realist rather than seeing things through rose-tinted glasses? 'I take it you like the guy she's marrying?'

She nodded. 'Aaron's a genuinely nice guy. And he loves Joni as much as she loves him. It's equal.'

Did that mean Bailey had been in a relationship that hadn't been equal, or was he reading too much into this?

'Plus,' she said, 'I happen to know the food's going to be good—and the music. Joni's brother has a band, and they're playing at the evening do.' She paused. 'Dinosaur rock. They're seriously good. So I think you'll enjoy that.'

'You don't need to sell it to me. I've already said I'll go with you, and I keep my word.'

Funny how brown eyes could suddenly seem so piercing. And then she nodded. 'Yes. You have integrity. It's better to be grumpy with integrity than to be charming and unreliable.'

That *definitely* sounded personal. And it intrigued him. But if he asked her any more, then she'd be able to ask him things he'd rather not answer. 'Let me know when and where the plus-one thing is, then,' he said instead.

'Thanks. I will.'

Bailey couldn't stop thinking about Jared on the way home. The world of football was pretty high profile—as much as the worlds of music and Hollywood were—and the gossip magazines were forever reporting divorces and affairs among sporting stars. But something in Jared's expression had made her think that it was a bit more personal than that. Was Jared divorced? Not that she'd pry and ask him. But it made her feel a bit as if she'd railroaded him into agreeing to be her partner at the wedding. And that wasn't fair.

When she got home, she texted him: You really *don't* have to go to the wedding.

The answer came back promptly: I said I'd do it. I'll keep my word.

Typical Jared. Stubborn.

Well, she'd given him the chance to back out. But hopefully he wouldn't hate it as much as he seemed to think he would. OK, thanks, she texted back, and added all the details of the wedding.

The next day was one of Bailey's clinic days at the London Victoria. Her first patient was a teenager who'd been injured playing tennis.

'Viv landed awkwardly in training,' Mr Kaine said.

'She said she felt her knee give and heard a popping sound. And her knee's started to swell really badly.' He indicated his daughter's knee. 'It hurts to walk.'

'It's just a sprain, Dad. It'll be fine,' Vivienne said. 'Let's stop wasting the doctor's time and go home.'

'No,' he said firmly. 'You're going to get this checked out *properly*.'

It sounded as if Mr Kaine was putting his daughter's welfare first and would support her through any treatment programme—which was a good thing, Bailey thought, because what he'd just described sounded very like the injury that had finished Jared's career. Damage to the anterior cruciate ligament.

She pushed Jared to the back of her mind. Not here, not now. Her patient came first.

'Thank you for giving me the background, Mr Kaine. That's very useful,' she said cheerfully. 'Vivienne, would you mind if I examine your knee?' she asked.

The girl rolled her eyes, as if she thought this was a total waste of time, but nodded. She flinched when Bailey touched her knee, so clearly it hurt to the touch and Bailey was very, very gentle as she finished examining the girl's knee.

'I'm going to send you for an MRI scan to confirm it,' she said, 'but I'm fairly sure you've torn your anterior cruciate ligament. I'm afraid you're going to be out of play for a little while.'

Again, she thought of Jared. He must have had a similar consultation with a doctor at a very similar age.

'What? But I *have* to play! I've got an important

tournament next week,' Vivienne said, looking horrified. 'I've been training for months. I can't miss it!'

However bad the girl felt about it, she had to face up to the severity of her injury. She wouldn't even be able to have a casual knockabout on the court for a while, let alone play an important match on the junior tennis circuit. Not even if her knee was strapped up.

'Viv, you have to listen to the doctor. She knows what she's talking about,' Mr Kaine said. 'I'm sorry, Dr Randall. You were explaining to us what Vivienne's done to her knee.'

Bailey drew a couple of diagrams to show Vivienne how the ligaments worked and what had happened to her knee. 'You have a complete tear of the ligament—it's the most common type, and I'm afraid it also means you've damaged the other ligaments and your cartilage.'

'Will it take long to fix?' Vivienne asked. 'If I miss this tournament, can I play in the next one?'

'I'm afraid that's unlikely,' Bailey said. 'You're going to need surgery.'

'Surgery?' The girl looked totally shocked. 'But—but—that means I'll be out for ages!'

'The injury won't heal on its own and unfortunately you can't just stitch a ligament back together. Vivienne, I'll need to send you to a specialist surgeon. I know Dr Martyn here quite well, and he's really good at his job, so I promise you'll be in the best hands.' She looked up at Vivienne's father and gave him a reassuring smile, too. 'He'll replace your torn ligament with a tissue graft, which will act as a kind of scaffolding for the new ligament to grow on. You'll be on crutches for a while afterwards.'

'Crutches. I can't play tennis with *crutches*.' Vivienne shook her head. 'This can't be happening. It just can't.'

'Crutches will stop you putting weight on your leg and damaging the structure of your knee further,' Bailey said. 'I can also give you a brace to protect your knee and make it more stable. But I'm afraid it's going to be at least six months until you can play sports again. After the surgery, you'll need a rehab physiotherapy programme—that means exercises tailored to strengthen your leg muscles and make your knee functional again.'

'Six months.' Vivienne closed her eyes. 'Oh, my God. My life's over.'

'Viv, it's going to take six months for you to get better. I know it feels bad, but it's not the end of the world. You'll come back stronger,' Mr Kaine said.

It was good that her dad was so supportive, Bailey thought. But Vivienne was clearly finding it hard to adjust.

'If you go back to playing too soon, you might do more damage to your knee and you'll be out of action for a lot longer,' Bailey said. 'The good news is that the way they do surgery today is a lot less invasive. It's keyhole surgery, so that means you'll have less pain, you'll spend less time in hospital and you'll recover more quickly.'

'When will the surgeon do it?' Mr Kaine asked. 'Today? Tomorrow?'

'Not straight away,' Bailey said. 'We need the inflammation to go down a bit first, or there's a risk of scar tissue forming inside the joint and you'll lose part of your range of motion.'

'And that means I won't be able to play tennis the way I do now.' Vivienne bit her lip. 'Not ever.'

'Exactly,' Bailey said. 'What you do next is going to make the biggest difference. For the next seventy-two hours you need to remember RICE—rest, ice, compression and elevation.' She talked Vivienne through the treatment protocols.

'What about a hot-water bottle to help with the pain?' Mr Kaine asked.

Bailey shook her head. 'Not for the first three days—and no alcohol, either.'

Vivienne rolled her eyes. 'Fat chance of that. Dad's part of the food police. We were told in sixth form that as soon as you're sixteen you're allowed a glass of wine with your meal in a restaurant. But Dad won't let me.'

'Alcohol slows your reactions and you can't play tennis with a hangover,' he said. 'At least, not well—and I should know because I've tried it.'

Bailey smiled at him. He was definitely going to need a sense of humour to help coax Vivienne through the next few months of a total ban from tennis. 'No running or massage, either,' she said. 'But I can give you painkillers—ones that will help reduce the inflammation as well as the pain.' She looked at Mr Kaine. 'Are there any allergies I need to know about?'

'No,' he confirmed.

'Good.'

'Six months,' Vivienne said again, making it sound like a life sentence.

'Better to make up a bit of ground in a couple of months,' Bailey said softly, 'than to go back too soon, do more damage and then have to spend even more time recovering.'

'She's right, love.' Mr Kaine rested his hand briefly on his daughter's shoulder. 'So what happens after the operation?'

'For the first three weeks the physio will concentrate on increasing the range of motion in the joint but without ripping the graft,' Bailey said. 'By week six Vivienne should be able to use a stair-climber or a stationary bike to maintain the range of motion and start strengthening her muscles, and then the plan will be to work to full rehab over the next few months. You need a balance between doing enough to rehabilitate the knee,' she said gently to Vivienne, 'but not so much that you damage the surgical repair and make the ligament fail again.'

'Six months,' Vivienne said again, looking totally miserable.

'There are other things you can work on that won't involve your knee,' Mr Kaine said cheerfully. 'Chin up.'

Vivenne just sighed.

Once Bailey had sorted out a compression bandage and painkillers, she said, 'I'll see you again in a couple of days and then we'll see the surgeon. Reception will make an appointment for you. Call me if you're worried about anything. But we'll get your knee fixed and you'll be back to playing tennis again.'

And, some time before their next appointment, there was someone she needed to talk to who might just be able to give her some really, really good advice to help Vivienne cope with the next few months.

She hoped.

CHAPTER FIVE

THERE WAS NEVER going to be a perfect time to ask Jared, Bailey knew, and she certainly wasn't going to ring him outside office hours to talk it through with him. But once the next training session with the team was under way and she was seated on the bench next to him, she turned to him.

'Can I ask you for some professional advice—something that's a bit personal?'

He looked completely taken aback. 'Why?'

She'd known before she asked that this was going to be difficult; Jared had never talked to her about his injury. But he was the only one who might be able to help. 'I have a patient, a teenage female tennis player. She landed awkwardly from hitting a ball.'

'And?'

'She, um, has a complete tear to her ACL.'

He went very, very still and guilt flooded through her.

'I know I'm being intrusive,' she said, 'and I apologise for that. I really don't mean to dredge up bad memories for you about your own injury. And, yes, I did look you up, so I know what happened. I could hardly ask you, could I?'

'I guess not.'

Talk about inscrutable. Jared's voice and his face were completely expressionless, so she had absolutely no idea how he was feeling right now. Worrying that she was risking their newfound truce, but wanting to get some real help for her patient, she said, 'The reason I'm asking you is because when it happened you were about the same age as she is now, so you know how it feels. Her dad's really supportive and he's trying to get her to rest her knee sensibly so she'll recover well from the operation, but she's distraught at the idea that she's going to lose a lot of ground over the next year. So I guess what I'm asking you is if there's anything I can tell her to help her deal with it a bit better.'

For a moment she thought Jared was going to blank her, but then he blew out a breath. 'That really depends on whether she's going to recover fully or not.'

Clearly he hadn't recovered fully enough to be able to resume his sports career. But she knew that if she tried to give him a hug—out of empathy rather than pity—he'd push her away, both literally and figuratively. So she kept the topic to a discussion about her patient. 'I think there's a very good chance she'll recover fully. The surgeon's brilliant,' Bailey said.

'Good.'

A complete tear to the anterior cruciate ligament. Jared knew exactly how that felt. Like the end of the world. When all your dreams had suddenly exploded and there wasn't any meaning in your life any more. You couldn't do the one thing you knew you were really good at—the thing you were born to do. In a few moments it was all gone.

At seventeen, it had destroyed him. Knowing that his knee wouldn't hold up in the future—that if he played again he was likely to do more damage to his knee and eventually he'd be left with a permanent limp. Knowing that he'd never play for his country again. He'd been so sure that nothing would ever be that good for the rest of his life.

Although it hadn't actually turned out that way. He enjoyed his job, and he was still involved with the game he loved.

He blew out a breath. 'It's a lot to deal with. Especially at that age. Tell her to take it one day at a time, and to find someone she can talk to. Someone who won't let her wallow in self-pity and will talk her into being sensible.' He'd been so, so lucky that the team's deputy coach had been brilliant with him. He'd let Jared rant and rave, and then told him to look at his options, because there most definitely *would* be something he could do.

What goes around comes around. It was time to pass on that same advice now. 'Tell her there will be something else. At first it'll feel like second best, but she'll find something else she loves as much. Even if it doesn't look like it right now.'

'Thank you,' Bailey said quietly. 'I appreciate it—and I'm sorry I brought back bad memories. That really wasn't my intention.'

He shrugged again. 'It was a long time ago.'

She said nothing, simply waited, and he was surprised to find himself filling in the gap. 'At the time, it was bad,' he admitted. 'I wanted someone to blame for the end of my dreams—but I always knew that the tackle wasn't deliberate. It was just something that went wrong and it could've happened to anyone. The guy who tackled me felt as guilty as hell about it, but it wasn't his fault. It wasn't anyone's fault. It was just an accident. Wrong time, wrong place.' He paused. 'And I found something else to do.'

'Did you think about coaching?' She put a hand across her mouth. 'Sorry. You don't have to answer that.'

He liked the fact that she wasn't pressuring him. There was no malice in Bailey Randall. She just wanted to help her patient, and he'd had first-hand experience of what her patient was going through right now. Of course she'd want to know how he'd coped. 'I thought about it,' he said. 'Though I knew I was too young to be taken seriously when my knee was wrecked. At seventeen, you don't really have enough experience to coach a team.'

'So why did you choose medicine? That's—well, a huge change of direction.'

'My family are all GPs,' he said. 'I'd always thought I'd join them. I guess it was a surprise to everyone when I was spotted on the playing field at school and the local team took me on for training.' He shrugged. 'Then I had to make a choice. Risk trying for a career in football, or do my A-levels. My parents said to give it a go—I could always take my A-levels later if it didn't work out. And when I was picked for the England squad...they threw one hell of a party.'

He smiled at the memory. 'When my knee went, it hit me pretty hard. But I was lucky in a way, in that I could fall back on my original plans—I just took my A-levels two years later than I would've done if I hadn't tried for a career in sport.'

'So you trained as a GP?' she asked.

'No. I ended up training in emergency medicine,' he said. 'I liked the buzz. Then, like you, I had a secondment to a sports medicine department. And then it occurred to me that I could have the best of both worlds—I could be a doctor in the sport I'd always loved.'

'That's a good compromise,' she said.

Again, to his surprise, he found himself asking questions and actually wanting to know the answers rather than being polite. 'What about you? Is your family in medicine?'

'No—my family has a restaurant. Mum's the head chef, Dad's front of house and my brothers are both kitchen serfs.' At Jared's raised eyebrows, she added swiftly, 'Joke. Gio is Mum's deputy—he's going to take over when she retires. And Rob's probably the best pastry chef in the universe and he makes the most amazing wedding cakes. They're planning to expand the business that way, too.'

'Didn't your parents expect you to join the family firm?'

She shook her head. 'Mum and Dad always said that we should follow our hearts and do what we love, and that they'd back us whatever we decided. Rob and Gio were always in the kitchen making stuff, so it was obvious what they wanted to do. And I was always bandaging my teddies when I was a toddler.' She grinned. 'And the dog, if I could get him to sit still.'

He could just imagine that. He'd bet she'd been

the most determined and stubborn toddler ever. 'A born doctor, then?'

'I've no idea where it came from. It was just what I always wanted to do,' she said. 'And I guess I was lucky because my family's always supported me. Even when I nag them about healthy eating and saturated fat.' She laughed. 'Though the nagging has at least made them put some super-healthy options on the menu—that's gone down really well with the customers, so I feel I've made some kind of contribution to the family business, apart from volunteering to taste-test any new stuff.'

Clearly Bailey was very close to her family and Jared had a feeling that they adored her as much as she obviously adored them. And she cared enough about her patients to do something outside her comfort zone; he knew that it must've been daunting to ask him about the injury he didn't talk about, but she'd asked him to see if he could help her patient rather than because she wanted to pry into his life.

'Your patient,' he said. 'When are you seeing her next?'

'Friday morning.'

'I could,' he suggested, 'come and have a word with her, if you like.'

'Really?' The way she smiled at him made him feel as if the sun had just come out at midnight.

'It might help her to talk to someone who's been there and come out just fine on the other side,' he said.

'I think it would help her a lot. If you're sure.' She bit her lip. 'I mean, I don't want to rip open any old scars.'

He smiled. 'It was a long time ago now. And I was

lucky—I had someone who helped me. It's my chance to pay it forward.'

She rested a hand on his arm; even through his sleeve, her touch made his skin tingle. 'Thank you, Jared. I really appreciate it.'

'No worries,' he said.

On Friday, Bailey saw Vivienne in her clinic at the London Victoria and examined her knee. 'Obviously you've followed my advice about rest, ice, compression and elevation,' she said.

Vivienne nodded. 'I want to play again as soon as possible. That means doing what you say.'

Bailey smiled. 'Well, you'll be pleased to know you're good to go for surgery and you can see the surgeon this afternoon.'

'That's great news,' Mr Kaine said, patting his daughter's shoulder. 'Thank you.'

'Actually, there is something else,' Bailey said. 'Obviously I wouldn't dream of breaking patient confidentiality, but I happen to know someone who had an ACL injury at your age, and I asked him for some advice for someone in your position.'

'Was he a tennis player?' Vivienne asked, looking interested.

'No, he was in a different sport,' Bailey said, 'but the injury and the rehab are the same. Actually, he offered to come and have a chat with you. He's waiting outside, if you'd like a word.'

Vivienne turned to her father, who nodded. 'That'd be great. Thanks.'

Bailey opened her office door and looked out;

Jared glanced up, caught her eye and came to the door. 'She'd like to talk to me?' he asked.

'Yes. And thank you. I owe you,' she said.

'No. I'm just paying it forward,' he reminded her. 'Just as your patient will pay it forward, one day.'

It was a nice way of looking at it, Bailey thought. She brought him into the room and introduced him to Vivienne and Mr Kaine.

'Well, I never. Jared Fraser—the England footballer. I remember watching you play years ago. You were amazing.' Mr Kaine shook Jared's hand. 'It's very good of you to come in and talk to us.'

'My pleasure,' Jared said.

'So do you still play for England?' Vivienne asked.

'No. Unfortunately, they couldn't fix my knee. Though that's *not* likely to be the case for you,' he emphasised, 'because Dr Randall tells me that you're a really good candidate for surgery. If you follow the rehab programme to the letter you'll be fine. Dr Randall asked me for my advice, and I thought it might be better for you to have it in person, just in case you have any questions.'

Vivienne nodded. 'Thank you very much, Mr Fraser.'

'Right now,' he said gently, 'it probably feels like the end of the world and you're worrying that you're going to lose so much ground against everyone else.'

She bit her lip. 'That's exactly how it feels.'

'So you need to take it one day at a time, and find someone you can talk to—someone who won't let you pity yourself, but will make you be sensible and get the right balance between doing enough work to strengthen your knee, but not so much that you damage it again and end up back at square one,' Jared said.

'That's good advice,' Mr Kaine agreed. 'I'll always listen, Vivi, but he's right—you do need someone else to talk to.'

'I was lucky,' Jared said. 'I had a great coach. And he made me see that although my knee wouldn't hold up enough for me to play at international level again, I had other options. I could learn to coach, or I could do what I ended up doing—I trained as a doctor, and I'm still part of the sport because nowadays I work with the youth team of a premiership division club. So even if there are complications in the future and you don't end up playing at this level again, you'll still have options—you can still be part of tennis.'

'I don't mean to be rude,' Vivienne said, 'but I don't want to be a coach or a doctor. I just want to play tennis. It's all I've ever wanted to do.'

'And you will play again,' Bailey said. 'But, as Dr Fraser said, you need to follow your rehab programme.'

'Waiting is the worst bit,' Jared said. 'You'll want to push yourself too hard. But don't. Use that time to study instead. Look at different techniques, look at the way your opponents play and use that to hone your strategy. To really succeed at a top level in sport you need just as much up here...' he tapped his head '...as you need the physical skills.'

'Vivi picked up a racket practically as soon as she could walk,' Mr Kaine said. 'I used to play—nothing like at her level—just at a club on Sunday afternoons, and her mum would bring her to watch. And she ended up joining in.' He ruffled her hair. 'When she started beating us hollow and she wasn't even ten years old, we knew we were seeing something special in the making. And you'll get that back, love. We just have to make sure we do everything the doctors tell us, OK?'

'OK,' Vivienne said.

Bailey smiled at them both. 'And I'll do my very best to help you get that knee back to how it was, so you can go and get those grand slams.'

'Can I be rude and ask, Mr Fraser, do you miss playing?' Vivienne asked.

'Sometimes,' Jared said. 'But I'm thirty-five now, so I'd be near the end of my professional playing career in any case. And I'm lucky because I really enjoy my job. It means I get the chance to help players fulfil their potential. If someone had told me that when I was your age, I would have laughed at them—but I really do feel I've achieved something when I see them grow and improve. So don't rule it out as something you might do when you're ready to retire from playing.'

Vivienne looked thoughtful, and Bailey could see that Jared's words had given her a different perspective—something that would make all the waiting during her rehab a lot easier. 'Thank you, Mr F—*Dr* Fraser,' she amended.

When the Kaines had left, Jared was about to follow them out when Bailey stopped him. 'Thanks for doing that, Jared—you've made a real difference to her.'

'No worries.'

'If I wasn't up to my eyes in paperwork and appointments,' she said, 'I'd offer to take you for lunch to thank you properly. Or dinner—but I'm doing bridesmaid stuff for Joni tonight. So please consider this a kind of rain check.' She took a plain white patisserie box from her desk drawer and handed it to him.

'What's this?' he asked.

She smiled. 'A little slice of heaven. Don't open it now. Tell me what you think later.'

'OK.' He looked intrigued. 'I'll text you. Good luck for tonight.'

'Thanks.'

Later that evening, she had a text that made her laugh.

Best chocolate cake in the universe. Would very much like to help with more patients. Quite happy to be paid in cake.

I'll see what I can do, she texted back.

Funny, when she'd first met Jared, she'd thought him grumpy and surly and a pain in the neck. Now she rather liked his dry sense of humour and the quiet, sensible way he went about things.

But she'd better not let herself get too close. After the way her marriage to Ed had splintered, she just didn't trust herself to get it right next time. It was best to stick to being colleagues. Friends, too, maybe; but she'd have to dampen down the attraction that sparkled through her veins every time she saw him. To keep her heart safe.

CHAPTER SIX

'JONI, YOU LOOK BEAUTIFUL,' Bailey said, surveying her best friend.

'So do you.' But Joni also looked worried. 'Bailey, are you sure you're OK?'

'Of course I am—why wouldn't I be?'

'Because I remember the last time that one of us was in a bridesmaid's dress and the other was the bride,' Joni said softly.

Bailey's wedding day. A day so full of promise. A day when she'd thought she couldn't be happier... And then, two short years later, she'd discovered that she couldn't be any more unhappy when her whole world crashed down around her. 'I'm fine. More than fine. Don't give it another moment's thought,' she said brightly. Even if she hadn't been fine, no way would Bailey rain on her best friend's parade on her wedding day.

'I can't believe you're actually bringing Herod as your plus-one.'

Bailey groaned. 'Please don't call him that when you meet him—he'll be mortified.'

'You've been very cagey about him. So you're getting on OK together now?'

'We've reached an understanding.'

Joni raised an eyebrow. '*That* sort of understanding?'

'Absolutely not. Even if I was looking for someone, Jared Fraser wouldn't make my list of potentials.' That was a big fat lie—Jared Fraser was one of the most attractive men she'd met, particularly when he smiled—but hopefully Joni would be too distracted by all the bridal stuff going on to call her on it. Bailey hoped. 'No, he's just doing me a favour and taking a bit of heat off me where my family's concerned.'

'As long as you're OK.'

'Of course I'm OK,' Bailey reassured her. 'I'm thrilled that my best friend's getting married to the love of her life, and I get to follow her down the aisle in the most gorgeous bridesmaid's dress ever. Now, the car's going to be here at any second, so we need to get moving.'

Jared took a deep breath and walked down the path to the church. He hadn't been to a wedding since his own marriage to Sasha. And, despite Bailey's assurances that the bride and groom were right for each other, Jared still felt awkward. A cynic who'd lost his belief in marriage really shouldn't be here to celebrate a wedding. He half wished Bailey was going to be there with him to take his mind off it, but as she was Joni's bridesmaid he knew that she would be the very last person walking into the church, and she wouldn't be sitting with him, either.

He really should have asked if he could at least meet the bride and groom before the wedding, so he would know someone there. Right at that moment he was really regretting the impulse that had made him offer to be Bailey's 'plus-one'.

His only consolation had been the text she'd sent him that morning: See you at the church. And thank you. I appreciate it.

And being appreciated was nice. It had been a while since he'd last felt appreciated.

The usher greeted him with a smile. 'Bride's side or groom's?'

'Bride's,' Jared said, feeling a total fake.

'Sit anywhere on the left except the front two pews,' the usher said with a smile, handing him an order of service booklet.

Jared remembered the drill: anywhere except the front two pews, where the bride's and groom's immediate family would be sitting.

Over the next few minutes the church filled up. Two men walked down to the front of the church; one of them was obviously the groom and the other the best man, Jared thought.

A wedding.

A room full of hope, with everyone wishing the bride and groom happiness until the end of their days. But how often did that hope turn sour? How many people did he know who'd actually stayed together, apart from his parents and two of his siblings? Not that many.

The organist started to play the wedding march, and the bride walked in on her father's arm, looking gorgeous and deliriously happy. Behind her, carrying the long train and a bouquet of deep red roses—to match her knee-length dress and incredibly high-heeled shoes—was Bailey.

Jared had never seen her wearing make-up before, not even on that morning when they'd trained together and she'd come to breakfast in a suit. It was barely there—mainly mascara and a hint of lipstick, from what he could tell—but it served to show him that she was jaw-droppingly beautiful and didn't need anything to enhance her looks. Right now, she looked incredibly glamorous, a million miles away from the slightly scruffy doctor he was used to—the one who walked around the football pitch in tracksuit pants and a hoodie.

He caught her eye as she walked by and she actually winked at him.

And all the blood in his body rushed south.

Oh, help. They hadn't set any ground rules, so this might just be one of his biggest mistakes ever. God. He really should've agreed it with her beforehand. At the very least they should've agreed on no touching and no holding hands. And yet he was supposed to be her fake boyfriend. Everyone would expect him to hold her hand, put his arm round her, gaze at her adoringly, maybe even kiss her...

The idea of kissing her sent him into such a flat spin that he was barely aware of the marriage ceremony. But then the registers were signed and the bride and groom walked down the aisle, all smiles.

The usher handed him a box of bird-friendly confetti on the way out. Jared lined up on the side of the path to the church with everyone else and waited until the photographer directed them all to throw confetti over the happy couple.

He took a couple of photos on his phone and managed to catch one of Bailey with her head tipped back, laughing. The kind of picture that would make a rainy morning feel full of sunshine.

She came over to him while the bride and groom were being photographed on their own. 'Hey. Thanks for coming.'

'Pleasure.' And, actually, it was now. 'You, um, look very nice.'

'Thank you. So do you. I've never seen you in a proper suit before.' She grinned. 'I would say a suit "suits" you, but I need to find a better way of saying it.'

Funny, her easy manner put him at his ease, too. It suddenly didn't matter that this was a wedding, and all the darkness associated with the end of his own marriage just faded away—because Bailey was there and she *sparkled*.

'I'll introduce you properly to everyone at the reception,' she promised. 'Sorry, I should have organised this a lot better so I was travelling with you or something.'

'It's fine. You're the bridesmaid and you have things to do. I'll see you at the reception.'

She gave him another of those incredibly sexy winks. *'Ciao, bello.'*

The Italian side of her was really coming out today. He'd never really seen this before; but then again she'd never flirted with him before, either.

Oddly, he found himself looking forward to the reception—and what he really wanted to do was dance with her. Which was crazy, because he didn't even like dancing very much; but he had a feeling that Bailey did and that she'd be good at it.

He made his way to the hotel where the reception was being held, and joined the line-up of people waiting to kiss the bride and shake the groom's hand. Bailey came and found him in the line. 'Hey, there.'

'Hey.' How ridiculous was it that he should feel suddenly intimidated?

But Bailey took charge, making small talk until she could introduce him to the bride and groom. 'Jared, this is Joni and Aaron. Joni and Aaron, this is Jared Fraser.'

'Very pleased to meet you, Jared,' Joni said with a smile. Jared caught the meaningful look she gave Bailey, and wondered just what Bailey had told her best friend about him. 'Thanks for coming.'

'Thanks for inviting me. It was a lovely service, and you look gorgeous,' he said.

She kissed his cheek. 'You're too sweet. I knew Bailey was lying when she said you were grumpy.'

He laughed. 'I can be.' He gave Bailey a pointed look. 'Though so can she.'

'No way—she's the endorphin queen,' Joni said. 'Bailey believes endorphins are the answer to absolutely everything.'

Jared went hot all over, thinking just how endorphins could be released and how much he'd like to do that with her. He really hoped nobody could read his thoughts. But he managed to pull himself together and shook Aaron's hand. 'Congratulations, both of you, and I hope you'll be very happy together.'

They exchanged a glance, and he could see just how much they adored each other. So maybe Bailey was right and this would have a happy ending. Maybe he should start to believe in love again.

'Righty.' Bailey tucked her arm into his. 'Let's get

this over with. Come and meet my lot. They're the nicest family in the world, but I'm going to apologise in advance because they're a bit—well—full on.'

'Italian,' he said.

She nodded. 'Even though Dad's English, living with my mum and the rest of us has kind of made him Italian.'

'That's nice,' Jared said, and let her lead him over to her family.

'Jared, this is my mother, Lucia, my brothers, Roberto and Giorgio—Rob and Gio for short—and my dad, Paul.'

Jared shook hands and kissed cheeks as expected, and then turned to Bailey. 'How come you don't have an Italian first name?' he asked.

'Because I was born on Christmas Eve, and in my family it's tradition to watch *It's a Wonderful Life* every single Christmas Eve—including the year I was born, because Mum had me at home. So she really had to call me Bailey, after George's family.'

'It could be worse,' Lucia said with a grin. 'I could have called you Clarence.'

'Clarrie. Yes. That's *so* me.' Bailey flapped her hands in imitation of an angel's wings and laughed.

'She's kept you very quiet, Jared,' Lucia said.

'Because we haven't known each other very long, and I know what you're like, Mamma,' Bailey said. She switched into rapid Italian; clearly she was asking her mother not to interrogate him or embarrass her, Jared thought. Mischief prompted him to ask her if she realised that he spoke Italian, just to tease her; but, knowing Bailey, she'd call his bluff and speak in

Italian for the rest of the evening, so he resisted the temptation. Just.

'Sì, sì, bambina mia.' Lucia pinched Bailey's cheeks, and then continued her interrogation. 'So where did you meet, Jared?'

'At work,' he said carefully.

'So you're a doctor?'

'For a football team, yes.'

Bailey's dad smiled at him. 'Which one?'

Jared named the premier division club. 'I work with the youth team—and they've got real potential.'

'Oh, the team Bailey's testing her box of tricks on?' Paul asked. 'I thought you said the team doctor was about to retire, Bailey?'

'He did. Jared took over from him,' Bailey said. 'Are you going to grill the poor man all night, or can we talk about something else—like how gorgeous my best friend looks in her lovely floaty dress?'

'She does indeed.' Paul gave her a hug. 'And so do you, darling. We don't see you dressed up like this very often.'

'If you came to see me with a sports injury and I looked like this when I treated you, you'd be worried that I didn't have a clue what I was talking about and think that you were going to be injured and in pain for the rest of your life,' she said with a grin. 'That's why I don't dress like this very often.'

It turned out that they were at a table with Bailey's family for the wedding breakfast, and Jared was surprised by how easily they included him in the conversation, as if they'd known him for ever. In turn, he got them to talk about the restaurant—and learned a lot about Bailey as a child. Her family was merciless in telling tales; but they clearly adored her, because she was laughing along with the rest of them and giving just as good as she got by telling tales about them, too.

He discovered that Bailey, when she was with her family, was incredibly tactile, so it was just as well they hadn't agreed a no-touching rule, because she would've broken it several times a minute. He already knew that she talked with her hands, but this was something else. She touched his arm, his shoulder, his face, his hair. He wasn't used to that at all, but he was surprised to discover that he liked it. That he wanted more.

Though that wasn't part of the deal. He was her fake partner for tonight, not her real one, he reminded himself.

The food was excellent, but best of all was the cake. 'This has to be the best cake I've ever had in my life,' he said.

Rob looked pleased. 'I'm glad you like it. Actually, it's one of mine,' he said diffidently.

'Bailey said you were good—but she didn't say you were *this* good. And I'm going to beg for seconds.'

'You weren't listening properly,' she said, cuffing his arm. 'I told you Rob was the best pastry chef in the universe. And who do you think made that chocolate cake I gave you?'

'Oh, now, with those two pieces of evidence, I agree completely,' Jared said with a smile.

Funny, he'd been faintly dreading the reception. But it was all easy, from chatting at the tables to listening to the speeches. And then finally the band started playing and the dancing began. The bride and groom danced together first, followed by Bailey and the best man. Jared couldn't take his eyes off her. The way she moved was so graceful, so elegant. This was yet another side to the clever, slightly acerbic doctor he was used to. She'd turned out to be full of surprises.

And then she came over to him. 'Dance with me?'

How could he say no? Especially when he'd been wanting to hold her close all day, and this was the perfect excuse.

When he danced with her, it was the first time he'd ever noticed her perfume; it reminded him of an orange grove in full bloom, yet with a sweet undertone. Sparkly and warm, just like her personality. And he could feel the warmth of her body against his.

To keep his mind off that fact, he asked, 'Why do I recognise the guy playing guitar with the band?'

'That's Olly, Joni's brother—he was one of the ushers, so you would've met him at the church,' she explained.

'Oh.'

'Sorry about my family earlier. As I said, they're a little intense.'

'Don't apologise—I like them. They love you,' he said, 'and it's pretty clear they worry about you.'

She rolled her eyes. 'I'm thirty years old. I can look after myself.'

'Families are supposed to worry about you,' he reminded her.

'Does yours worry about you?' she challenged.

He smiled. 'When I let them, yes.'

'So you're as bad as I am—except I bet you keep yours at bay by being grumpy.'

'And you keep yours at bay by sparkling,' he fenced.

'Sparkling?'

'Like vintage champagne in candlelight,' he said.

Oh, for goodness' sake. Anyone would think he'd been drinking way too much of the vintage champagne. He simply didn't wax poetic like that. But something about Bailey made the words flow and he couldn't stop them.

She smiled. 'You think I'm sparkly?'

'Very,' he admitted.

'Thank you—that's a really lovely thing to say. Especially as I've pretty much neglected you today, and you're doing me a huge favour by being here in the first place.'

'You haven't neglected me.' And he was suddenly really glad that he'd agreed to do this. Because he was seeing a new side to Bailey Randall—a side he really liked. Sweet and playful and totally charming; yet it was totally genuine.

He held her closer. Somehow they were dancing cheek to cheek, and his hand was splayed at the top of her dress. He could feel the warmth of her skin against his fingertips and it sent a thrill right through him. Right at that moment it felt as if it was just the two of them on the dance floor, with nobody else around for miles and miles and miles.

'Your back is perfect,' he murmured.

'Why, thank you, Dr Fraser.'

'Sorry.' He sighed. 'I didn't mean to say that. Ignore me.'

She pulled back slightly to look him straight in the eye. 'I wasn't being sarcastic—and I wasn't offended. Seriously, Jared, thank you for the compliment.'

Her mouth was beautiful; her lower lip was full and he itched to catch it between his.

Oh, this was bad.

Why was he thinking about kissing her?

'I noticed how perfect your back was when we trained together,' he said. And now he was making things much worse. He really needed to shut up.

She ran one finger down his sleeve. 'And I noticed your biceps when we trained together.' Her voice had grown husky. 'I like your biceps. They're perfect, too.'

He knew that he was supposed to be just playing the part of her partner, but right now he wanted to make it reality. So he dipped his head. Just a little bit. Just enough that his mouth could brush against hers.

She tasted of champagne and wedding cake—and he liked it. A lot.

He pulled back so he could look her in the eye and take his cue from her. If she wanted him to back off, he'd do it.

But her lips were ever so slightly parted and there was a sparkle in her eyes that he'd never seen before.

'Bailey, I really want to kiss you,' he whispered.

'I want you to kiss me, too,' she whispered back.

That was all the encouragement he needed. He dipped his head again and took his sweet time kissing her. Every brush of his mouth against hers, every nibble, made him more and more aware of her. And she was kissing him back, her arms wrapped as tightly round him as his were round her.

He wanted this to last for ever.

But then he became aware that the music had changed and become more uptempo, and he and Bailey were still swaying together as if the band was playing a slow song. He broke the kiss, and he could see the exact moment that she realised what was going on, too. Those gorgeous dark eyes were absolutely huge. And she looked as shocked as he felt. Panicked, almost.

This wasn't supposed to be happening.

'I, um…' she said, and tailed off.

'Yeah.' He didn't know what to say, either. What he really wanted to do was kiss her again—but they were in a public place. With her best friend and her family in attendance. And doing what he really wanted to do would cause all kinds of complications. He didn't want to get involved with anyone. Apart from that one awful evening when his best friend had persuaded him to try speed dating—an experience he never wanted to repeat—Jared hadn't dated since his divorce. No way was he setting himself up to get hurt again, the way he he'd been with Sasha—even though he knew that Bailey wasn't a bit like Sasha.

'I guess I ought to do some chief bridesmaid stuff and get the kids dancing,' she said.

And he ought to offer to help her. Except there was just a hint of fear in her eyes. He didn't think she was scared of him; maybe, he thought, she was just as scared of getting involved as he was. Especially given that she'd asked him to be her fake partner to keep her family happy. Bailey had obviously been hurt at some point, too, and they clearly worried about her.

'I guess,' he said. 'Do you, um, want a hand?'

'Do you like kids?'

That was an easy one. 'Yes, I do.' And he'd always thought he'd have children of his own one day. Sasha had taken the choice of keeping the baby away from him, and at that point he'd realised just how much he wanted to be a dad. But unless he took the risk of giving someone his heart—the right woman, someone he could really trust—that wasn't going to happen.

He pushed the thought away and concentrated on helping Bailey organise the children. She was a natural with them—they responded to her warmth. Just like him.

'If you could dance with some of the wallflowers,' she said quietly to him, 'that would be kind.'

Kind wasn't what he was feeling right now, but kind would be a hell of a lot safer. 'Sure,' he said.

Even though he was polite and made conversation with the women he danced with, he was totally aware of Bailey throughout the entire evening. Her smile, her sparkle, her warmth. And she made him ache.

He wanted her. Really wanted her. But he knew she'd panicked as much as he had when they'd kissed, so it was a bad idea. They needed to go back to being strictly colleagues. Somehow.

At the end of the evening he said his goodbyes to Bailey's family, trusting that she'd manage to get him out of a promise to see them soon.

'I guess this is it, then,' she said as she walked him to the door of the ballroom.

'I'll call a taxi and see you home first,' he said.

She shook her head. 'You don't have to do that.'

He smiled. 'Yes, I do. I'm old-fashioned. So let's not argue about it—just humour me on this one, OK?'

She didn't argue and let him organise a taxi. She didn't say much on the journey back to her place; although Jared desperately wanted to reach for her hand, he kept a tight rein on himself and simply joined her in sitting quietly.

When the taxi stopped, he paid the cabbie.

'Isn't he taking you home now?' Bailey asked, and he could see the panic in her eyes. Did she really think that he expected her to invite him in for a nightcap—or more?

'No. I'm seeing you to your doorstep and waiting until you're safely inside, then I'm taking the Tube home,' Jared said. 'And, yes, I know you can look after yourself, but it's been a long day and you're wearing incredibly high heels.'

'Point taken.' Her expression softened. 'Thank you.'

She let him escort her to her doorstep.

'Thank you for today,' she said. 'I really appreciate it.'

'No worries.' He leaned forward, intending to give her a reassuring—and strictly platonic—kiss on the cheek. But somewhere along the way one or both of them moved their head, and the next thing he knew his lips were skimming against hers.

What started out as a soft, sweet, gentle kiss quickly turned to something else entirely, and he was kissing her as if he was starving. She was kissing him right back, opening her mouth to let him deepen the kiss. And this felt so right, so perfect.

When she pulled away, his head was swimming.

'No,' she said. 'We can't do this.'

The panic was back in her face.

Her ex, whoever he was, must have really hurt her badly, Jared thought.

And he had no intention of making her feel worse.

'It's OK.' He took her hand and squeezed it. Just once. The way she'd squeezed his hand when he'd talked about his knee injury. Sympathy, not pity. 'You're right. We're colleagues, and *just* colleagues.'

And he needed to keep that in mind. He didn't want the complication of falling for someone, either. The risk of everything going wrong. Been there, done that and learned from his mistakes.

The fear in her eyes faded—just a fraction, but she'd clearly heard what he'd said.

'I'll see you at work,' he said.

'Yeah. I'll see you.' She swallowed. 'And I'm sorry.'

'There's nothing to be sorry for,' he said.

He waited until she'd unlocked her front door and closed it again behind her, and then he left to find the Tube station. It was better this way. Being sensible.

Wasn't it?

CHAPTER SEVEN

BAILEY SLEPT REALLY badly that night. Every time she closed her eyes, all she could see was Jared in that wretched suit, looking totally edible. Worse, her mouth tingled in memory of the way he'd kissed her.

OK, she'd admit it. She was attracted to Jared Fraser. Big time.

But, after the way her marriage had imploded, she wasn't sure she could risk getting involved with anyone again. Letting herself be vulnerable. Risking the same thing happening all over again. After the ectopic pregnancy she'd ended up pushing Ed away—physically as well as emotionally—because she'd been so scared of getting pregnant again.

So, as much as she would like to date Jared—and to take things a lot further than they had at the wedding—she was going to be sensible and keep things between them just as colleagues. Because she didn't want to hurt him, the way she'd hurt Ed.

Do you like kids?

And he'd said yes. She could imagine him as a father, especially after she'd seen him with the children at the wedding. And that was another sticking point. She wanted children, too. But the ectopic pregnancy had shredded her confidence. What if it happened again and her other tube ruptured, leaving her infertile?

She'd been terrified of getting pregnant again, and that had made her scared of sex—a vicious circle she hadn't been able to break. Technically, Ed had been unfaithful to her; but Bailey blamed herself for it, because he'd only done it after she'd pushed him away and refused to let him touch her. She knew that the break-up of her marriage was all her fault.

Since her divorce, until Jared, she hadn't met anyone she'd wanted to date. But how could she expect him to deal with all her baggage? It wouldn't be fair.

So, the next morning, she sent Jared a text to clear the air—and also to make it very clear to him how she felt. And hopefully it would ease any potential awkwardness at work.

Sorry. Too much champagne yesterday. Hope I haven't wrecked our professional relationship.

Jared read the message for the fourth time.

Too much champagne? Hardly. He'd been watching Bailey. She'd had one glass, maybe two. With a meal. Most of the time she'd been drinking sparkling water—as had he.

It was an excuse, and he knew it. She'd looked so scared. As panicky as he'd felt. But why?

Next time he saw her, he decided, he'd get her to talk to him. For now, he'd try to keep things easy between them.

Medicinal recommendation of a fry-up for the hangover, he texted back. See you on the pitch later in the week.

* * *

Facing Jared for the first time since the wedding made Bailey squirm inside. In the end, she decided to brazen it out. Hadn't he said she was sparkly? Then she'd go into super-sparkly mode. So she chatted to all the players, gave Archie a smacking kiss hello on the cheek—while making quite sure she was out of grabbing reach half a second later—and gave Jared a lot of backchat about being too old and too stuck in his ways to do yoga with the boys in the team.

To her relief, he responded the same way, and things were back to the way they used to be. Before he'd kissed her.

Almost.

Because during the training session she looked up from her laptop and caught him looking at her; those amazing blue eyes were filled with wistfulness.

Yeah.

She'd like to repeat that kiss, too. Take things further. But she just couldn't take the risk. She knew he'd end up being just as hurt as she was. She couldn't destroy him, the way she'd destroyed Ed.

'Can we have a word?' Jared asked at the end of the training session.

'Um—sure.' Bailey looked spooked.

He waited until the players and Archie had gone into the dressing room. 'Are you OK?' he asked gently.

'Of course. Why wouldn't I be?'

'You and me. Saturday night,' he pointed out.

'Too much champagne,' she said swiftly.

'I don't think so.' He kept his voice soft. 'I think you're running scared.'

She lifted her chin and gave him a look that was clearly supposed to be haughty, but instead he saw the vulnerability there. 'I'm not scared.'

'That,' he said, 'is pure bravado. And I know that, because this thing between us scares me, too.'

The fight went out of her. 'Oh.'

'So what are we going to do about it?' he asked.

'I'm not looking for a relationship. I'm fine being single.'

'That's what I've been telling myself, too.' He paused. 'Maybe we could be brave. Together.'

'I…' She shook her head. 'I'm not ready for this.'

'Fair enough.' He held her gaze. 'But when you are…'

She swallowed hard. 'Yeah. I, um, ought to let you get on.'

He let her go. For now. And he could be patient, because Bailey Randall was definitely worth waiting for.

Everything was fine for the next week, until Bailey's system picked up a marked problem. Maybe it was a glitch in the system, she thought, and decided to keep it to herself for the time being. But when the same result showed after the next session, and after she'd caught the tail end of the lads gossiping outside the dressing room, she knew that she was going to have to do something.

'Jared, can we have a quick word?' she asked quietly.

He frowned. 'Is something wrong?'

'I think so.' She gestured to her laptop, so he'd know that it was to do with the monitoring system and one of the players.

'Hadn't we better talk to Archie if you want to pull someone from the team?' he asked.

She shook her head and kept her voice low. 'This is a tricky one, and you're the only person I can talk to about it.'

'OK,' he said. 'I assume you mean somewhere quiet, away from the club.'

'Definitely away from the club,' she said. 'Yes, please.'

'Are you free straight after training?'

She nodded.

'We'll talk then.'

'Thank you.' And just knowing that she could share this with him and he'd help her work out what to do made some of the sick feeling go away.

After the session, Jared took Bailey to a café not far from the football club. 'Sit down, and I'll get us some coffee.' He remembered what she'd drunk at the gym. 'I take it you'd like a latte?'

She smiled. 'I'm half-Italian. You only drink lattes at breakfast. Espresso for me, please.'

He smiled back. 'Sure.'

'And can I be greedy and ask for some cake, too?' she asked. 'I don't care what sort, as long as it's cake.'

'It's not going to be up to your brother's standards,' he warned.

'Right now, I don't care—I need the sugar rush.'

Worry flickered down Jared's spine. Whatever she wanted to discuss with him was clearly something serious if she needed a sugar rush. And he'd noticed that she'd been much quieter than normal during the training session.

He came back with two coffees, a blueberry muffin and a double chocolate muffin. 'You can have first pick.'

'Thank you.' She took the blueberry one.

He sat down opposite her. 'Spit it out. What's worrying you?'

'You know how my system picks up if someone's underperforming?'

'Yes.'

'I'm worried about one of the players. I've heard the rumours that he's in danger of losing his place on the team because he hasn't been playing well for a while.'

'Darren,' Jared said immediately.

She nodded. 'And I heard the boys talking. He's not coping with the pressure.' She sighed. 'It's hearsay and I don't want to accuse him of something when he might be perfectly innocent, but...' Her eyes were huge with concern. 'I think he's drinking. Apart from it making his performance worse, he's not even eighteen yet—he's underage.'

Jared blew out a breath. 'I've known a few players over the years who started drinking to handle the pressure, and it finished their careers.'

She looked miserable. 'I don't know what to do. If I tell Archie, then Darren will definitely lose his place. He'll be kicked out.'

'For breaking his contract,' Jared agreed.

'But if he *is* drinking, then it needs to stop right now, Jared. He's going to damage himself.'

'Agreed.'

'Maybe I'm being a bit paranoid and overthinking it. Have a look and see what you reckon.' She opened her laptop and drew up the graphs. Darren's performance had been very near his average in every session apart from the last two, where there was a marked difference.

'So you suspected it last time as well?' he asked.

She nodded. 'I wanted to monitor a second performance, just in case the first one was a one-off—a glitch in the programme or something.'

'No, I think your analysis is spot on. We need to tell Archie and Lyle Fincham.'

'But they'll kick him out.'

'Not necessarily. We can both put in a good word for him. He's not a bad kid—he's just made a mistake and he needs some help.' Jared shrugged. 'Extra coaching might make things easier for him, and I can design a workout programme tailored to his needs.'

'You'd do that for him?' She sounded surprised.

'Everyone makes mistakes. And everyone deserves a second chance,' he said. 'A chance to put it right.'

He hoped she'd think about it. And that she'd give them a second chance, too.

Mr Fincham wasn't available, so Jared and Bailey tackled Archie.

'So there's a problem with one of the players?' Archie asked.

Bailey nodded and talked the team coach through the computer evidence.

Archie frowned. 'So you think he's drinking?'

'You know as well as I do, some players do when they can't cope with the pressure,' Jared said.

'And it only makes things worse. Plus he's underage. If he can't cope, then he'll have to leave the team,'

Archie said with a sigh. 'I can't have him being a bad influence on the rest of the lads.'

'Or,' Bailey said, 'you could give him another chance. We could talk to him and tell him what damage he's doing to himself—in graphic enough terms to make him stop.'

'And I can give him an extra training programme to help him brush up his skills and make him feel that some of the pressure's off,' Jared said.

'If the papers get hold of this, the muck will really hit the fan,' Archie said, and shook his head. 'No. He'll have to go.'

'Archie. It's happened *twice*. That's not so bad—he'll be able to stop. Give the boy a chance to come good,' Bailey urged.

'And what message does that give the others? That I'm soft on the kind of behaviour that destroys a team?'

'No. It tells them that you understand they're still very young and some of them need a bit more guidance than others,' Jared said.

'Lyle won't be happy about it,' Archie warned.

'But you can talk him round. You're the team coach. He'll listen to you,' Bailey said.

Archie didn't look totally convinced. 'And what if Darren does it again?'

'Then there are all kinds of disciplinary options,' Jared said.

'But if we all give him the right support,' Bailey added, 'he won't do it again.'

Archie went silent, clearly thinking about it. 'All right,' he said. 'I'll square it with Lyle. But I'm going to read young Darren the Riot Act and make sure he knows that if he puts a single toe out of line from now on, he'll be out.'

'Thank you,' Bailey said.

'Everyone deserves a second chance,' Jared added. 'I think he'll make the most of it.'

Everyone deserves a second chance.

Could that be true for them, too? Bailey wondered.

Jared had clearly been thinking about it, too, because later that evening he called her. 'Are you busy?'

'I'm studying,' she said.

'Have you eaten yet?'

'Yes.' A sandwich at her desk. But it counted.

'Oh.' He paused. 'I wondered if you'd like to have dinner with me.'

Was he asking her on a date? Adrenalin fizzed through her veins. Strange how Jared made her feel like a teenager. 'As colleagues?' she asked carefully.

'No.'

So he *did* mean a date. Excitement was replaced by skittering panic. 'I'll think about it.'

'Is my company really that bad?' he asked.

'No—no, it's not that, Jared. Not at all.' She sighed. 'It's complicated.'

'I can take a hint.'

She *would* like to have dinner with him; it was just that the whole idea of dating again scared her. How could she tell him, without dumping all that baggage on him? Telling him what had happened to her, and why her marriage had ended? She couldn't. She just couldn't. 'I, um, haven't dated in a while,' she said.

'Me, neither,' he said, surprising her. 'I'm seriously out of practice, too.'

Something else they had in common. Who, she wondered, had hurt him?

'I was thinking,' he said, 'we were a good team, this afternoon.'

'Yes.'

'And I was thinking,' he said, 'maybe we should give ourselves a chance to see if we could be a good team outside work.'

'Maybe,' she said.

'I could,' he suggested, 'cook dinner for you.'

'You can cook?'

He coughed. 'Don't be sexist. Especially as your brothers are both chefs.'

She smiled wryly. 'Yeah, I guess.'

'So—how about it?'

'If I say yes,' she said, 'then it's just between us?'

'You want to keep it a secret?' He sounded slightly hurt.

'I want to keep life simple,' she said. 'Can I think about it?'

'It's just as well I'm a sports doctor. My ego could really use some liniment right now,' he said dryly.

And now he'd made her laugh. He was the first man to do that in a long while. Maybe, just maybe, she should give this a try. Maybe everyone was right and it was time she learned to live again. And Jared might just be the man to help her do that.

'All right. Thank you, Jared. I'd like to have dinner with you. I don't have any food allergies and I'm not fussy about what I eat.'

'That was a quick decision.'

And she still wasn't sure it was the right one. Part of her really, really wanted to do it; and part of her wanted to run. 'When do you want to do it?' Oh, and that sounded bad. She felt her face heat. Worse still, that was a definite Freudian slip. Because any woman with red blood in her veins would want to go to bed with someone as sexy as Jared Fraser. 'Have dinner, I mean,' she added hastily.

'Tomorrow night?' he suggested.

'That's fine.' Big, fat lie. Now they'd actually set a date, the panic was back. In triplicate. 'I'll need your address.'

'Got a pen?'

'Give me two seconds.' She grabbed a pen. 'OK, tell me.' She scribbled down his address as he dictated it. 'What time?'

'Seven?'

'Seven,' she confirmed. 'Can I bring anything? Pudding, maybe?' She could get Rob to make something special. Then again, Rob would tell their mother, and Lucia would go straight into interrogation mode. OK. She'd cheat and buy it from a top-end supermarket instead.

'No, that's fine. Just bring yourself,' he said.

And how scary that sounded.

Bailey was feeling antsy the next morning, and she was really glad that she was busy all day in clinic. There were the usual sprains and strains, although she did feel a bit sorry for the middle-aged woman who'd managed to give herself tennis elbow from taking her weightlifting training too hard and was horrified to learn it could take several months of rest before the tear in her ligament healed.

'Rest, ice it every couple of hours, take painkillers and use a support bandage when you exercise and whenever it's really sore,' Bailey said. 'And when you do go back to using weights, you'll need to drop the weights right down and take it very steadily. And don't do anything above your head before it's healed fully, or your rotator cuff in your shoulder will over-compensate for your elbow and you'll have to get over the damage to that, too.'

Mrs Curtis grimaced. 'I knew I shouldn't have done that last set. I just wanted to finish the last few reps, but I should've just admitted that I was tired and stopped there.'

'You'll know next time,' Bailey said. 'Come back and see me if it's not any better within a couple of weeks. It should heal on its own, but if it doesn't then a corticosteroid injection could help.'

'Thank you.' Mrs Curtis smiled wryly. 'That'll teach me to remember how old I am, not how old I feel.'

Bailey patted her shoulder. 'We all do it. Don't beat yourself up about it.'

She bought wine and chocolates on the way home, and changed her outfit three times before deciding that smart casual was the way forward—a little black dress would be way too much. Black trousers and a silky long-sleeved teal top would be better. She added her nice jet earrings to give her courage, put on a slightly brighter shade of lipstick than she would nor-mally and then stared at herself in the mirror.

How long had it been since she'd gone on a first date? Or since someone had cooked for her? How did you even behave in these sorts of situations? She thought about calling Joni and asking for help—but, then again, it would make Joni think she was really serious about Jared, and… No, it was all too complicated. She had no idea how he made her feel, other than that he put her in a flat spin.

'It's dinner. Just dinner,' she told her reflection. 'Treat him as a friend. A colleague. And then everything will be fine.'

Except she knew she was lying. Because since that kiss, she hadn't thought of Jared as a colleague—or as a friend. And he hadn't asked her to dinner as a colleague or friend, either.

Would he kiss her again tonight?

And she wasn't sure if the shiver down her spine was anticipation or fear.

CHAPTER EIGHT

BAILEY'S PANIC GREW as she walked up the path to Jared's door. She almost didn't ring the bell and scuttled home to safety instead, but she knew that would be unkind and unfair. He'd gone to the effort of cooking her a meal, so the least she could do was turn up to eat it—even if she did feel way more jumpy than the proverbial cat on a hot tin roof.

She took a deep breath and rang the bell.

When he answered the door, she was glad she'd opted for smart casual, because he'd done the same. He was wearing black trousers and a dark blue shirt that brought out the colour of his eyes. She could feel herself practically dissolving into a puddle of hormones, and her social skills had all suddenly deserted her.

How had she forgotten just how gorgeous the man was?

And his biceps.

Don't think about his biceps, she told herself. Concentrate. Friends and colleagues.

She handed him the wine and chocolates. 'I forgot to ask you if I should bring red or white, so I played it safe—and I should've asked you if you like milk, white or dark chocolate.' Oh, help. Now she was gab-bling and she sounded like a fool.

'These are just fine, and you really didn't need to bring them—but I appreciate it,' he said.

And, oh, that smile was to die for. The butterflies in her tummy went into stampede mode.

'Come in.' He stood aside and gestured for her to enter.

How come he didn't look anywhere near as ner-vous as she felt? How could he be so cool and relaxed when she was a gibbering wreck?

She followed him inside, her tension and anticipa-tion growing with every step.

'We're eating in the kitchen. I hope that's OK,' he said, obviously trying to put her at ease.

'That's very OK, thanks.' His kitchen was gor-geous: a deep terracotta tiled floor teamed with glossy cream cabinets, dark worktops and duck-egg-blue walls. There was a small square maple table at one end with two places set. 'I really like the way you've done your kitchen,' she said.

'I'm afraid it's all my sister's idea rather than mine,' he confessed. 'When I bought this place and did it up, she offered to paint for two hours a day until it was done if I would let her choose the kitchen.'

It sounded as if he was as close to his family as she was to hers. 'So you're not really a cook, then?'

'Given that you come from a family of restaura-teurs and chefs, I wouldn't dare claim to be a cook,' he said.

She smiled. 'I promise I won't go into food critic mode.'

He pretended to mop his brow in relief, making her smile. 'Can I get you a drink?'

'Yes, please—whatever you're having.'

He took a bottle of Pinot Grigio from the fridge and poured them both a glass. Bailey noted that all his appliances were built-in and hidden behind doors to match the rest of the cabinets. Efficient and stylish at the same time. She liked that. It was how she organised her own kitchen.

'Have a seat,' he said, indicating the table.

'Thanks.' She bit her lip. 'Sorry. As I said, it's been a while since I dated.'

'Me, too. And it's hard to know what to say. We could make small talk about the team and work—but then it wouldn't be like a date.'

'And if we ask each other about ourselves, it'll feel like—well—we're grilling each other,' she said.

'Or speed dating.' He grimaced. 'I let my best friend talk me into that one six months ago. Never, *ever* again.'

Speed dating was something she'd never done—along with signing up to an online dating agency or letting anyone set her up on a blind date. She'd made it clear to everyone that she was just fine as she was. 'Was it really that bad?'

'Probably slightly worse,' he said. 'But how do you meet someone when you get to our age?'

'You make us sound middle-aged.' She laughed, even though she knew what he meant. By their age, most people had already settled into a relationship or had a lot of baggage that made starting a new relationship difficult. It wasn't like when you were just out of university and there were parties every week-end where most of the people there were still single.

'I'm thirty-five—and sometimes I feel really middle-aged,' he said wryly, 'especially when I hear the seventeen-year-olds talking in the changing room about their girlfriends.'

She raised an eyebrow. 'They don't do that in front of me. Probably because they think I'll tell them off.' Then she groaned, 'Which means they think I'm old enough to be their mother, and at thirty I'm not *quite* that old.'

'Or maybe they've got a secret crush on you and don't want to sound stupid in front of you,' Jared suggested.

'I think,' she said, 'that might be a slightly worse thought. They're still practically babies!'

He laughed and raised his glass. 'To us,' he said, 'and finding some way to talk to each other.'

'To us,' she echoed, feeling ridiculously shy.

'I forgot to ask you if you like fish,' he said.

'I do.'

'Good. Though I'm afraid I cheated on the starter,' he admitted. 'Which is ready right now.'

He took two plates from the fridge: baby crabs served in their shell with a salad garnish, and served with thin slices of rye bread and proper butter.

'I don't care if you cheated. This is lovely,' she said.

The main course was sea bass baked in foil with slices of lemon, rosemary potatoes, fine green beans and baby carrots. 'This is fabulous,' she said. 'Super-healthy and super-scrumptious.'

He inclined his head in acknowledgement of the compliment. 'Thank you.'

Pudding was a rich dark chocolate mousse served in a tiny pot with raspberries.

'Now, this,' Bailey said after the first mouthful, 'is what you'd use to make any woman say yes.'

And then she realised what she'd said.

She put one hand to her face in horror. 'Please tell me I didn't say that out loud.'

'I'm afraid you did.' His voice had grown slightly husky, and his pupils were huge, making his eyes look dark.

She blew out a breath. 'Um. I don't know what to say.'

'If it helps, I didn't actually make it with the intention of using it to seduce you,' he said. 'Only…you've put an image in my head now.'

'An image?'

He nodded. 'Of me feeding you this, one spoonful at a time.'

So much for telling herself to treat this as just dinner with a friend. Right now, he'd put exactly the same image in her own head and she could hardly breathe. Especially as she could vividly remember what it had felt like when he'd kissed her.

What would happen if she held out her spoon to him? Would he let her feed the rich chocolate mousse to him? Or would he lean forward and kiss her?

Time hung, suspended.

Which of them would make the first move?

Dark colour was slashed across his cheekbones. And she could feel the heat in her own face. The beat of desire.

Would he kiss her again?

'I think,' he said, his voice even huskier now, 'we probably need coffee.'

And some distance between them so they could both calm down again. 'Yes,' she whispered.

Though she couldn't help watching him while he moved round the kitchen. For someone who was over six feet tall and so muscular, he was very light on his feet. He'd moved lightly when he'd danced with her, too. What would it be like if he...?

No.

Do not think of Jared Fraser naked, she told herself.

Except she couldn't get the idea out of her head.

What would it be like, making love with Jared?

Her face heating even more, she tried to push the thought to the back of her mind and concentrated on her pudding. He did likewise when he'd finished making them both an espresso.

Silence stretched between them like wires, tighter and tighter.

They needed to break the tension now. Right now. Before they did something stupid. Like kissing each other until they were both dizzy. Right at that moment it was what she really wanted him to do. And she didn't dare look at him in case he didn't feel the same—or, worse, in case he did. She wasn't sure which scared her more.

She sipped the coffee. 'This is good,' she murmured. Oh, for pity's sake. Where was her stock of small talk when she needed it? Why couldn't she talk to him about books and films and theatre?

Probably because her tastes were on the girly side and his would be decidedly masculine.

'I'm glad you like the coffee.' He paused. 'Would you like to sit in the living room?'

'Can I help you wash up first?'

'No. That's what a dishwasher is for,' he said.

Actually, it probably wouldn't be a good idea to work with him in the kitchen. It would be way too easy to brush against each other. Turn to each other. *Touch each other...*

She followed him into his living room. Everything was in neutral tones and comfortable. There were several framed photographs on the mantelpiece and she couldn't resist putting her coffee down so she could look at them more closely. His graduation, three more graduation photographs of what had to be his brothers and his sister as they looked so like him, wedding photographs of his brothers and sister, and various family portraits—including one of him with a small child.

His daughter? Or maybe she was his niece or his godchild. If he'd had a daughter, he would've mentioned it when they talked about kids at Joni's wedding, surely?

'Your family?' she asked.

'Yes. Also known as the doctors at Lavender Lane Surgery.' He smiled. 'They try to poach me onto the team every so often, but I like what I'm doing now.'

Then she came to a picture of a football team. Judging by the haircuts, she'd say the picture was nearly twenty years old. So it was pretty obvious what that represented. His first ever international match. But something had puzzled her for ages. 'So how come, given that you have a Scots accent and a Scots surname, you played for England?'

'I was born in London,' he said, 'and my mum's English—so technically I could have played for either team, but as I lived in London I guess it made more sense to play for England.' He smiled. 'Dad said if my team ever played the under-twenty-one Scotland team, his loyalties would've been really divided.'

'Like in our house. Whenever England plays Italy in the World Cup the boys end up cheering both sides.'

She picked him out immediately in the middle of the photograph. Mainly because that was the one she'd seen when she'd snooped on the Internet—not that she was going to tell him that. 'That's you at seventeen?'

'Yes—the first time I played for England.' He smiled. 'It was an amazing feeling. And when I scored that goal, it felt like all my birthdays and Christmases at once.'

'I bet.' On impulse, she turned round and hugged him.

Big mistake, because then his arms came round her, and he dipped his head to kiss her. His mouth was warm and sweet and tempting, and she found herself responding, letting him deepen the kiss.

He picked her up and carried her over to the sofa, still kissing her, then settled down with her on his lap.

Right at that moment she really wanted him to carry her to his bed. To take her clothes off, bit by bit, and kiss every inch of skin as he uncovered it. And then to touch her again, make her forget about everything in the universe except him...

But then reality rushed back in. She wasn't on the Pill. She hadn't needed to be, because she'd steered clear of relationships, let alone sex. Condoms weren't always effective. If they made love, what if she got pregnant, and what if…? She swallowed hard. She could still remember being rushed into the emergency department, the crippling pain in her abdomen followed by an even worse pain in her soul. And it froze her.

Jared was aware that Bailey had stopped kissing him back. He pulled away slightly and he saw she looked incredibly panicky. Something had clearly happened in her past, something that had put absolute devastation in her eyes.

He stroked her face. 'Bailey, it's all right. We can stop right now and I'm not going to push you.'

But the fear didn't seem to go away. She remained where she was, looking haunted.

'If you want to talk to me,' he said, 'I'll listen, and whatever you tell me won't go any further than me.'

'I don't want to talk about it,' she muttered.

'That's OK, too.' He kept holding her close. He had a few trust issues, too, thanks to Sasha cheating on him and then not giving him any say in keeping the baby. But he really liked what he'd seen of Bailey. It would be worth the effort of learning to trust and teaching her to trust him. They just needed some time.

Maybe it would help if he opened up a little first.

'I used to be married,' he said.

Bailey still looked wary, but at least she hadn't pulled away.

'I loved her. A lot. Sasha.' Funny, saying her name didn't make him feel as if he'd been put through the shredder any more. 'We were married for three years. I thought we were happy, but I guess she wanted more of a WAG lifestyle than I could give her—so that meant seeing a footballer rather than the team doctor.'

Bailey looked surprised. 'She left you for a footballer?'

Sasha had done a lot more than that, but Jared wasn't quite ready to talk about that bit. About how she'd totally shattered his world. How she'd had an affair, got pregnant, decided she didn't actually know who the father of her baby was as she'd been sleeping with them both, and had a termination without even telling him. 'Yes,' he said. 'She'd been seeing him for a while.'

'That's hard,' Bailey said.

He shrugged. 'It was at the time. But it was a couple of years ago now and I'm over it. We could probably just about be civil to each other if we were in the same room.'

'It's easier when you can be civil to each other,' she said.

'You're on civil terms with your ex now?'

It was her own fault, Bailey thought. She'd practically invited the question.

And she had to be honest with Jared. 'It wasn't Ed's fault that we broke up.' She'd shut her husband out and pushed him away. Sex had been out of the question because the fear of getting pregnant and having another ectopic pregnancy had frozen her. Ed had tried to get through to her, but her barriers had been too strong. And so he'd given up and turned elsewhere for comfort. She couldn't blame him for that. She hadn't been in love with him any more, but the way her marriage had ended still made her sad. 'Jared, I don't want to talk about it. Not right now.' She wriggled off his lap. 'And I think I ought to go home.'

'I'll drive you. I only had one glass of wine so I'm under the limit.'

'I'll be fine on the Tube,' she said. 'To be honest, I could do with a bit of a walk to clear my head.'

'Would you at least let me walk you to the Tube station?'

She shook her head. 'I'll be fine. But thank you—that was a really nice meal, and I appreciate it.'

And she needed to get out of here now, before she did something really stupid—like resting her head on his shoulder and crying all over him. It wouldn't be fair to dump her baggage on him, and it really wasn't fair to lead him on and let him think that this thing between them was going anywhere, because it couldn't happen. She wasn't sure she was ready to get that involved with someone again—especially someone who'd been hurt in the past and had his own baggage to deal with. She was attracted to Jared, seriously attracted, but that just wasn't enough to let her take that risk. She didn't want it all to go wrong and for him to get hurt because of her.

When Bailey still hadn't texted him by lunchtime the next day, Jared knew that he'd have to make the first move.

But what had spooked her?

She'd flatly refused to talk about it, so it had to be something huge. He wasn't sure how to get her to talk to him without making her put even more barriers up.

In the end, he called her. He half expected her to

let the call go through to voicemail, but she answered.
'Hi, Jared.'

'How are you doing?' he asked softly.

'OK. Thanks for asking.'

'Want to go and get an ice cream or something?'

'Thanks, but I have a pile of work to do.'

It was an excuse, and he knew it. He could hear the panic in her voice, so he kept his tone calm and sensible. 'So if you have a lot of work to do, a short break will help refresh you.'

She sighed. 'You're not going to let this go, are you?'

'Nope,' he agreed.

'OK. What time?'

'Now?' he suggested. 'It's a nice afternoon.'

'Are you standing outside my flat or something?' she asked.

He laughed. 'No. I'm sitting in my kitchen, drinking coffee. Which is the alternative offer if you don't want ice cream.'

'You're pushy.'

'No. I'm not letting you push me away, and it's a subtle but important difference. I like you, Bailey,' he said. 'I think you and I could make a good team.'

There was a pause, and for a moment he thought he'd gone too far. But then she said, 'I like you, too.'

It was progress. Of sorts.

'I'll see you here in, what, an hour?' she asked.

'An hour's fine,' he said.

Jared turned up with flowers. Nothing hugely showy, nothing that made a statement or made Bailey feel under pressure; just a simple bunch of pretty yellow gerbera. 'They made me think of you,' he said.

Funny how that made her feel warm all over. 'Thank you. They're lovely.' She kissed his cheek, very quickly, and her mouth tingled at the touch of his skin. 'I'll put these in water.' Which was the perfect excuse for her to back away, and she was pretty sure he knew it, too.

They ended up going for a walk in the nearby park. And when Jared's fingers brushed against hers for the third time Bailey gave in and let him hold her hand. He didn't say a word about it, just chatted easily to her, and Bailey knew they'd turned another corner. That she was letting him closer, bit by bit.

Everything was fine until they walked past the children's play area.

'I used to take my niece to the park when she was small. Before she grew into a teen who's surgically attached to her mobile phone,' Jared said. 'The swings were her favourite. That and feeding the ducks.'

So that picture back at his place was of his niece. Even though Bailey's mouth felt as if it was full of sawdust, she had to ask the question. She needed to know the answer. Clearly he loved being an uncle— but would that be enough for him? 'Do you want children of your own?'

'Yes,' he said. 'I'd love to have kids—someone to kick a ball round with and read bedtime stories to. One day.'

Was it her imagination, or did he sound wistful? She didn't quite dare look at him. Besides, panic was flooding through her again.

He wanted children.

OK. So this thing between them was new. Fragile. There were no guarantees that things would work out. But it wouldn't be fair of her to let things go forward without at least telling him about her ectopic pregnancy. If he wanted kids, he needed to know that might not be an option for her. Yet, at the same time it felt too soon to raise the subject. As if she were presuming things.

She'd have to work out how to tell him. And when.

'What about you?' he asked.

How did she even begin answering that?

It was true. She did want children. But that would mean getting pregnant, and the whole idea of that terrified her. It was a vicious circle, and she didn't know how to break it. 'One day,' she said. Wanting to head him off the subject, she added, 'The café's just over there. The ice cream's on me.'

To her relief, he didn't argue or push the subject further. But he didn't let her hand go, either. He was just *there*. Warm and solid and dependable, not putting any pressure on her.

So maybe, she thought, they might have a chance. She just had to learn to stop being scared.

CHAPTER NINE

EVERYTHING WAS FINE until the following Monday, when Bailey was having her usual chicken salad with Joni after the yoga class.

Joni had been a bit quiet all evening, looking worried.

'Is everything OK?' Bailey asked.

'Ye-es.'

But she didn't sound too sure. Bailey reached across the table and squeezed her hand. 'What? You've had a fight with Aaron? It happens. One or both of you is being an idiot, one or both of you will apologise and it'll be fine.'

'It's not that.' Joni bit her lip and there were tears in her eyes. 'Bailey, I don't know how to say this—I mean, it's good news, but I also know that...'

At that moment Bailey knew exactly what her best friend was going to tell her. And, even though it was ripping the top off her scars, no way in this world was she ever going to do anything other than smile—and she was going to try and make this easy for Joni, because she knew exactly why her best friend was worried about telling her. 'Joni, are you about to tell me something really, really fantastic—that you and Aaron are going to be…?'

The sheer relief in Joni's eyes nearly broke her.

'I've been dying to tell you since before the wedding, but…'

Yeah. Bailey could remember how it felt. The moment she'd suspected she was pregnant, the moment she'd done the test and seen the positive result, the way Ed had scooped her up and swung her round when she'd shown him the test stick. The sheer joy and happiness of knowing that they were going to have a baby, start their own family… She'd managed to keep the news to herself for four whole days before it had been too much to keep it in any more; she'd sworn both her mum and her best friend to total secrecy and had burst into happy tears when she'd told them. And whilst Ed had been worried about her jinxing it by telling everyone too early and not waiting until the twelve-week point was up, she'd been so happy that she just couldn't contain her news any longer.

Maybe Ed was right—maybe she *had* jinxed it by telling everyone too soon.

She pushed the thought away. Not now. This was about her best friend's future, not the wreck of her own past.

'Oh, Joni, I'm so pleased for you.' And she was, she really was. Just because it had gone bad for her, it didn't mean that she couldn't appreciate anyone else's joy. 'That's fantastic news. How far are you?'

'Ten weeks. I went for the dating scan today,' Joni said almost shyly.

'Good.' So Joni definitely wasn't going to go

through the pain and fear of an ectopic pregnancy. Bailey almost sagged back in her chair in relief. 'So do I get to see a photograph, then?'

'Are you sure you want to see it?'

At that, Bailey got up, walked round to the other side of the table and hugged her friend. 'Don't be so daft! Of course I want to see the scan picture—I'd be really upset if you didn't show me.'

Joni blinked away tears. 'Sorry. I just didn't want to bring back…you know. And I'm being so wet.'

'Hormones,' Bailey said with a grin. 'You'll be crying at ads with puppies and kittens in them next.'

She sat down again as Joni reached into her bag for a little white folder and handed it to her. She studied the ultrasound photograph. 'You can see the baby's head, the feet, the spine—this is incredible, Joni.'

'And the heart—it was amazing to see the baby's heart beating.'

Bailey hadn't even got to do that bit, so it wasn't as if this was bringing back memories; it was more the shadow of what might have been. And she wasn't going to let any shadows get in the way of her best friend's joy. She was fiercely determined to share that joy with her.

'Bailey, there's something else I wanted to ask you,' Joni said. 'Will you be godmother?'

'Of course I will! I'd be utterly thrilled.' Bailey blanked out the fact that she'd wanted Joni to be godmother to her baby, too. 'So that means I get to do all the fun things, all the cuddles and the smiles and the messy toys, and then I hand the baby back to you for nappy changes and the night feeds. Excellent.'

She could see in Joni's eyes that her best friend

knew exactly how much effort this was costing her and how much she was holding back, but to her relief Joni didn't say it. She simply smiled and said, 'Bailey Randall, you're going to be the best godmother in the history of the universe.'

'You can count on that,' Bailey said. 'And you can still do yoga during pregnancy, though maybe…' She took a deep breath. 'Maybe you need to switch to a water-aerobics class, one of the special antenatal ones. And I'll do it with you for moral support.'

She meant it, she really did—even though it would be hard seeing all those women with their bellies getting bigger each week and trying not to think about how that hadn't happened for her.

Joni reached across the table and squeezed her hand. 'I know you would. This is yet another reason why I love you. But I'm not going to make you do that. I'll stick to yoga—I'll talk to Jenna before the next class and ask her where I need to take it down a notch.'

Bailey kept it together at the restaurant, but all the way home she could feel the pressure behind her eyes, the sobs starting down low in her gut and forcing themselves upwards. Once her front door was closed behind her, she leaned against the wall and slowly slid down until she was sitting with her knees up to her chin and her arms wrapped round her legs. Then and only then did she let the tears flow—racking sobs of loss and loneliness, regrets for what might have been.

She didn't hear the doorbell at first. She was dimly aware of a noise then recognised the sound. Who was it? She wasn't expecting anyone. She scrubbed at her face with her sleeve and took a deep breath. Right at that moment she wished she hadn't cut her hair short, because then at least she could've hidden her face a bit. As it was, she'd have to brazen it out. She opened the door just a crack. 'Yes?'

'Bailey, are you all right?'

'Jared?' She frowned. 'What are you doing here?'

'We have a meeting to discuss Darren, remember?'

She remembered now. Joni's news had knocked the meeting completely out of her head.

She couldn't let Jared see her in this state. 'Can we do it tomorrow?'

'Are you all right?' he asked again, and this time he pushed the door open. He took one look at her and said, 'No, you're not all right.' Very gently, he manoeuvred her backwards, closed the door behind them and cupped her face between his hands. 'You've been crying.'

'Give the monkey a peanut,' she muttered, knowing that she was being rude and unfair to him but hating the fact that he'd caught her at a weak, vulnerable moment.

But he didn't pay any attention to her words. 'Come on. I'll get you a drink of water.' He put one arm round her. 'Your kitchen's at the end of the corridor, yes?'

'Yes.'

She let him lead her into the kitchen and sit her down at the bistro table. He opened several cupboard doors before he found where she kept her glasses, then poured her a glass of water; she accepted it gratefully.

Jared waited until Bailey had composed herself for a bit before he made her talk. He knew she'd been to yoga with Joni and then out for dinner; it was their regular Monday night catch-up. But he'd wanted to have a quick chat with Bailey about Darren, their problem player, so she'd agreed to be home for nine o'clock and meet him at her place. Jared had been caught up in a delay on the Tube after a signal had broken down, so he'd been all ready to apologise for being twenty minutes late for their meeting, but that didn't matter any more. Clearly something bad had just happened.

'What's happened? Is Joni all right?'

'She's fine.' Bailey dragged in a breath. 'It was good news.'

'Good news doesn't normally make you cry or look as if you've been put through the wringer,' he pointed out.

'I'm fine.'

They both knew she was lying.

'It's better out than in,' he said softly. And he should know. He'd bottled it up for a while after Sasha, until his oldest brother had read him the Riot Act and made him go to counselling. And that had made all the difference.

'I can't break a confidence.'

'Under the circumstances, I think,' he said softly, 'that Joni would forgive you. Or maybe I can guess. Good news, from someone who's just got married—it doesn't take a huge leap of the imagination to know what that's likely to be.'

And it didn't take a huge leap of the imagination to put the rest of it together, either. What would make someone bawl their eyes out when they learned that their best friend was going to have a baby? Either Bailey couldn't have children or she'd had a baby and lost it. Miscarriage, stillbirth, cot death…a loss so heartbreaking that she'd never really recovered from it. And neither had her marriage.

Was that why she'd been so adamant that the break-up hadn't been her ex's fault? And was that why she'd suddenly been so antsy at the park, when she'd asked him if he wanted children?

The way she looked at him, those beautiful dark eyes so tortured, was too much for him. He came round to her side of the table, scooped her out of her chair, sat in her place and settled her on his lap, his arms tightly wrapped round her. 'I'm not going any-where until you talk to me. And whatever you say isn't going any further than me, I promise you.'

She didn't really know him well enough to be com-pletely sure that he wouldn't break his promise, but he hoped that she'd got to know him enough over the time they'd worked together to work out that he had integrity.

'What happened, Bailey?' What had broken her heart?

'I was pregnant once,' she whispered.

He stroked her face. 'When?'

'Two and a half years ago. I was so thrilled. We both were. We wanted that baby so much.'

He said nothing, just holding her close and wait-ing for her to tell him the rest.

'And then I started getting pains. In my lower ab-domen. It hurt so much, Jared. I was worried that I might be having a miscarriage. And my shoulder hurt—but I assumed that was because I was worried.'

Jared knew that when you were stressed and tense you tended to hold yourself more rigidly and the mus-cles of your shoulder and neck would go into spasm, causing shoulder pain. Clearly that hadn't been the reason for the pain in this case.

'I went to the toilet,' she said, 'and there was spotting.' She closed her eyes. 'I felt sick. Light-headed.' She dragged in a breath. 'Then I collapsed. Luckily one of my colleagues found me and they got me in to the department. I told them I was pregnant, but I knew what was happening. I *knew*.'

A miscarriage? Heartbreaking for her.

'They gave me a scan. I was six weeks and three days. The pregnancy was ectopic.'

Even harder than he'd guessed. The fertilised egg hadn't implanted into the uterus, the way it should've done. Instead, it had embedded in the Fallopian tube and stretched the tube as it had grown, causing Bailey's lower abdominal pain.

'My Fallopian tube had ruptured. They took me straight into Theatre,' she said, 'but they couldn't save the tube.' Her voice wobbled, and then a shudder ran through her. 'I wanted that baby so much. And I—I…'

'Shh, I know.' He stroked her hair. 'And it wasn't your fault.' It happened in something like one out of eighty pregnancies. Often it sorted itself out and the woman hadn't even known she was pregnant in the first place. But Bailey had been unlucky, caught up in one of the worst-case scenarios.

And clearly the fact her best friend had just shared the news of her pregnancy had brought it all back. Joni had doubtless been one of the first people that Bailey had told about her own pregnancy, and Jared would just bet that Joni had agonised over telling her best friend the news, knowing that it would bring all these excruciating memories back. And he was equally sure that Bailey had gone into super-sparkly mode to reassure her that it was fine, all the while her heart breaking into tiny pieces again.

'The ectopic pregnancy wasn't my fault,' Bailey said, 'but the rest of it was.'

The rest of it? He'd obviously spoken aloud without meaning to, or maybe the question was just obvious, because she started talking again.

'I pushed Ed away afterwards. I—I just couldn't cope with the idea of it happening all over again.'

Jared knew that a second ectopic pregnancy was more likely if you'd had a first. He'd never worked in obstetrics, but he was pretty sure that the statistics weren't shockingly high. Bailey's fears had obviously got the better of her.

'I was so scared of getting pregnant again. So scared of losing another baby. So scared of losing my other Fallopian tube, so I'd never be able to have a baby without medical intervention. I wouldn't let Ed touch me. I knew he was hurting and he needed me, but I just *couldn't* let him touch me. I couldn't give him the physical comfort he wanted.' She leaned her head against his shoulder. 'I was such a selfish bitch.'

'You were hurting, too, Bailey,' he reminded her softly. 'You weren't being selfish. You were hurting and you didn't know how to fix it—for yourself or for your husband.'

'In the end, Ed found comfort elsewhere. But he—he wasn't like your ex,' she whispered. 'He wasn't out there looking for someone else. He would never have done it if I hadn't pushed him away and made him feel as if I didn't care. It was all my fault.'

And now he understood why her family worried

about her so much and were so keen for her to meet someone. Not because she was 'on the shelf', but because they knew how much she'd been through and they wanted her to find someone to share her life with and to cherish her, someone who'd stop her being lonely and sad.

If she'd let him, maybe he could do that. Maybe they could both help each other heal.

But Bailey had pushed her husband away, terrified of getting pregnant again. She'd ended her marriage rather than risk another pregnancy going wrong.

And that explained why she'd responded to him and then backed off again so swiftly. She'd felt the pull of attraction between them just as much as he had, but she was too scared to act on it. Too scared to date, to grow intimate with him, to make love with him—in case she became pregnant and she ended up having another ectopic pregnancy.

'It takes two to break a marriage,' he said. 'Your ex gave up on you.'

'You gave up on your marriage,' she pointed out.

He knew she'd only said it because she was hurting. Clearly she thought that sniping at him would make him walk away and leave her to it. Maybe that was one of the tactics she'd used to push her husband away, but it wasn't going to work on him. 'Yes, I did,' he said. 'I'll take my share of the blame. Just as long as you accept that not all the blame of your break-up is yours.'

'It feels like it is,' she said, sounding totally broken.

If only he had a magic wand. But this wasn't something he could fix. The only one who could let her trust again, let her take the risk of sharing her life with someone, was Bailey herself. Until she was ready to try, it just wouldn't work.

So he said nothing, just held her. If necessary, he'd stay here all night, just cradling her on his lap and hoping she'd be able to draw some strength from the feel of her arms around him.

Eventually, she stroked his face. 'Thank you, Jared. For listening. And for not judging.'

Unable to help himself, he twisted his face round so he could drop a kiss into her palm. 'No worries.'

'I'm sorry I cried all over you.'

'It probably did you good,' he said.

'And we were supposed to be talking about Darren,' she said.

He smiled. 'Don't worry about it. Darren can wait. We'll talk about him tomorrow, maybe. Right now, this is a bit more important.'

'I don't normally cry over people.'

No. He'd guess that normally she sparkled that little bit more brightly, pretending everything was fine and waiting until she was on her own before letting her true feelings show. 'It's fine. Really.'

'I, um, ought to let you go. It's getting late.'

'I'm not going anywhere,' he said softly.

'But…'

'Bailey, do you really think I can walk away and just leave you here alone, upset and hurting?' he asked.

She just looked at him, those huge, huge eyes full of pain.

'It's your choice,' he said. 'I can sleep on your sofa tonight—just so I know you're not alone, and I'm here if you need anything. Or…' He paused.

'Or?' she whispered.

'Or I can hold you until you fall asleep. Sleep with you.'

Even though she tried to hide it, he could see the panic flood into her face. 'I said *sleep*, Bailey,' he reminded her quietly. 'Which isn't the same as having sex.'

'I—I'm sorry.'

He kissed the corner of her mouth. 'You're upset, you're trying to be brave and all your nightmares have come back to haunt you. Some people might use sex as a way of escaping it all, but you're not one of them. And I would never push you into anything you're not happy with.'

'I know.' She swallowed hard. 'I'm a mess, Jared. And you've been hurt in the past, too. I'm the last person you need to get involved with.'

'Let me be the judge of that,' he said gently. 'And let me be here for you tonight.'

Bailey knew it was a genuine offer. It would be, oh, so easy to take him up on it. To lean on him. To take comfort from the warmth of his body curled round hers.

But it would also make things really complicated.

'You're going to be stubborn about this, aren't you?' he asked wryly.

She nodded. 'And you said I had a choice.'

'Sofa?' he asked.

'Go home,' she said. 'Really. I'll be fine.'

'How about we compromise?' Jared suggested. 'You let me hold you—on the sofa—until you're asleep. Then I'll tuck you in and I'll leave—though if you wake at stupid o'clock and you need to talk, then you call me.'

So, so generous. She stroked his face. 'I'm sorry I called you Herod.'

He smiled. 'That was the autocorrect on your phone.'

'But I never took it back. And you're not a tyrant at all. You're more like Sir Galahad. A knight on a white charger coming to the rescue.'

He laughed. 'Hardly. I'm just a man, Bailey.'

'There's no "just". You're a good man, Jared Fraser. Kind. You do all that gruff, dour Scotsman stuff—but that's the opposite of who you really are.'

'Thank you,' he said. 'Now lead me to your sofa.'

'Don't you want a drink or anything? I've been horribly rude and haven't even offered you a coffee.'

He kissed the tip of her nose. 'In the circumstances, that's not so surprising. And I don't want a coffee. I just want to hold you until you fall asleep.'

'Yes,' she said softly, and led him through to the sofa in her living room.

CHAPTER TEN

THE NEXT MORNING, Bailey woke to find herself still fully clothed on the sofa, with her duvet tucked round her.

Falling asleep in Jared's arms last night had felt risky—but it had also felt so, so good.

She grabbed her phone, but a wave of unexpected shyness stopped her calling him. What would she even say?

Instead, she sent him a text: Thank you for last night.

Her phone pinged almost immediately with his reply: No worries. Sleep well?

Yes. Thank you.

Good. See you at work. And this time he'd signed his text with a kiss.

Maybe this was going to work out after all. Jared made her feel brave. And his ex, Bailey thought, really needed her head examined. Why would you throw away the love of a kind, decent, thoughtful man for a shallow, publicity-obsessed lifestyle?

Then again, unhappiness made you do stupid

things. Cruel things. Bailey knew she was just as guilty when it came to the way she'd pushed Ed away. And didn't they say you shouldn't judge someone until you'd walked a mile in their shoes?

She showered, changed and headed for the football pitch. But when she got there she was surprised to find that the players weren't warming up as usual on the field. Instead, they were sitting in the dressing room, and the mood was extremely subdued.

'What's the matter, lads?' she asked.

'You need to go in and see Mr Fincham in his office,' Billy said. 'Archie and Jared are already there.'

Mr Fincham? Why would the football club's chairman of directors want to see her? 'Why?' she asked.

'I can't say.' He bit his lip. 'But there's trouble, Bailey.'

Worried, Bailey hurried along to the office. Mandy, Lyle Fincham's PA, was typing furiously on her keyboard. 'Mandy, what's going on?' Bailey asked.

Mandy shook her head. 'That's for Mr Fincham to say, not me.' She inclined her head towards the door. 'They're in there, waiting. You'd better go in.'

Bailey knocked on the door out of courtesy and walked in. 'Sorry I'm a bit late. There was a delay on the Tube.'

Then she saw Darren sitting between Archie and Jared. And Jared was looking every inch the dour, unsmiling Scotsman.

'It's in all the papers this morning,' Lyle said, indicating the stack of newspapers on his desk. 'And all over the Internet.'

'What is?' she asked.

'The video of laddo here.' Lyle jerked his head towards Darren. 'In a club, getting drunk. Underage.'

She looked at Darren, who was white-faced and looked utterly guilty. So much for making the most of his second chance. Or maybe they just hadn't given him enough support. After all, Jared had originally wanted to talk to her last night about the boy; they hadn't got round to discussing the situation, because she'd been in meltdown.

And yet…something didn't quite stack up. The last couple of weeks, since she'd picked up Darren's underperformance and she and Jared had persuaded Archie to give the boy another chance, his stats had all been back to normal. 'When did all this happen?' she asked.

'Last night,' Archie said grimly.

Darren shook his head. 'I wasn't out last night. You can ask my mum. She'll tell you.'

'Actually, my stats show that Darren's performance has been normal ever since we talked to you, Archie,' Bailey said. 'If he'd still been drinking, it would've shown up on my graphs.'

'Graphs, schmaphs,' Lyle Fincham said, flapping a dismissive hand. 'Archie should never have let that box of tricks of yours cloud his judgement. This is a total mess, and I can't afford to let this affect the club. As from today, you're out, Dr Randall. I don't care how much of your research project's wasted. It's over.'

'Actually, I agree with Bailey,' Jared cut in. 'It would show on the graphs. And if she goes, I go.'

No. No way was she letting Jared risk his career. For her, this was a research project. Yes, there would be repercussions about the way it had ended, but it would eventually blow over. For Jared, it would be his whole career on the line. This wasn't fair.

'I was the one who talked Archie into giving Darren another chance, so don't take this out on Jared,' she said swiftly. 'Don't make him leave because of me.'

'And that video's from weeks back, I swear. I haven't touched a drop since you said I could stay, Mr McLennan,' Darren added desperately, giving Archie a beseeching look. 'I know I was stupid to do it before.'

'But you've still dragged the club's name into disrepute.' Lyle shook his head. 'No. You're out, boy, so go and pack your things.'

'That's not fair—he's owned up to his mistakes, and this is just bad timing,' Bailey said. 'Nobody's perfect. Can you honestly put your hand on your heart and say that you've never, ever made a decision you haven't later regretted?'

Lyle gave her a speaking look.

'We all have the potential to make the wrong choice somewhere along the way. It's hard to own up to it. But Darren admitted his mistake and he's doing something about it.' Bailey grimaced. 'Look, can Darren just go and wait in another room while we talk about this like the professionals we are? It's horrible, all of us standing round like vultures pecking at the poor lad.'

'I agree,' Jared chipped in. 'And I also think we can turn this around so the club can make this a positive. We'll need your PR manager to help us, but we can do it.'

For a moment, she thought Lyle Fincham was going

to refuse, but then he tightened his mouth and nod-ded. 'Darren, go and wait next door with Mandy. You don't move a muscle, you don't phone anyone or talk to anyone and you don't go anywhere near the Inter-net, do you hear? Leave your phone with us.'

Looking hunted, the boy handed over his phone and went to wait with Lyle's PA next door.

Lyle picked up his phone. 'Max? My office. Now. There's a situation that needs handling.' He put the phone down again. 'Right. So we'll sort this out be-tween us.'

'Darren's only seventeen. He's still just a kid, re-ally. He's not going to think things through properly, the way someone more mature would do. Instead of coming to you to ask about extra training, Archie, he got drunk to blot out how he felt. You agreed to give him a second chance. He's stayed clean since then—and I bet if you ask any of the other lads they'll be able to tell you that, too,' Bailey said.

'I let you persuade me into giving him another chance, yes,' Archie said. 'But if one player goes wrong, then all the players get tarred with the same brush. You know what the press is like about how much money is in football. They'll have a field day with the kid—and with the club. This isn't fair to the rest of the players, or to the fans.'

'Or the shareholders,' Lyle added. 'His behaviour's put everything at risk.'

'But we can turn this round,' Jared said. 'Really.'

There was a rap on the door and Max Porter, the PR manager, came in. 'So what's this situation?'

'Darren. There's a video of him drunk and under-age.' Lyle's colour was dangerously high again, and

Bailey was really beginning to worry that the chairman of directors was about to have a heart attack or a stroke.

'Right,' Max said calmly. 'Talk me through it.'

'We picked it up on Bailey's system,' Jared said. 'He admitted he'd been drinking. Archie agreed to give him another chance.'

'And he hasn't touched anything since,' Bailey said. 'All his stats since we talked to him about it match his average. And it would show up if he was still drinking.'

'I've analysed the way he plays and designed a training programme to help him improve his weak spots,' Jared added.

'So you both obviously think he should stay,' Max said. Then he looked at Archie and Lyle. 'And I take it you both think he should go?'

'And not just him,' Lyle said with a pointed look at Jared and Bailey.

'We can turn this around,' Jared said again. 'This is a classic example of what the pressures of professional football can do to young players. We brought Darren into the club. We set the bar high. And what do we do with the players who can't handle the pressure? Do we just abandon them, in a cold-hearted business decision? Or do we treat them like a family member—knowing he has flaws, knowing he's human and helping him to get over the problem?'

'That's a good spin,' Max said. 'I do hope you're not planning to change career and go after my job, Jared.'

The joke was just enough to dissipate some of the tension in the room. *Just.*

'We don't just need to teach our young players ball skills,' Jared said. 'We need to teach them life skills, because this is a kind of apprenticeship and we're responsible for the way our players develop as people, not just as players. We need to show them how to own up to their mistakes and how to start to make things right.' He paused. 'When my knee was wrecked by that tackle, I was the same age as Darren and it felt like the end of the world, knowing I was never going to be able to play professional football again.'

Knowing how rarely he spoke about this, Bailey held her breath for a moment.

'I could so easily have gone off the rails,' Jared continued. 'But my family and my coach were brilliantly supportive. They stopped me doing anything stupid. And we need to do that for Darren.'

'Actually, Darren could be a good ambassador for the club,' Max said thoughtfully. 'We could get him to talk about his mistakes to kids at school, how he's overcome them and how he managed to get back on the right path with our help. They can learn from his mistakes rather than making those mistakes themselves.'

'So he gets away with it?' Lyle asked, his nostrils flaring in disgust.

'No. Because you could always fine him,' Bailey suggested. 'Donate the fine to a charity specialising in alcohol abuse among kids. Then his mistake will help people who also made mistakes.'

'Making the punishment fit the crime,' Archie said. 'I like that. And he's not a bad lad, Lyle. He's not wild. We need to give him a bit more pride in himself.'

'And what's the press going to think? That I condone all sorts of nonsense at the club?' Lyle demanded.

'No. They'll think that you expect the best from people, but you don't just throw them to the wolves if they get it wrong. You help them be the best they can be,' Max said. 'You're going to get all the mums on your side.'

'Mums don't buy season tickets,' Lyle grumbled.

'Maybe, but they can talk their partners into buying a season ticket for a club that gives a damn about the kids and doesn't just see them as future cash cows,' Jared said.

Lyle threw his hands up. 'I give up. All right. The boy gets a second chance. But you make sure everyone knows we fined him for doing wrong, and that we donated that money to help kids who made the same mistake.'

'Thank you,' Bailey said. 'And I'm sorry I didn't talk it over with you and Archie. I understand why you don't want me here again after today.'

'You know, it would be a shame to lose all that PR—it shows that we care so much about our players' well-being, we've worked with them using the latest technology to help reduce soft-tissue injuries,' Jared said, looking at Max and then Lyle.

'He's right,' Max said. 'It's a brilliant story and it would be a real pity to lose it.'

This time, Jared looked straight at Bailey. 'Everyone deserves a second chance,' he said softly.

She knew he didn't just mean Darren, or their work on the team. He meant them. A second chance to get it right. And it made her go hot all over.

'All right, all right,' Lyle grumbled. 'You can finish your research, Dr Randall. But one foot out of line from you in future…or you,' he warned, gesturing to Jared, 'and that's it.'

'I promise,' Bailey said.

'Me, too,' Jared said. 'Should we send Darren back in to learn his fate?'

'Do that,' Archie said, clapping them both on the back. 'And we'll postpone training until this afternoon. Two-thirty, sharp. Tell them for me, will you?'

Bailey and Jared went next door into Mandy's office. 'Darren, you can go back in now,' Jared said.

'What did Mr Fincham say?' Darren asked, looking anxious.

'He'll listen to you and be fair about it. Just go in, tell the truth and you'll be fine,' Bailey advised him.

Then they went into the dressing room to see the rest of the players. They were full of questions, all talking together and not giving anyone a chance to answer them.

'Has Darren been sacked?'

'Is the boss mad because of all the stuff that happened in that nightclub?'

'Are the rest of us going to be sacked?'

'Shh—calm down,' Bailey said. 'Archie will be in to see you later and he'll explain everything. In the meantime, training today has been postponed until two-thirty. I'm sure you lot have stuff you can get on with in the meantime—and stay out of trouble, OK?'

'Nicely done,' Jared said when they left the dressing room.

'I've got everyone into quite enough trouble as it is,' she said ruefully. 'And I'm sorry, Jared. I really thought you were going to lose your job because of me back there.'

'Lyle always blows up. He'll calm down again.' Jared gave her a wry smile. 'Though I was worrying about him back there. I didn't like his colour.'

'Me, neither,' she agreed.

'Maybe you could teach him some of your yoga stuff to help him relax and reduce his blood pressure.'

'Suggesting that,' she said, 'is probably more than my life's worth right now—and yours.'

'Well, it looks as if we have some unexpected free time.' He paused. 'Want some cake?'

'I think that's a really good idea,' she said.

'My place isn't far. And there's a good patisserie on the corner.'

'That sounds good to me,' she said. 'Though I insist on buying, considering I nearly got you the sack.'

'No, you didn't—but I'm not going to turn down the offer of cake,' he said with a smile. 'Let's go.'

CHAPTER ELEVEN

THEY BOUGHT CAKE at the café and walked back to Jared's place in comfortable silence. Jared made them both a mug of coffee; Bailey was relieved that they sat in his kitchen, given how they'd ended up kissing on his sofa. She didn't quite trust herself not to repeat that, especially as the more time she spent with Jared, the more attractive she found him.

He'd hinted at a second chance. Did she dare take it?

'I was wondering,' he said, 'if you were doing anything at the weekend.'

'Nothing out of the ordinary,' she said. What did he have in mind? Adrenalin fizzed through her at the possibilities.

'I know it's ridiculously short notice, but there's this football function on Saturday night—a charity ball thing. I, um, have two tickets.'

'And you've been let down at the last minute?'

He frowned. 'Bailey, I'm not the kind of man who asks someone to go to a dinner with me and then kisses someone else stupid.'

'No, of course not.' But he was obviously remembering those kisses, too. Had he been planning to ask her to the ball all along? Or had he just bought the tickets to do his bit to support the charity, not actually intending to be there on the night?

She blew out a breath. 'Sorry. I didn't mean to insult you. Honestly. First I nearly lose you your job, and then I practically accuse you of being a philanderer... I'm not doing very well today.'

'The job thing was just as much my fault,' he said. 'And I think you and I...' He blew out a breath. 'It's complicated.'

'Just a tad.' She paused. 'So is this an official date? In public?'

He held her gaze. 'It could be. Or it could be the same deal as you had with me at Joni and Aaron's wedding.'

A fake date, to take the heat off him?

'Sasha's going to be there?' she guessed.

'Possibly.' He shrugged. 'I have no idea.'

There was something she needed to know. 'Are you still in love with her?'

'No. Actually, I don't care whether she's there or not. That isn't the reason I asked you. I only bought the tickets to support the charity,' he admitted. 'I wasn't actually going to go.'

Just as she'd half suspected.

'But I've been thinking about it. And I'd like to go.' He paused. 'With you.'

It was tempting. So very tempting. And maybe the sugar rush of the cake was to blame for her opening her mouth and saying, 'Yes.'

His smile made her feel warm all over.

'So where do I meet you, and what time?' she asked.

'I could pick you up from your place at seven?' he suggested.

'That works for me.'

And how crazy it was that this made her feel like a teenager all over again.

A second chance. If you counted the wedding, this would be their third attempt at a date. At the wedding, and when they'd had dinner together, she'd ended up panicking and backing away. Would this be third time lucky? Would she be able to get over the fear this time?

Jared was a good man. He'd stuck up for her. He'd been there for her when she'd needed a shoulder. He ticked all her boxes. All she had to do was get rid of the fears inside her head.

All.

The training session that afternoon was pretty much as usual. The lads were a little subdued but did their best, including Darren. She was busy at clinic the rest of the week.

And all too soon Saturday night arrived.

Rather than going all out for a ballgown, Bailey had chosen a black lacy dress and patent black leather high heels. Simple yet sophisticated enough for the function, she hoped. And as soon as she opened the door to Jared, she knew from the flare of heat in his gaze that she'd made the right decision. He definitely liked what she was wearing.

'Hello,' she said, feeling ridiculously shy.

'You look fabulous,' he said softly.

'So do you.' She'd seen him in a suit before, but not a dinner jacket. How crazy that something as simple as a dark red bow tie should look so incredibly sexy on him. Just to stop herself doing something stupid—like grabbing him and kissing him and dragging him off to her bed instead of going to the ball—she said, 'Though I was half expecting you to wear a kilt.'

He laughed. 'That would be a wee bit clichéd.'

But, to her relief, laughter broke the tension just enough to get her common sense back.

Jared had seen Bailey dressed up before, but it did nothing to stop the shock of how attractive he found her. Right at that moment he didn't want to go to the charity ball and share her; he wanted her all to himself. He wanted to kiss her until they were both dizzy, and then take her to bed and spend the whole night finding out what gave her the most pleasure. But he held himself in check. Just.

He ushered her to the taxi. When he reached for her hand on the way to the dinner-dance, she curled her fingers round his.

Maybe, just maybe, this thing between them was going to go right.

At the dinner, Bailey went into sparkle mode. She chatted to absolutely everyone, not in the slightest bit fazed by the incredibly glamorous WAGs there or how famous some of the players were. But Jared noticed that she didn't only talk to the famous ones; she talked to everyone and drew them out.

Bailey Randall had a gift for making people feel special.

He watched her sparkle and thought, *I could really lose my heart to this woman.* He knew she was as special as she made people feel, but he also knew that she had a protective shell round her. He wasn't sure if he'd be able to persuade her to let him past it.

He turned round to see Sasha there with her third husband in tow. Jared had expected to feel some kind of reaction at seeing her again—but he was surprised and relieved to discover he didn't. What had happened was in the past. It couldn't be changed. And it didn't matter any more—it didn't *hurt* any more.

And he knew why: because Bailey was in his life. Being with Bailey made his world a much brighter place.

After he'd introduced Bailey to Sasha and her husband, Jared made his excuses and drew Bailey towards the dance floor.

'Are you OK?' Bailey asked.

'Sure. Why wouldn't I be?'

She coughed. 'Sasha's not exactly a common name. I take it she's *the* Sasha.'

'Yes. Actually, I thought I'd find it difficult to see her,' he admitted, 'but there's just nothing there any more. It's fine,' he reassured her. But he also noticed that Bailey didn't look fine. 'What's wrong?' he asked softly.

'Well—she's incredibly beautiful.'

'And?' He didn't get it.

She shook her head. 'Nothing.'

Then he got it. And it surprised him that Bailey was feeling vulnerable. The Bailey Randall he'd got to know was incredibly together and was comfortable in her own skin, and he really liked that. 'I know you're not fishing for compliments,' he said, 'but, just for the record, you can more than hold your own with her. You're just as beautiful, except yours is a natural beauty.' He paused. 'And I'm so glad you're nothing like her as a person.'

'Hmm,' she said.

'Just to make it clear,' he said softly, 'right now I'm dating a woman I really, really like. A woman I respect for who she is.' He held her gaze. 'And whom I happen to find very, very attractive.'

Had he gone too far?

Panicking that he might make her back off, he added, 'Anyway, your hair's shorter than Sasha's.'

'I used to wear it long.'

He held her closer. He could guess when she'd cut it. After she'd lost the baby. 'No shadows tonight,' he said softly. 'This is just you and me.' He pulled back slightly so she could see his eyes and know that he was telling the truth. 'I've put the past to rest.'

'Good.'

For a moment he wondered if she was going to say that she'd put her past to rest, too.

But she didn't. And he knew he was going to have to take this at her pace.

When he'd been younger he wouldn't have had the patience to do that. But Bailey Randall was going to be more than worth his patience, he thought. So he wasn't going to push her until she was ready.

During the evening, Bailey danced with both Lyle Fincham and Archie.

Archie tipped his head towards Jared. 'Are you and Jared…you know?'

She smiled. 'I'm taking the Fifth Amendment on that one.'

He laughed. 'You can't. You're not American.'

'I'm still doing it. Anyway, under English law you have the right to remain silent, too,' she pointed out.

'I guess.' He smiled. 'He's a good man. I know you two didn't exactly hit it off at first.'

'Jared's not the grumpy Scotsman he likes everyone to think he is,' she said with a grin.

'Exactly. And I think you'll be good together.'

'It's early days, Archie,' she said softly. She wasn't quite ready to believe this was all going to work out. But she really was going to try and put the past behind her.

Eventually Jared claimed Bailey back. Perfect timing, too, because the music changed to soft and slow, which meant that she was right where he wanted her—up close and personal. And she was holding him just as tightly. He wasn't going to embarrass her by kissing her stupid in public, but maybe…

'Shall we get out of here?' he murmured into her ear. 'Go and have a glass of wine back at my place?'

He didn't realise he was holding his breath until she said yes.

He held her hand in the taxi all the way back to his place.

And once the front door was closed behind him, he was able to do what he'd wanted to do all evening and kiss her.

He could drown in her warmth and sweetness.

He broke this kiss before he did something stupid, like carrying her upstairs to his bed. Too fast, too soon. 'I promised you a glass of wine,' he said hoarsely.

'I don't really want a drink,' she said softly.

Then what did she want?

Anticipation thrummed through him. Did she want the same thing that he did? Did she want to lose herself in him, the way he wanted to lose himself in her?

'Last time I was here, you put pictures in my head,' she said. 'Do you happen to have any more of that fabulous chocolate pudding?'

'No, but I can improvise,' he said. Then he went very still as he took in what she'd just said. Not quite sure he'd got this right, he asked, 'Bailey, are you saying we can…?'

'Yes. Provided,' she said, 'we're really careful and you use protection. I'm not on the Pill. I never thought I'd…' She tailed off, wrinkling her nose and looking awkward.

He knew what she meant. When she'd told him about her ectopic pregnancy, she'd also told him how scared she was of getting pregnant again and how she'd pushed her husband away physically. And so what she was offering him now was *hugely* brave. So generous it made him catch his breath. She was going to trust him. To let him prove to her that having sex again wasn't going to make her life implode. 'I'll take care of you,' he said softly, 'and I want you so badly it hurts—but I know this is really scary for you. If you change your mind at any point tonight and say you want to stop, that's also fine. We can take this as slowly as you like.'

Tears glittered in her eyes. 'Thank you, Jared.'

He needed to ask. 'Do you want me to stop now?'

She took a deep breath. 'Yes. And no. Both at the same time. I'm scared, Jared,' she admitted.

'I know. And I understand.' He held her close for

a moment. 'But maybe, just maybe, you can be brave with me. Maybe we can be brave with each other,' he said, and drew her hand to his mouth. He kissed each fingertip in turn, then her palm, folding her fingers over his kiss.

She stood on tiptoe and kissed the end of his nose. And then the corner of his mouth. And then she caught his lower lip between hers, in silent demand that they deepen the kiss.

He was more than happy to comply. And happier still when she kissed him back, matching him touch for touch and nibble for nibble.

'I want you,' he whispered. 'So very, very badly.'

'I want you, too,' she said, her voice low and husky and sensual.

He didn't need a second invitation. He scooped her up and carried her up the stairs to his bedroom. He'd already closed the curtains before he'd left that evening, so all he had to deal with was the light, once he'd set her back down on her feet.

In the soft light of the table lamp he could see the strain on her face. The fear.

'It's OK,' he said. 'We can stop.'

She shook her head. 'Not now.'

'Are you sure?'

She took a deep breath. 'I'm sure.'

He knew she wasn't yet she was clearly trying to push herself past the fear. So he'd do what he could to help. He kissed her lightly, then slid the zip at the back of her dress all the way down. He pushed the lacy material off her shoulders and the dress slid to the floor. She stepped out of it, and he hung it over the back of a chair, not wanting the dress to be spoiled.

And then he held her at arm's length. 'You take my breath away, Bailey,' he said huskily.

'Right now,' she said, with the tiniest wobble in her voice that told him she was still panicking inside, 'I think I'd feel a bit better if you weren't wearing quite so much.'

He smiled. 'I'm all yours. Do what you will with me.'

She slid his jacket off and placed it over her dress on the chair. Then she checked his bow tie. He could see the moment that she realised it was a proper one. 'Very flash,' she said, rolling her eyes, and pulled both ends. The knot came apart in her hands, and she draped the tie over his jacket.

Next was his shirt, and he noticed that her hands were slightly unsteady as she undid the buttons. She pushed the material off his shoulders. 'Oh, your biceps,' she breathed, and stroked the muscles. 'I've wanted to do this since we trained together. They're so beautiful.'

And so was she. He needed to see her. Properly. All of her. 'Can I play caveman now?' he asked. Stupid, because he'd already done that by carrying her up the stairs.

'I was thinking superhero,' she said. 'One with really, really sexy biceps. Though I can live with the fact you're not wearing a cape.'

'That works for me.' At her nod, he unclipped her bra and turned her round. 'Oh, my God, Bailey. You're glorious.' He kissed his way down her spine. 'If I could paint, I'd want you to model for me.' He stroked her back. 'You're perfect.' He drew her back against him so she could feel his erection pressing against her and would know that he meant every word of what he said. He cupped her breasts and kissed the curve of her shoulder. 'Right now, I want you so badly. You make me ache, Bailey. In a good way.'

She turned round in his arms. 'Then take me to bed, Jared.'

He didn't need her to ask again. He picked her up and carried her to the bed, then laid her gently against the covers.

Time seemed to stop. Bailey wasn't sure which of them had removed the rest of his clothes and her underwear, but finally they were skin to skin.

Then she froze as she realised what was just about to happen. She wanted this—she really, really did—but supposing this all went wrong?

'Stop thinking, Bailey,' he whispered. 'Let yourself go. Let yourself *feel*.'

He kissed her again; she tipped her head back against the pillows, and he kissed the curve of her throat, lingering in the hollows of her collarbones.

She could feel her nipples tightening; he nuzzled his way down her sternum and then took one nipple into his mouth, sucking hard. Bailey pushed her hands through his hair, urging him on, and his mouth moved lower, lower.

She almost forgot how to breathe when she felt the long, slow stroke of his tongue along her sex. And it was like a starburst in her head when he teased her clitoris with the tip of his tongue. Her climax was shockingly fast. Oh, God. She'd forgotten what this was like. Forgotten how it felt. Forgotten how good it could be. And it had been so long…

He waited until the aftershocks had died away, then came up to lie beside her and drew her into his arms. 'OK?'

'I think so,' she said. 'Which planet am I on again?'

He chuckled softly. 'I wanted that first time to be all for you.'

He cared that much? She felt a single tear leak out of the corner of her eye.

He kissed it away. 'Bailey, I think we're going to be good together.'

The panic threatened to spill over again, but she pushed it away. She'd said that she'd be brave with him. She wasn't going to back out now.

'Show me,' she whispered.

He took a condom from his drawer and handed her the packet. 'You're in control.'

She knew exactly why he'd done that—so she could be quite, quite sure that there was no chance of getting pregnant, because she'd know they'd used the condom properly—and had to blink back the tears, but she ripped open the packet and rolled the condom over his shaft. And then finally, finally, he was inside her. He held himself very still so her body could adjust to the feel of him, then began to move.

He was a concentrated lover, she discovered. One who didn't talk and who focused on his goals. And, oh, having that focus entirely on her... She was aware of every touch, every kiss, and she knew that he was exploring her and paying very, very close attention to what she liked, and what she liked even more.

It shouldn't be this good. Not their first time. It should be awkward and embarrassing and faintly ridiculous.

But then she stopped thinking as she felt a climax spiralling through her again. She clung onto him for dear life and knew the very second that he'd fallen over the edge, too.

When they'd both floated back to earth, he moved. 'I'd better deal with the condom,' he said softly, and kissed her shoulder. 'Stay there. You look comfortable.' She *was* comfortable. And even though there was a slow burn of panic deep inside her, knowing that Jared was there—that he was solid and dependable and real—helped her to ignore that panic. It was time she stopped letting what had happened to her dictate her life. Time she stopped letting it scare her away from what she wanted. With Jared by her side, supportive and compassionate, she could have everything.

That night, she fell asleep in his arms, just as she had on her sofa. But this time when she woke she was still in his arms. In his bed. Skin to skin. Warm and comfortable. She kept her eyes closed for a little while longer, just luxuriating in the feeling of being held. Of being cherished. She'd forgotten how good this could be.

'Good morning,' he said softly when she opened her eyes at last.

'Yes. It is,' she said with a smile. 'Because you're here.'

'It's the same for me. I don't care if it's raining outside, because it feels like the brightest summer day.' He stroked her face. 'So will you stay for breakfast?'

She kissed him lightly. 'Thank you. I'd love to.'

He made her pancakes with maple syrup and some truly excellent coffee. They went back to her flat so she could change from her lacy cocktail dress into something casual, and spent the rest of the day wandering hand in hand along the South Bank, enjoying the market stalls and the art installations and the street performers.

'No regrets?' he said on her doorstep when he finally saw her home.

'None,' she said. 'Today's been fantastic. Actually, it's the first time in a long while that I've felt this happy.'

'Me, too,' he said.

'So I was wondering,' she said. 'I'm not promising pancakes, but I make a mean bacon sandwich.'

His eyes widened. 'Are you asking me to stay for breakfast, Bailey?'

She took a deep breath. 'Yes.'

'Sure?' he checked.

'It still scares me a bit, the idea of having another relationship,' she admitted. 'But yes. You make me feel brave. I can do this, with you.'

In answer, he kissed her. And she opened her front door and ushered him inside.

CHAPTER TWELVE

FOR THE NEXT three weeks Bailey was really happy. She and Jared were so in tune—and she really liked the funny, kind, gentle man beneath his dour exterior. She also enjoyed the occasional sarcastic text he sent her, signed 'Herod'. He was never going to let her forget that, was he?

This was all still so new that she wasn't quite ready to share it with her family or her best friend, but she found herself looking forward to every evening that she spent with Jared, every night that she slept in his arms and every morning that she woke and he was the first one she saw.

Work was fantastic. She'd always enjoyed her clinic work, and she'd been accepted as one of the team at the football club, so both strands of her job suited her perfectly.

Life didn't get any better than this, she thought.

Until the middle of the day when she suddenly realised that her period was late. She calculated mentally. Not just late—*a whole week late*, and she was never late.

For a moment she couldn't breathe. *What if she was pregnant?* And why, why, *why* hadn't she waited to go on the Pill and insisted on using condoms as well, before she'd made love with Jared?

She took a deep breath, knowing that she was being ridiculous. OK, so the only form of contraception that was one hundred per cent effective was total abstinence, but condoms still had a pretty good success rate. She and Jared had been really, really careful. And she was thirty years old, so her fertility level was lower than when she'd fallen pregnant last time. She only had one Fallopian tube working, making the chances of falling pregnant even lower. This was probably just a stupid glitch.

But how many other women had been caught out that way? How many teenage girls had fallen pregnant after just one time? How many women, nearing menopause and thinking that their fertility was practically zero, had taken a risk and discovered they were having a 'happy accident'? She knew of several colleagues who hadn't planned their last babies.

And what if history repeated itself? What if she was pregnant and it was another ectopic pregnancy? What if, this time, she lost absolutely everything?

There was only one way to find out. And she was going to have to be brave and face it.

At lunchtime she went out and bought a pregnancy test kit. With every step back towards the hospital her legs felt as if they were turning into lead, heavy and dragging.

The last time she'd bought a pregnancy test she'd been so excited, so hopeful. She had actually run to the bathroom, because she'd so desperately wanted it to be positive—she'd wanted to know the result that very second.

This time, taking a pregnancy test felt more like a sentence of doom. Something she had to nerve herself to do. Panic made her hands shake as she opened the box. It took her three goes to open the test kit itself.

Oh, God. Oh, God. Oh, God.

Please don't let her be pregnant.

Please don't let the nightmare happen all over again.

Please don't let that low, dragging pain start as a nag and then flare into agony.

Please don't let her lose her last chance.

Time felt as if it was wading through treacle as she washed her hands and kept an eye on the test stick. One line in the window to let her know that the test had worked.

She felt sick. The line in the next window would tell her yes or no.

'Please let it be no. Please let it be no. Please let it be no.' The words were ripped from her, low and guttural.

But she knew that begging wasn't going to change a thing. The test stick was measuring the level of a hormone in her urine: human chorionic gonadotropin, which was produced by the placenta after fertilisation.

Then again, a negative result could be just as bad because it might mean that the embryo hadn't implanted yet—or that it had implanted in the wrong place. Just as it had before.

She stared at the next window. One line formed, and then a second.

Positive.

Her knees went weak and she sat down heavily.

And then there was the window to tell her how many weeks since conception...

She stared at the window until the words finally penetrated her brain. *Three weeks plus.* She and Jared had first made love three weeks and two days ago. Now she thought about it, it had been smack in the middle of her cycle. The most fertile stage. Which would make her five weeks and two days pregnant now.

No, no, no, no, no.

Nearly three years ago, at this stage, that meant that in one week and one day's time...

Her stomach heaved, she dropped the test stick and was promptly sick in the sink.

Bailey washed her face afterwards while she tried to think about what to do.

She was going to have to tell Jared; but she had absolutely no idea what she was going to say. Or what was going to happen next. He'd said he wanted kids one day. But they hadn't been together that long. This was way too soon. She didn't think Jared was the kind of man who'd walk away, or who paid towards a child's upbringing but had no emotional involvement with the baby whatsoever—yet something else worried her. Would he want the baby more than he wanted *her*?

Panic really had turned her into a gibbering, raving idiot. She was always so together, so organised. Not knowing what to do next just wasn't in her make-up. And it freaked her out even more that she was reacting like this. That all her common sense had vanished into thin air. That she couldn't think rationally.

What the hell was she going to do?

Right now, her parents were in Italy. She knew that all she had to do was pick up the phone and her mother would get on the next plane to London to be with her but that wasn't fair; her parents deserved a chance to enjoy having a holiday around their wedding anniversary. Her brothers were up to their eyeballs running the restaurant, so it wouldn't be fair to talk to them about it, either.

Then there was Joni. But how could Bailey dump something like this on her best friend, when Joni should have the chance to enjoy her own pregnancy without any shadows?

Besides, Jared was the one she *really* needed to talk to.

Today was one of her clinic days, so she wouldn't see him during working hours. She knew she could call him—but she didn't trust herself to make any sense on the phone. She had a nasty feeling that she'd start crying as soon as she heard his voice. The last thing she wanted to do was to panic him by sobbing uncontrollably and mumbling incoherent fragments at him. This conversation needed to be face-to-face. Rational. Together.

But her brain was so fried that she couldn't even remember what they'd arranged to do this evening. Was she meeting him at his place? At hers? Somewhere else?

'For pity's sake, Bailey Randall, get a *grip*,' she told herself sharply.

But she couldn't. She felt as if she was scrabbling around in the dark, wearing oversized boxing gloves.

She grabbed her phone and texted Jared. Can you meet me at my place after work?

* * *

Jared looked at Bailey's message on the screen of his phone: Can you meet me at my place after work?

Odd. They'd planned to go out for a pizza after work and then to the cinema. He was meeting her at the Tube station. Had she forgotten? Or had something happened that meant they had to change their plans?

Sure. Is everything OK? he texted back.

OK, she replied.

That was very un-Bailey-like. She was normally much chattier than this. Or maybe she was having a rough day in clinic and she was up to her eyes in work. Being busy might explain her forgetting their plans.

He was busy that afternoon, too, and didn't think anything more of it until she answered the door to him. Then he saw that her face was pale—paler than he'd ever seen it before—and her eyes were puffy, as if she'd been crying. 'Bailey? What's happened?' he asked.

She backed away before he could put his arms round her. 'You'd better come in and sit down.'

And now he was really worried. This definitely wasn't normal for her. The woman he'd been dating was warm and tactile. She liked being hugged, and he really enjoyed the physical side of being close to her. The fact that she'd just backed away... What was happening?

He followed her into the kitchen and she indicated the chair opposite hers.

'Do you want a drink?' she asked.

'No. I want to know what's wrong,' he said, sitting down. And his worry increased exponentially when he reached across the table to hold her hand and she pulled away.

'I'm, um…' She dragged in a breath. 'Well, the only way I can tell you is straight out. I'm pregnant.'

Jared wasn't sure what he'd been expecting, but it sure as hell hadn't been this.

Pregnant?

'But—how?' He knew the question was stupid as soon as the words left his mouth. They'd had sex. Which meant the risk of pregnancy. He shook his head in exasperation at his own ridiculousness. 'I mean, we were careful.'

'I know.'

'How far along are you?'

'Just over three weeks, according to the test.' She dragged in a breath. 'Five weeks since the start of my LMP.'

'OK.' He blinked, trying to clear his head.

Bailey was pregnant.

With his baby.

He'd been here before—sort of. When Sasha had told him that she'd had a termination. Saying that she didn't know whether the baby was his or not. Saying that she didn't want a baby anyway. Saying that she didn't want to be married to him any more.

This wasn't the same thing. At all.

But it was a hell of a lot more complicated. The last time Bailey had been pregnant it had been ectopic. She'd gone through enormous physical pain—and she'd lost part of her fertility as well as the baby. And the fear of it happening again had led to the breakdown of her marriage.

Right now, she was clearly panicking, worrying

that history was about to repeat itself. Would that panic make her consider having a termination even before the embryo had implanted—and would she make that decision without him?

He pushed the fears away. Bailey wasn't Sasha. And Bailey needed his full support. He had to put his own concerns and feelings aside and put her first. And he needed her to know that he'd be there. Given how she'd pushed Ed away, she was likely to do the same thing with him—he was learning that this was the way Bailey coped. She'd already begun pushing him away by not letting him hold her and comfort her when she was clearly so upset.

Well, Jared wasn't Ed, either. He wasn't going to let her push him away. The future might be tricky, but they had a lot more chance of surviving it if they faced it together.

He didn't think she'd listen to him right now—panic would've stopped up her ears. Which left him only one course of action. He stood up, walked round to her side of the table, scooped her out of her chair and sat down in her place. Once he'd settled her on his lap, he wrapped his arms tightly round her. Now she'd know for sure that he wasn't going to let her go.

She wriggled against him. 'Jared, what are you doing?'

'Showing you,' he said simply. 'That I'm here. That we're in this together. That I'm not going to let you push me away.'

She looked utterly confused. 'But—'

'But nothing,' he cut in gently. 'Oh, and just so you know—Bailey Randall, I love you.'

CHAPTER THIRTEEN

He loved her?

Bailey couldn't quite take this in. 'But…we've hardly…'

'It's too soon. I know. We haven't been dating long, we've both got baggage and we should both be taking this a hell of a lot more slowly.' Jared shrugged. 'But there it is. I don't know when it happened or how. It just *is*. I love you, Bailey. You make everything sparkle. My world's a better place with you in it. I know the very second you walk onto the football pitch at work, even if my back's to you and I haven't heard you speak, because the world immediately feels brighter.'

It was the nicest thing anyone had ever said to her.

But still the worry gnawed at her. He'd told her he wanted children. And she'd just told him she was pregnant. Why else would he say that he loved her? 'Are you saying this because of the baby?' she asked.

'No. The baby doesn't change anything about the way I feel about you.' He blew out a breath. 'But I guess there's something I ought to tell you. It's the wrong time to tell you, but if I don't tell you now then you'll be hurt that I didn't tell you when you eventually find out, and… Oh, hell, you'll be hurt if I do tell you.' He rested his forehead against her hair. 'I don't know how to say this.'

'You and Sasha had a baby?' she guessed.

'Not exactly,' he said.

She frowned. 'I don't understand.'

'She was pregnant,' he explained, 'but she didn't know whether the baby was mine or someone else's, because she'd been sleeping with another man, too. Until she told me, I didn't have a clue that she'd been having an affair, much less anything else.'

Bailey was too shocked to say anything. So Jared had been here before. Been hurt. And she'd just brought back all the bad memories for him, too.

'She, um, had a termination,' Jared said quietly. 'When I thought she was going on a girly weekend with her mates.'

'She didn't tell you until afterwards?'

'She didn't tell me,' he corrected softly, 'until the bank statement came through and it turned out she'd accidentally used the wrong debit card to pay for it.'

'How do you mean, the wrong debit card?'

'Sasha didn't work,' Jared explained. 'I used to put money into her account every month, because I didn't want her to feel that she had to check with me or ask me for money before she went out to lunch with her mates or had her hair done. That might've been the way our grandparents did things, but I thought it was important she should feel that she had money of her own.'

So Jared had done what he'd thought was the right thing, and it had come back to bite him.

He sighed. 'When I saw the payment to a private medical clinic, I realised something was wrong.' He gave a wry smile. 'I know I'm a sports medicine doctor, but I was a bit hurt that she hadn't talked to me about whatever medical thing was worrying her. I could've reassured her and maybe helped her get the right treatment. When she came home that night I asked her about it, and that's when she told me about the affair.' He swallowed hard. 'And the reason she'd been to the clinic was because she'd had a termination. She'd got rid of the baby without telling anyone what she was doing—without telling anyone at all. Not me, and not the other guy whose baby it might have been.'

Clearly the double betrayal had cut him to the bone.

'Don't get me wrong,' he said. 'I believe there are circumstances where a termination is the right choice. But I do think you should at least talk over all the options with your partner before you make a decision as life-changing as that.'

'And it wasn't the decision you would've made?' Bailey asked.

He shook his head. 'As I said, even if the baby hadn't been mine, we could've worked it out. Or at least tried to work it out. But then she came out with all this other stuff and I realised that even if the baby had definitely been mine, she would've done exactly the same thing. She didn't want a baby at all. She didn't want the changes it would make to her body.'

'That's… I don't know what to say,' Bailey admitted. 'That was hard on you.'

'On both of us,' Jared said ruefully.

'It wasn't your fault she had an affair, Jared.'

'Maybe, maybe not. My work took me away a lot, and that wasn't fair on her.'

Sasha had taken the choice away from Jared. Did he think Bailey would do the same? Was that why he was telling her this? Or was he telling her that he definitely wanted the baby? She swallowed hard. 'You said in the park, that time, that you wanted kids.'

'I do.' He paused. 'But that's not the be-all and end-all of a relationship, Bailey. You're pregnant with my baby, but that's not why I want to be with you. I want to be with you for *you*.' He took a deep breath. 'And right now I'm guessing that you're in a flat spin, worrying that history's going to repeat itself. This must be your worst nightmare. Your biggest fear come true.'

Her breath hitched. 'Yes.'

His arms tightened round her. 'I know you've had one ectopic pregnancy, but it doesn't mean that this one's definitely going to be ectopic as well.'

Brave, she thought, but misguided. 'We both know the risks of having another ectopic are higher in subsequent pregnancies.'

'It's a *risk*, not a guarantee,' he said. 'Let's start this again. You've just told me that you're pregnant. I know you're scared. I think I am, too. It's a huge thing. But this is amazing, Bailey. Really *amazing*. We're going to be parents.'

'What if…?' Again, she couldn't breathe. Couldn't say the words that haunted her.

'If it's another ectopic pregnancy or you have a miscarriage? Then we'll deal with it if and when that happens,' he said. *'Together.'*

And then she realised that he wasn't going to let her push him away. Even if she tried. He wasn't going to repeat his mistakes, and he wasn't going to let her repeat hers, either.

The bleakness and fear ever since she'd taken the pregnancy test suddenly started to recede. Only a little bit, but it was a start. 'You reckon?'

'I reckon.' He didn't sound as if he had any doubts. 'And I'll be brave and lay it on the line. I want you, Bailey. Yes, I'd like us to have children together—whether they're our natural children, whether we need IVF to help us or whether we adopt. But the non-negotiable bit is you. I love you, Bailey, and I want to be with you.'

He meant it. She could see that in his eyes. He'd been honest with her, and she owed him that same honesty. 'I want to be with you, too,' she said. 'But I'm scared that I'm going to make the same mistakes again. My marriage collapsed because I pushed Ed away, and I know I hurt him. I feel bad about that.' She blew out a breath. 'I don't want to hurt you like that, Jared. Especially as I know you've already been through a rough time.'

'Then maybe we both need to do something different this time,' he said softly. 'Maybe we need to take that leap and trust each other—and ourselves.'

She nodded. 'This is a start.'

He took a deep breath. 'If you decide that you can't go ahead with the baby, then I'll support you. I'll be right by your side.'

Even though a termination was clearly a hot button for him, he'd support her if that was what she wanted.

But that was only one option. What about the really scary one? 'And what if—what if I *do* want to go ahead?' she asked.

'Then I'll still be right by your side. Nothing changes.'

He'd be there for her. Whatever. Regardless. Because he loved her.

'I'm not going to wrap you up in cotton wool—even though part of me wants to—because I know it will drive you insane. So I'll be whatever you need me to be. Though, to be fair, I'm not a mind reader,' he added, 'so you'll have to tell me if I get it wrong, instead of expecting me to work it out for myself. Because I'm telling you now that I probably won't be able to work it out.'

Trust him.

Take the risk.

Could she?

She thought about it. When she'd told him about her ectopic pregnancy, he'd been brilliant. He hadn't pushed her, he hadn't told her what to feel—he'd just held her and listened. He'd backed her in front of Lyle Fincham; he'd even said that if she left the club, so would he. And he'd just opened his heart to her, been totally honest with her.

She knew he'd be by her side all the way through her pregnancy. Not smothering her, not making the decisions for her—but he'd be there to discuss things, to help her see a way forward through all the worries. Just as he was here for her now—holding her, letting her know that he was there, supporting her.

So, yes, she could take the risk.

But there was something else she needed to tell him. Something important.

'I love you, too,' she said softly. 'Even when you're being stubborn and awkward and I want to shake you.'

'I'm glad we cleared that up,' he said dryly.

'And here I am, insulting you again when I'm trying to tell you something really important.' She leaned forward to kiss him. 'I didn't date anyone after my divorce. I never wanted to be with anyone again. I didn't want to take the risk of loving and losing. But I noticed *you*. Even though you annoyed me the very first time I met you, at the same time I noticed your eyes were the colour of bluebells.'

'Bluebells...' He looked amused.

She cuffed him. 'Stop laughing at me. I'm trying to be romantic.'

'Are you, now?'

She loved that sarcastic Scottish drawl. 'And then you trained with me.' She went hot at the memory and her breath caught. 'Your biceps,' she whispered.

He nuzzled her earlobe. 'Yeah. Your back. I hope you know you gave me some seriously hot dreams.'

Just as she'd dreamed about him. 'You danced with me at my best friend's wedding. You kissed me.'

'I wanted to do a lot more than dance with you. And kiss you. Except you got spooked.'

'I know. It scared me that I wanted you so much, Jared. I didn't want to be attracted to anyone. I didn't want to love anyone again. But then,' she said simply, 'there you were. And it happened. I fell for you. As you said, I don't know how or where or when. I just *did*.' She paused. 'I love you.'

'Good.'

She kissed him again. 'So what are we going to do about this?'

'Given that you're expecting my baby and we haven't had a proper courtship?' he asked. 'I guess we're just going to have to take each day as it comes. But one thing I promise you is that I'll always have your back,' he said. 'Just as I know you have mine—I haven't forgotten the way you stood up to Lyle Fincham on my behalf.'

'You stood up for me, too,' she pointed out. And then suddenly it was clear as the panic ebbed further and further away. 'You make me feel safe, Jared. And you make me feel as if I can do everything I'm too scared to do.'

'And you make me want to be a better man,' he said.

'You're already enough for me, just as you are,' she said.

He held her closer. 'So I'm going to ask you properly. I don't have a ring, but that's something we'd choose together later in any case.' He kissed her, then gently moved her off his lap and dropped to one knee in front of her. 'Bailey Randall, will you do me the honour of being my wife?'

'Yes. Absolutely yes,' she said, drawing him to his feet and kissing him. 'I think I'd like a quiet wedding, though.' Particularly as it would be second time round for both of them. Their second chance.

'We can do whatever we want,' Jared said. 'Whether you want a tiny church or a deserted island or a remote castle—whatever you want, that's fine by me. I don't care where we get married or how, just as long as you marry me.'

'I'd like just our family and closest friends there—the people who mean most to us,' she said. 'And then maybe a meal afterwards.'

'Maybe a little dancing. I quite like the idea of dancing with my bride,' he mused. 'And a wedding cake made by Rob.'

'White chocolate and raspberry,' she suggested.

He grinned and kissed her. 'Good choice. I agree.'

'When did you have in mind?'

'I would say as soon as we can, which means a fortnight, but that might be rushing it a tad,' he said. 'So how about…say…six weeks from now?'

Around the time of the twelve-week scan. *If* the baby was even viable. If she wasn't in the middle of another ectopic pregnancy.

'What if it goes wrong?' she whispered.

Luckily he seemed to realise that she was talking about the baby and not them. 'It's not going to stop me loving you and wanting to be married to you,' he said.

'But what if everything goes wrong and I can't have children?' She dragged in a breath. 'You said you wanted children.'

'There are other ways,' he said. 'Adoption. Fostering. Or even if it's just the two of us and a dog and a cat, and we just get to spoil our nieces, nephews and godchildren. We'll still be a family. We'll be together.'

He really, really believed in them.

And the strength of that belief nearly made her cry.

'Agreed. Six weeks,' she said. 'On a weekend?'

'Or a weekday. Whenever they can fit us in.' He paused. 'I need to buy you an engagement ring. Maybe we can go shopping at the weekend.'

She smiled. 'That's not important. It's not about the jewellery. It's about how we feel.'

'I know. But I still want to buy you an engagement ring.' He hammed up his accent. 'I'm traditional, you know.'

'And you're going to marry me in a kilt?'

That made him laugh. 'No.'

She rolled her eyes. 'Spoilsport.'

'It might clash with your dress. Anyway, we need a ring first. We're going to do this properly, Dr Randall.'

She laughed and kissed him. 'OK. An engagement ring it is.'

He paused. 'Though maybe you should meet my family before I give you the ring.'

'And we need to tell mine,' she said. 'Be warned, there will be a party. And nobody parties like Italians.'

'No? Try the Scots,' he said. 'Now, *we* can party all night.'

She smiled. 'So your family likes partying as much as mine? We might have a bit of trouble talking them into a quiet wedding.'

'No. They love us. They'll back us in having exactly what we want,' Jared said. 'My family's going to love you.'

'Mine already likes you.'

'Then we're going to be just fine.' He sat down on the chair again and pulled her back onto his lap. 'I love you, Bailey.'

'I love you, too.'

'And I know you're still scared—so am I,' he admitted. 'But we can talk to the experts and make sure we know what all our options are.'

'They did tell me last time,' she said, 'but I didn't really take any of it in. I guess I was a bit too shell-shocked.'

'Then we'll ask again,' he said. 'We'll get the first appointment we can and ask for an early scan—maybe even more than one, until we're sure this pregnancy definitely isn't ectopic—and the one thing I promise you is that your other tube isn't going to rupture. Because if it *is* another ectopic, we'll do something before that happens.'

She swallowed hard. 'Have a termination, you mean.'

He nodded. 'But it won't be because we don't want the baby. It'll be because the baby doesn't have a chance of survival and it's a risk to your health, which isn't the same thing at all. And I will be right by your side, holding your hand, all the way.'

Giving her courage when she faltered. And letting her give him courage in the bits he found difficult. A true partnership. The same team. That worked for her. 'That,' she said, 'is a deal.'

The next morning, Bailey booked an appointment with her GP. She texted Jared to let him know the time and where to meet her, just in case he could make it.

He made it. She was pretty sure he'd had to call in some favours to do it, but she was glad that he'd kept his promise to her: he was right by her side, all the way.

He held her hand while she told the GP about her previous pregnancy and the GP rang through to the hospital to book her in for an urgent scan.

And he was right by her side as they walked through the corridors towards the ultrasound department at the hospital later that afternoon.

'I'm scared,' she whispered.

'I know you are, but I've got a good feeling about this.' His fingers tightened round hers. 'And, whatever happens, I'm here and I'm not going away.'

No matter what she did or said, he wasn't going to let her push him away. He wouldn't let her repeat her mistakes. Funny how that made everything feel so much safer.

Jared held her hand while the trans-vaginal scan was done, and he didn't say a word about the fact that her fingers were so tightly wrapped round his that she must've been close to cutting off his circulation. He was just there. Solid. Immovable. Her personal rock.

'Dr Randall, I'm absolutely delighted to say,' the ultrasonographer said with a broad smile, 'that you have an embryo attached very firmly to the wall of your placenta.'

The picture on the screen was just a fuzzy blob to both of them; they couldn't really make anything out at all.

But it was their baby.

In her womb, not in her Fallopian tube.

And the nightmare that had happened last time definitely wasn't going to happen again. *It wasn't an ectopic pregnancy.*

Bailey felt the tears spilling out of her eyes as she looked over at Jared; and she could see that his eyes were shiny with tears, too. 'Are you crying?' she whispered. Her big, tough, dour Scotsman, in tears?

'Yes, and I'm not ashamed of it. We're seeing our own little miracle,' he whispered back. 'I'm so happy. I want to climb on top of the hospital roof and yell it out to the whole world.'

The picture that put in her head made her smile but then the panic came crashing back in to spoil it. 'Not yet. We don't say a word to anyone, not until twelve weeks,' she said. Just in case she lost the baby. There were still no guarantees that everything would be all right. But at least they'd passed the first hurdle.

CHAPTER FOURTEEN

JARED'S PREDICTION ABOUT his family turned out to be spot on. Bailey adored Jared's family—particularly when Aileen, Jared's sister, took her quietly to one side and confided in her. 'We've all been so worried about him.'

'After Sasha, you mean?'

Aileen nodded. 'But he's seemed a lot happier lately. Now I've met you, I can see exactly why. And I'm so pleased you're joining our family.'

'Me, too,' Bailey said, and hugged her impulsively.

And her family was just as ecstatic when Jared and Bailey dropped in to announce the news of their wedding. And they insisted on having a small party with cake and champagne—including Jared's family—when Jared bought Bailey a very pretty sapphire-and-diamond knot.

To Bailey's relief, Jared didn't wrap her in cotton wool. Instead, he insisted that her life should be pretty much as it always was—only just not quite so intense on the exercise front. But he did move into her place, and he insisted on bringing her breakfast in bed every morning.

Bailey couldn't ever remember being this happy before.

It was hard not to share the news about the baby with her mum and Joni, especially as Joni was blooming with her own pregnancy, but Bailey was completely superstitious about it. She wasn't going to do anything the same this time. She wasn't even going to start looking at baby clothes, or nursery furniture, or baby name books, until they'd reached the twenty-week mark.

But she was glad that Jared had suggested getting married in six weeks' time, because planning everything would keep them both occupied. He'd already booked the register office and asked his oldest brother to be his best man. Her family had immediately offered to sort out the wedding breakfast and the wedding cake—raspberry and white chocolate, as she'd suggested. So all she had to do was sort out her bridesmaid, the dresses, the invitations and the flowers.

On Monday evening, after the yoga class—and luckily Joni had told Bailey exactly which bits Jenna had suggested to tone down during pregnancy, so she was able to do the same without having to ask—she and Joni had their usual catch-up over a chicken salad.

'There was something I wanted to ask you, Joni,' she said. 'How do you fancy being a bridesmaid again?'

Joni stared at her in shock. 'You and Jared, you mean? But…you stopped talking about him. I thought it had gone wrong. And, um—well, I thought you'd tell me about the break-up when you were ready.'

Bailey grinned. 'In answer to your questions—

yes, yes, yes, and we've sorted it out so there's nothing to talk about.'

'You and Jared,' Joni repeated.

'Me and Jared,' Bailey confirmed.

Joni hugged her. 'That's the best news ever.'

'Don't cry, or you'll start me off,' Bailey warned, seeing the telltale glitter in her best friend's eyes.

'Sorry. It's hormones making me so wet and crying over everything,' Joni said.

Me, too, Bailey thought, but hugged the secret to herself.

'So when is it all happening?'

'Um, that would be…a little under six weeks.'

Joni looked shell-shocked. 'That soon?'

Bailey shrugged. 'We couldn't see any reason to wait. The reception's going to be at the restaurant, Rob's doing the cake, the register office is booked… so all I need to do is sort out flowers, dresses, and ask you if Olly's band would come and play during the meal.'

'I'm sure they will—in fact, I'll ring him now.' A couple of minutes later she hung up. 'Deal. Olly says he needs to know what the "our song" is.'

'I have no idea.' Bailey spread her hands. 'I guess I'll have to ask my fiancé what he thinks.'

'And I'll go dress-shopping with you any time.'

'Good. That means this Saturday,' Bailey said.

And by the end of Saturday she had the perfect dress—a skater-style strapless dress in deep red velvet that wouldn't let her pregnancy show, even in another five weeks' time, with matching shoes. Joni had a similar dress in ivory with red shoes and a red sash, and her mother found a champagne-coloured suit.

'Look at us. We rock,' Bailey said, when they were dressed up and standing in front of the mirror.

'Jared's going to be totally bowled over. You look so beautiful,' Lucia said. 'You both do.'

They agreed on simple flowers—ivory roses for Bailey and red roses for Joni. The invitations were written and posted. And all they had to do then was hope for a sunny day.

Finally it was the Thursday of Bailey and Jared's wedding day. Bailey had spent the previous night at her parents' house, to preserve the tradition of not seeing the groom until the actual wedding. Jared had sent her a single red rose, first thing, with the message, 'I love you and I can't wait to marry you'—in his own handwriting, she noticed, rather than the florist's.

Joni and Aaron came over to help them get ready, and finally they were ready to go to the register office. As Bailey had been expecting, she and Jared were both interviewed by the registrar—in separate rooms so they wouldn't see each other until the wedding—and then finally the guests were all seated and it was time to walk into the room itself.

They'd arranged for Olly to play a song on acoustic guitar as she walked down the aisle on her father's arm—a love song from Jared's favourite rock band, with the mushiest words in the world, and she'd nearly cried the first time Jared had played it to her.

And her dour Scotsman—wearing morning dress rather than a kilt, but with a velvet bow tie to match her dress—lit up in smiles as he turned to watch her walk up the aisle.

'You look amazing,' he said. 'I love that dress. But, most of all, I love you.'

'I love you, too,' she whispered.

Every moment of the ceremony felt as if it had been engraved on her heart—from the registrar welcoming everyone to declaring all the legal wording.

'I do solemnly declare that I know not of any lawful impediment why I, Jared Lachlan Fraser, may not be joined in matrimony to Bailey Lucia Randall,' he said, and she echoed the declaration.

He took her hand. 'I call upon these persons here present to witness that I, Jared Lachlan Fraser, do take thee, Bailey Lucia Randall, to be my lawful wedded wife.'

And then, once they were legally married, the registrar smiled. 'You may kiss the bride,' she said, and Jared took Bailey into his arms, kissing her lingeringly to the applause of their family and friends.

Once the registration was complete and they'd checked the entry was correct before signing it, there was time to take photographs on the marble staircase. And then, outside the register office, everyone threw dried white rose petals over them.

She smiled at Jared. 'This is even better than snow,' she said.

'Especially as it won't result in broken bones on the football pitch,' he said.

She grinned. 'Indeed, Dr Fraser.'

'Absolutely, Dr Fraser.' His eyes were full of love.

He helped her into the wedding car. There were some last photographs, and then the chauffeur drove them off. It was only when Jared stopped kissing her that she realised they weren't heading in the right direction for her family's restaurant.

'Um, excuse me, please?' she said to the driver. 'I think we're going in the wrong direction.'

'No, we're fine, ma'am,' he said with a smile.

'But we're going the opposite way to the restaurant. Would you mind turning round, please?'

'Sorry, ma'am, I have my orders,' he said.

'Orders?' She frowned. What orders? 'Jared, do you know anything about this?'

He looked blank. 'We already made the arrangements. We're going to your family's restaurant—aren't we?'

She frowned. 'Can I borrow your phone?'

'Sure.'

She rang her mother. Lucia made some completely unsubtle noises that were clearly meant to be static and didn't sound remotely like it. 'Sorry. This mobile phone signal is breaking up,' she said, and hung up.

'I'll try Joni,' Bailey said, but her bridesmaid did exactly the same as the mother of the bride.

'Let me try my mother,' Jared said. Bailey handed the phone back to him, but the result was the same.

'This is obviously their idea of a surprise,' he said. 'Whatever they've planned, they're all in it together.'

'I'm not very keen on surprises,' Bailey said.

'Me, neither, but right now I don't think there's anything we can do but go with it.' Jared smiled at her. 'Their hearts are in the right place.'

'I know,' she said ruefully. 'Sorry. It's hormones making me grumpy. I love you.'

He kissed her. 'I love you, too, Dr Fraser.'

Then she realised they'd pulled up outside the football club. 'What are we doing here?' she asked.

'I have no idea,' Jared said.

Bailey's father opened the door with a beaming smile. 'Dr and Dr Fraser, this way, if you please.' He helped Bailey out of the car.

There was a red carpet unrolled outside, and Jared and Bailey exchanged a glance; both of them had a glimmer of an idea now of what was happening.

They followed the red carpet into the room that the club used for functions. As soon as they walked in, there was a massive cheer from everyone in the room and a flurry of confetti in the air. The walls had been decorated with hearts, balloons and a huge banner saying 'Congratulations, Bailey and Jared'.

She could see everyone there—their families and friends, everyone from the football club, and all her colleagues at the sports medicine unit.

Archie and Darren came up to them. 'We know you wanted to keep it quiet—but we wanted to throw a party for you because you're both so special,' Darren said, and hugged them both.

Bailey had to blink back tears. 'Did you arrange all this, Darren?'

The boy nodded shyly.

'It was all his idea,' Archie said. 'He went to see Lyle about it, and Lyle got Mandy to help him with the details. He's been talking to both sets of parents and to your best friend, Bailey.'

'I don't know what to say,' Bailey said, 'except this is fantastic—thank you so much!'

The food was fabulous, and the centrepiece was an amazing wedding cake made by her brother. No wonder he'd refused to let her see it, as it was a lot bigger than the one she'd planned—it was the same raspberry and white chocolate cake, but scaled up for many more guests.

'I can't believe you kept it all a secret,' she said to Rob. 'And that cake is just stunning.'

'Anything for my little sister,' he said, 'and the man who made her smile again.'

Finally it was time for the speeches. Jared stood up. 'This wasn't quite what we'd planned for the reception, so I don't have a huge speech. I'd just planned to thank my bride for making me the happiest man alive and I'm going to stick with my plan—well, almost.' He smiled. 'Some of you know that something quite special happened to me when I was seventeen. I thought when I scored the winning goal in the championship that it was the happiest moment of my life, but I was wrong—because today is even better than that. Today, the love of my life married me. So I'd like to make a toast to her. To Bailey.'

'To Bailey,' everyone echoed.

'And I'd also like to thank our family and friends, who managed to surprise us this afternoon as much as we surprised them with the announcement of our wedding,' he said. 'You're all fantastic and we love you.'

Jared's oldest brother gave a short, witty best-man's speech. And then it was the turn of the father of the bride; Paul was almost in tears. 'There's so much I could say—but I want to keep it short and sweet. Bailey's the apple of my eye, and I couldn't find a better son-in-law than Jared. So I want to wish Bailey and Jared a long, fabulous life together.'

Darren stood up next. 'I know I don't really have the right to do this, because I'm not family, but I wanted to make a tiny speech, too.'

'You organised our reception, so I think you earned the right,' Jared said with a smile. 'Go for it.'

Darren took a deep breath. 'I think most of you know that I got into a bit of trouble a few months back, when I wasn't doing very well and I started drinking. Between them, Bailey and Jared straightened me out and gave me a second chance, and I owe them everything. Jared's been a brilliant father figure to me and I just wanted to say thank you. To Jared.'

A brilliant father figure. Yes, Bailey thought, he's going to be a brilliant dad. She squeezed her husband's hand under the table. He caught her eye and at her raised eyebrow he gave a small nod.

'In that case, I think I need to make a speech, too,' Bailey said, standing up. 'Doing this research into soft-tissue injuries at the football club has turned out to be the best decision I ever made, because it's how I met Jared. But what Darren just said really struck a chord with me. Jared's a brilliant father figure. And we've been keeping things under wraps a bit because—well, some of you know it's been a bit tricky for me in the past. But we'd like the world to know officially that Jared's going to be a dad in about six months' time.'

And the room erupted in a froth of cheering and champagne.

EPILOGUE

Six months later

JARED SAT ON the edge of the hospital bed, one arm round his wife and the other resting on the pink-swathed sleeping bundle in her arms.

'She has eyes the colour of bluebells—just like yours,' Bailey said dreamily.

'All babies have blue eyes,' Jared pointed out. 'She'll have brown eyes like you when she's older.'

'Not necessarily—my dad's eyes are blue,' she reminded him.

Jared stroked his daughter's cheek. 'She has your mouth.'

'And your nose.'

'She's beautiful. Our Ailsa.' He leaned over to kiss his new daughter. 'I thought on our wedding day I could never be happier than at that moment, but seeing her safely here in your arms and knowing you're both OK—life doesn't get any better than this.'

She smiled at him. 'Oh, I rather think it will. We have the first smile, the first word, the first step, the first "I love you, Daddy"—there's all that to come.'

'We're lucky. We got our second chance,' he said softly. 'And I love you, Bailey Fraser.'

'I love you, too,' she said. 'Always.'

* * * * *

COMING SOON!

We really hope you enjoyed reading this book.
If you're looking for more romance
be sure to head to the shops when
new books are available on

Thursday 22nd May

To see which titles are coming soon, please visit

millsandboon.co.uk/nextmonth

MILLS & BOON

THE HEART OF ROMANCE

A ROMANCE FOR EVERY READER

MODERN
Prepare to be swept off your feet by sophisticated, sexy and seductive heroes, in some of the world's most glamourous and romantic locations, where power and passion collide.

HISTORICAL
Escape with historical heroes from time gone by. Whether your passion is for wicked Regency Rakes, muscled Vikings or rugged Highlanders, awaken the romance of the past.

MEDICAL
Set your pulse racing with dedicated, delectable doctors in the high-pressure world of medicine, where emotions run high and passion, comfort and love are the best medicine.

True Love
Celebrate true love with tender stories of heartfelt romance, from the rush of falling in love to the joy a new baby can bring, and a focus on the emotional heart of a relationship.

HEROES
The excitement of a gripping thriller, with intense romance at its heart. Resourceful, true-to-life women and strong, fearless men face danger and desire - a killer combination!

From showing up to glowing up, these characters are on the path to leading their best lives and finding romance along the way – with plenty of sizzling spice!

To see which titles are coming soon, please visit

millsandboon.co.uk/nextmonth

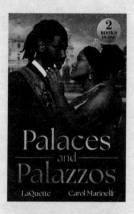
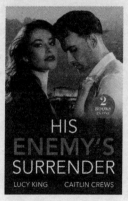
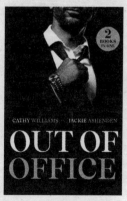

LET'S TALK
Romance

For exclusive extracts, competitions
and special offers, find us online:

f MillsandBoon

X @MillsandBoon

O @MillsandBoonUK

♪ @MillsandBoonUK

Get in touch on 01413 063 232

afterglow BOOKS

Afterglow Books is a trend-led, trope-filled list of books with diverse, authentic and relatable characters, a wide array of voices and representations, plus real world trials and tribulations. Featuring all the tropes you could possibly want (think small-town settings, fake relationships, grumpy vs sunshine, enemies to lovers) and all with a generous dose of spice in every story.

🎵 @millsandboonuk
📷 @millsandboonuk
afterglowbooks.co.uk

#AfterglowBooks

For all the latest book news, exclusive content and giveaways scan the QR code below to sign up to the Afterglow newsletter:

SCAN ME

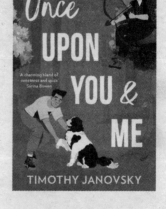

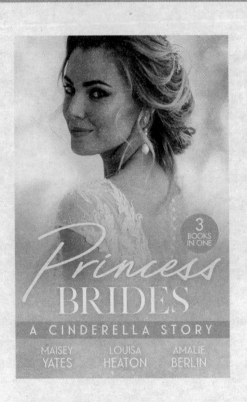